D1165917

C. John Tupper, M.D.

The Aesculapian

Joe Hawkins (h) IS
Ed Annis, Past AMA Pres.
(Florida)

He spoke in an empty
Madison Sq. garden &
was nominated (from the floor)
of the Hse of Delegates to
run for AMA Pres. — & Won!
He also visited us in
Ann Arbor in 1963 & '64

Letitia
is Jim Sammons?

The Aesculapian

Dan Cloud

FOR MARY —
WHO KNOWS ORGANIZED
MEDICINE CAN BE FUN!
FROM LINDA + MANSFIELD
JUNE 1999

FREDERIC C. BEIL

Published in the United States by
Frederic C. Beil, Publisher, Inc.
609 Whitaker Street
Savannah, Ga. 31401

First Edition

LIBRARY OF CONGRESS CATALOGING-IN-PUBLICATION DATA
Cloud, Dan, 1925–
The aesculapian / Dan Cloud
p.   cm.
ISBN 0-913720-98-4
I. Title
PS3553.L589A68   1998   97-36389
813′.54—dc21   CIP

Beil website address: http://www.beil.com

This book was set in the Galliard typeface by SkidType, Savannah, Georgia;
printed on acid-free paper; and sewn in signatures.

TO

Virginia
who graced my life lo these many years
and lovingly endured the writing of this book—
I adore her

and

Priscilla, Andy, Toadie, Mike, Stephanie,
Annie, Katie, Andy, David, and Kevin

Preface

Although *The Aesculapian* is a work of fiction, parts of the story deal with organizations and places that exist, as well as actual happenings. However, the characters portrayed and their activities are purely imaginary and bear no relation to real people or activities, past or present, except by coincidence.

Many have tendered support, for which I am deeply grateful. Edward R. Annis, M.D., of Miami, Florida, former president of the American Medical Association and a valued friend and counselor for many years, inspired the central event of the novel with a powerful speech he presented on behalf of the AMA in an empty Madison Square Garden, and televised by NBC on May 21, 1962. That performance by Dr. Annis was among the finest I have ever seen.

Special thanks must go to Rochelle Tigner, Kathy Holder Viele, and Miriam Weckerly, who continually reinforced and encouraged me, and to Paul Eckstein and Ann Hobart, who offered sound guidance. Frederic Beil summoned the courage to publish this first novel, and Mary Ann Bowman Beil, my tolerant and gracious editor, made the whole thing a reality. And of course, my wife, Virginia, and our children and grandchildren provided daily inspiration, and always with love.

A word about the American Medical Association, an extraordinary organization of which I am honored to have been a member and its president. Many have said that if the AMA were suddenly to vanish, someone would quickly have to create another to take its place. I believe this to be true, for the AMA is the only body in the world committed solely and without compromise to the betterment of our health. Without the AMA the remarkable achievements of medicine could not have been realized, and patients would not have been so ably served by their physicians.

During my tenure on the board of trustees of the AMA, which included the presidency, my fellow board members and our dedicated staff afforded me some of the most gratifying years of my life, as did members of the house of delegates of the AMA, which elected me, and the many physicians I was privileged to meet throughout the country. All bestowed a rich endowment of memories and friendship, and I am grateful.

And finally, my profound gratitude to the profession of medicine for giving me a lifetime of exhilaration and fulfillment. I am proud to be a physician, and I would give anything to be starting all over again.

The author, with fond memories, gratefully acknowledges the following beautiful songs and their creators: "Memories of You," by Andy Razaf and Eubie Blake; "I'll Be Seeing You," by Sammy Fain and Irving Kahal; "Stardust," by Hoagy Carmichael and Mitchell Parish; and "Deep Purple," by Peter DeRose and Mitchell Parish.

The author also acknowledges this beautiful passage written by George Sand in a letter to Lina Calamatta, March 31, 1862: "There is only one happiness in life, to love and be loved."

Aesculapius

Aesculapius, the god of healing, was the son of Apollo and the maiden Coronis of Thessaly. While heavy with the child of Apollo, Coronis dallied with a mortal, and Apollo, furious at her faithlessness, had Artemis slay her with arrows. But Apollo suffered a pang of grief when he saw flames rising above the funeral pyre and plucked the unborn infant from its mother's body. He bequeathed the infant to Chiron, the wise and kind old centaur, and had it called Aesculapius. From Chiron Aesculapius learned the art of healing and in time surpassed his teacher. He gave relief to those suffering from ailment or injury, even those near death. Thousands came as his fame spread, and great temples of healing were built in his name. Then, in a moment of folly, he raised a man from dead for a fee of gold. This angered the gods, and Zeus slew Aesculapius with a thunderbolt. But earthlings revered Aesculapius as no other mortal, and for hundreds of years those with every malady journeyed to his temples in search of healing. It was said that serpents mysteriously served the extraordinary powers of Aesculapius. Indeed, his familiar gnarled staff entwined with a single serpent became a symbol of healing and, in modern times, the revered emblem of the American Medical Association.

Prologue

Ten Years Earlier

It was the dinner hour in Washington, and the government was in repose.

David Chamberlain hated the moment. The call from Geneva that morning had exploded his brain, and now he must seek favor from a man he loathed. He entered the offices of Senator Jonathan Ridge. The waiting room was drenched in brown. Chairs of brown-leather lined the paneled walls, and beneath a brass chandelier rested a sprawling, brown-leather sofa and a mahogany table covered with ashtrays and magazines. The smell of tobacco and old leather tainted the air.

A white-haired lady in yellow gingham sat behind a desk tending papers. Her face brightened as she greeted him. "Good evening, Senator Chamberlain. How nice to see you."

"Good evening, Martha," David Chamberlain said, smiling to conceal his agitation. He was expensively attired in single-breasted pinstripe of navy, and was handsome in an angular way with thick, dark hair and strong features. "You're working late."

"I always work late, sir," she answered cheerily in a soft Carolinian drawl. "Senator Ridge is expecting you." She nodded toward an open door.

David Chamberlain moved into a spacious room consumed by a massive oak desk, cluttered bookcases, more brown-leather chairs, and a long table laden with stacks of papers. In the corner stood an illuminated globe the size of a beach ball. A frail man in a black, three-piece suit—chicken neck, waxen face, thin white hair, squinty gray eyes with arcus senilis, and wire spectacles—rose behind the desk and came forward. This was the famous Senator Jonathan Ridge. Once he had been a country lawyer, and the ambience of his office in the Dirksen Building was remindful of the antebellum house in the tobacco fields where he was born and raised and, as a young Southerner, practiced law. Jonathan Ridge had evolved in the once raging tide of the Ku Klux Klan and

3

white supremism and now was among the powerful men of Washington—a member of the Committee on Appropriations; chairman of the Subcommittee on Defense, overseer of the Department of Defense, the military, the nation's intelligence community; and an impassioned advocate of states' rights. The Central Intelligence Agency was his pet, and his sword. It was a matter regarding the CIA that Senator David Chamberlain intended to discuss with Senator Jonathan Ridge.

"Good evening, David." Jonathan Ridge smiled and extended his hand. He spoke in a whispery rasp, and his upper lip curled unappealingly, baring stained teeth and rose-colored gingivae. "It's nice to see you."

"Good evening, Jonathan." David Chamberlain accepted the slender hand. He towered over the kyphotic figure of the elder statesman.

"May I offer you a drink?"

"Scotch please, thank you."

Jonathan Ridge opened his cabinet bar and puttered with the glasses and bottles, then turned, holding a highball in each hand. "Will Chivas be satisfactory?"

"Perfect."

"I still prefer my Wild Turkey."

"You wouldn't be Jonathan Ridge without Wild Turkey," David Chamberlain said.

Jonathan Ridge smiled again—it was more of a grimace—and raised the glass in salute. He opened a copper humidor on the desk. "Care for a cigar?" The humidor exuded the rich aroma of expensive tobacco.

"No, thank you."

"Do you mind if I smoke?"

"Not at all," David Chamberlain lied, wondering what would happen if he said yes.

Jonathan Ridge extracted an oversized Cuban from the humidor, trimmed the tip, and flamed it with a kitchen match, then puffed until the leaf burned to his satisfaction and a cloud of blue smoke had enveloped both men. David Chamberlain blinked to relieve his eyes.

"I'm sorry I couldn't meet you earlier," Jonathan Ridge said. "I had the military boys here most of the day. You know how that goes."

"Of course."

"Well, I hope you didn't come at this late hour to quarrel about my tobacco subsidies."

"No sir."

"Good." The two men sat facing each other across a small table. "Do we have a social call then?"

David Chamberlain crossed his long legs and tried to relax. He didn't like Jonathan Ridge, had always thought him an arrogant, patronizing old bastard. "Not exactly, Jonathan. I need your help."

"What kind of help, David?"

"My son, Bryce, is in serious trouble."

"I see. I thought you seemed a bit restive."

"As you know, Bryce is in Geneva working for the CIA. He started out as I did, worked in a state attorney's office after law school, then joined the CIA. He's been stationed in Geneva for a year."

"Yes, I know."

"This morning I received a call from a man named Pierre Globa."

"Dr. Globa?"

"Yes."

"I remember Dr. Globa. He fought in the French underground. Had quite a record. After the war he became a physician. He's wealthy now and lives in Geneva." Jonathan Ridge puffed his cigar. "A good man."

"Your memory is correct. Pierre is an old and trusted comrade. We met in Geneva when I was an agent. We had some good times, and a few bad ones. We drank together in Geneva, and in Lyon, and Beaulieu. Sometimes we drank too much. When Bryce went to Geneva, I asked Pierre to keep an eye on him. My calling was more of a pleasantry, an excuse for a chat. I really didn't expect to need Pierre's services. When he telephoned this morning, I immediately knew something was wrong. He told me

5

that Bryce—this is difficult, Jonathan—that Bryce had been apprehended while engaged in a homosexual act with a young man from the Russian embassy and is now being held incommunicado in the American consulate."

"Did you know Bryce was homosexual?" Jonathan Ridge asked. His face remained expressionless.

The question irritated David Chamberlain. "No, Jonathan, and I don't know it now."

"Has he communicated with you recently?"

"He wrote two weeks ago. The letter was cheerful and unremarkable. I called this morning, but they wouldn't let me talk to him."

"How did Pierre Globa find out?"

"Pierre has ways of knowing things."

"What do you want of me, David?"

"I want you to ask Admiral Busey to release Bryce to my custody. I'll bring him home. I can guarantee security. I have the resources."

"As a matter of fact," Jonathan Ridge said, "Admiral Busey briefed me on your son yesterday."

David Chamberlain flushed angrily. "For God's sake, Jonathan, why didn't you tell me?"

"The admiral asked me not to disclose the matter at this time, David, not even to you. Your son is a security risk and will be held incommunicado pending the investigation."

"Jonathan! I'm a United States senator!"

"The admiral had hoped to brief you personally after obtaining all the facts. He will be chagrined to learn that Dr. Globa has already contacted you."

"Pierre called out of friendship with me. He broke no rules."

"As a courtesy to you, and to Dr. Globa, I will so inform the admiral. I'm sure he'll let it go at that."

"My son is not a security risk, Jonathan."

"In matters regarding the CIA, there is always a presumption of guilt. You understand."

"Because you regard him as a homosexual?"

"Of course."

"Did he pass classified information? Did he breach security?"

"That's yet to be determined."

"Bryce is no spy. He'll be cleared within the week."

"He's subject to incarceration, regardless."

"It's no crime to be a homosexual."

"In the CIA it's forbidden to engage in unnatural sexual acts. You know our policy about homosexuals, David. From your experience in the agency, you know that sexual deviates are always security risks. They're vulnerable to blackmail. Worse, they tend to have political beliefs as bizarre as their behavior. It's unfortunate that your son is one of them. His knowledge of the CIA, and the fact that you are a United States senator, poses a serious threat to national security."

"Bryce is a sensitive, intelligent young man. He wouldn't know how to be disloyal."

"You're ignoring reality. However, I can't fault you for that. He's your son, and I pity you."

"The reality is, I'm trying to help my boy. I know the rules. I recognize the implied security risks. But this is my son. I love Bryce. I won't abandon him. He's a scared kid who needs his father."

"Face it, David. Homosexuals are sick. They're bad for government, bad for business, bad for the professions. They should be ostracized."

"That's cruel, Jonathan."

Jonathan Ridge stiffened and his voice turned shrill. "Those are facts, senator." Contempt distorted the face of the older man.

David Chamberlain struggled to contain his outrage. "Jonathan, I ask you as a fellow senator, call Admiral Busey. Tell him to satisfy himself there's been no breach of security, then release Bryce to me. Let it end there. Don't punish the boy needlessly."

"That won't be possible."

"I'm flying to Geneva tonight to see Bryce."

"You cannot see him."

"Why not?"

"Those are the rules."

"I would be in your debt, Jonathan."

"I'm sorry, senator. This is a matter of national security."

"What about Bryce's rights? Certainly he's entitled to counsel."

"In the CIA, at this point, he has no rights. He is not entitled to counsel."

"For God's sake, Jonathan! We're dealing with a young man's life. Bryce has done nothing to warrant this kind of treatment."

"Your son is a homosexual, senator. That is repugnant. He deserves whatever he gets."

David Chamberlain sickened. With all his heart he hated this wretched old man. "Who are you to be judge and jury, Jonathan? Who are you to crucify my son?"

"Senator!" Jonathan Ridge barked. "They caught your son sodomizing the goddamn Russian!"

David Chamberlain glared at Jonathan Ridge, then abruptly stood and jerked the old senator erect by the lapels. He held him nose-to-nose, and the gray eyes dilated and a great blue vein bulged grotesquely across the center of the forehead. David Chamberlain ached to smash a fist into the yellow teeth. "You rotten bastard!" David Chamberlain's voice turned to cold steel. "Sooner or later, Jonathan, I will cut your fucking balls off and shove them down your miserable throat."

Françoise Globa was a tall, patrician woman with shining blond hair gathered into a tight bun. She poured coffee for the two men and served bowls of fresh blueberries and sugar. "The blueberries grow in France." She spoke slowly with a heavy, sensual accent. "We are fortunate to live at the border. I purchased them in Ferney-Voltaire. Pierre enjoys fruits and berries.

"Do blueberries not grow in Switzerland?" David Chamberlain inquired.

"Blueberries grow in Switzerland," Françoise Globa replied. "But, they are better in France. French farmers grow very good things."

David Chamberlain tasted the colorful berries. "They're delicious," he said.

Pierre Globa smiled and his leathery face crumbled into a million wrinkles. "Françoise takes excellent care of me. She is a good woman."

"A very good woman," David Chamberlain said. "She is a wonderful cook. The scallops were elegant. The Montmelian was superb. She does take excellent care of you. You are lucky, my friend."

"It is good to have you visit us," Pierre Globa said, "even under these trying circumstances. I am sorry you cannot relax and enjoy Geneva. The lake is pretty these days."

"Yes. The lake is pretty. I love Geneva. I love your home. I often think of you and Françoise. We had good times here, and in France."

"Very good times. I treasure them."

"I'm grateful for your friendship. I would not have fared well this week without it."

"I regret we cannot do more. The cloak of secrecy is very strict. Admiral Busey allows no word to escape. I hear nothing. Every door is closed."

"I'll demand to see Bryce tomorrow. If they refuse, I'll call the President and ask him to intercede. They've held Bryce incommunicado for a week. Enough is enough."

"I am surprised the admiral treats a United States senator with such discourtesy."

"It's a travesty," David Chamberlain said.

"I am also surprised at Senator Ridge."

David Chamberlain frowned. "So am I. But for the moment, Jonathan Ridge is calling the shots."

"I know something of him. He is a hard man, an evil man."

"I almost killed the son of a bitch with my bare hands when I saw him last week. He refuses to take my calls. I don't understand his behavior. He must know I'll retaliate."

"Possibly he is counting on your desire to keep the matter secret."

"He's right about that. I don't want Bryce publicly humiliated. But my time will come. Jonathan Ridge is a contemptible man. I'll even the score. Wherever he goes, whatever he does, I'll be there, waiting. And he'll see me when it happens."

Pierre Globa smiled. "I know how relentless you can be, David. I would not want to be your enemy. Fortunately you are a civilized man. You are not likely to kill Jonathan Ridge, although you are quite capable of doing so. Anyway, that would be too merciful. You will find another way."

"I will do the appropriate thing, my friend. Count on it. But first, I want Bryce out of Geneva."

"Agreed."

"I believe the President will act on my behalf. I am one of his staunch allies."

"Well, it's time for cognac. I have a bottle of Martell." Pierre Globa prepared three glasses of the cognac, and Françoise replenished their coffee. "This is a Grande Champagne cognac," he said. "It is distilled from wine made of grapes grown in the chalky soil south of Cognac. Grande Champagne is the best of the cognacs, and hard to find."

"And powerful," David Chamberlain said upon tasting the strong spirit. "I don't recall cognac like this ten years ago."

"Ten years ago we could not afford a Grande Champagne," Pierre Globa said, smiling.

"And now you are wealthy," David Chamberlain said. "You have earned your wealth. I admire that."

"I have been fortunate," Pierre Globa said.

"You should retire and enjoy life," David Chamberlain said.

"I would not know what to do."

"He will never retire," Françoise Globa said. "He loves to work." She produced a dish of chocolate wafers.

"That is the hallmark of a good doctor," David Chamberlain said. He tasted a chocolate wafer. "Umm, bittersweet. You remember what I like, Françoise." His hostess smiled affectionately.

"Are you going to run for President of your country?" Pierre Globa inquired.

"Perhaps, some day," David Chamberlain replied.

"You would make a fine President," Pierre Globa said.

The telephone rang and Françoise rose to answer. Her eyes widened and she quickly handed the phone to David Chamberlain. "It's Admiral Busey," she whispered.

David Chamberlain looked surprised. "Good evening Admiral Busey. This is David Chamberlain."

The admiral spoke deliberately. "Senator Chamberlain. I have bad news, sir. Your son died an hour ago. He hanged himself in the consulate."

Three Weeks Earlier

The man whispered guardedly into the phone. "I'm HIV positive . . . last month . . . my own physician . . . I'm making arangements . . . there's no mistake, it's been rechecked . . . who knows? . . . I've decided to reveal my contacts . . . no, my mind's made up . . . it's the least I can do. . . ."

Two Weeks Earlier

Leonard Breslow, the chief financial officer of the American Medical Association and a confidant of Letitia Jordan, the executive vice-president, stayed late to finish loading a computer file named LEDGER. He had created the secret file a month ago, and only he knew it existed. He bolted the door to his private office and from a leather portfolio extracted a packet of documents. Then he accessed LEDGER on his personal terminal and meticulously entered the contents of the documents, concluding with the cryptic message:

Y–1—BRAZIL—JENO—CHECK IT OUT!

Satisfied, he turned off the computer and fed the packet of documents to the shredder and, after straightening his desk, called for a taxi, picked up his briefcase, and departed. That afternoon he had placed the clue in his lockbox at the bank, and tomorrow he would face Letitia Jordan. Now it was time for a Chardonnay and a quiet dinner at home with his wife.

He stepped out of the taxi in front of his condominium on Lakeshore Drive. It was the dead of winter in Chicago, and he wore a heavy overcoat and muffler and a wool hat and gloves.

The wind off the frozen lake stung his cheeks. He doffed the gloves, handed the driver a folded bill, pocketed the receipt, then, carrying his briefcase, walked briskly across the sidewalk to the entrance. The guard in the foyer waved and triggered the security door, and Leonard Breslow walked past the elevators to the stairwell.

He attacked the stairs two at a stride. He was lean and very fit and often ran up the cement stairs. Running the stairs was a nice finale to a long day of crunching numbers, and customarily he made it from the ground floor to the front door of his condo on the fifth floor in less than a minute without getting winded or breaking a sweat, even when laden with winter clothes and a heavy briefcase. Tonight he was in good form.

On the fourth landing he encountered a big man wearing jeans and a blue turtleneck, a knit cap, and thick gloves. He saw the man's face and pulled up, surprised, and smiled. The man nodded recognition and stepped forward, as if to shake hands, then seized Leonard Breslow by the arm and spun him and with a looping bolo punch, drove a gloved fist powerfully into his flank.

It was a vicious blow, and the rib snapped with a sound like splintering kindling. Leonard Breslow gasped and the briefcase tumbled across the landing. In an instant the man had applied a vicious chokehold. Unable to scream, Leonard Breslow clawed frantically at the muscular arms gripping his neck, but was driven to his knees. Then, with a wrenching motion, the man deftly cracked Leonard Breslow's cervical spine. The bones snapped and instantly the body fell limp, like a dangling puppet. The man wrenched the neck again, and again, twisting as far as it would go. When he was certain the spinal cord was severed, the man flung the lifeless body down the stairs, and Leonard Breslow's face splattered on the cement.

[1]

JOE HAWKINS crawled into the cockpit of his vintage Jag roadster and turned the key. The big V-12 caught on the first try and quickly settled into a mellow purr. It was a February dawn in Arizona and cold in the foothill where he lived. Joe had donned a cap and leather jacket, and when he hunkered down in the seat, the leather squeaked like cowboy chaps working a saddle. He buckled the safety harness and punched a cassette into the stereo, pulled on a pair of gloves, lit the headlamps, and backed out of the carport. Then he spun the big Michelins, loudly rousting the loose gravel on the driveway, and gunned the impatient cat onto the narrow road in front of the house.

Old love ballads poured from the stereo as he drove . . . *waking skies . . . at sunrise . . . every sunset too. . . .* It had rained in the night, a very good rain that had cleansed the air and soaked the desert grass—the filaree and blue grama—and the ocotillo and cholla and the great saguaro with the fledgling bud on top, and the young wild flowers, and had bestowed a pleasing smell of freshness . . . *seems to be . . . bringing me . . . memories of you. . . .* Now the sky was clear and moonless, and above the mountain behind the foothill the stars sparkled like exquisite diamonds and seemed close enough to touch. As he drove, puddles of fresh rainwater on the road splashed the belly of the Jag, and the first orange of sunrise faded the stars in the east and silhouetted a jagged mountain range in the distance known as Four Peaks . . . *sometimes I wonder . . . why I spend . . . my lonely night . . . dreaming of a song. . . .* In moments the sun would paint a red flame along the shadowy crest of Four Peaks, then the sun would rise and kindle the wondrous textures and tones and rhythms of the great desert and lavender mountains . . . *the nightingale . . . sings its fairy tale . . . of paradise where roses bloom. . . .* The blast of cold air in the open cockpit brought tears to Joe's eyes. By noon, if he wants, he can peel to his shirtsleeves and bask in the hot sun, but now he was on the verge of shivering. He sped down the switchbacks, down-shifting and double-clutching, jazzing the powerful V-12 on the straightaways . . . *though I dream in vain . . . in my heart it will remain . . . my stardust melody . . . the memory of love's refrain.* . . . Then he cleared the switchbacks and cruised on a boulevard headed for the heart of the city. In the distance he could see the red beacon blinking over the helicopter pad at the hospital. He sank even deeper in the seat, grateful for the warm jacket and cap . . . *I'll be seeing you . . . in all the old familiar places . . . that this heart of mine embraces . . . all day through.* . . . Traffic was sparse on the boulevard, and he amused himself by striving to hit the intersections when the lights were green, for there was nothing to do now but steer and keep an eye on the tachometer and listen to the ballads and the purr of the V-12 and the rubber tires whining on wet pavement . . . *in that small café . . . the park across the way . . . the children's carousel . . . the chestnut tree . . . the wishing well.* . . . As he neared Palo Verde, he idly counted the beacon flashes and wondered when the first helicopter would arrive and what agony it would bring . . . *when the deep purple falls.*

Joe Hawkins can never forget a moment twenty years ago in a country by the South China Sea, in the heart of an Asian peninsula the French called Indochina, a place lush and green, mysteriously beautiful, but underneath, an ocean of shit—a bloody firefight on a steaming, rain drenched day and a slimy stream in the rice paddies of Quang Ngai, where Sergeant Cobb, the marine they called "Mad Dog" and believed to be immortal, got blown away, where Lieutenant Joe Hawkins took a bullet in a femoral artery and bled nearly to death.

"All right, shitheads!" the foulmouthed D.I. at Quantico had screamed. "You worthless scum are all mine now, all mine, for ten miserable weeks."

He was the toughest, meanest son of a bitch they had ever seen, with a black moustache and chest full of ribbons, and he terrified them. "Never jeopardize the mission!" he screamed, over and over. "Never fucking jeopardize the mission, shitheads!"

"Sir! No sir!"

"Keep moving, shitheads! Keep moving! Never look back. Never fucking jeopardize the mission!"

"Sir! Never fucking jeopardize the mission. Sir! No sir!"

"Mad Dog" got shot as he crossed the shallow. A steel jacket from a banana clip in a Cong AK 17 across the stream ripped his chest wide open. Joe heard the sickening whomp of the bullet smacking live flesh, heard the cry, saw the great sergeant go down and thrash and flail and choke and bleed as the putrid water poured into the gaping hole and flooded the torn lung, saw the eyes, the haunting eyes, searching, pleading.

"Sir! Never fucking jeopardize the mission. Sir! No sir!"

Joe hesitated, turned, fought his way across the hip-deep shallow, twenty agonizing yards in sucking mud, a mile, an eternity, cradled his sergeant, struggled to hold the tortured face above water and plug the jagged wound, with only a fist for a tampon, and felt life drain from the strong body. Sergeant Cobb died in Lieutenant Hawkins' arms, and blood spilled on the muck and a great red clot floated lazily on the stench, clinging to the flimsy rushes, dimpling under the pounding raindrops—in that fleeting, final moment of serenity that accompanies even violent death.

Joe clung to the dead sergeant, unbelieving, numb, oblivious to the screams of his men. Then a steel jacket ripped Joe's thigh, tore the flesh, splintered the great bone. In those last seconds of remembrance, his own blood gushed in a scarlet torrent.

"Sir! Never fucking jeopardize the mission! Sir! No sir!"

❦

Joe Hawkins, somehow, had survived and tonight would go home to Grace, their children, the perfection of his life, perhaps a cognac, and the nightmares . . . always the fucking nightmares. Christ!

❦

Joe made it to Palo Verde in half an hour. The dawn had flourished, and the air was warmer and his thoughts had turned to the morning surgery and the speech he was to make at noon.

He parked the Jag and doffed his jacket and cap and slipped into a blazer he had tossed on the seat, then walked smartly across the ramp to the back entrance of the hospital. He was tallish and trim and militarily erect, a bit leggy, well shouldered, with a wide jaw and brown eyes and a nose twice broken. A maroon tie and blue oxford button-down distinguished nicely his tan face and brown hair. The blazer and gray slacks and ox-blood loafers completed the outfit, what he called his "speaker's uniform." In the corridors the nurses of Palo Verde maneuvered to catch his eye and greet him.

Jerry Sax waited in the intensive care unit. He was a third-year surgery resident with peach-fuzz cheeks and a sickly pallor emblematic of the confinement of surgical training.

"Good morning, Jerry. How are we doing?"

"Pretty good, sir. Mrs. Rutherford had a fair night. Her vitals are okay, temperature is thirty-nine, respirations are up some, gases are normal, her pulse is good. She's had a fair amount of bloody drainage, but not bad considering the adhesions in that apex. The crit dropped. I slipped her two units of packed cells about midnight. It was thirty-seven an hour ago. She vomited once this morning. Seventy-five of Demerol holds her about four hours."

"You always lose more blood than you think with an abscess," Joe said. "She may need more cells." He slipped on his half-glasses and perused Mrs. Rutherford's chart. "What's the bug juice?"

"Ampicillin, one million q 6, IV, Keflex, one gram q 6, IV."

"Good." Joe smiled. He liked the young resident's concise answers. "Stay with that drainage. Better grab a film this morning. She'll make it. We can deal with infection. She's lucky it wasn't a damn cancer."

"Mr. Barnard had a good night. He's stable. No bleeding. Minimal drainage. I skipped his gases. The Demerol holds him nicely."

"Pathology should have the slides out today," Joe said. "Clamp the tube and leave it in. The oncologists may want to infuse their magic potion. He'll be all right for now. God knows, we did little enough for him yesterday."

Joe walked across the unit and studied a thin figure lying on a surgical bed amidst the cluttered paraphernalia of intensive care. Harry Barnard was asleep and his chest, strapped with an elastic surgical bandage, gently rose and fell. He looked well enough; the ravages of terminal disease had not yet appeared. He was forty-three, a hard driving, successful realtor, and for twenty years a three pack-a-day smoker. Last week he coughed up a blood clot, and yesterday they found an inoperable bronchogenic carcinoma. He would undergo the customary radiation and chemotherapy. It would make him sick, buy a little time, maybe a year or two, then Harry Barnard would die miserably, thirty years too soon.

"Only one case today?" Jerry inquired.

"That's right. The patent ductus in the four-year-old. I'm speaking to Rotary at noon. I want out of here by ten. I need to pull some things together."

"I understand you give a lot of speeches."

"Probably too many."

"What are you talking about today?"

"I was going to do the 'What's New in Medicine?' routine, but maybe I'll try something political. Want to come?"

Jerry grinned enthusiastically. "Yes, sir. I'm always happy to escape hospital food."

Joe smiled. "Fair enough." He handed back the charts. "See you in the OR. I'm going by pre-op to say hello to the parents."

A little boy was sleeping on a gurney in the holding area

outside of surgery. They had administered sedation before wheeling him from his room and, mercifully, he would not remember the scary hospital corridors and the mysterious noises and smells that terrify children. He lay curled under an afghan and seemed small for four years. His parents stood beside the cart.

"How are you folks this morning?" Joe asked.

"Nervous," the father replied, forcing a smile.

"You're entitled to that. We'll be starting soon. The operation will take about an hour. You can wait with the surgical hostess down the hall. She'll have coffee and rolls. I'll find you when I'm finished. Try not to worry. He's a healthy boy. We'll take good care of him. He'll do fine." Joe grinned. "So will you."

The father wrapped an arm around his wife. Joe had explained the diagnosis and the risks. Ductus surgery is safe surgery, many times safer than the drive to the hospital, whatever that's worth. They were solid people, sensible, not likely to panic. It felt good to have their trust.

In the surgeons' lounge he changed into blue scrubs and a pair of cross-trainers spattered with dried blood. He inspected himself in the mirror and tucked a few strands of loose hair under the cap, then tied on a surgical mask, the paper kind with the smell of antiseptic that he hated, and pinched it to his nose under the glasses so his breath wouldn't fog the lenses. When satisfied, he joined Jerry Sax who was already scrubbing at the sink outside the operating room.

"Is this your first ductus?" Joe asked.

"Yes, sir."

"Talk to me."

"Well, the ductus arteriosus is derived embryologically from the sixth aortic arch on the left . . ."

Joe quickly interrupted him. "Signs and symptoms." He knew Jerry would have the embryology and anatomy memorized cold.

"The child usually appears normal, maybe a bit small for the age," Jerry said. "The diagnosis is usually made when someone picks up the typical murmur on a routine examination."

"Describe the typical murmur."

"A harsh, rumbling, systolic murmur, loudest in mid-systole, usually carries through diastole, heard best in the second or third interspace to the left of the sternum, also known as a machinery murmur."

"Right," Joe said. "The machinery murmur is pathognomonic. In an uncomplicated ductus, the diagnosis can be made on the murmur alone."

"There's usually a thrill over the murmur. This kid has a hellacious thrill. The interspace actually quivers."

"Very good. What else?"

"Bounding femoral and radial pulses, indicative of high pulse pressure. On the chest X-ray, increased pulmonary vasculature, prominent pulmonary artery, mild cardiomegaly. Hilar dance under fluoroscopy."

"Cyanosis?"

"Only with severe pulmonary hypertension."

"How do you explain that?"

"In an uncomplicated ductus the aortic pressure is higher than the pulmonary arterial pressure, as in a normal child. Therefore, blood shunts left to right, aorta to pulmonary artery. With pulmonary hypertension, the pulmonary arterial pressure may exceed the aortic pressure, and the shunt reverses. The unsaturated blood from the pulmonary artery dumping into the aorta causes cyanosis."

"Severe cyanosis?"

"No, sir. The cyanosis is usually mild compared to, say, Tetralogy of Fallot, where you have a major anatomic shunt inside the heart."

"Why is this important?"

"Pulmonary hypertension carries a bad prognosis. Occluding the ductus in the presence of pulmonary hypertension could be fatal."

"Very good," Joe said. "It's important for the surgeon to know the essentials. As a practical matter, though, the cardiologist makes the diagnosis. It may take some fine tuning to ferret out subtle variations or associated cardiac anomalies. These days, though, with sophisticated imaging techniques, the cardiologist can practically take a stroll through the heart and eyeball what's going on."

Then he asked, "What about the political significance of the ductus?"

"Political significance?"

"Discoveries in medicine have political significance."

"I'm not sure I understand."

"At the turn of the century the big killers were pneumonia, gastroenteritis, and tuberculosis. Antibiotics changed all that, wiped those suckers clear off the charts, doubled life expectancy. Thanks to medical progress we have a bigger population, which means more people in the job market and millions of older folks to look after. All of this adds up to a helluva strain on welfare, Social Security, and Medicare. That's politically significant.

"Tuberculosis was one of the great scourges of all time. Then streptomycin took it out, saved thousands of lives and billions of dollars. But, the sanitaria closed, and people lost their jobs. The old chest surgeons, the 'rib strippers,' had to find a new gig.

"The same for poliomyelitis. Salk and Sabin put the iron lungs in the junkyard and the Polio Foundation out of business. That also eliminated a lot of jobs, but polio is gone, thank God.

"The operation you're about to witness has saved the lives of thousands of children. That's important enough, but it's only part of the story."

They filed into the operating room looking like surgeons in the movies—arms bent, hands high, water running down their arms and dripping off their elbows.

"Good morning, Muriel," Joe said.

"Good morning, Dr. Hawkins. Good morning, Dr. Sax."

Muriel Jackson was Joe's scrub nurse and she adored him. She was black, buxom, and too short to pass instruments from her Mayo stand without standing on a platform. She had scrubbed a half-hour early to set up for the case. "You're looking awfully sharp this morning," she observed when handing Joe a towel. Muriel well knew his habit of primping in front of the dressing room mirror before scrubbing and liked to tease him.

Joe simply grunted.

The circulating nurse, a young woman named Carnation Mc-Gillicuddy, began prepping Charlie's chest. She wore a skin-tight, blue scrub dress tied with a sash, was swarthy, sultry eyed, and astonishingly endowed; and it was said that any man who came near Carnation would sustain an instant, uncontrollable erection.

Carnation prepped with a frenzy. She lathered the skin to and fro with bounding strokes, and her buns jiggled like great globs of jello. Joe glanced at Jerry Sax, who seemed mesmerized at the spectacle. Then Muriel confronted them with surgical gowns and a wink to say she had detected their rapture.

Carnation finished the prep, and Joe shrugged her off and returned to the matter at hand. Nothing could appear more help-less, he thought, than the limp body of an unconscious child strapped to a surgical table. He draped the young chest with sterile towels and sheets, leaving a snug, rectangular window for the incision. The moist film of soap on the skin glistened under the powerful surgical light.

"Let's go," he said.

Muriel passed him a scalpel and Joe incised swiftly, from the pink nipple in front of the chest to the scapula behind. The blade cut and the skin fell open and instantly ran crimson.

"I'll be goddamned, Muriel. You finally found me a knife with a decent blade."

"Yes, sir."

Moving rapidly, he and Jerry sponged blood and incised the layers of heavy muscle and intercostals and opened the chest cavity, blotting and sucking blood, clamping vessels, coagulating myriad bleeders with an electric forcep that charred bits of tissue and blood vessel between its tips.

"Keep 'em coming, Muriel, goddammit. I don't have all morning."

"Yes, sir." Muriel expected the banter that was part of the ritual with Joe. It would trouble her if he remained silent.

Once, however, in their early days, he had truly infuriated Muriel when in haste he grabbed for an instrument on her Mayo stand and accidentally pawed her ample breast. "Goddammit, girl," he had rudely scolded. "Your tits get in the way."

Later she confronted him in the office. "Dr. Hawkins. You are a fine surgeon. I respect you and will do my best to please you.

But I refuse to be treated like a goddamn trained orangutan."

The delicate infantile lung, glistening pink, unstained by the sooty inhalants that blacken the lungs of adults, ballooned into the incision. Joe positioned the steel blades of a Finochietto retractor and spread the slender ribs, then he packed the fragile lung under a moist laparotomy pad and fiddled with the Deavers and lights until he was satisfied.

"We'll find the ductus here," he said, pointing his dissecting scissors to the lucent pleura over the mediastinum at the root of the lung, deep in the chest. "Aorta, pulmonary artery, vagus." He touched each of the structures with the tip of the scissors. "With a patent ductus the pulmonary artery heaves with the heart beat. This is the hilar dance the radiologists talk about. Put your finger on the artery." Jerry obeyed. "Feel the jet from the ductus?" Joe said. "Feel the bruit? There's your machinery murmur."

"We open the pleura along the aorta and slip an umbilical tape around the vagus." Joe dissected as he talked. "There's no fat under this kid's pleura, a few nodes around the hilum . . . no problem. This little vein is the hemiazygos, the 'half-ass-igos.' We ligate it for exposure. It's only a remnant. The counterpart in the right chest, a big baby, the azygos, drains into the superior vena cava above the heart. It can be troublesome with procedures requiring bypass. Are you boned up on the embryology of the azygos system?"

"No, sir," Jerry admitted.

"Well." Joe relished the opportunity to show off. "The azygos system originates in the embryo with the supracardinal veins. The left supracardinal fades leaving only the hemiazygos, which you see is unimportant. The right supracardinal enjoys a more exalted destiny. It forms the azygos and also gives rise to the caudal portion of the inferior vena cava. Look it up in Arey when you have time."

"Yes, sir."

"This is the recurrent nerve coming off the vagus. The recurrent is the key to the dissection. It leads you to the ductus. Always, I mean always, identify the recurrent as the first order of business and keep it in sight at all times. The recurrent must never be damaged. It descends from the neck with the vagus, then takes off around the ductus and runs up the postero-lateral aspect of the trachea, behind the thyroid, to the larynx. You've seen it in thyroidectomies. If you ding the recurrent, you may paralyze his vocal cord and make him hoarse for the rest of his life.

"Now we have the ductus exposed. See the recurrent encircling it? We dissect the adventitia and reflect the pericardial lappet. It's considered bad form to snip the lappet. Pericardial fluid leaks out, a bit of a nuisance. It's a harmless mishap, but it gives the cardiologists something to gloat about. They love to pick up the friction rub post op and announce to the world that the surgeon snipped the goddamn lappet.

"It's also bad form to snip a lymphatic duct, but that's not so harmless. The area around the ductus may be full of lymphatics because of proximity to the thoracic duct behind the esophagus. Small lymphatics are almost impossible to visualize in situ. You avoid them with careful dissection. You know you've snipped one if you see milky fluid—chyle. If you don't stop the leak, you get a chest full of chyle, which means repeated chest taps, maybe a long term chest tube, extra days in the hospital. So far, I see no chyle.

"The ductus must be absolutely clean before applying the clamps. Take a good look.

"Robert Gross performed the first successful ductus operation in 1938. He was a young surgeon in Boston, barely out of his residency. The story goes that he snuck it in on a Saturday when the boss was out of town. The patient was a girl of seven, not much bigger than this kid.

"He managed to tie a single, braided silk ligature around that little girl's ductus. Sounds simple enough, but in 1938 it was a monumental achievement. Unfortunately ligation in continuity was plagued by recurrences. Gross then developed the divide and suture technique that we use today. Now recurrence is almost unheard of.

"A few years later Willis Potts, a Chicago surgeon back from the war in the Pacific, perfected a sweet little clamp that made the ductus operation even safer."

He turned to Muriel. "Show Dr. Sax one of my Potts clamps. Take a close look. Each jaw has a double row of tiny, needle-sharp teeth that interdigitate precisely one-third the length of the teeth. They have the virtue of gripping like a bulldog without crushing the tissue. It's an ingenious principle. They say Potts got the idea from an Indian fakir lying on a board of nails. That's probably bullshit, but it makes a good story. A Potts clamp will never let you down. A pair of those babies, and a damn good surgeon, once saved my leg."

The ductus pulsated in the crevice between the aorta and pulmonary artery. "Looks innocent, doesn't it," Joe said. Gingerly he applied a Potts clamp to each end of the squatty vessel. "Voila! The bruit vanishes. That rules out other pathology, like a ventricular septal defect, which might have been obscured by the ductus murmur. Feel the pulmonary artery. It softened dramatically when we occluded the ductus. That rules out pulmonary hypertension."

With thin-bladed scissors he transected the ductus between the Potts clamps. "You have to leave enough lip on each side to hold the sutures. There's a full head of pressure behind those clamps. If one popped off, this kid would exsanguinate in seconds. Reliable clamps are essential."

Muriel passed him a diamond-jaw needle holder loaded with arterial suture. "The suturing technique is crucial. Place the stitches one millimeter from the edge and one millimeter apart. Rotate your wrist to go with the curve of the needle as you pull it through. I like 5-O Deknatel on a T-1 needle. Some surgeons use a monofilament suture, but Deknatel is easier to handle. Hold the suture with medium tension. If you suture properly, you'll have no bleeding." He demonstrated the movements.

"Today ductus surgery is routine. The technique is a piece of cake, the mortality is practically zero, and you cure the patient —a seventy-year cure for this little guy. Our forebears made it easy for us. All we Johnny-come-latelies have to do is follow the book.

"Gross opened the door to modern cardiovascular surgery. Congenital defects, the heart-lung machine, coronary bypass, heart transplants, lasers, angioplasties, the mechanical heart—it all started in 1938 with that first ductus.

"Potts was only trying to make the Gross technique a little safer. He found a hardheaded German instrument maker named Bruno Richter, and they came up with these clamps. As it turned out, the multitooth clamp made some operations possible and many operations safer. Now multitooth clamps are an integral part of surgical armamentarium. Potts patented his clamp, but only to prevent imitations that might be inferior. He never accepted a cent of royalty money. Incidentally, my set are originals. Take care of them.

"Gross and Potts lived in the heyday of free enterprise. They had courage and ingenuity, and no federal bureaucracy was telling them how to do surgery. They were brilliant guys who saw a problem and had the balls to solve it. The result was a multibillion dollar industry affecting the lives of millions of people, and still growing. That's politically significant. Neither of them envisioned anything of such magnitude. Today both are legends. That's the nature of discovery. That's why exploring the unknown must never be suppressed.

"Times have changed. Some want to kill free enterprise. They say medical care costs too much. Unfortunately, a few of our selfish brethren are making it easy for the critics. This bodes evil for medicine."

Joe put aside the needleholder. "Always time the lecture to end with the last stitch. Corollary—the slower the surgeon, the longer the lecture."

"That was anything but slow, Dr. Hawkins," Jerry said with admiration.

Joe tied the Deknatel at the completion of each row, setting neat square knots. Then he cautiously disengaged the clamps— first, the pulmonary side, then the aortic side. The stubby stumps of the ductus pulsated with the heart beat. The suture lines bulged, oozed momentarily while the gods of coagulation worked their magic, then bled not a drop.

"Aha! Neat, but not gaudy." Joe eyed the suture lines. "No bleeding. No chyle. The recurrent is intact. Be sure to mention those points in the op note. Close him up, will you Jerry. Slip a bit of Gelfoam between the stumps and suture the pleura over it. Gelfoam doesn't do much, but humor me. Muriel will give you a hand. He's just a little boy. Make him a nice scar."

He peeled off his gown and gloves. "The practice of medicine is fundamentally unchanged. People get sick, suffer pain, injury, fear death, need care and comfort, like always. What's changed is the goddamn economics."

Joe turned and strode from the operating room, and Muriel snapped a needle holder into Jerry's palm, harder than usual. Jerry was a lowly resident, and it was her prerogative to abuse him now and then.

"Did you hear enough?" she asked.

"Wow!" Jerry replied.

After reporting to the Merkles, Joe changed and retired to his office in the annex. Soon Muriel appeared in the door.

"Everything okay?" he asked.

"Everything's okay. The kid's in recovery. Drainage is minimal. He's awake. Jerry is with him."

"Jerry is a good boy."

"You bamboozled him with your lecture."

Joe smiled. "I know."

"You have a message from the American Medical Association in Chicago."

"*The* American Medical Association?"

"No less. The director of public relations, someone named Kate Murphy, wants to see you after your speech today."

[2]

HE WAS A SHORT man, and in the odd glow of the mercury streetlamps his round face resembled that of a cherub. He wore an overcoat of navy cashmere and a dark scarf and fedora and leather gloves, but shivered when the cold brushed his face.

Quickly he mingled with the city dwellers crossing the damp pavements and appeared to go unnoticed, for little about him was distinctive other than expensive clothing and a determined Napoleonic strut.

The orders had been precise: "Taxi to Clark and Deming. Walk toward the lake on the south side of Deming. Eight o'clock. Sharp. Bring the money." The short man glanced at a clock in the drugstore window, then proceeded, skirting the berms of crusty snow peppered with soot that lined the crowded sidewalk.

Deming is among the ordinary little streets that lattice the bank of dwellings north of Chicago's Old Town. Its biggest intersection is with Clark Street, where there is a drugstore, a bar, and a delicatessen, where in a garage not far away, on a sunny Valentine's Day years ago, mobsters held a famous massacre. The dwellings start a few yards from the intersection, and at night the curbs of Deming fill with the cars of unlucky ones without garages.

One by one the city dwellers cut away to their destinations leaving him nearly alone. The traffic noise faded and the streetlamps were fewer. He quickened the pace and wondered how and when contact would be made. The exertion warmed him, and he stopped shivering but was nervous and felt the sweat collecting in his armpits. A jogger came suddenly from behind, startled him, swept quickly past, rubber soles padding the sidewalk, and vanished into the fog and darkness ahead.

He continued walking and glanced impatiently at an approaching walker in vain search of a signal. He was inexperienced in clandestine matters and uneasy at the thought he might walk into a setup and get mugged, maybe worse. He walked faster near the end of Deming where it fed into Lincoln Park, hoping to find late visitors to the zoo and perhaps a measure of safety.

Now what? He approached the end of Deming, crossed the parkway and leaned against a steel railing with his back turned to the dark expanse of Lincoln Park, scanned the street, the parkway, and the sidewalks. The fog, heavier near the lake, shrouded the streetlamps with pearly halos. An empty taxi drove by, and he was tempted to flag it down and go home. He checked the time . . . twenty past eight . . . wait another ten minutes.

It took less. At eight twenty-five the jogger reappeared, loping effortlessly along the parkway. He was about to pass, then abruptly pulled up, gripped the railing beside the short man, and began a standing dogtrot. He was wearing a black warm-up suit with a metallic stripe down the arms and legs, a dark baseball cap, black running shoes, and a white Turkish towel around his neck, tucked in like a scarf.

"Are you my man?" the jogger asked.

The short man hesitated, then nodded.

"Do you have it?" The jogger looked straight ahead and spoke in a curious monotone.

The short man turned, unsure, trying to decide if the voice was the one he had heard on the telephone. The jogger stared poker-faced into the darkness and maintained the dogtrot. He was lean and fairly tall with a sloping neck and a contour of strength in his shoulders. The straight lines of the warm-up suit hugged his extremities, and he bounded on the balls of his feet with the ease of a conditioned athlete.

The jogger spoke again, "Clark and Deming, eight o'clock sharp," with no hint of exertion.

The short man nodded agreement. He had been told only that he would recognize the signal. "I have it," he rumbled and eyed the jogger.

"Thirty thousand in hundreds."

That confirmed the identification. "In the envelope," the short man replied.

"Details?"

"It's all there."

"Name?"

"Breslow."

"Connection?"

"I'd rather not say," the short man answered nervously. He didn't like the questions.

"Can they pin a motive on you?"

"No. I'm the only one who knows."

"If you finger me, you're dead."

The short man winced. "I won't finger you."

The jogger dropped a hand from the railing and without breaking the dogtrot, opened the zipper in his jacket and turned to the short man. "Let's have it."

He glimpsed the jogger's face. The jaw was square, the masseters well-defined below prominent cheekbones, the eyes wide-set and pale and cold. Droplets of sweat clung to the forehead. It was a sturdy face of which little was memorable except the cold look of the eyes.

He handed a thick envelope to the jogger. The jogger tucked the envelope into his jacket and gripped the railing again without missing a beat of the dogtrot.

"Are you going to count it?" the short man asked.

"Not here. I'll find you if it's not right."

"How do I know you'll do the job?"

"I'll do the job. I have a reputation."

"It must look like an accident."

"It will."

"How will you do it?"

"You'll know when it's done."

"When?"

"Three, four weeks."

"Fair enough."

"It's a pleasure doing business with you," the jogger said, almost cheerfully, still in the curious monotone. He released his grip on the rail and trotted away and in seconds vanished in the fog and darkness.

❦

"This morning I operated on a little boy with congenital heart disease. When the operation was first performed half a century ago, it was hailed as a miracle. On that occasion there was no bureaucracy to overcome and no red tape. The young surgeon, a true pioneer, knew what had to be done and simply did it. He gave life to thousands of children.

"Today the operation is routine and endures as a splendid example of American free enterprise.

"I am only one member of one profession, but I believe I speak for all of us here today. Freedom is the lifeblood of excellence. We must guard our great system of free enterprise from the ravages of bureaucratic suppression. The day we fail will be the day the miracles cease. I urge you, don't let that happen. . . . Thank you."

The Rotarians applauded as Joe stepped back from the lectern and his friends came forward to congratulate him. Jerry Sax said, "I enjoyed your speech, Dr. Hawkins. I understand what you were talking about this morning. Thank you for inviting me."

"I'm glad you could make it, Jerry. Is Charlie okay?"

"He's fine, sir."

"Good. Call me later. I'll be in the office."

Joe walked to the door of the banquet room and mingled with the people strolling out. He noticed a pretty young woman lingering at the edge of the crowd. She had chestnut hair and unusually blue eyes and wore a trim, navy suit that tastefully revealed the fullness of her bosom and hips. Their eyes met and he looked away, then their eyes met again and he moved closer and she smiled and stepped forward and offered her hand.

"Hello, Dr. Hawkins. I'm Kate Murphy."

Christ! Those are the bluest eyes I've ever seen. . . . "Hello, Miss Murphy."

"Congratulations. The audience loved your speech."

"Thank you," Joe replied. "They're friends."

"Friends can be tough critics."

Joe laughed. "I received your message. When did you arrive?"

"Two hours ago. I came straight from the airport."

"Are you staying over?"

"I plan to catch the three o'clock flight back to Chicago."

"You've come a long way."

"I have an important mission. Can we talk?"

"Of course. There's a little cocktail lounge off the lobby."

They walked across the lobby to the lounge and settled into a pair of captain's chairs.

"Something to drink?" Joe asked.

"A Chablis spritzer with crushed ice and a lime."

"Some lunch? They have sandwiches."

"No, thank you."

"Make it two spritzers," Joe said to the bartender, then looked at Kate. "I'm a little surprised."

"What do you mean?"

"You're so young."

She laughed. "I hope you're not disappointed."

"I'm delighted."

"Thank you."

"Are you really the director of public relations for the American Medical Association?"

"I am."

"So . . . you report directly to Letitia Jordan?"

"I do."

"You have a very important job."

"It's exciting. Do you know Dr. Jordan?"

"Of course. She's the first woman to become chief executive officer of the AMA, no small achievement. She's an extraordinary lady. I've seen her on 'Newsline.' She addressed our state association last year, did a phenomenal job."

"You know Dr. Jordan," she concluded.

"How old are you, may I ask?"

"You may. I'm twenty-eight."

"Tell me, how did you get lined up with the AMA?"

"I was lucky. I graduated from the University of Missouri School of Journalism when I was twenty-two. I shopped around and hired on as an intern in the PR department of the AMA. After a year they offered me a job. It was a small department, and I had a lot of responsibility. I loved it, and I worked hard. Three years later the director resigned, and I became acting director—fortuitously they were short-staffed. Dr. Jordan took a liking to me and appointed me director a couple of years ago."

"That's quite remarkable."

"Dr. Jordan has appointed a number of young women to important positions in the AMA." She smiled. "We all think she knows top talent when she sees it."

The bartender brought the spritzers. Joe's mouth was dry and the first sip of the icy Chablis and soda felt good.

Then Kate said, "Tell me, Dr. Hawkins, what do you think of the American Medical Association?"

Joe thought a moment, then replied, "It's a great organization. Covers a lot of territory, does good things. On balance, I like the AMA. It's a good outfit."

"I agree," Kate said. "And I'm one of its toughest critics."

Joe leaned back and cradled his drink in both hands. "Now that we have that settled, what's this all about?"

"It's about you and the President of the United States."

"Oh?"

"Next week President Chamberlain will address a political rally in Madison Square Garden. The address will go live on television to an audience of sixty million. He plans to attack the American Medical Association. Of course the AMA will respond. We've secured Madison Square Garden and a half hour of prime time on CBS the following night."

"What does that have to do with me?"

"We want you to deliver the rebuttal."

"You must be kidding."

"I'm not kidding."

"Why me?"

"I want a new face. Our field service rates you a fine speaker and definitely not the 'old boy' type. They spotted you a long time ago. I ran your computer profile—age, practice, family, war record. And, I heard you speak today. You're exactly what I want."

"Is the decision yours?"

"I have to clear it with Dr. Jordan, but for practical purposes, yes. You're fabulously qualified: bedrock conservative, long on values, short on nonsense, a marine war hero. And you're a busy surgeon, a mainstream doctor. You see patients every day. You'll look great on television, by the way."

"Now you're blowing smoke up my ass."

"I'm being objective, Dr. Hawkins," Kate snapped, "call it what you will. My job is to analyze these things. I happen to be very good at it."

Joe immediately regretted his cynicism. "No offense. This is a bit sudden."

Her voice softened. "Sometimes I come on a little strong."

"Please continue."

"Chamberlain will attempt to destroy the AMA. He'll castigate doctors and brand the AMA as a self-serving monopoly controlled by rich charlatans in dire need of regulation. Then he'll tout his National Health Policy as the salvation of the country. The NHP is his euphemism for socialized medicine. He loves not, the AMA. He's convinced we fought his election."

"Did we?"

"In a manner of speaking, yes. Federal law prohibits the AMA from engaging in election activities. That's for AMPAC, the political action committee, and AMPAC deals only with congressional races. The AMA runs one of the most powerful lobbies in Washington, but theoretically lobbying and electioneering don't overlap. Unfortunately, during the campaign Dr. Jordan openly criticized Chamberlain. In fact, on one occasion she called him a 'dumb shyster.' God knows, that was a mistake. Chamberlain is neither dumb nor a shyster. For sure, he'll retaliate. He's out to break Dr. Jordan."

"Can't say as I blame him," Joe said.

Kate took a moment to sip her spritzer. "The rally next week will kick off the President's new campaign for socialized medicine. This year congressional support is stronger. He may win."

"All because of Letitia Jordan?"

"Something like that."

"If he wants to fix health care, he should go after the insurance companies. They're the real villains."

"At the moment he's not mad at them. He's mad at Letitia Jordan. I'm sure you realize that Chamberlain is a formidable man with all the attributes of a successful politician. He's bright, personable, ruthless, extremely articulate; has a huge ego; covets power; thinks he can do no wrong; knows when to cut losses; and has damn little humility."

Joe laughed. "I know surgeons like that."

"But Chamberlain has a unique vulnerability."

"And what is that?"

"Everything leaks in Washington, especially the White House. We have quite a book on President Chamberlain. The word is, Don't piss him off. To put it bluntly, the man is a vindictive son of a bitch. Revenge is an obsession with him. It's also his blind spot."

"I'm sure you know what you're talking about, but where is this taking us?"

"Chamberlain wants Dr. Jordan. With that it mind, we've arranged for certain, shall I say, 'special information' to become available. You might call it 'bait.'"

"What kind of 'special information'?"

"Have you heard of the notorious 'fatcats,' the doctors who allegedly were paid a hundred thousand dollars or more last year by Medicare."

"I've heard."

"Well, last month Al Menghini, President Chamberlain's secretary of Health and Human Services decided it was his sovereign duty as guardian of the nation's health to publish the names of the 'fatcats.' That would make the public believe every doctor in the country is bilking Medicare, and it would help Chamberlain's campaign. We stopped it with an injunction, but only temporarily. Currently the matter is waiting trial.

"We obtained a copy of the list. It was shocking. They pulled names out of raw files without validating the data. 'Careless' would be a charitable word for it. The list is full of lies—phony names, botched payment records, pediatricians who've never treated Medicare patients. One poor doc who died three years ago was reportedly paid two-hundred thousand dollars after he was dead. Furthermore, we don't think Menghini is aware of the falsehoods."

"Funny, if it weren't sad," Joe said.

"We were planning to go public and try to embarrass Menghini into a retraction. Then we heard about the President's rally. We know Menghini presented the flawed list to the President, and the President doesn't know it's flawed. It's a good bet Chamberlain will wave those names, lies and all, in front of the camera next week and proclaim to the whole world that the doctors are a 'bunch of greedy bastards.' When he does, we, that is, you, will emasculate him."

"The 'fatcats' are the bait?"

"Precisely."

"Come on!"

"It's worth a try."

"What about his speech writers, his advisors? What about the injunction?"

"They'll probably tell him to back off. But this President is a killer. He'll jump on the 'fatcats.' Screw the speechwriters. Screw the injunction. What can a court do to the President of the United States? I tell you, Chamberlain won't be able to resist."

"Jesus!" Joe said. "You want to sandbag the President of the United States!"

"Look, Dr. Hawkins. I know it's a stretch, and I know it's crazy, but the man is out to destroy your profession. He may very well succeed. You have nothing to lose."

Joe smiled at his spunky young companion.

"I hope the smile is a good sign," she said.

"I'm not sold, but I am interested."

"Fair enough. Now, why do we want Joe Hawkins? Frankly the AMA has an image problem. We need a new face, a genuine doctor, someone to belie the traditional old-boy stereotype of the AMA. The current president, Dr. Hollings, is a retired radiologist. He had a coronary bypass four years ago. He's a sweet old man, but a disaster on television."

"I've seen Hollings. I agree."

"If Chamberlain takes our bait, it'll set the stage for a giant presidential confrontation. Chamberlain is tough. We need a powerful personality to take him on."

"Can't someone on the board of trustees handle it?"

"The chairman of the board, Dr. Devlin, makes the board assignments. When something good comes along, he takes it himself or gives it to Dr. Hollings. Unfortunately neither would be a match for the President, and they know it. Dr. Rodansky is on the executive committee and could probably handle it, but

Devlin won't let Rodansky do it because he's not a Devlin lackey. Ergo, no one from the board. Dr. Rodansky is an interesting man, by the way. He was a Big Ten wrestler, a tough guy. I think you'd like him."

"Why not Letitia Jordan? She's damn good at this sort of thing."

"Agreed, Dr. Jordan is damn good, and she would dearly love to do battle with Chamberlain, particularly on national television. But the press regards her as a hired gun, and she's been too personal in her attacks on Chamberlain to be a credible opponent. Furthermore, she's been out front too much. There's pressure internally to let others speak for the association."

"What kind of pressure?"

"Dissension in the board and the house of delegates. Dr. Jordan can be uncommonly abrasive. People are saying, 'Here comes Letitia Jordan again, having one of her tantrums.' She's too much of a hatchet man. We need someone new, a fresh face, from the mainstream, a real doctor who can match the President's charisma, someone who will command attention and respect."

"How did you persuade Letitia Jordan to go along with that line of reasoning?" Joe asked.

"I convinced her the plan might fail, and because she's already under fire, this is a good time to put someone else's head on the block. She knows the troops are restless. If you succeed, she takes the credit. If you fail, it's your ass, not hers."

"That's not very comforting."

"I did what I had to do to make her see it my way. Be assured, though, I do not contemplate failure."

"No, I don't suppose you do."

"Incidentally, Dr. Jordan will be gracious and seductive when you meet her, but she'll never concede that anyone can do anything for the AMA as well as she."

"Will Devlin go along?"

"Of course. Dr. Jordan controls him."

"You're revealing company secrets."

"I'm realistic, not disloyal," Kate said. "Ego reigns supreme in the AMA. You work around it. What counts are results. I'm asking you to take on a big job. The least I can do is be candid. This is too important to play cat and mouse over."

"Why do I believe you slyly manipulate Letitia Jordan and the whole damn crowd to do everything your way?"

"I'm absolutely shocked that you would even think such a thing," Kate said with a straight face.

Joe grinned. "Exactly what would I have to do?"

"Very simple. Be yourself. Deliver a sober, reasoned rebuttal, much as you did today. That was perfect. Then crucify Chamberlain on the fatcats."

"What if he decides not to wave the fatcat list in front of the camera?"

"I'll be surprised, but we still need a powerful rebuttal. We have material drafted to cover every contingency, and we simply piece your speech together after we hear the President. There'll be plenty of time to polish and rehearse. You're already well prepared—I'm sure you could wing it this afternoon if necessary. Have you done live television?"

"A couple of interviews. No speeches."

"We'll coach you on the TelePrompTer and the camera setup. No trouble."

"Where do you find fifteen thousand people to fill Madison Square Garden? No one knows Joe Hawkins from a boatload of shit."

"That's the kicker. We don't fill Madison Square Garden."

"What do you mean?"

"There'll be no live audience."

"I beg your pardon."

"No live audience. Picture this . . . Madison Square Garden . . . dead empty. Trash from the rally the night before . . . banners, posters, pennants, balloons, paper cups. We pay to have the damn place not cleaned up. You'll be speaking to a deserted arena with acres of empty seats," she leaned forward and swept her arms over the table, "and silence, like the circus tent after the clowns, the stadium after the game. You alone, on stage, facing the lens, millions out there in television land. Facts, not flamboyance.

Reason, not rhetoric. Common sense, no hyperbole." She flopped back in her chair.

Joe looked at her for a moment. "Did you dream this goddamn thing up all by yourself?" he finally asked.

"More or less."

"It's outrageous."

"Yes."

"Daring."

"I hope so."

"Ingenious."

Kate grinned. "You'll do it?"

"It's awfully short notice."

"Yes, and I apologize for that. I wanted to contact you sooner, but a terrible thing happened. Leonard Breslow, our chief financial officer, died suddenly two weeks ago. Everything came to a halt."

"I read something about that. What happened?"

"He fell down a stairway in his condo and broke his neck. We were told it was an accident. The police are still investigating."

"Foul play?"

"Don't know. I hear rumors."

"What kind of rumors?"

"Leonard was an athletic man. They think it's odd that he got killed the way he did. There's talk about his personal life. He was married, but some say he was gay. The fact that he was the money guru raises the specter of financial irregularities. The auditors descended like a bomb squad. They're still poking around."

"This is a poor time for a crisis like that."

"For damn sure. We have trouble enough already. Everyone is paranoid. The AMA is paralyzed. I thought this little deal had collapsed, but yesterday morning Dr. Jordan's secretary notified me to proceed."

"Obviously you have the boss's confidence."

"I hope so."

"What's our next move?"

"I want you to come to Chicago this Friday. Dr. Jordan promised to meet with you. You'll also get together with Ben Green—

Ben's our best speechwriter—and check out on the TelePromp-Ter. By the way, I need a copy of the speech you gave today."

"I have only my notes. You're welcome to them." Joe pulled some folded papers from inside his blazer.

"Fine. I made a tape, but the notes will be helpful. By all means, bring Mrs. Hawkins to New York. All expenses paid, of course, first-class airfare, and a thousand dollar honorarium."

"No honorarium."

"That's entirely up to you."

"I'll check my calender and call tomorrow."

"Fine." She took a card from her bag. "This is my private number."

Joe left money for the spritzers, and they walked through the lobby to the entrance of the hotel.

"Do you think the AMA is a troubled organization?" he asked.

"The problem is the dictator in charge. Dr. Jordan has been good for the AMA, but she's still a dictator. Unbridled power always means trouble." Kate picked up her trench coat at the checkroom and tossed it over an arm.

"Do you need a ride to the airport?" Joe asked.

"No thanks. I rented a car."

"Luggage?"

"Nothing," she said cheerily. "Just my Burberry and my shoulder bag—the working girl's rig."

"I'm sorry you can't stay over and enjoy the weather."

"So am I. I can't believe how good that sun feels. Chicago was twenty-four this morning. We may have two feet of snow by tonight. Bring warm clothes."

"I will."

Outside the entrance she looked up and the sun livened the chestnut in her hair and illuminated her eyes. "You have the biggest, bluest eyes I've ever seen," Joe said.

"I'm told they turn violet sometimes."

"They're spectacular."

"Thank you." She smiled and extended her hand. "Look, Dr. Hawkins. I'm asking you to take on the most powerful man in the world. That's quite a chore."

39

"I think I understand the risk."

"I'm also asking you to throw in with a tough crowd. I mean, it could get rough."

"So be it."

Then she said, "You're going to be famous, you know."

"What if I say no?"

Kate tossed her head and laughed. "I'll simply kill myself."

[3]

GRACE HAWKINS loved gin on the rocks. She opened her refrigerator and scooped a handful of ice cubes into a brandy snifter, then frowned. The cubes were actually half-moon-shaped wafers, the home refrigerator variety, cloudy and soft, and they made decidedly unattractive, watery cocktails. She liked pretty ice cubes like the bartender served at the country club, the kind that sparkled and tinkled and made really sharp martinis that held their bite. The bartender had explained that when you freeze water it captures millions of minuscule air bubbles that cloud the ice; that commercial ice makers purge the air to make clear ice; and that homemade ice is soft and melts rapidly, too quickly diluting the gin. Unfortunately the bag of clear, hard crystal ice that she picks up regularly at the grocery just for making cocktails had run out and, this evening, the homemade ice would have to do.

Oh well. She poured enough Gordon's to float the ice in the snifter, cradled the snifter in the cup of her hand, swirled it, inhaled the sensuous coriander and sweet juniper, then, resigned to ugly ice, drank the cold gin with relish.

Grace was a tall, slender woman with brown eyes and long curls of flaxen hair that tumbled adventurously over her shoulders. She had on a baggy denim shirt, the sleeves rolled up and the tail hanging out, faded jeans, and a pair of red Botegas. On her wrist was a gold Rolex with diamonds and on her ring finger, the wedding band Joe Hawkins had placed there twelve years ago.

Dinner was in the oven—tuna casserole, easy to prepare and a family favorite. Grace swirled the snifter and strolled into a sprawling room at the back of the house with oak ceiling beams and adobe walls, Navajo rugs, and a massive, fieldstone fireplace primed with mesquite logs. She sunk into a leather chair and idly listened to the children chattering in their rooms down the hall. Joe had called to say he was on his way home, and for the moment she was content with her gin.

❦

"Your father has been asked to make a speech on television," Joe announced after they had said the blessing and loaded their plates with the casserole.

The children waited for him to continue. All were nicely suntanned. Tracy, the ten year old, was a pretty blond with blue eyes, tall, like Grace, and borderline gangling. Young Rosie was pugnacious with dark hair and riveting brown eyes. Two years separated them, but Rosie's muscles made the difference seem less. Little Jake, named for Joe's father, was a towhead whose toddler legs pumped like pistons.

"It happens next week, on CBS, Madison Square Garden, in New York," Joe said.

"What's it all about?" Grace asked.

"It's for the AMA."

"What's the AMA?" Tracy asked.

"The American Medical Association," Joe said. "A—M—A. It's a bunch of doctors."

They nodded as if they understood.

Joe then told of Kate Murphy's visit and her proposal.

"That's a tall order," Grace said.

"It certainly is."

"What did you say?"

"That I would check my calendar and call in the morning." Then he added, "I can clear the time."

"And?"

"I want to do it."

"Then go for it," Grace said.

41

"You can handle it," Tracy said.

Joe laughed. "What makes you so sure, young lady?"

"You're my dad," she answered.

"I'll have to fly to Chicago on Friday to meet Letitia Jordan and the speechwriter. Then, next week, New York." He turned to Grace. "Come to New York with me."

"That would be fun," she said.

After dinner the children took a last run at Joe, then disappeared and Joe and Grace retreated to the sofa in front of the fireplace. Joe put a match to the fire, and the dry mesquite quickly filled the room with its rich fragrance.

"You're determined, aren't you?" she asked.

"I really want to do it," he replied.

Grace sensed the exhilaration. "It's time for you to have a new project," she said. "It'll be good for both of us."

"Yes. It'll be good for both of us." He took her hand. "Grace, I love you."

"I love you too." She kissed and cuddled him.

"At first I thought it was a crazy idea," he said. "But now, I'm getting excited."

"That's the way you are."

"The stakes are pretty high."

"Is it possible they're using you?"

"It's possible."

"So what—huh?" Grace anticipated his answer.

"That's right. So what?"

"What's Kate Murphy like?"

"Bright. Intelligent. Persuasive. Sincere."

"Is she attractive?"

"Very. Pretty hair, unusually blue eyes, dresses tastefully. She represents the AMA extremely well."

"Is she married?"

"She didn't say, but I presume not."

"Is she in love with you?"

"For God's sake, Grace."

"Women fall in love with you all the time."

Joe smiled. "I'll keep that in mind."

"What do you know about Letitia Jordan?"

"She's a political animal, and she's in trouble. The troops are restless, and now she's got a problem concerning her chief financial officer."

"Like what?"

"The man died a couple of weeks ago falling down some stairs. The police are still investigating, and the auditors are poking around. The place is in a turmoil."

Grace thought a moment, then said, "Maybe Lady Letitia is using you."

"For what?"

"I don't know. Maybe to deflect attention from her."

He sipped his cognac. "What the hell—we all use each other."

"Can you back out after you go to Chicago?"

"I suppose so, but I don't want to string them along."

"I'll have trouble getting away. I have a League meeting."

"Come on."

"It's an important meeting."

"Work on it. I want you to come to New York."

"I'll try, but I can't promise."

"Can you drive me to the airport Friday morning? I'll book a seat on the seven-thirty flight. The kids can ride out with us, and you can drop them at school on the way back."

"They'd love that." She drank some gin.

"For the life of me, I don't see how anyone can handle gin after dinner," Joe said.

"I like the taste."

Cold air poured into the bedroom when Joe opened the Arcadia door and by the time he had pulled the curtains back and hurried to bed, he was goosebumped and shivering. Grace had already crawled under their big down comforter. In the winter they liked to sleep under the comforter with the room wide open to the cold. He pulled her warm rump against his belly, but the shock of his cold skin failed to elicit the customary recoil and little squeal. He rearranged the comforter and draped his arm across her body. Grace was sound asleep and her breathing was labored. She had consumed more gin than he realized. His thoughts churned with ideas for the speech, and he was impatient to call Kate in the morning. Now he was tired and the warmth of Grace's body settled him, but it was a while before he dozed off.

❦

Joe arrived in Chicago at noon and the weather was clear and very cold. It was sunny across the country, and with a seventy-knot tailwind at thirty-seven thousand feet, the 727 coasted into O'Hare a half-hour early. How can it be so damn cold here, Joe thought, and so warm and balmy only three hours away in the desert, on the same continent, in the same winter, under the same sun? He walked from the warm terminal across an icy sidewalk to the taxi stand and shivered in spite of his overcoat and the fur hat with ear muffs.

The American Medical Association headquarters was north of the loop near Michigan Avenue. Kate was waiting in the lobby.

"Welcome to cold Chicago," she said cheerily.

"Thank you."

"Good trip?"

"Very good."

She led him to the elevator. "Dr. Jordan is waiting." Kate's dress, oyster white with blue stripes and long sleeves, clung provocatively to her hips.

They entered a luxurious lobby on the third floor. "That's the board room," she said, pointing to a big double-door, "where they make the 'godlike decisions.'"

"You lack reverence, Miss Murphy," Joe remarked.

"I do indeed, Dr. Hawkins." They crossed the lobby. "The executive offices are down the hall."

"Is this where the top brass hang out?"

"Right."

"It seems awfully quiet."

"The board met last week. It's always a crisis when they're in town and a big letdown when they leave. Actually, more like terminal shock. It was worse this time because of the Breslow thing."

"How often does the board meet?"

"Five times a year, plus special meetings."

"Is that all?"

"That's all."

"I take it Letitia Jordan runs the AMA more or less single-handedly."

"That's about the size of it."

They turned a corner and entered a waiting room where a statuesque woman with sleek black hair sat at a desk by a door marked "Executive Vice-President."

"Dr. Hawkins, this is Sarah Mason, Dr. Jordan's personal secretary," Kate said.

"How do you do, Dr. Hawkins?" Sarah rose and came around the desk. "Let me take your things. Dr. Jordan has been expecting you. Please go right in."

"Thank you." He followed Kate through the door.

Letitia Jordan walked across the room to greet them. She was young forties, petite, in elegant black, round face, clear skin, the palest of blue eyes, strawberry blond hair pulled snugly back into a tight chignon, Evita style, and she walked with loping strides that stretched her thin legs. Beneath it all she was pleasingly filled out and Joe thought, "My God, she's as beautiful as she is deadly."

"Afternoon, Kate. Hi, Joe?" Letitia smiled affably and grasped Joe's hand. "Good to see you again. A year ago, wasn't it, in Phoenix?" The husky voice was almost too big for the diminutive body.

"That's right," Joe replied. "Nice to see you, Letitia. I know you're busy. It's good of you to make time for me."

"Not at all, not at all," Letitia replied. "Glad to do it. I'm sure Kate told you that Len Breslow, our CFO, died a couple of weeks ago, in a fall. That was a shocker, but things are settling down now. I'm delighted you could make it."

Joe wondered if Letitia truly remembered their previous meeting. It was a year ago at a medical society dinner in Phoenix. She had delivered one of her trademark stemwinders—a bombastic, locker-room, half-time fight talk. "We will never submit to government hoodlums," she had screamed and the doctors had

45

cheered. She was an orator, all right. It was somehow reminiscent of newsreels of the Anschluss in the thirties and Adolph Hitler mesmerizing hysterical masses with the sheer power of his words.

The three of them sat down. "How are things in sunny Arizona?" Letitia asked.

"Warmer than Chicago," Joe replied.

"Chicago is a bitch in the winter."

"Come visit us, anytime. They're still talking about that speech you gave in Phoenix last spring."

"Thank you. It was a great crowd. I probably got carried away."

"They loved it."

"Kate tells me you're a pretty good talker yourself."

"I had a friendly audience when she was there."

"That always helps."

They laughed and it reminded Kate of two fencers meeting for the first time—measuring, sparring, each testing the firmness of the other's blade.

"We have a problem," Letitia said. "This clown Chamberlain is hell-bent to nail us."

"So it appears," Joe said.

"He gave Health and Human Services to that son of a bitch, Menghini. Menghini kisses his ass every day."

"Former Senator Menghini?"

"Now Secretary Menghini. Last year he introduced a bill that would have forced medical students and residents to pay back their training by serving equal time in deprived areas, under the authority of Uncle Sam, of course. We killed it, but he'll be back. Now that he's got cabinet rank, he fancies himself the goddamn king of medicine."

"What's his problem?" Joe asked, wondering if she fancied herself as the "queen."

"That's easy," Letitia replied. "Menghini wants to make chattels of us. He's an old enemy. Now he's in cahoots with Chamberlain—signed on early in the campaign, delivered his state, and got HHS in return. He's positioned himself well, and he inspires Chamberlain, as if that son of a bitch needs inspiration."

"Have you met Menghini?"

"Oh yes. I saw him two weeks ago and told him just what I think of him."

"Did it do any good?"

"I don't know, but I want that son of a bitch and his boss to know, by God, we're not going to roll over."

"I imagine you made that perfectly clear," Joe said, smiling.

"I did, and it made me feel better," Letitia said. Then she looked sternly at Joe. "Chamberlain and Menghini are out to destroy medicine. They plan to start by destroying me."

After a moment her frown relaxed and she turned to Kate. "Well, young lady, this is your show. Proceed."

Kate spoke smartly. "Dr. Hawkins, now we have lunch with Ben Green to talk about the speech."

"Ben's a good speechwriter," Letitia said.

Kate continued. "We've compiled everything President Chamberlain might say. We'll go over the material until you're comfortable. We want you ready for anything when you come to New York.

"After lunch we'll stop in the TV room. We have a good clip of the President, and you can check out on the TelePrompTer. We'll make a tape, see how you look."

"I don't want to see how I look," Joe grumbled.

Kate laughed. "How about a tough Q and A for practice. That's always fun."

"Ugh," Joe said.

"Don't worry," Kate said. "All practice tapes are erased. No one, but no one, rats outside the TV room. Right, Dr. Jordan?"

"Right."

"That will finish the afternoon. You should be able to make the dinner flight to Phoenix."

"Great," Joe said.

Kate continued. "Next Wednesday Dr. Hawkins, Ben Green, and I will meet in New York. I've reserved a suite at the Plaza in your name, Dr. Hawkins. It has a TV with a VCR. At seven Ben and I will join you in the suite for dinner. The President will speak at nine. We'll critique the speech and have the rest of the evening and all next day to prepare your remarks."

"What time do I go on?"

"Nine o'clock, same time as the President. We'll have dinner in the suite about six. Dr. Jordan, Dr. Devlin, and possibly Dr. Hollings will join us and wrap up the details. Dr. Jordan, of course, must approve the draft. You and I will head for the Garden about eight. The others will watch in the suite."

"You'll have a bar for us?" Letitia inquired.

"Of course," Kate replied. "However, I prefer that Dr. Hawkins not imbibe before the speech."

"You make the rules," Letitia said, grinning. "However, I'm not the speaker, and I know Hollings will want his drinks."

"That about covers it," Kate said.

"Well, Joe?" Letitia asked.

"Frankly, I'm nervous."

"We've had a good look at you," Letitia said. "You'll do just fine."

"I hope so."

They departed Letitia's office and Kate led him to a small conference room down the hall. Fresh coffee and sandwiches and cookies waited on the credenza. "Ben will join us in a moment," she said. "May I pour your coffee? It smells awfully good."

"Please," Joe said.

They sat down. "Brandy would go well with this," she said.

"That it would."

"Perhaps next time."

"Well, what do you think of the great Letitia Jordan?"

"I thought you might ask."

"I'm only curious. I won't tell." Kate folded her legs and arranged the dress over her knees. She was prettier than Joe remembered from their first meeting.

"She's a powerful woman—smart, deadly, strikingly beautiful, egotistical, ruthless, and probably perfect for her job," Joe said.

"Don't sugarcoat it," Kate said, grinning.

"She likes strong language."

"Do you like her?"

"Yes. I like her."

"It's hard not to like her."

"How does the staff feel?"

"By and large, they respect her. Some think she's a genius. Some are uneasy around her."

"Like I said, she's probably perfect for the job."

"Now do you understand why I can't let her give the speech?"

"I do indeed. I'm surprised, though, that you're getting away with it."

"It's a matter of ego. Her big fear is looking bad. I convinced her the whole idea might backfire, and that she personally should not run that risk. If someone has to take a fall, better you than she—it's that simple."

"Very clever."

"Ego is the soft underbelly of powerful people."

"What if it does backfire?"

"No way," Kate said. "You're a winner."

"You're still blowing smoke up my ass."

"No. I mean it."

"I hope you're right," Joe said. "Whatever happens, I'm grateful for the opportunity."

"It will be a memorable occasion."

"Incidentally, is Letitia married?"

"Funny you ask," Kate replied. "Yes, she's married, to Dr. Luther Agostelli, a psychiatrist of all things, a quiet little guy no taller than she. He sticks to her like glue."

[4]

SARAH MASON called on the intercom. "The gentlemen from the police department are here."

She escorted two men, youngish and wearing brown seersucker suits, into Letitia Jordan's office. One was tall, the other, average height and stocky, and the tall man carried a large, manila envelope. Each produced a wallet with a badge.

"Good morning, Dr. Jordan," the tall man said. "I'm Detective Caliano. This is Detective Stubbs."

Letitia smiled and shook their hands. "How do you do, gentlemen?"

"Thank you for seeing us," Caliano said.

"Anytime," Letitia said. "Please, come in."

"Something to drink?" Sarah inquired.

"Black coffee would be fine," Caliano replied.

"The same," Stubbs said.

They settled into the chairs in front of Letitia's desk. The brown suits were rumpled, and she calculated it must have been at least three wearings since they had been pressed. Had she not known they were Chicago cops, she might have figured them for a pair of small-time car salesmen.

"Well, gentlemen, I understand you're interested in one of my former employees."

"Yes, ma'am," Caliano replied, quickly concluding the woman was a hard-assed broad. "We're investigating the death of Leonard Breslow."

"Poor Len—killed himself falling down the stairs in his condo," Letitia said.

"That was the initial determination," Stubbs said.

"Is there a problem?" Letitia asked.

"We're not certain the fall killed him," Caliano said.

"Oh?"

Sarah Mason returned with two coffees and a Coca-Cola for Letitia and arranged the drinks on the desk, then departed.

"You have my attention, gentlemen," Letitia said.

Caliano sipped his coffee. "How long did you know Leonard Breslow?"

"About five years," Letitia replied.

"We understand that you appointed him chief financial officer of the American Medical Association eight months before his death."

"That's correct. I hired him out of the Martin Ross firm. He was my vice-president for finance and corporate planning."

"What did his responsibilities include?"

"The AMA and its subsidiary corporations."

"Subsidiary corporations?"

"It's a little complicated," Letitia said. "The AMA owns an insurance company and a holding company with a number of subsidiary components."

"Is it fair to say that Breslow looked after all financial matters involving the AMA and its holdings?"

"That's fair," Letitia replied.

Caliano produced a notebook. "Breslow and his wife lived alone in a condominium on North Shore Drive near Fullerton Avenue. They sold their home in Evanston five years ago, after their children had grown, and moved to the condo."

"That was my understanding," Letitia said.

"Breslow arrived home by taxi at seven-fifteen on the evening of February 20, the day he died. The cab company records verify his pickup in front of the Dearborn Street entrance of the AMA building at six-fifty-five and arrival at the condo at seven-fifteen, twenty minutes later. The doorman remembers seeing him come in. Breslow lived on the fifth floor. He made it a practice to run up the stairs for exercise. Each flight was ten stairs, and there was a landing between each of the floors. That evening he apparently started up as usual, but didn't make it. At seven-forty-five one of the tenants found his body lying face down on the landing between the third and fourth floors. His watch was still running. At first blush it appeared to be a straightforward case of accidental death. However, certain inconsistencies came to our attention."

"Inconsistencies?"

Caliano continued. "Why did Breslow fall? He was fifty years old and in good physical condition. His blood was negative for alcohol. He hadn't been ill. He was athletic and liked exercise. He jogged and played racquetball regularly at the Uptown Club. He had navigated the same stairs hundreds of times. Furthermore, he was going up the stairs. The vast majority of stairway falls occur when someone loses control trying to go down too fast.

"His body was found at the bottom of the stairs, but his briefcase was found on the landing above. Why would a relatively young man, sober and in good physical condition, reach the top of the stairs, then fall in an uncontrolled manner all the way back to the bottom?

"The briefcase was leather, full of papers and fairly heavy. It was dented on one corner and freshly scraped. Well and good. It was damaged on the cement. But the briefcase wound up across the landing six feet from the top of the stairs. Why didn't it fall down the stairs with him?

"He was found face down. His nose was smashed, but there was minimal blood in the nostrils and only a spot on the cement under his face. The septum was severely lacerated. Nasal bleeding should have been profuse."

Caliano sipped his coffee and continued. "A fresh ecchymosis twelve centimeters in diameter was found on the body over the tenth rib on the right. The ecchymosis was the diameter of a fist. The rib was fractured. The proximal end had punctured the pleura and the lower lobe of the lung. The autopsy showed fresh bleeding at the fracture site and in the pleural cavity.

"The force required to cause such an injury would have been extraordinary. Breslow was wearing an overcoat over a suit and vest and a shirt and undershirt, a goodly amount of padding. And he was fairly muscular. Something hit him like a pile driver, but we found no object or protuberance that might have caused such an injury. Furthermore, no other bruises were found on the body. If he had tumbled down ten stairs hard enough to cave in his chest, you would expect bruises."

Caliano pulled two X-rays from the envelope and handed them to Letitia. "These are the anterior and lateral decubitus views of the chest taken on the autopsy table."

She leaned back and held the films up to the ceiling light. "The broken rib is displaced."

"Do you make out the pneumothorax?" Caliano asked.

"Yes, of course," Letitia said, pointing to a thin rim of translucency on the lateral view.

"We thought that as a physician you would be interested in the films," Caliano said.

"I am interested. What about a skull fracture? With a fall, that's the first thing I would think of."

"No skull fracture. The only injury to the head was the broken nose."

"Was anything found that might have dropped him in his tracks, like a myocardial occlusion, a stroke, a ruptured aneurysm?"

"Nothing," Caliano said. He pulled more X-rays out of the envelope and passed them to Letitia. "These are the postmortem head and neck films."

On the lateral film she saw the ghost-like outline of the skull of Leonard Breslow. Something caught her attention, and she focused on the intricate pattern of shadows where the spine joined the base of the skull.

"You've spotted it," Caliano said.

Letitia studied the films. "I'm no radiologist, but that's one helluva busted neck."

Caliano pulled a report from the envelope and read: "There is anterior subluxation of the atlas, C-1. The odontoid process of the axis, C-2, is fractured at its base. There are comminuted fractures of both pedicles of C-2 with anterior dislocation and apparent levorotation of C-2 on C-3 and evidence of extensive soft tissue damage throughout the adjacent tissues. This represents a massive injury of the upper cervical spine with complete bony dislocation, rotation, and certain spinal cord severance. Such injuries are caused by a powerful, snap-like twist of the neck coupled with extreme hyperextension. The resultant fracture complex is known as, 'hangman's fracture.'"

"He sure as hell didn't hang himself," Letitia said.

"No, sir," Caliano said.

"Whoever dictated that report has a certain flare," Letitia said.

"The coroner's pathologist," Caliano said. "He's something of a ghoul."

"You have a certain flare yourself." Letitia had noticed Caliano's expert use of medical terminology.

"Thank you, ma'am," Caliano said, half smiling, then continued. "We found a four centimeter strand of navy blue wool snagged under the edge of the nail on the middle finger of the left hand. It appears to be out of a sweater." He produced a photograph of the dead man's hand and handed it to Letitia.

"We don't know where it came from. Nothing Breslow wore matches the fiber. No other garments or fabric of any kind were found in the stairway."

"What about the lining of his gloves?"

"Good point. We checked. He had leather gloves with no lining. They were in his coat pocket when he fell. He took them off when he paid the driver. The receipt for the cab fare was also in the pocket."

"Could he have picked it up somewhere else?"

"We searched all of his and Mrs. Breslow's clothing, the cab, and his route through the building to the stairway and came up with nothing. Furthermore, you can see from the photograph that the strand was big enough to be bothersome. You would have expected him to remove it from the nail as soon as he noticed it."

The two detectives sat quietly while Letitia pondered the X-rays and the photograph.

"You're extremely thorough," she finally said.

Detective Stubbs replied. "It's unlikely, if not impossible, that the fall alone produced a fracture like that in his neck."

"Well then, what did?"

"A man," Stubbs answered softly.

"A man?"

"We believe Mr. Breslow was murdered," Stubbs said.

"You can't mean it. By whom, for God's sake?"

"A powerful man, trained in silent, noninvasive killing techniques. A man who could deliver a lethal bolo punch to the ribs and snap his neck with a choke hold."

Letitia contemplated the detective's statement for a moment, then said, "That's far-fetched. It could have been a freak fall."

Stubbs persisted. "The broken neck was no accident, maam. I'll stake my life on it. Breslow was killed by an expert. Properly applied, a choke hold can snap the victim's neck and sever the spinal cord in a second. The bones crack and the body goes limp. Death is instantaneous."

"Good Lord! How do you know something like that?"

"I served four years in the special services branch of the army, ma'am."

"Detective Stubbs is our expert," Caliano said, again half smiling. "He knows all about choke holds."

The stocky detective continued. "The doorman saw Breslow enter the front door of the apartment building at seven-fifteen carrying the briefcase in his right hand. He walked across the lobby to the stairwell and began climbing the stairs. When he reached the fourth floor landing, he took a step or two and was attacked by an unknown assailant. We'll demonstrate what we believe happened."

The detectives stood up, and Stubbs positioned himself behind the taller man.

"The assailant was waiting on the landing," Stubbs said. "They were alone. Breslow was unsuspecting and therefore off-guard. They pass, the assailant turns and drives his fist into Breslow's flank, hard enough to fracture the rib. A bolo punch." Stubbs simulated the blow from behind Caliano.

"He probably used a lead gauntlet, a glove with strips of lead sewn in to add weight, something like a boxing glove with lead in the padding. A lead gauntlet weighs four, maybe five pounds, and can turn a strong man's fist into a bludgeon.

"The blow causes Breslow to rear back in an uncontrolled manner." Caliano arched his back and threw up his arms.

"As Breslow's arms come up, he releases the briefcase. It's thrown forward on the landing in the direction he's facing at the moment of the attack. That's why it didn't fall down the stairs behind him. The cement floor caused the fresh scuffs on the briefcase.

"Breslow is instantly helpless. The assailant throws one arm around the neck and hooks the crook of his elbow under the chin. With his other hand he locks the head into the crook. Then he drives Breslow to his knees. Now he has leverage." Stubbs went through the steps of applying the hold.

"The assailant is wearing a blue wool sweater. Breslow clutches at the arm that's choking him"—Caliano clutches Stubbs's arm—"and snags his finger nail in the sweater. When his hand pulls away, a strand of wool hooks under the nail and comes with it. That strand of wool is the only tangible evidence we have that someone other than the victim was present.

"Breslow is helpless. The assailant brings the full strength of his arms and shoulders to bear. He snaps Breslow's head forward, then snaps it back and gives it a sharp twist. The twist severs the spinal cord." Stubbs demonstrated on Caliano.

"Forward, backward, and twist. Sort of a rocking motion. Forward, backward, and twist. If you do it properly, it's like pithing a frog."

"Easy does it," Caliano said.

Stubbs smiled and released Caliano. "The assailant maintains the hold until he's certain Breslow is finished. He repeats the maneuver if necessary. He probably checks the pulse in the neck before he lets go. When he's sure Breslow is dead, he throws the body down the stairs face first. Breslow's nose is smashed by the fall, but it doesn't bleed. His heart had already stopped. He was dead before the fall, which is why there was no bruising. Of course, his heart was beating when the rib was fractured, which explains the ecchymosis on the chest and the bleeding around the fracture site."

The detectives sat down across from Letitia.

"That's quite a story," Letitia said. "How did the man get in and out without being seen?"

"The condo had only one doorman," Caliano said. "Our man had no trouble. He was a pro."

Letitia thought for a moment. "Maybe it was a mugging."

"He wasn't robbed," Caliano replied. "He had his wallet and his jewelry."

"Well," Letitia said, "he could have lost his balance, dropped the briefcase, fallen backward, cracked a rib against the edge of the stair, jammed his neck. I've seen broken noses that didn't bleed much."

"What about the strand of wool?" Stubbs asked.

She shrugged. "That seems like damn little evidence to hang a murder on."

"It's circumstantial," Caliano admitted.

"Assuming you're correct, who would do it?"

"A professional killer," Caliano replied. "Trained in the military. Probably taller than Breslow. Very strong. Owns a lead gauntlet and a blue wool sweater."

"We've identified a list of suspects," Stubbs said. The FBI maintains a file on persons known to be skilled in noninvasive killing, based on military and civilian records. They also have a file of known professional killers and their MO's. They ran a check."

"Did you find a connection with Breslow?"

"No, ma'am," Stubbs replied.

"Organized crime?"

"We're checking that out," Caliano said. "However, this has the earmarks of a private contract. The killer made it look like an accident. Mobs generally don't work that way. They want their hits recognized as executions."

"So, you believe Len Breslow was murdered by a hired killer."

"Yes, ma'am," Caliano said.

"Who tried to make it look like an accident."

"Yes, ma'am."

"Working for someone unknown."

"Yes, ma'am."

"Why, for God's sake?"

"That's the big question," Caliano replied. "We have no motive, no idea who would want Breslow killed, or why—not even a hint."

"Maybe you have no murder."

"Maybe," Caliano said.

"This is bizarre," Letitia murmured.

"Hired killers don't work for the hell of it," Caliano said. "Somebody paid. And there has to be a motive. That's why we're here. Do you know anything that can help us?"

"Certainly not."

"Breslow was your chief financial officer. Did he leave any financial irregularities?"

"None. We conducted an immediate audit."

"Who performed the audit?"

"Martin Ross. They've been our audit firm for several years. I mentioned that Len worked for them."

"I assume you had internal audits."

Letitia bristled. "The board of trustees does not feel obliged to have internal audits. That function is carried out by the CFO under my direction."

"Did Breslow perform that function when he was CFO?"

"Yes he did."

"And he reported no irregularities?"

"That's right."

"Could he have covered up something?"

Letitia responded cautiously. "Nothing worth getting killed over. The internal audit deals with lesser matters, like expense accounts. Martin Ross would have picked up any significant discrepancies."

"We understand you paid Breslow a signing bonus of one-hundred thousand dollars."

"Correct."

"That's a generous sum."

"It was generous, but not out of line. Bonuses of that order are often required to recruit top executives. Len was well worth it."

Caliano smiled apologetically. "I mean no offense, Dr. Jordan. I'm sure you realize that if a motive is found, in all probability it will have to do with money. This is particularly true when the victim is the financial officer of an enterprise with the largesse of the American Medical Association."

"I understand," Letitia replied.

"I assume you maintain your financial records on a computer."

"Correct."

"We would like to examine the records that were under Breslow's supervision."

"Very well. I'll advise our general counsel to cooperate in whatever way is appropriate."

"One last thing," Caliano said. He pulled a folded paper from his jacket. "Mrs. Breslow found this in their personal lockbox. It's one of Leonard Breslow's AMA letterheads. The word 'LEDGER' is handprinted in capital letters."

Letitia studied the paper. "'LEDGER?' What does it mean?"

"Mrs. Breslow is certain it's her husband's handwriting, but she doesn't know what it means."

Letitia returned the paper to Caliano. "I can't help you."

"Do you maintain other financial records?"

"No, sir."

"Could it be a code?"

"Not that I know of. We use standard numerical identifiers."

Caliano folded the paper and returned it to his jacket. "That's about all for now. Thank you for your time, doctor." The detectives rose to leave. "We'll make arrangements to see the financial records."

"You're convinced he was murdered?" Letitia asked.

Caliano smiled. "I'm beginning to doubt it. But we're obliged to investigate."

[5]

TWENTY THOUSAND friends of President David Chamberlain packed Madison Square Garden. They cheered, waved flags, drank beer, clapped, and were lavishly rewarded with an old-fashioned political rally. The President, as Kate had predicted, savaged the doctors. He took the bait about the fatcats and waved a fistful of papers and pounded the lectern and shouted: "These doctors are cheating the American people." It was vintage Chamberlain, the politician. Phase one of her plan had worked. Now it was time to drop the sandbag. But the President of the United States is not someone to trifle with, and this particular President was vindictive and very able.

Joe flew to New York on the day of the President's speech. Grace had decided to stay home for the League meeting, and they had quarreled.

"Please come with me," he had pleaded. "Your friends won't care."

"I've made a commitment."

"You'll just sit around all afternoon with those women and babble and get drunk." He often wondered how Grace and her cronies managed to accomplish anything, let alone find their ways home afterward.

"I promised Jackie."

"Bullshit, Grace, it can't be that important."

"It's important to her."

"You say yourself the League is a bunch of phonies."

"No they're not," she snapped.

"I didn't mean that," he said. "I love you, Grace. I'm just disappointed you're not coming with me."

She kissed him. "I'm disappointed too, and I love you."

"I know the League means a lot to you."

"I want to hang in there a while longer—for the little girls, if nothing else."

"What parents endure for the goddamn sake of status."

"The goddamn Junior League, the goddamn debutante's ball, the whole goddamn bit," Grace said. "Anyway, it's cold in New York, and you'll be too busy to have any fun. Maybe in the spring we can go alone, just the two of us. Spring would be perfect. Maybe we can see *La Bohème* or *Butterfly*. Central Park will be pretty. The stores will be full. In the spring we can have New York to ourselves."

"I called mom," Joe said. "She's excited."

"Wonderful. How is she? How's Janie?"

"They're both fine. Janie is the more excited. They're having some friends over to watch. All of Jacksonville has been alerted, naturally."

"I'm going to watch with the kids. One night we watch the President of the United States, the next night we watch Dad, and we keep score."

"God help me!"

"God help us all if you don't win."

❦

On the evening of the President's rally, Kate and Ben Green joined Joe in his suite in the Plaza. They ordered up strip sirloins and a cabernet and watched the rally on television.

Kate was elated when it was over. "We anticipated every point he made. We're ready."

"He sure tore into the 'fatcats,'" Joe said, "as you predicted."

"We've got him," Kate said.

"Menghini must have snookered the hell out of him," Joe said.

"You're not sorry for him, are you?" Kate chided.

"I pity the poor bastards who fed him the wrong information. You don't do that to a President."

They huddled around the dining table and worked on Joe's speech until they were exhausted, then Kate and Ben retired to their rooms and Joe crawled under the covers of his big bed and fell asleep.

At ten the next morning they met again and called room service for scrambled eggs and sausage. Ben pulled some papers from his briefcase. "I fleshed out a speech. The 'fatcats' are the centerpiece."

"Great," Joe said.

"I included the usual spiel about the great and wonderful things the AMA is doing," Ben said.

As Joe read the speech, his face showed disappointment. "Forgive me, Ben," he said. "This sounds like a damn commercial."

Kate frowned. "We thought you might say that."

"What do you mean?" Joe asked.

"Dr. Jordan won't approve the speech without the commercial, as you call it."

"So?"

"So, you finesse it," she said.

Ben folded his hands on the table. "Dr. Hawkins. I listened to the tape of your speech last week in Phoenix. It was a fine performance. You came off as a caring doctor talking to a patient."

"You don't need our speech," Kate said. "Chamberlain was devastating, but you can top him if you look straight into that television camera and go one-on-one with those twenty million people out there. You're their doctor, not Chamberlain. They want to hear from you, not a politician, not a speechwriter."

Joe leaned back and stared at his friends. Kate—bright, eager, her pretty face chapped from the winter cold, and Ben—intense, professorial, thick glasses, probing eyes, a bit frazzled.

"You're saying, do it my way?" Joe asked.

"You got it," Kate replied.

Joe shuffled the pages of the draft. "Okay. What do you suggest?"

"Use the factual material, delete what you don't like, and extemporize the rest," Ben said.

"To hell with the party line," Kate said.

"What about Letitia?"

"We'll give her my draft for approval," Ben said.

"You mean, switch speeches," Joe said.

"Right," Ben said.

"At the last minute you get confused and decide to wing it," Kate said. "That's perfectly understandable. She'll scream like hell, but she'll get over it. In fact, she'll take the credit."

"This is a goddamn conspiracy," Joe said.

"Of course it is," Kate said.

"Why chance it?" Joe asked.

"Why not?" Kate replied. "The AMA is a magnificent organization, but it could become a cold, political monster. There are damn good doctors out there, and I like to think I work for them. I do whatever it takes to protect what they stand for. I know you see it the same way. Besides, you couldn't handle a canned speech."

"You're a brazen wench," Joe said.

"Whatever it takes," she repeated. "One thing, though. If Letitia Jordan finds out Ben was in on this, she'll have him for breakfast. You must take full responsibility."

"What about you?"

She grinned. "I can take care of myself. Scheming and conniving are part of my job description."

They spread the papers across the dining table, and in two hours Joe was ready. Then Kate and Ben departed to prepare the bogus draft for the TelePrompTer.

Joe decided to skip lunch and go for a walk. It was a wintry afternoon. He strolled along Fifty-ninth Street across from Central Park, turned on Fifth Avenue, and entered Tiffany's. He browsed the tables of elegant china long enough to get warm, then walked on to the Gucci store and ran the gauntlet of smug salespeople in their brown dresses and jackets. They scornfully eyed his Johnson and Murphys until he engaged one of them to purchase a gift for Grace, a small and outrageously expensive black evening bag with a gold chain. Then he returned to the Plaza and the warm suite and after an oatmeal cookie and hot tea, slipped into his pajamas and crawled into the big bed. The audacity of Kate's plan troubled him, but he soon fell asleep.

At five o'clock Joe awakened and quickly showered and shaved. The knocker sounded and at the door stood a big man, fiftyish, with a square jaw and heavy eyebrows and thick, graying hair. His shoulders filled a tweed jacket and his face was furrowed and tough looking; then he grinned and the toughness melted.

"You're Joe Hawkins?" the man inquired.

"Yes."

"I'm Duke Rodansky, member of the board of trustees." The voice was leathery and friendly. "I was in New York and decided to stay over for your speech."

"Please come in."

They shook hands and Duke Rodansky entered. He was slightly pigeon-toed but moved with surprising agility. Joe remembered Kate saying he was a Big Ten wrestler.

"Kate told me about you," Joe said.

"She told me a lot about you," Duke replied. "Bless her heart. Is she here?"

"Not yet. The bar is open. Would you like a drink?"

"Believe I would." Duke rummaged behind the bar and came up with a bottle of Black Label. "Can I fix one for you?"

"No thanks."

"Following Kate's orders?"

Joe laughed. "You're damn right."

Duke dropped ice cubes into a highball glass and poured a serious shot of the Scotch, then downed a big swallow. "Who's in town?"

"Kate and Ben Green. Letitia Jordan is coming. We're expecting Devlin, Hollings, and Mrs. Hollings."

"What do you think of Letitia?"

"Beautiful and deadly."

"That pretty well sums it up."

"So far, I like her."

"Did you meet her husband?"

"No. Kate told me a little about him."

"Name's Luther Agostelli. He's a psychiatrist. You can imagine the comments that draws."

"I can imagine," Joe said, smiling.

"He's a little guy—no taller than Letitia. A strange cat. Talks like a professional Southerner. He'll be here. She never travels without him. Curiously, for all her ability, she depends on him."

"She's a powerhouse. It's hard to believe she depends on anyone but herself."

Duke smiled. "Ben is an excellent speechwriter. He and Kate make a good team. Incidentally, you can count on Kate. She gets the job done."

"I've noticed that," Joe said.

"Letitia is the boss, but Kate knows how to manipulate her. Kate is a very capable young lady."

"Letitia seems to like her."

"Letitia fancies her as tough, like she is. She goes for that."

Joe smiled.

"Letitia is smart as hell. But she's got an ego that won't quit. Sooner or later it'll finish her."

"Docs have big egos," Joe said.

"True, but Letitia is exceptional," Duke said and upended his Scotch. "Well, Dr. Hawkins, last week you were leading the orderly life of a busy surgeon, saving lives, stamping out disease, minding your own business."

"That I was."

"And tonight the American Medical Association is spending half a mill to stick you on TV in front of twenty million people. Have you wondered why the AMA would put out that kind of money on a harebrained scheme to sic an unknown joker from Arizona on the President of the United States?"

"I have indeed," Joe replied.

"Well, you heard Chamberlain last night. He was mean as hell. We have to fight the son of a bitch, and you're the man. We have nothing to lose."

"Only my ass."

Duke smiled. "No way, amigo. You're no loser."

"I hope you're right."

"You were Kate's idea. She's always wanted to pull someone in from the trenches, a mainstreamer, a new face, to do something spectacular. This thing with Chamberlain is perfect. Kate knew the heat was building to let someone else speak for the association. She convinced Letitia that now would be a fine time to be magnanimous, throw the critics a bone, and, incidentally, duck the risk."

"I can't imagine Letitia ducking anything."

"You're absolutely right. She's fearless, sometimes to the point of being foolish. However, we've had complaints about her too frequent public appearances."

"Doesn't the board decide those things?"

"Theoretically, yes."

"Why is Letitia so pivotal?"

"She's our gal," Duke replied. "She knows everything about the AMA."

"Kate filled me in last week. The whole thing is a little hard to comprehend."

"We need a new image."

"That's what Kate said."

"This is one of those brainstorms that's elegant for its sheer simplicity."

"I'm still not sure about Letitia."

"You'll reinforce Letitia's ego. She figures if you do well, it's because of her. But if you screw up, it's your ass, not hers, and the complainers on the board take the blame. Either way, tomorrow we all eat humble pie. She'll still think she's the greatest, and it's back to business as usual."

"You're spending a lot of money on humble pie."

"Letitia Jordan doesn't give a damn about that. She also doesn't give a damn what happens to you."

"She was friendly," Joe said.

"Of course. She's very likable."

"And effective."

"Enormously effective," Duke agreed. "She's a powerful leader—been great for the AMA. But you have to know how to deal with her. Another thing: for the moment she regards you as a flash in the pan. That will change the instant she realizes you're a threat."

"I'm no threat to Letitia Jordan."

"The hell you aren't," Duke said.

"I'll probably screw up."

"No way. Follow your instincts."

"I'll try to remember that," Joe said. He liked this big guy with the blunt talk and wondered if Kate had told him of the plan to switch speeches.

"I'm a little surprised that Letitia is coming in tonight," Duke said. "She's been swamped. Did Kate tell you what happened to Len Breslow?"

"She mentioned it."

"It's a frigging mess. The auditors froze the books. We have bean counters all over the place. On top of that, we just had a board meeting. Poor Letitia has been running on fumes lately."

"What's the deal on Breslow?" Joe asked.

"Don't know for sure. First we were told he fell down a stairway and broke his neck. Then we heard the cops were still investigating. He broke his neck, all right, but they seemed to think it was unusual. And, there was something about a secret file. When the head bean counter croaks, all hell breaks loose. Our jungle drums have been working overtime."

"Secret file?" Joe said.

"That's all I know. So far it's only rumor."

"Tell me about the neck injury."

"I was told it was a fracture subluxation that severed the cervical cord, and that death was instantaneous. Must have been a C-1–C-2 fracture. It struck me as pretty unusual too, for that kind of fall."

"Do the police think someone killed him?"

"I suppose they do."

"It could have been a chokehold."

"I agree. But who would want to kill him?"

"Maybe a mugger."

"A damned skillful mugger, I'd say. I suppose that's why the cops are still investigating."

"Kate said she heard Breslow may have been gay."

"I heard that too, but it's hard to believe. Len had a charming wife and two kids. It doesn't add up."

"I agree," Joe said. "It doesn't add up."

"Funny things happen."

"What do you mean?"

"Nothing, really," Duke replied. "So, you're a rib stripper."

"That's right."

"Me, I'm a head cutter."

"You're too relaxed for a neurosurgeon."

"Not relaxed; just tired."

Again the knocker sounded. It was Letitia and a man Joe presumed was her husband. She was strikingly beautiful in a black dinner dress. "Good evening, Joe."

"Good evening, Letitia."

"This is my husband, Luther Agostelli. Luther, this is the soon-to-be-famous Joe Hawkins."

Luther Agostelli was indeed short, scarcely taller than Letitia, with fat, blustery cheeks and thin dark hair receding from the temples, and stiff-necked, with the backward thrust of head and shoulders that short men, like Bonaparte, or Cagney, acquire trying to look taller. Joe resisted an impulse to check his feet for elevator shoes.

"Haaah you, Joe," Luther said. "Letitia's been singing your

praises." The soft, resonant voice oozed catfish and hush puppies.

They smiled and shook hands and Joe replied, "Hi Luther."

Kate and Ben appeared. Then came Mike Devlin and Dick and Mary Hollings, and Letitia introduced them to Joe, and they chatted about how nice it was to meet him and how cold it was in New York and was he ready for the big speech. They moved into the living room, and Duke Rodansky hoisted a fresh Scotch and greeted them with a rousing, "Hurrah for the 'clan.'"

"Duke!" Letitia called out with matching vigor. "I thought you were on your way back to Michigan."

"I would have been, but this is a big night. I wouldn't miss it."

"Great. Glad to have you." She moved in behind the bar and loaded five cocktail glasses with ice cubes, poured two full jiggers of Tangueray into each, then a single drop of vermouth. "My little mother used to tell me, 'If you want a good martini, don't spoil it with vermouth.' Well, those weren't her exact words." She plunked green olives into the drinks and stirred with a swizzle stick. "One of my solemn duties, as your loyal and dedicated EVP, is to prepare martinis fit for the discerning pleasure of the president and Mrs. Hollings, the chairman of the board, and my husband and me, of course. You other cats are on your own." She tasted the Tangueray and smacked her lips, "Ahhh, magnificent."

Duke Rodansky whispered, "Her little mother never heard of a martini, much less Tanqueray."

"Now, Ben," Letitia said. "While we're waiting for dinner, let's have a look at your timeless prose."

Ben passed out copies of the speech and sipped his wine while they read. Mary Hollings was disinterested, but since none of her compatriots from the "board wives" were there, she sat in silence and drank her Tangueray and waited for the next phase of the proceedings. Letitia Jordan read quickly, and when finished, said, "It's fine, Ben. You know what I like. What do you think, Joe?"

"I'm satisfied," Joe replied, a little uneasy because Letitia seemed so pleased.

"Only satisfied?"

"It's an excellent speech. I hope I can do it justice."

"Good," Letitia said. "Did you time it?"

"Twenty-five minutes," Joe said.

"Perfect."

"A bit long."

"That's expensive air time. Fill it."

"I understand."

Mike Devlin said, "I'd like to add our names where it says, 'On behalf of the American Medical Association . . .'"

"Good idea," Letitia said. "Mike, then Dick, then me. Can you remember that, Joe?"

"I can remember," Joe replied. "Doesn't Dr. Hollings come first?"

"The chairman of the board comes first," Letitia replied.

Joe marked his copy and noted the amusement in Duke's eyes.

"Anything else, anybody?" Letitia asked.

"It's a good speech," Richard Hollings said.

Luther Agostelli nodded but said nothing.

The cocktails and wine were plentiful, and Mike Devlin and Richard Hollings continued sizing up Joe. They were appropriately cordial, but Mike Devlin, who was fidgety and a chainsmoker, seemed pointedly suspicious. Grandfatherly Richard Hollings, with the demeanor of one who had achieved his pinnacle and had nothing to do but act wise, was content to listen and fondle his Tangueray. Later, while they were dining on the prime rib Kate had ordered, Mary Hollings giggled and quizzed Joe about why Grace hadn't come to New York and about his children and his home and his family history and a tiresome list of banalities until even Richard Hollings, who usually drank Mary out of his awareness, became annoyed and unceremoniously declared, "Shut up, Mary!"

"But Richard, darling," she demurred in a hurt voice, "I want to know more about Dr. Hawkins."

"It's perfectly all right," Joe said. "I'm delighted to visit with Mary—anytime."

Short, plump Mary Hollings smiled, and Richard Hollings returned to his prime rib and Tangueray. Joe looked relieved. Kate, who had listened to the exchange, caught his eye and nodded approval.

Letitia Jordan loved nothing better than talking politics, and she and Mike Devlin and Richard Hollings cornered Joe with speculation about the Chamberlain speech and what influence "that son of a bitch Menghini and his gang of clowns in HHS" might have on the President, and what to do about it. The discussion was more vituperative than constructive. Mary Hollings fell inattentive, and Kate, who always reveled in an opportunity to eavesdrop on the "clan," tried not to appear too fascinated. Soon it was time for Joe, Kate, and Ben to leave for the Garden.

"What exactly is the 'clan'?" Joe asked as they waited for the elevator.

"The 'clan,'" Kate replied, "is what we lowly staff people call the power barons of the board of trustees—privately, of course. Dr. Rodansky was needling them, probably for my benefit."

"Letitia Jordan certainly takes charge."

"That she does."

"Luther is a laid back little guy. You hardly know he's around."

"That's his style. I've never seen him animated."

"Do they always drink gin like that?"

"I believe they do."

"It was nice of Duke to come," Joe said.

"Yes," Kate said. "I'm a little surprised. He must have really wanted to meet you. He's a bit of a loner."

Joe smiled. "What if I don't make it the full twenty-five minutes?"

"Worry not. I have a plan."

[6]

"IF I'M GOING to get my ass shot off," Joe Hawkins said upon emerging from the taxi with Kate and Ben, "Madison Square Garden is as good a place as any."

Madison Square Garden, the pride of New Yorkers for more than a century, is one of the famous arenas of the world. Aficionados know that in the century of its existence there have been four Gardens, of ascending eminence, in three locations, all in Manhattan. The first arose some fourteen years after the Civil War in a roofless, red brick building on the old Madison Square on Twenty-sixth Street, where nineteenth-century New Yorkers came seeking pleasure at what was known at different times as Gilmore's Gardens, or P. T. Barnum's Hippodrome. Today the Garden stands on top of the Pennsylvania Station at Eighth and Thirty-first, more or less in the middle of things. Twenty thousand people can squeeze inside, more with extra seats. They come to watch games, prizefights, rodeos, circuses, conventions, ice shows, concerts, and political rallies like the raucous Chamberlain affair the evening before.

No matter, the Garden is the Garden, a palace of wonder where feasts of the world are lavished on millions. Like Boston was to George Apley, Madison Square Garden, to New Yorkers, is a state of mind. Tonight would be momentous. For the first time in its incomparable history, the show in Madison Square Garden, a one-man show starring an unknown, Dr. Joe Hawkins, would play to an empty house.

They entered from a side door and walked across the outer rotunda and through a door at the back and down a long aisle to the stage. The arena was a giant cavern, empty and silent.

"It's spooky in here," Kate said.

Two minutes before air time, Kate asked, "Are you ready?"

"I'm ready," Joe replied.

"When we go on the air, the cameras will pan around the arena to dramatize the emptiness. This will give the audience time to settle in and get curious. No audio, no music, just a simple message across the bottom of the screen announcing the program. Then comes a one time voice-over, and you walk across the stage to the lectern. Be crisp, but deliberate. Build suspense. Hook the audience. And remember your eye contact. The hot camera will show a red light. Always look in that camera. You'll be staring straight in the eyes of all those millions out there. Think one-on-one. You're their doctor. Okay?"

"Okay."

"I'll be in the control room with Ben. Just be yourself." She smiled. "We'll make you look good."

"I hope so."

Joe watched the monitor. The cameras panned the silent Garden picking up the eerie shadows and rows of empty seats and the litter from the President's rally the night before. Then a silky voice announced: "The following program is presented in the public interest by the American Medical Association."

"Good luck," Kate whispered and gave him a pat.

Joe climbed the stair and walked across the stage to the lectern. He moved confidently and the cameras followed, prolonging the moment. He arrived at the lectern and squared himself. So far, so good. Goddamn! This is scary—blinding lights—darkness beyond —like shadows across the stream—no banana clips, though— that's something—he planted his feet and found the camera with the red light—then came the old adrenalin rush—combat— exhilaration—euphoria—he stared into the lens, took a breath, and began.

Kate and Ben were in the control room with Maurie Wells, the director. "He looks good," Kate said.

"Good evening. My name is Dr. Joe Hawkins. I am a thoracic surgeon in private practice in Phoenix, Arizona. I have an important message for the President and the people of the United States.

"Mr. President, last night you stood at this very podium and said terrible things to Americans about their doctors. This great Garden was packed with your friends, Mr. President, who believe what you tell them. They love you, Mr. President. They cheered and ate hot dogs and drank beer and waved flags like we Americans do at our good, old-fashioned, political sideshows.

"But what you said about doctors, Mr. President, was simply wrong. I believe you were misinformed. So tonight, with no crowd or band or hullabaloo to distract us, I will explain the truth about your American doctors, doctors who care and were hurt by what you said. I will tell you what they stand for and some of the wonderful, miraculous things they do."

"Great! Absolutely great!" Maurie said. "Check that eye contact."

"He's off the script already," Ben said. "No mention of the AMA."

"Now, Mr. President, you charged that doctors are ripping off Medicare. You said elderly citizens receive poor care while their doctors make fortunes. You called those doctors, 'Medicare Fatcats.' Mr. President, your charges are categorically false."

"Jeez! He's really winging it," Kate said. "He didn't even turn on the TelePrompTer."

"For example, you identified Dr. John Grossman as a 'Fatcat' from Ohio who was paid $235,000 by Medicare last year. The truth is, Dr. Grossman no longer lives in Ohio. He retired to my home state of Arizona twelve years ago. Mr. President, Dr. Grossman is an eighty-year-old senior citizen who has not practiced medicine since he retired. Medicare paid him not a single dollar last year, let alone $235,000. Some 'Fatcat,' Dr. Grossman.

"You identified Dr. Robert Carlyle as a 'Fatcat' from Chicago who was paid $115,000 by Medicare last year. Mr. President, you are simply wrong about that. Robert Carlyle collected not a cent from Medicare, or anyone, last year. Robert Carlyle was dead. The poor man passed away three years ago. Furthermore, Robert Carlyle was a pediatrician. He took care of children, not senior citizens. Never in his entire professional career did Robert Carlyle treat a single Medicare patient, or collect a single cent from Medicare. Some 'Fatcat,' the deceased Dr. Carlyle.

"Then, Mr. President, you talked about Dr. Lane Ferguson, a family doctor in Wilson County, Illinois. You accused him of neglecting his Medicare patients and pocketing $195,000 last year, and you dubbed him the 'Fatcat of Wilson County.'"

Kate pointed to the monitor. "Two souls just slipped in the side entrance. They look interested."

"I see them," Maurie said. "There's another in the back and a couple more in the upper tier."

"Part of the cleanup crew," Kate said.

"Let's pick up their faces," Maurie said.

"There's one on the other side, an older gentleman, a guard. God! Look at him. He's mesmerized."

". . . and the Ferguson Clinic is the only doctor's office in Wilson County. Last year Dr. Ferguson and his two assistants, in addition to caring for their other patients, treated some two thousand Medicare patients a total of thirteen thousand times—including office visits, hospital visits, minor surgery, emergency room, and house calls—and provided drugs and supplies. They averaged forty-four patient visits a day, six days a week. To help with his Medicare patients, Dr. Ferguson employs two young physicians, two nurses, two aides, and three secretaries. Last year Medicare paid the Ferguson Clinic $195,000 for the care of these two thousand patients, which incidentally comes to about $15 per visit. This barely covered Dr. Ferguson's costs.

"You say, what's the catch? Well, there is no catch. Lane Ferguson's father and grandfather were physicians who served the people of Wilson County before him. In sixty years the good Doctors Ferguson never turned a patient away. Lane Ferguson doesn't know how to practice medicine any other way.

"I might add, Mr. President, the American Academy of Family Practice recently named Dr. Ferguson 'Family Physician of the Year.' He is revered by the people of Wilson County, and by his colleagues. 'Fatcat,' indeed, Dr. Ferguson.

"Where is the rip off, where is the neglect, where are your 'Fatcats'? Clearly your staff gave you false information, Mr. President. And in your haste to make political capital, you maligned and dishonored these fine physicians."

"Wow!" Ben said. "He's laying it on."

"The man is good," Maurie said.

"Then, Mr. President, you said that we doctors are responsible for what you called the 'skyrocketing costs of medical care.' Well, sir, let me point out some facts about medical costs."

Kate and Ben sat quietly in the control room and stared at the monitors. Twelve cameras were stationed about the Garden—in the wing behind the lectern, close in front, along the sides, in the balconies. A bank of color monitors lit up the control room and a central monitor displayed the image on the air. Maurie Wells sat behind his console surveying the images as Joe spoke. He gave orders to the cameramen over the intercom and modulated the audio to create a faint echo when a distant camera was on line, and he called for zooms and pans and fades and closeups and wide-angles—head and shoulders, ultra close, eyes only, from the side, the back, high in the balcony, the faces and eyes of the interlopers who had wandered in, a cluster of last night's balloons trapped under the balcony, rows of empty seats and scattered pennants and papers and empty paper cups—images shifting and blending, masterfully creating motion and drama around the lone figure of a man on a lectern speaking before an enormous, vacant, trash-littered amphitheater.

"Our nation suffers a towering epidemic of self-inflicted death and disability caused by smoking, drinking, accidents, and poor habits—an epidemic that kills nearly 700,000 Americans every year, as many as all the Americans killed on all the battlefields in all the wars Americans have fought from the Revolution in 1776 through Vietnam—an epidemic that injures millions, cripples tens of thousands, and accounts for half the total cost of our health care."

"My God!" Kate said. "Is that true?"

"It's true," Ben replied.

"Mr. President, doctors don't cause this epidemic—people do. So, Mr. President, don't trash your doctors. Control the epidemic.

"Cigarette smoking, the greatest single threat to public health in the world, the principal cause of heart disease and cancer and strokes, alone kills more than 400,000 Americans every year. And every year millions of teenagers take up smoking and remain smokers for life.

"Why? Because nicotine, the drug that puts the kick in cigarettes, is profoundly addictive. Cigarette manufacturers profit from addiction, just as drug pushers profit from addiction. But, unlike cocaine and heroine and the like, cigarettes are legal. Furthermore, tobacco farmers are subsidized by the government.

75

"Mr. President, you can do something about that subsidy and still help those farmers.

"You can do something about cigarette manufacturers who manipulate the nicotine in tobacco to promote addiction.

"And, Mr. President, you can do something about a tobacco industry that seduces teenagers with subliminal advertising, knowing that a kid who starts smoking will likely become addicted and a customer for life.

"For decades doctors have known about the consequences of nicotine and addiction, Mr. President. We are ready to help, and we want to help."

"This is incredible," Kate said.

"Now we have AIDS, a devastating killer. What is your plan for AIDS, Mr. President? How will you prevent AIDS from sweeping our country, maybe the world? Certainly not by blaming doctors. You should help doctors find ways to stop AIDS.

"In fact, Mr. President, prevention across the board will do far more to promote good health and control costs than anything.

"I admit that doctors have not done enough to encourage prevention. And as I call on you to curtail the atrocities of the tobacco industry, I admit that we all must do more to prevent those atrocities. And we will do more. And we will some day conquer AIDS. But you must work with, not against, us.

"Obviously, sir, the problems are not simple, and the solutions not always apparent."

Maurie leaned over. "The station checked in. They're swamped with calls."

As Joe continued, Kate and Ben listened. "I wonder what possessed him to wing it," Kate said.

"He's better that way," Ben answered.

"That may be the understatement of the year."

"He's covering everything I wrote."

"Letitia Jordan will shit a brick."

"Two bricks."

"So will the others."

"We'll have to watch where we step when we get back to the hotel," Ben said, chuckling.

"Maurie's great. Look how he moves things around and makes the whole production come alive."

"Four minutes to go."

"He was afraid he couldn't make the full twenty-five."

"He's getting ready to close now."

"Mr. President, last night you unjustly villified American doctors. You said it is time to bring us under control. You outlined your plan for a national health policy designed to do exactly that. Well, we both know you were talking socialized medicine. We both know you were talking bureaucratic suppression, which will undermine our health care system and render it mediocre. Do you really want mediocrity? Do you really want to crush the profession of medicine? Do you really want to destroy our tradition of excellence?

"I remind you, Mr. President, our great country was founded on freedom. My profession, like all successful American enterprise, achieved greatness because doctors were free, because our insatiable thirst for knowledge was unrestricted, and because Americans were free to shop for their own doctors and make their own decisions about their own health care."

Then Joe's voice softened. "My father, Jake Hawkins, a young marine captain in World War II, died on a tiny Pacific atoll named Tarawa while fighting for freedom. He was awarded the Congressional Medal of Honor."

"I didn't know that," Kate whispered.

"Years later I became a young marine lieutenant, attempting to emulate my father. I fought and nearly died in Vietnam. My mother, who is watching this broadcast tonight from her home in Jacksonville, Illinois, endured great anguish over me, as she had over my father, as have millions of American wives and mothers, for the sake of freedom. And today, as one who loves freedom, who fought for freedom and lost his father in the fight for freedom, and who is deeply honored to be a surgeon in the mainstream of a free and noble profession, I know we cannot flourish without the freedom to explore the unknown and provide for those in need.

"The American Medical Association arranged for my appearance tonight, Mr. President, and paid for this half hour of prime television time. But I speak not just for the American Medical Association—I speak for all Americans."

"Oh my God!" Kate said. "Letitia Jordan will definitely shit a brick."

"Mr. President, good health is a national treasure, a treasure born of freedom. . . .

"Do not constrict us. . . .

"Do not strip our heritage. . . .

"Do not consign sick people to a nightmare of bureaucracy. . . .

"Abandon your national health policy. . . .

"Work with your doctors. We are willing to work with you. Together, let us preserve the freedom essential for the good health of our nation. . . .

"We are ready."

A pause, a smile, a parting look into the camera, then—"Thank you, Mr. President. Good evening." Joe turned and walked away from the lectern, and the announcer intoned the final voice-over.

". . . in the public interest sponsored by the American Medical Association."

Kate and Ben bolted from the control room, and Kate cried and hugged Joe and Ben pumped his hand.

"That was fantastic," Kate said.

"Unbelievable," Ben said.

"Thank you."

"How do you feel?" Kate asked.

"Drained. Your mascara is running."

"I can't stop crying." She backed away and produced a tissue from her pocket.

"Helluva way to tell me you didn't like my speech," Ben chided.

"Forgive me, Ben. It just happened."

"You were sensational, doc."

Maurie Wells spoke from the door of the control room. "Dr. Hawkins, you have a call. It's the White House."

"My God!" Kate said.

Maurie extended his hand as Joe entered the control room. "Dr. Hawkins," he said. "Before you take that call, I want you to know that was one of the best crazy damn performances I've ever seen."

"Thank you." Joe smiled and picked up the phone.

"Dr. Hawkins?" a crisp, female voice inquired.

"Yes."

"One moment for the President."

"Good evening, Dr. Hawkins." President Chamberlain's unmistakable baritone came over the phone.

"Good evening, Mr. President."

"Congratulations on your excellent presentation."

"Thank you, sir."

"Whose idea was it to stage it in the empty Garden? That was pure genius."

"The genius is a young lady named Kate Murphy, Mr. President, the director of public relations for the AMA. She's full of it, if you know what I mean."

"I do indeed know what you mean. Please extend my compliments to Ms. Murphy. If I ever have occasion to publicly castigate the President of the United States, I want her to show me how."

"She's standing beside me," Mr. President. "I'll be delighted to tell her."

"You roughed me up pretty good, Dr. Hawkins."

"I meant no disrespect, Mr. President. I believe you were given incorrect information, particularly about the three doctors."

"My staff will check the facts. If I was misinformed, and I suspect I was, I will apologize and correct the record appropriately."

"Thank you, Mr. President."

"Your data about preventable illness was impressive."

"That information came out of the almanac, sir."

"Is that a fact?"

"Yes, sir."

"You roughed up the tobacco folks too."

"They deserve it, sir, but not the farmers."

"I like your style, Dr. Hawkins. Will you help me on health matters?"

"Of course, Mr. President. However, I don't like your national health policy."

"I promise, we shall talk about that."

"I look forward to it, Mr. President."

"I'm glad you came forward for the country, not just the AMA. Candidly, I distrust the AMA. I sense that you are a man of integrity, that you spoke your personal convictions."

"It was my speech, Mr. President."

"I thought so. Someday tell me how you managed that."

"I'll be happy to sir—if I survive."

The President laughed. "I understand. Again, my congratulations. You are much too formidable to be an opponent, Dr. Hawkins. I want you on my side."

"I hope we can work that out, Mr. President."

"Have a good trip home. You're lucky to live in Arizona. It's one of my favorite places. Good night."

"Thank you for your gracious call, Mr. President. Good night."

Kate exploded. "What did he say?"

"He was very cordial—not at all angry. He congratulated me, complimented you, said he would like to talk to me again. And, he likes Arizona."

"I taped it," Maurie said.

"Great," Kate said.

"Don't play it for Letitia," Joe said.

"God, no."

"Good news," Maurie announced. "The studio said they're deluged with calls, all positive. They now estimate thirty million viewers. Justin Carter picked up on your speech. He's going to run excerpts on the eleven o'clock news. They say he's going to call you 'the exciting new voice of American medicine.'"

"You're a celebrity," Ben said.

Joe laughed with them but then felt very tired. "Let's head back to the hotel. We might as well face Letitia and get it over with."

They thanked Maurie and the crew, then found a taxi and returned to the Plaza.

The "clan" had watched the broadcast from Joe's suite. Letitia Jordan and Mike Devlin asked why he changed the speech, and Joe explained he had become nervous at the last minute and lost his place on the TelePrompTer. He apologized for failing to mention their names, blaming it on forgetfulness. Then he told them the President had called, and Duke Rodansky proclaimed "Bullseye!" Letitia and Mike said little but were cordial and joined in the champagne toast. Finally they all retired to their rooms.

Joe barely stayed awake for Justin Carter but managed to see the excerpts and hear himself referred to as "the exciting new voice of American medicine." He called home and told his kids he had talked to the President of the United States. Grace said that all Phoenix had called and she was very proud and loved and missed him, then he collapsed into the giant bed.

At one o'clock the phone awakened him. "Dr. Hawkins, this is Kate. I just had a terrible row with Dr. Jordan."

"Are you all right?"

"Yes. But I've never seen her like this. Can I talk to you."

"Now?"

"No. I'm exhausted. Can you meet me for breakfast? The Edwardian Room at nine."

"Of course."

[7]

KATE WAS waiting at a table in the Edwardian Room next to a tall window heavily streaked with frost. The table was set with a pink tablecloth and napkins, Georgian silver, and a quaint little hurricane lamp with a lighted candle that painted a flickering daub of yellow on the window pane. It was wintry outside, and across Fifty-ninth Street people bundled in heavy coats and fur caps and scarves struggled along the sidewalk and through Central Park, fighting the cold wind. Their breathing blew puffs of white condensate into the frigid air and a man slipped and in a flurry of arms and legs almost fell, then recovered and went on his way. Fresh snow covered the park and clung like sugar frosting to the barren, black tree limbs and the sky was gray.

"Good morning," Joe said.

"Good morning. How do you feel?"

"Fine. I slept very well." He sat down. "How about you?"

"Much better now."

"Have you been waiting long?"

"Only a couple of minutes."

"It looks awfully cold out there," he said, peering out the window.

"I've been watching the people," Kate said. "They're freezing."

Joe inspected the oak-paneled room. Crystal chandeliers hung from the high ceiling and cast a bright, cheerful light. Men and women in chic suits and dresses, appearing nonchalant, sat at the tables; and waiters in white jackets rustled about and the sounds of voices and silver and china melded into a tinkly murmur.

"So this is the Edwardian Room," he said admiringly.

The waiter arrived with two goblets of a tomato-red drink garnished with lime wedges, sprigs of mint, and celery stalks, and a bottle of Tabasco.

"I hope you like Bloody Marys?" Kate said.

"I'm going to like this one," Joe replied.

"Better try it before you add Tabasco."

Joe tasted the Bloody Mary, then whistled softly. "You're right. Tabasco it needs not." The waiter poured the steaming coffee. It had an exhilarating vanilla fragrance. "This is great. Hot coffee, a spicy Bloody Mary, a charming companion, and I'm starving."

"May I order for you?" Kate asked.

"Please do."

"Blueberries and eggs Benedict?"

"Perfect. You know what I like."

"It's part of the VIP treatment. You're a genuine VIP now."

"Have the others gone?"

"They had nine o'clock flights out of La Guardia." She gave the order to the waiter, then asked, "Did you listen to Justin Carter last night?"

"I did."

Kate pulled a folded newspaper from her bag. "You made the front page of the *Times*, no less." She read aloud. "'AMA Speaker Appears in Empty Madison Square Garden.'

"'Dr. Joe Hawkins, a thoracic surgeon from Phoenix, Arizona, last night defended American doctors in a dramatic television speech aired to thirty million viewers from an empty Madison Square Garden.'

"'Hawkins countered charges against doctors brought by President David Chamberlain twenty-four hours earlier in a televised address to a political rally in the Garden.'

"'Hawkins said he spoke before an empty arena to contrast truth with political rhetoric.'

"'Chamberlain called some doctors 'Medicare Fatcats.' Hawkins labeled the president's charges, 'categorically false.'"

Kate raised her brow and smiled. "Now listen to this: 'In delivering his stinging rebuttal to the President, Hawkins emerged as the leading spokesman for the AMA and has been called by some, 'the exciting new voice of American medicine.' How about that?"

"Holy smokers!" Joe replied.

"ABC and NBC picked it up on the late news. You made all three networks this morning. CBS is still getting calls. Doctors are contacting the AMA from all over the country. The reaction is uniformly favorable. The New York media want a press conference at one o'clock. They know the President telephoned you last night. You can hold the press conference and still make your three o'clock flight."

"Why so much fuss?"

"You only blew the socks off the President of the United States, on national television, that's why."

The waiter served their blueberries—cobalt, lush, and sweet. "Where do you suppose they find blueberries like this in February?" Joe wondered aloud.

Kate folded the paper. "Dr. Jordan summoned me to her room last night. She called after the Justin Carter broadcast. I could tell by her voice that she was terribly agitated."

"She seemed okay when she left the suite."

"She lost it when she heard Justin Carter call you the 'exciting new voice of American medicine.'" Kate dawdled with her blueberries. "I've heard about Dr. Jordan's legendary tantrums, but I had no idea how awful she could be." Her eyes moistened.

"When I went to her room, she grabbed my arm and jerked me inside. Then she shook me, literally shook me. I was amazed how strong she was for a little woman. Her face turned beet red and she hyperventilated. I thought she was going to have a stroke."

❦

"You bitch," Letitia shrilled. She shoved her livid face at Kate. "What are you trying to do?"

"Dr. Jordan—please. You're hurting my arm."

"I'll hurt more than your arm if you don't tell me what the hell is going on." But she relaxed the grip and Kate pulled away.

"Nothing is going on. I don't know what you're talking about."

"Don't lie to me, Kate. It was your goddamn idea to put this show on tonight. You hauled that son of a bitch marine in here from Arizona, switched speeches, said nothing about his old man, didn't warn me the fucking President was going to call. You sure as hell didn't tell me you were going to spread him all over the news like the second coming of Christ."

"Dr. Jordan, please, I'll explain, but if you don't calm down, I'm going to walk out of here."

Letitia glared. They stood eye to eye. "All right, young lady. Explain."

Kate rubbed her arm. "As a matter of fact," she said, angrily, "it was a damn good idea, and it worked. I'm delighted to take credit."

"You told me he would fuck it up."

"No, I said it was risky. Better he than you if something went wrong. And I did not use that word."

"You changed the goddamn speech."

"I did no such thing. Dr. Hawkins told you what happened. He used the material that you approved. You know he's inexperienced. At the last minute he became uncomfortable with the TelePrompTer, then lost his way and decided to extemporize." She prayed Letitia would never discover the truth.

"Bullshit. He sure as hell forgot who put him on that podium." Letitia stepped back and posed, clutching her chest. "'I speak not for the American Medical Association—I speak for all Americans . . . ya, de ya, de ya.' I wanted to puke. Christ! Hawkins sounded like a goddamn Kennedy. He was telling the AMA to fuck off. Who the hell does the high and mighty son of a bitch think he is?"

"Dr. Jordan, he gave the AMA full credit. Believe me, it was effective."

"He screwed me big-time with the tobacco folks. You know we're supposed to lay off that."

"He didn't know. He's a chest surgeon. He hates smoking."

"He sold us down the river, and you know it."

"Wrong," Kate retorted. "He clobbered the President of the United States. He made us look good."

Letitia Jordan teetered on the balls of her feet and again shoved her face at Kate. "Goddamn you. Why do you defend him?"

Kate stood firm. "I'm trying to make you understand the reality."

"You always have a smart answer."

"That's what you pay me for."

Letitia Jordan glared, then stepped back. "What about his father?"

"That was news to me. Our computer didn't have it. Dr. Hawkins never mentioned it before the speech. Frankly, the possibility that his father might be a Medal of Honor man never occurred to me."

"Not funny. What about the Chamberlain call? Did you arrange that?"

"I did not. It was a complete surprise."

"Hawkins extended an olive branch to him."

"The President apologized and said he would correct the record. That's a major concession."

"You taped the call, of course."

"No," she lied. "We were too surprised." God help me if she finds out I have a tape.

Letitia glared. "Don't try and tell me you didn't fix it with Justin Carter."

"I tried beforehand, but no deal. You know very well Justin Carter is not friendly to us."

"He's a bleeding heart, commie, son of a bitch," Letitia growled.

"The empty Garden bit caught Justin Carter's attention. That's why he decided to run it."

"Did you plant that shit about the 'exciting new voice of American medicine'?"

"I planted nothing," Kate replied. "Those were Justin Carter's words."

"Goddammit!" Letitia screamed, and Kate thought surely Luther Agostelli could hear the commotion. "Hawkins doesn't speak for American medicine, I do. And don't you forget it. Christ! I had a feeling this would turn bad."

"Dr. Jordan. The speech was successful. We took a big piece out of the President. That's what we set out to do."

"You made Hawkins look like a God."

"He's only a flash in the pan," Kate said. Jeez! How she could lie when she had to. "This will all blow over in a couple of days."

Letitia glowered. "You make goddamn certain it blows over, young lady. I mean, put Hawkins on ice. No press releases, no interviews, no speeches, no television—nothing."

"Dr. Jordan, I can't stop the media. If they want him, they'll find him. They'll dig all the harder if we don't cooperate."

"You heard my order. Stonewall those bastards. Return Hawkins to obscurity. I'm holding you personally responsible."

It was, of course, an impossible order. Tomorrow Joe Hawkins would be a celebrity and nothing Kate or anyone else could do would prevent it. But it was futile to argue with an irate Letitia Jordan, and Kate was suddenly very, very tired.

Letitia reared back like a strutting hen. "We'll see who speaks for American medicine."

"All right, Dr. Jordan, I'll do my best." Then Kate took a deep breath and faced her down, her nose inches from hers. Kate's eyes boiled. Enough of the little bitch. "Now understand this. I love my job. I believe in the American Medical Association. I know the pressure you're under. I'm willing to put up with your obscenities, and your tantrums, and your peccadillos." Her voice hardened and she punched a finger into Letitia's chest. "But if you ever again call me a bitch, or manhandle me, or even scream at me, I'll bloody your fucking nose!"

❦

"Jesus Christ! What did she say?" Joe asked.

"Not a word. I walked out and slammed the door."

Joe laughed aloud. "That's the funniest damn thing I've ever heard."

"I'll probably get fired."

"She won't fire you," Joe said, still laughing. "She can't fire you."

"I was mad."

"No kidding!"

"I meant it. If she touches me again, I'll do just what I said. My brothers taught me how to fight."

"Did you see her husband?"

"No. We were alone."

The waiter arrived with the eggs Benedict and fresh coffee. The ham slice under the poached eggs was lean and thick, and the English muffin was crisp to perfection. "I'm ready for this," Joe said. "You've doubled my appetite." They ate hungrily.

"She frightened me," Kate said.

"I doubt that."

"Not physically—I'm pretty strong. I mean the whole, crazy scene. She was out of control."

"Probably had too much to drink."

"I don't think that was it," she said.

"She has a lot on her mind."

"The Breslow matter has taken its toll."

"Duke Rodansky told me a little about Breslow. That kind of neck injury is difficult to explain on the basis of a simple fall."

She looked up. "What do you mean?"

"Maybe someone broke his neck."

"Wow!"

"Letitia is paranoid, isn't she?"

"That's an understatement," Kate replied.

"I'm not surprised she blew up."

"I don't know. I think she's sicker than paranoid. She's a ticking time bomb." They ate silently.

"A beautiful, blond time bomb."

"Tell me about your father," Kate then said.

"It's quite a story."

"I want to hear it."

Joe leaned back. "My father was Captain Jake Hawkins, 2nd Battalion, 2nd Regiment, 2nd Division, United States Marines. He was killed on November 20, 1943, on Betio, a miserable little island in a tiny, coral atoll named Tarawa, in the Gilbert Islands in the Central Pacific, a few hundred miles this side of Australia, eighty miles above the equator. The Marine Corps fought one of the bloodiest battles of World War II on Tarawa.

"My father was on a landing craft in the first wave. It was blown up a few yards from the beach. He was nicked in the shoulder. Wounded marines were slipping under the water and drowning. My father helped two men to the beach, then he went back and brought in two more.

"His colonel and most of the officers in the regiment got killed wading in. He organized the survivors and set up a command post. Then he crawled over the seawall. The men followed. The Japs were only yards away. His men covered him. He took out three pillboxes with grenades and a flamethrower. At the last pillbox he got hit in the leg. A platoon of Japs charged. He killed most of them with the flamethrower and an M-1. He took a bullet in the chest. Then he took a twenty millimeter in the shoulder. His men carried him back to the beach. He bled to

88

death and they could do nothing. They had no corpsman, no plasma."

Kate had listened quietly. "How do you know the details?" she asked.

"Colonel Shoup wrote to my mother and sent a map. Two marines came to talk to her. The main points are covered in the citation. Others have written and visited over the years. She was able to reconstruct the story pretty accurately."

"It's so sad." Kate was on the verge of weeping.

Joe spoke softly. "I'm extremely proud of my old man. I've read his letters over and over. He wrote beautiful letters. I've studied every picture. Mom told me everything about him. He's a big part of me."

He pulled out his wallet and extracted a small photograph mounted in plastic. "This was my father and me when I was nine months old. It's the only photograph I have of us together."

He turned the plastic over. "This is my mother, my little sister, and me. Janie was six months old. I was two. My father never saw Janie. He had these with him when he died."

Kate studied the photographs. Joe's mother was a beautiful young woman with a big smile. The faces were small, but the pride of the marine officer was evident.

"I think about him every day. I remember nothing, of course, but he seems real. I've gone over his whole life, retraced his steps. The only piece missing is Tarawa. I'll go there someday. I know exactly where he died. I want to wade in on the same beach, lean against the same pier, sit on the sand, think about him, maybe talk to him."

"Where is he buried?"

"In Hawaii in the Punchbowl, with many of the men who died in the Pacific. The Punchbowl is one of the beautiful cemeteries of the world. I hope you see it someday."

"Tell me about your mother and your sister."

"My mother's name is Betty. She's a brilliant lady, sometimes a bit zany, great smile, always irrepressible. Somehow she managed to raise Janie and me. After my father was killed, we went to live with her parents in Champaign. Her father was a professor at the university. My mother earned a Ph.D. in chemistry. Then we moved to Jacksonville. She taught there, at Illinois College. We grew up in Jacksonville."

"Ph.D.'s in chemistry don't come easy," Kate said.

"My mother never married again. She gave all of herself to Janie and me. She still does.

"Janie was born with a cleft palate. Fortunately her lip was intact. She's not disfigured. She had a good repair, but she has that flat, nasal voice typical of palate kids. She's a pretty girl, but self-conscious."

"Is she married?"

"Not yet. I hope she will marry. She lives with my mother and teaches handicapped children.

"I was a rebellious teenager. Nothing serious, I suppose, but I gave my mother fits. I resented not having a father.

"I was determined to be a marine. I quit college when I was a freshman to enlist. I wanted to be like Jake Hawkins. Mom and Janie didn't want me to go. I guess I broke their hearts. I shouldn't have done it. I thought I was indestructible, but I came back all shot up and crazy. They suffered, more than I'll ever know, but there were no recriminations. If I had known what war was all about, maybe I wouldn't have gone. I don't know. In a way I'm glad. I found some of what my father went through. The difference was, he was proud of his war."

"What happened in Vietnam?"

"Another time," Joe said.

"Sure."

"I was lucky to have a good home to return to. It was a loving home—caring and full of wonderful memories. Jacksonville is a little midwestern college town . . . the county seat in the heart of Abe Lincoln country.

"I had posttraumatic stress syndrome—guilt, nightmares, depression, anxieties, the whole bit. In World War I they called it shell shock. Medication helped, but Mom and Janie saved me. Without them I might have wound up spending my life in the loony bin of a veterans hospital. Mom made sure I had everything I needed. Janie never left my side. She read to me, talked to me, coached me, motivated me. That was a switch. She was always the dependent one."

"When did you decide to go to medical school?"

"Six months after I came home. I had my strength back. My head was better. Mom always wanted me to study medicine. She knew I needed a challenge to get my mind off of Vietnam. She was the premed adviser at the college. She set me up."

"You were fortunate to have her."

"Indeed I was. I do okay now, mentally, that is. A few ups and downs." Joe sipped his coffee. "I shouldn't unload on you."

"I don't mind," Kate said. "God knows, you've listened to me."

"Which brings us back to you and Letitia Jordan."

"I feel better now that we've talked," she said.

"I suggest you go back to work. Ride it out. Act as though nothing happened. She'll move on to the next crisis."

"Yes, but she won't forget. She's vindictive. That worries me. Last night she lost control. What will she do next?"

"Nothing. I'll go home, back to work, out of her way. That'll end it."

"We should capitalize on your speech."

"You have your orders," Joe said. "Don't give her an excuse to fire you. Hang in there."

"We could get you on one of the morning shows, maybe a talk show, maybe McNeil-Lehrer."

"Forget it."

"What about the press conference? It's scheduled for one o'clock."

"Cancel it."

"All right." She was disappointed.

"Can we stay in touch?" Joe asked.

"I'll call in a couple of days and let you know what's happening. Do you mind if I call after work?"

"That'll be fine."

Kate took a card from her purse. "This is my home number."

"Do I have to let it ring twice, then hang up and call back?" Joe asked, smiling.

Kate laughed. "We don't have to be that clandestine."

"This has been quite an experience."

"That it has. I now know that success can backfire."

"And that hell hath no fury like that of a woman scorned."

"A particular woman," Kate said, then added, "You made a great speech. I'm proud of you."

"It was your idea. It was a stroke of genius."

"I'll take credit, I say in a moment of lost modesty. But the show was all yours, Dr. Hawkins."

"Call me Joe. Okay?"

"Thank you," she said. "I'll be honored to call you Joe, under the appropriate circumstances."

Joe signed the check and they made their way to the door. They stopped for a last look about the great room with the crystal chandeliers and pink table cloths and hurricane lamps, then they strolled alongside the Garden Room and past a bank of red and yellow tulips to the lobby.

"I'm checked out," Kate said. "I'll grab my bag and head for the airport." She held out her hand. "I'll cancel the press conference. Thanks for everything."

"I'm sorry for the trouble I caused."

"It wasn't your doing."

"Call me."

"I will." She hesitated. "Someday, will you tell me about Vietnam?"

"Of course."

"Good-bye, Joe." She kissed him on the cheek and turned and walked to the bell captain's desk. Joe stepped inside the elevator and watched her until the door closed.

❦

Letitia and Luther lay naked in bed with her head on his shoulder. She sobbed convulsively and clung to him, like a frightened child, and her warm tears dampened his chest. He pulled her close and stroked the small of her back with his palm, and the sobbing eased and she relaxed. Then he turned her face up and gently kissed her lips. For all her power and genius, she was still only a little girl.

"It's okay, babe," he said.

"I'm so afraid," she whispered. "Why do I get so afraid?"

"It's over now," he said, and she snuggled and they kissed again.

"I swear she lied to me. I swear she set the whole thing up."

"I doubt it. Too many loose ends."

"You're sure?"

"Positive. You have nothing to worry about."

"I couldn't help myself."

"You hyperventilated, and you panicked."

"I mustn't lose control like that. You've got to help me."

"I will," he said. "I will."

"Promise you'll always take care of me."

"I promise." Gently he moved his hand to her belly and massaged the smooth skin. "I'll always take care of you, and you'll always take care of me."

"Oh honey," she groaned. "It's good."

"It's all yours."

"Please don't stop."

Grace and the children were waiting amidst a cluster of young men and women when Joe walked off the boarding ramp in the airport in Phoenix. One young man carried a television camera on his shoulder with Channel 10 painted in big red letters on the front. With him was a thin girl in jeans and tennis shoes lugging a ponderous set of batteries on a leather belt and a blinding spotlight that she poked in Joe's face.

The children kissed their father, then Grace wrapped her arms around his neck and kissed him longingly on the mouth. "You were absolutely beautiful," she whispered.

"I love you," he said.

She kissed him again, then turned to the people watching them. "I believe these people invading our privacy are the press."

"Why are they here?"

"You're a celebrity."

A young woman shoved a microphone into his face. "Dr. Hawkins," she cried. "Are you now the official spokesman for the American Medical Association?"

[8]

"Dr. JOSEPH HAWKINS, please?"

"This is Dr. Hawkins."

"Ah, Dr. Hawkins." The voice, that of a man, was clear, faintly accented, and precise. "I call from Tokyo on behalf of Dr. Taro Kajimoto, president of the Japan Medical Association. Will you speak with Dr. Kajimoto?"

"Yes, of course," Joe replied.

"Thank you, sir. My name is Gihachi Miyoshi. My American friends do not easily pronounce Gihachi, so they call me George. I hope you will call me George."

"All right, George, I'll do that," Joe said, amused.

"I presume you do not speak Japanese."

"You presume correctly."

"I will simultaneously translate your conversation with Dr. Kajimoto. Dr. Kajimoto and I are seated in his office with a speaker phone."

A guttural voice rumbling in Japanese filled the earpiece. "That was Dr. Kajimoto," George said. "Do you hear us clearly?"

"I hear you clearly," Joe said.

"Very good. Dr. Kajimoto offers his greetings and is pleased that you can speak with him. He is aware that you traveled from New York to Phoenix today and hopes that he is not imposing."

"Not at all," Joe replied.

Then Kajimoto spoke. "I offer my congratulations for your speech in Madison Square Garden."

"Thank you, sir," Joe replied. "I was not aware it had appeared in Japan."

"The Japanese ambassador had a tape flown to me," Kajimoto

said. "Also, a tape of President Chamberlain's speech. President Chamberlain was powerful. However, you were brilliant."

George proved to be a facile translator, and the conversation flowed smoothly.

"You flatter me, sir," Joe said.

"How did President Chamberlain receive your comments?"

"He telephoned me. He was complimentary and agreed to withdraw the incorrect statements issued by Secretary Menghini or himself."

"I met President Chamberlain many years ago in Switzerland when he was employed by the CIA. He is an astute politician and an honorable man."

"He was very gracious."

"I follow the affairs of the American Medical Association with interest. I was surprised that Dr. Jordan did not respond to President Chamberlain."

"I too was surprised," Joe said.

"Why were you chosen?"

"I was informed the AMA decided to put a new face on the firing line."

"Perhaps they did not expect you to succeed so admirably," Kajimoto said.

Joe laughed. "Perhaps."

"Will you continue to be a spokesman for the AMA?"

"I doubt that Dr. Jordan will call on me again."

"Ah. That is unfortunate. However, the physicians of your country may hold a different view. You are a credible man, Dr. Hawkins."

"Thank you, sir."

Kajimoto then said. "Dr. Hawkins. We have something more in common. In your speech you stated that you are the son of Marine Captain Jake Hawkins, who died honorably in the battle of Tarawa."

"Yes, sir," Joe said, immediately curious.

"I fought as an Imperial Japanese Marine in the battle of Tarawa. Captain Hawkins spared my life."

"Good Lord!" Joe exclaimed.

95

"At Tarawa, American marines overcame superior Japanese forces with bravery. I personally witnessed the heroism of Captain Hawkins for which your nation awarded him the Congressional Medal of Honor. He advanced from the beach under heavy fire and destroyed Japanese pillboxes with grenades and a flame-thrower. He killed many Japanese. My platoon attacked when his flamethrower was exhausted. I fell only twenty meters from where he stood. He observed that I was alive and raised his rifle to kill me. I waited for death. Our eyes met. He saw that I was helpless, and we became human beings instead of animals. Then he lowered his rifle. In the next instant he suffered a mortal wound. I lost consciousness. I was taken prisoner and treated by American navy doctors. Eighteen Japanese marines survived Tarawa. Five thousand Japanese died and remain entombed in the battle-ground. After the war I studied accounts of the battle and identified Captain Hawkins as my savior. Nearly five decades have passed. I was surprised when you identified the same Captain Hawkins as your father."

The lucid narrative of the old Japanese doctor stunned Joe. "Dr. Kashimoto, that is an incredible story. I don't know what to say."

"I hope not to awaken painful memories. You have reason to harbor malice for Japanese."

"When I was a boy, I hated the Japanese for killing my father. I admit, I still experience anger. However, my father died a long time ago, and I have since had my own war in Vietnam."

"I too experienced anger," Kajimoto said. "Sometimes in war it is more painful to live than die. Those who die find peace."

"Yes."

"Now I am old and travel with difficulty. Possibly you will visit me in Tokyo. I would be honored to describe my remembrance of the battle of Tarawa. We can also discuss our profession."

Joe was elated. "I would like to visit you, Dr. Kashimoto. Perhaps I can arrange also to see Tarawa. I have always hoped to retrace my father's steps."

"An excellent plan," Kajimoto said.

"Will George be available to translate for us?" Joe asked.

Kajimoto chuckled. "Of course."

"I agree," George quickly added.

"Then it's done," Joe said.

"Ah, that is settled," Kajimoto said. "In the meantime, I will follow your career with interest."

"You have given me a great deal to think about, sir," Joe said. "Thank you for calling."

❦

Grace strolled in with a pair of icy martinis as Joe hung up the phone. "That, my dear, was an old Jap doc, who says he's the president of the Japan Medical Association, calling from Tokyo. He says my father saved his life on Tarawa." Joe enthusiastically described Kajimoto's revelation.

"Wow!" Grace said. "Do you believe him?"

"He knew all the right details."

"You sound like you liked him."

"As a matter of fact, I did like him."

"You, liked a Jap? That's a first."

"I really want to meet him. Maybe later this year. Maybe I can swing by Tarawa on the way."

"Can I go with you?"

"I wouldn't go without you."

Then Grace purred, "Now it's time for you to drink your very dry, very cold, very major martini."

Joe looped an arm around her head and kissed her lips. "That was one helluva phone call." Then he inhaled the aroma of the martini and took a sip. "Damn, that is good." He kissed her again. "And I'm excited."

"I hope you're hungry. I have fresh, honey-baked ham, Indian bread, and Dijon."

"Perfect."

"I fed the kids early so we could dine alone."

Within minutes she had the sandwiches on the table. He bit into the ham. "Delicious." He took another bite and then another sip of his martini. "Since when does a martini fit with a ham sandwich and hot mustard?"

"Some occasions simply transcend beer."

"Sound reasoning," he said and again sipped the martini. "This is a big drink."

"It's mostly ice."

"Yours is almost gone."

"I gave you the double."

He knew that was a fib but didn't care. Grace disappeared and in a moment returned with a bottle of Gordon's gin. She winked and poured a splash into her glass. "There. We're even again."

"I've been thinking," Joe said. "I want you to switch to Beefeater."

"Why?"

"I like the grenadier on the bottle."

"It's a yeoman of the guard."

"How do you know that?"

"I learned it in the Junior League."

"Figures."

"I figured you'd figure it figures."

Joe then said, "I'm sorry I snapped at you the other day about the League."

"I should have gone to New York. I was furious with myself afterwards. Screw the Junior League."

Joe leaned back. "That would be a tall order."

Grace laughed. "You could handle it. They would be grateful."

Joe munched on the sandwich and drank the last of his martini. "I still think you should go to Beefeater."

"Gordon's is cheaper and just as good, but I'll give serious consideration to Beefeater when the next boatload arrives from England." She kissed him. "I love you very much, Dr. Hawkins, and I am very proud of you."

"If I'm not too drunk, I'll try to make at least one member of the League happy tonight."

The next morning was clear with a few lenticulars in the southern sky, a sign to aviators of high winds aloft. After breakfast of coffee and grapefruit, an English muffin, and crisp bacon, Joe slipped on a sweater and shades and settled into a lounge in the warm sun on the patio. He studied the city below the foothill and the lavender hues and textures of the White Tanks and Sierra Estrellas and Superstitions that circled the valley. Then Grace brought fresh cups of steaming coffee and snuggled against him on the lounge.

"What are you doing today?" she asked.

"I'm signed out until Monday. I'll check with Jerry Sax and Muriel. Nothing else. Maybe take the kids for a drive."

"I want you to loaf all weekend."

Joe gazed at the mountains and gingerly brought the cup of hot coffee to his lips. "I feel really good. That call from the old Jap was incredible."

"Are you tired?"

"A little. I was tired when I woke up in the hotel yesterday morning, but it was a good tired. Actually I feel better than I have in years."

"You were enthusiastic last night. It must have been that Spanish fly I slipped into your martini."

Joe laughed. "Who needs Spanish fly with you?"

"I wish we were in Antibes," Grace said, "in the Cap, dinner tonight at Eden Roc, perhaps a good Meursault, or a Bordeaux. When we were there last year, you were so restless and irritable. We wasted that romantic cottage and the Mediterranean."

"I know. I was not good." He looked at the valley. "This is a beautiful place. Anywhere with you is beautiful. I adore you."

She kissed him. "I love you."

"I keep thinking about Kajimoto."

"You'll call your mother, of course?"

"Yes. When it's lunchtime back there and they're home from church."

"She'll be excited."

"That she will. We haven't talked about dad in a long time."

"Tell her I love her for having you."

"Thank you," he whispered and stroked her smooth rump.

❦

"Kate is on line one," Muriel announced. "She's ecstatic."

Joe picked up the phone and settled back in his chair. "Good afternoon, or is it good evening there?"

"Good evening. It's dinnertime in Chicago."

"Where are you?"

"In my apartment."

"Safe from the talons of Letitia Jordan?"

"I've raised the drawbridge and loosed the alligators in the moat."

"Did you see her?"

"No. I stayed away from the third floor today."

"I crack up when I think about how you told her off."

"I'm so glad you found it entertaining."

"What's up?" Joe asked.

"I came home from work and poured myself a big glass of Chablis. Then, I had to call."

"You don't sound like someone who's just finished a long day at the office."

"I'm on a roll. Do you have any notion of the sensation your speech caused?"

"Can't say that I do. I hung around the house all weekend, and I operated today."

"We had a bunch of mail this morning, and a bunch of calls—mostly from doctors. They love you."

"You exaggerate."

"The big thing was, ABC called. Marvin Leonard wants you on Newsline tomorrow evening."

"That's awfully short notice."

"It'll be easy. Just drive down to your ABC affiliate in Phoenix. They'll pipe you into the network."

"What's it all about?"

"How you stuck it to the President. What else? You're hot copy. They're having three other guests: Jerry Dixon, for the administration; someone for the Consumer Advocates, most likely that asshole Melvin Johnson; and Dr. Walter Sexon, president of the New York State Medical Association. ABC was specific; they don't want Letitia Jordan, or any other AMA type but you."

"She'll be furious," Joe said. "She gave you explicit orders to keep me under wraps."

"This is ABC's show. I explained the situation when the gal

called. She's a friend of mine. Officially I turned down their request. So ABC will contact you this evening and negotiate directly."

"Letitia will see through that."

"My friend will cover me. She had her boss send a telegram to Dr. Jordan protesting my lack of cooperation in making you available." She paused to sip the Chablis. "I'm out of it. However, I can tell you what to expect. Marvin Leonard is going to advertise you as the bold new voice of American medicine."

"Come on."

"Marvin is the best interviewer in the business."

"Will he trick me?"

"He couldn't if he tried."

"You want me to do this?"

"Of course. It'll be wonderful exposure."

"I had a fairly stable life until you came along."

She giggled. "Forget it. You're big time now."

"By the way, a Dr. Taro Kajimoto called me from Tokyo Friday evening when I got home."

"The president of the Japan Medical Association?"

"That's right. He'd seen a tape of the speech and called to congratulate me."

"I'm impressed," Kate said. "Kajimoto is a big shot. He's a power in the World Medical Association and a good friend of the AMA."

"Turns out, he was a Jap marine on Tarawa. He fought against my father. He says my father spared his life. That was almost fifty years ago."

"Wow!" Kate said.

[9]

Kate TELEPHONED Joe in the studio within a minute after the Newsline show was over. "Chamberlain issued a retraction," she said, elated. "That's incredible."

"And an apology," Joe said.

"Did you know in advance?"

"I had no clue. I don't believe Marvin Leonard did either. When he brought up the 'fatcats,' the President's man simply reached in his pocket, produced a statement, and read it. He surprised all of us."

"It was a smart move," Kate said. "When the President himself takes full responsibility, that ends it."

"A preemptive strike," Joe said. "Cut the losses."

"You backed Chamberlain down."

"I don't want to offend him. He's been pretty decent to me."

"Perhaps our appraisal of him was too harsh."

"I like him. I hope he senses that."

"I'm sure he does. You were gracious in your remarks. You let him save face."

"I would prefer to have David Chamberlain as a friend."

"Definitely," Kate said.

"It was nice of you to call."

"I must look after my protégé. Incidentally, I'm sending tapes of tonight's program and the Garden speech and the call from the President. You can play them for your grandchildren someday." She signed off with a cheery, "Stay in touch."

In the ensuing month Joe settled into the rigors of a busy surgical schedule and father to three young children. Then Duke Rodansky called. "I need to see you," he said. "I'm flying to Los Angeles tomorrow. I can arrange to lay over a couple of hours in Phoenix."

Joe met him at the airport. "I'll come right to the point," Duke said. "I want you to run for president of the American Medical Association."

❦

Joe stared at the big guy with genuine shock, then Duke said, "I'm serious."

"Jesus Christ, Duke. Why would I want to do a stupid thing like that?"

"Because it needs to be done. Besides, any dumb fuck who would give a speech to an empty Madison Square Garden like you did is fool enough to try anything."

"Point well taken," Joe said. "I'm listening."

"My friend, as a result of your extraordinary speech in the Garden, the media coverage, the appearance on Newsline, and the apology you extracted from President Chamberlain, you are now regarded as the imminent leader of American medicine. I represent a sizable coalition in the house of delegates who want to capitalize on that situation and elect you president of the AMA."

They were walking in the long corridor to the main terminal. Joe stopped and looked at his friend. "Cut the bullshit, Duke. We both know you're really out to rat-fuck Letitia Jordan."

Duke grinned. "No. Only shake her up."

They found a cocktail lounge and settled into a leather booth. "I know enough about the AMA to know you don't just walk in and take over," Joe said.

"My friend, believe me, we could not find a better president than you. He paused and tapped his fingers on the table. "At least, hear me out."

Duke ordered Black Label and Joe, iced tea.

"I've been meaning to ask you," Joe said, "why do you drink that strong stuff?"

"Neurosurgeons never have a good day," Duke said. "We require hard liquor."

Joe laughed. Then Duke said, "Let's go back six years. The AMA was in financial trouble, spiraling inflation, a busted budget, real estate holdings, but no cash, big debt."

"I remember."

"Carmichael was the EVP. He was a dignified, scholarly type, but apparently his financial managers let him down, and the board lost confidence in him. At least that was the story. One night they decided to fire him—someone called it 'the night of the long knives'—and poor Carmichael was out on his ass the next day."

"How did Letitia Jordan get the job?"

The waitress came with their drinks, and Duke sampled the Black Label. "The search for a new EVP came down to two candidates—a professor of surgery named Richard Arnold, and Letitia."

"I know Dr. Arnold by reputation," Joe said. "He's a top transplant investigator."

"Quite true. Other than an excellent record as a student, Letitia has no academic credentials. But, she's smart. She went straight from her internship in Pittsburgh to family practice in Bolton, Mississippi, a little town near Jackson. In short order she organized and ran a small, prepaid health plan that became a model for rural communities. That's how she honed her management skills."

"Where did she meet her husband?" Joe asked.

"In Mississippi. He was a psychiatrist practicing in Jackson. They had been married a couple of years when she got the job with the AMA. He closed his practice and came with her. Now he practices part-time in Chicago."

"He didn't say much when we were in New York."

"He never does. He's a strange duck. But Letitia is your quintessential activist, and that's an understatement. Four years before the Carmichael firing, she wangled an appointment to AMPAC. Those were tough times for AMPAC—some docs don't believe in political action committees. Letitia turned AMPAC into a force. Her political skills are legendary.

"Through AMPAC she developed strong friendships on the board. It was a man's world, but the power barons took a liking to her. She was one of their kind. So they decided to replace Carmichael with Letitia."

"Power barons?"

Duke smiled. "The guys on the board with the power. Here's

Right!

the way it works. You have fifteen voting members on the board. The critical vote takes place at the annual board reorganization, right after the June meeting of the house of delegates, when the board picks its new officers for the year. It takes eight votes—one more than half—to win. A block of eight or more join up and vote for a slate—the chairman, vice-chairman, secretary-treasurer, executive committee, and so on. Each man on the slate gets what he wants in exchange for his vote for the others. The majority rules, so what it boils down to is, the AMA can be controlled by eight votes—the power barons." He laughed. "It's a goddamn cabal."

"What happens to the losers?"

"That depends on the chairman. If the election is contested, the reorganization can be pretty bloody. The chairman has to play the game to get elected, but a good chairman will close ranks and heal the wounds. A bad chairman will figure, 'fuck 'em, to the victor go the spoils.' That's the way Devlin plays it. The 'ins' are in, and the 'outs' are out—way out, behind the privy. Devlin is a vindictive bastard. If you don't support him, you're on his shit list.

"There's a pecking order in the board room. The power barons —the chairman, officers, and executive committee sit around the head of the table. The other bastards sit to the foot."

You bet

"Where do you sit?" Joe asked.

"Right in the middle, in the last slot for the executive committee."

"You must have been on the slate."

"I was a compromise. The barons either disagreed or got confused over the last slot, so I got it. Maybe it was a screw-up. With a secret ballot, a promise made is not necessarily a promise kept.

"Sooner or later the bastards at the foot of the table find a way to retaliate. If they swing a couple of votes their way, they cancel out the bastards at the head of the table. That happened once. I thought Letitia was going to have a stroke."

"Who's on the board, anyway?"

"A bunch of guys like you and me. Dedicated, highly successful practitioners out of the mainstream of medicine from all over the country. Family practice, surgery, internal medicine—everything. They're all good people and strong leaders. Most of them labored years climbing the ladder of organized medicine before making it to the board. They're ambitious, and they all want to be president. They enjoy power, and they play the standard political game, like everyone else in positions of leadership, and they play hard. They'll push the envelope, but they would never knowingly tolerate corruption or sell out their profession."

"No women on the board?"

"Not yet. Letitia is the first female to crack the leadership, which some think is extraordinary. But I can tell you, she was no token. She got the job because she had the stuff."

"So, you're saying she's wrapped in a cabal."

"Something like that. When she was a candidate for EVP, she let it be known she would take care of her supporters. That did it. The cabal solidified, and Letitia won. It was close. Arnold had a powerful lobby in the house of delegates pushing for him. The vote was eight to seven." Duke chuckled. "That's one of Letitia's nicknames—'eighty-seven.'"

"Did you vote for her?" — who?

"I wasn't on the board then, but I would have voted for her. It boiled down to an academician or a smart, mean, tough son of a bitch. We needed the son of a bitch."

"I'm inclined to agree."

"We had a helluva crisis. Had to borrow money to make payroll. Letitia turned us around. She put through an assessment, then orchestrated a dues increase, reorganized management, jacked up advertising revenues—made the AMA solid financially and a respected political force. No doubt about it, she's a goddamn genius."

Then Joe said, "Frankly, this all sounds like politics as usual. So what's the big deal? If you don't like what's going on, organize your own cabal. Throw the bastards at the head of the table out."

"It's more than board room shenanigans."

"How so?"

"I was elected to the board three months after Letitia was appointed EVP. The AMA was in an uproar over finances. Letitia's appointment infuriated the Arnold lobby, and they attacked the board. In fact, that's the reason I got elected. The house of delegates dumped the incumbents."

"I remember reading about it."

"Those were rough times, but the board saw its duty and closed ranks behind Letitia. No one wanted the American Medical Association to go down. We backed her all the way. The turnaround was fun." Duke took another swallow of Scotch. "We straightened out the financial problems, and a new AMA materialized—Letitia Jordan's AMA. Then Letitia changed. Her power consolidated with her success. And she became arrogant, ruthless, and paranoid."

"Does she still take care of her friends?"

"Absolutely."

"You're still talking like a sore loser."

"Maybe that's what I am, but hear me out. Martin Ross is the AMA's accounting firm. Leonard Breslow was the partner who ran the AMA account. Leonard was the quintessential big-city accountant—pin stripes, alligator briefcase, the whole bit. We relied totally on him during the financial crisis.

"Last year Leonard presented the annual audit. It was a glowing report. He praised Letitia, of course, and put out the usual boilerplate shit about no material weaknesses in the financial affairs of the association. However, one of the new trustees, an internist, Cleve Randall, asked to see the internal audit—that's where a staff member is assigned to examine sensitive matters like expense accounts and confidential management policies. The purpose, of course, is to head off improprieties. Well, there was no internal audit. Leonard argued we didn't need it. That was too much for Cleve. He demanded an independent audit of top management."

"And the shit flew," Joe said.

"Exactly," Duke replied. "If Letitia had shut up, it would have gone her way. Instead, she hit the ceiling and, in effect, dared the board to fire her. It was a classic paranoid fit. Peter Conlan, the chairman of the finance committee and, incidentally, a loyal member of the cabal, took umbrage and backed Cleve. That was a switch, and it looked like it might go against Letitia. That would have been tantamount to a vote of no confidence. The chairman realized a disaster was in the making and decided we should sleep on it. He wisely adjourned the meeting.

"That night they summoned Conlan to the chairman's suite, and the next day Conlan announced that upon reconsideration he believed an independent audit was unnecessary. So it died."

"Wait a minute," Joe said. "Isn't Peter Conlan now the senior vice-president?"

Duke smiled. "You got it. Second to Letitia."

"Son of a bitch! Letitia bought him off."

"Right, but we didn't know how until the December board meeting six months later when Letitia announced Conlan's appointment as senior vice-president. It was a done deal. Conlan had signed a contract, and none of us knew anything about it. As Cleve Randall said, 'It took six months for the other shoe to drop.'"

"Letitia didn't advise the board in advance?"

"No, and she should have. However, Letitia was determined to block that audit. She got Conlan to change his vote by promising him a five-year contract at a fat salary and a shot at EVP when she retires. Of course only the board can hire the EVP, but Letitia and Conlan would have five years to nourish the cabal and make it happen. When Conlan gets the job, he in turn makes Letitia a consultant with a fat retainer and an expense account. In effect Letitia will have chosen her own successor and picked up a nice payola in the deal. God knows, Letitia won't need the money. She'll be a millionaire when she retires. But she could never bring herself to quit the AMA cold turkey. Furthermore, she's greedy."

"Why was she so afraid of the audit?"

"I don't know, but for damn sure, she was. And there's more. At the previous board meeting, while Conlan was still chairman of the finance committee, and after he had secretly cut his employment deal with Letitia, he recommended that her salary be upped thirty grand."

"Did the board approve?" Joe was incredulous.

"Of course. It was wired. And no one knew that Conlan was already working for Letitia."

"What did Cleve Randall do?"

"Cleve ate shit, like the rest of us."

"I'll bet."

"Then Leonard Breslow got himself killed. Talk about a shocker."

Joe shook his head. "What a coincidence."

"For sure."

"What's Conlan like?"

"He's a slick operator. Always out for Conlan. He set Letitia up to squeeze a deal out of her."

"Why did he quit practice?" Joe asked.

"Good question. He said he wanted a new challenge. They all say that. He's making a helluva lot more than he did in practice. Conlan's something of a loner. Has an apartment downtown. His family lives in New York."

Joe eyed the big man. "That's one helluva story, Duke. Why doesn't the board control Letitia?"

"Most of them concede that Letitia is a little high-handed at times, but the good outweighs the bad, that sort of thing. As long as the AMA is doing well, they'll tolerate her peccadilloes. Her attitude is all or none. If you don't like what I do, fire me, and so far she's won. All she needs is eight votes. Unless something happens, she'll be around until she dies, or goes to jail."

Joe laughed. "Well, it all sounds like normal political games to me. What's the problem?"

"Nothing, if this were a fucking widget factory. But it's not. It's the American Medical Association. There's a small matter of public trust."

"The AMA is in good shape financially."

"That's true. In six years the AMA has become the wealthiest professional organization in the world. The budget is 150 million, the assets, 200 million. It sounds wonderful. But hard core membership has fallen. Less than half of the mainstream docs support the AMA. That's a disaster.

"When Letitia took over, membership dues were the principal

source of income. But every time we jacked up the dues, we lost members. It wasn't only the dues. Some people simply didn't agree with the AMA.

"Letitia built a powerful financial enterprise: subsidiary corporations, real estate, publishing. Over a hundred million a year and growing—investments, advertising, rentals, subscriptions, you name it. The outside income is twice the dues income. It looks beautiful on the financial reports. She gets eulogized every year. The truth is, she's changing the AMA."

"What do you mean?"

"The less we depend on dues income, the more the hired hands run the show."

"What is Letitia really after?"

"Power," Duke said. "Power for the sake of power. The woman is obsessed with power."

"Not money?"

"I don't think so. She's well paid, but for her that's incidental to power."

"Power corrupts," Joe said.

"Absolutely," Duke said.

"Is the cabal still solid?"

"They lost Conlan's vote when he went to management, but they're recruiting. They still trust Letitia."

Joe was skeptical. "Listen, Duke, even if you are on to something, what could I do?"

"Help even the odds. Mike Devlin is running for president in June. So far he's unopposed. If you knock him off, the cabal loses a big vote."

"Then you dump Letitia?"

"Hell no." Duke laughed. "Believe it or not, I don't want to fire her. I only want her to show a little deference to her employers and the docs we represent. Besides, if we fired her, we'd have to find another genius just like her. It wouldn't be worth it."

"Seriously, can anyone beat Devlin?"

"Hell yes. You can beat him. Devlin is a phony. The delegates are smart. They see through phonies."

"You mentioned a coalition."

"California, Texas, Illinois, maybe New York. There'll be others after you announce."

"Why don't you run?"

"I can't win. Until you came along, Devlin was unbeatable. It's tough to beat a chairman, even if he is a jerk. I have my niche. I'm content to sit tight."

Duke downed the last of his Scotch, then said, "Your strong suit, you're nobody's toady. That's what I like about you. That and your goddamn pretty face."

"Fuck you, Rodansky."

Duke laughed. "You're what the AMA needs, and you'll never have another opportunity like it. Even if you lose, you'll shake the cages so fucking hard they'll never stop rattling."

"If I run, I don't intend to lose."

"You'll run. It's in your blood. I can tell. And you'll win."

"Did Kate put you up to this?"

"No, but she would approve."

"Give me forty-eight hours."

"Done."

"By the way," Joe said. "Do you know a Jap doctor named Kajimoto?"

"The president of Japan Medical?"

"That's the one. He called to congratulate me on the Garden speech. He was a Jap marine on Tarawa. He says my father spared his life. He says he saw my father go down."

"No kidding!"

"He invited me to visit him in Tokyo."

"By all means, go," Duke said. "Kajimoto is a powerful man. He's also a strong AMA supporter."

Joe grinned and hoisted his tea glass. "To the rat-fuckers of the world."

"To the rat-fuckers."

[10]

GRACE HAWKINS had lived in Phoenix five years before she drank her first martini. Then someone at a cocktail party said, "Why don't you try a man's drink?" and handed her the martini. It was a Saturday night, and Joe was at Palo Verde cracking the chest of a Mexican whose signora had blasted him point blank with a .38 Special. Grace was milling around on her own. A lonely woman's drink, she thought. But the martini slid down easily, and she had another at the next party, then another. In time she came to prefer straight gin and this evening was nursing her usual snifter of Gordon's over ice.

Grace was in the kitchen when Joe arrived. She was dressed in a denim dress and a sash belt and sandals with her hair tied in a ponytail with a red ribbon. He hugged her. "It's time for me," he said, and when he kissed her could taste the gin in her mouth.

"Always," she murmured.

"What's for dinner?" He kissed her again.

"Your favorite."

"Hamburgers?"

"You got it, doctor."

"Did you eat with the kids?"

"No. I waited for you."

"Wonderful. I'll slip into my sweats." He disappeared through the door, and she heard him jousting with the children on his way to the bedroom.

Grace dropped a pair of beef patties onto the hot skillet and tossed a bowl of Bibb lettuce with mustard dressing. Then she turned the hamburgers, fetched a can of Coors and a frozen stein, and replenished the gin in her snifter. Finally she slid the crisp hamburgers into warm sesame buns and retrieved the salad plates and forks from the freezer. Everything was ready when Joe returned.

"I put a Coors out for you," she said.

"Great." He poured the beer into the frozen stein. "It's so cold I can hardly hold it," he said. "I love frosty beer."

"I rinse the steins before putting them in the freezer. The water droplets freeze then float off in the beer. That's what makes it frosty."

Joe smiled. "So you've explained, many times." He leaned over the edge of the table and kissed her. "I can't stand warm beer."

"I know."

"Everything is perfect, sweetie. Hamburgers well done, Bibb lettuce, mustard dressing, chilled forks, frosty beer."

"You seem excited," she said.

"I am. Remember Duke Rodansky? He came through this afternoon on his way to Los Angeles. I just met him at the airport."

Joe slathered a knifeblade of Dijon on the hamburger and took a big bite. "Damn! That's good. . . . He wants me to run for president of the American Medical Association."

"What are you saying?"

"President of the American Medical Association. He wants me to go for it."

"When?"

"In June at the big meeting in Chicago."

Grace stared at him. "You're serious."

"Absolutely."

"What did you say?"

"That I'd think about it."

"When must you decide?"

"Forty-eight hours. We don't have much time to organize a campaign."

"Campaign?"

"Speeches, posters, balloons, the whole schmear." Grace said nothing and Joe drank more beer. "What do you think?" he asked.

"I don't know what to think."

"You're not pleased?"

She touched his hand. "I am pleased."

"It would be a tremendous honor."

"I know. I'm very proud of you."

"What, then?"

"Would you travel a lot?"

"I suppose so."

"We hardly see you now."

"You can travel with me."

"What about the kids?"

"It's only three years. President-elect, president, then immediate past-president." He added, "First, I have to get elected."

"You'll get elected. God help anyone who gets in your way."

"Come on," he scolded.

"It's true," she said.

"I'll be going against the establishment. They lined their man up a long time ago. But Duke says a faction in the house of delegates wants to change that. They want me to run this year to capitalize on the Garden speech. Duke says I'm the best man for the job."

"He hardly knows you."

"He knows me well enough. We hit it off."

"I take it you've made up your mind," Grace said.

"I wanted to talk to you first."

"That's a charade."

"I won't run without your approval."

"Do I have a choice?"

"I thought you'd be thrilled."

"I am thrilled, for you."

"Then, what's the problem?"

Grace drank some gin. "Our life together is pretty thin as it is."

"Please, don't start that."

"You're a busy man. You leave early in the morning, work hard all day, come home late, get called out at night, make plenty of money. We have three beautiful children, a house on a pretty mountain, the country club, the Junior League, Rotary, great friends, everything."

"Well?" He spoke impatiently.

"It's all so goddamn perfect." Grace toyed with her salad and drank more gin. "Would you like another Coors?"

"Please."

She rose and put the dishes in the sink.

"You didn't finish your hamburger," Joe said.

"I had enough." Grace pulled another Coors and a fresh stein from the refrigerator and placed them in front of Joe. "Don't drink this one so fast."

"Thanks," Joe said.

"I can warm some apple pie and cheddar."

"I'm full."

"So am I," Grace said. "Let's take our drinks to the fireplace. I think the kids have vamoosed."

The fire she had started before dinner was still smoldering. She dropped a pair of mesquite logs on the coals and prodded them with a poker. The logs caught and the dry bark crackled smartly, then yellow flames darted out and curled around the logs. She and Joe sat on the sofa, and the fire cast a glow and a pleasing warmth on their faces.

"Man will never lose his fascination with fire," Joe said.

Grace rested her head on his shoulder. "Remember our picnic at Half Moon Bay, how cold the ocean was, the fire on the beach. We had a blanket and snuggled against a big log and watched the sunset and the fire and listened to the waves."

"And the magnificent drive down the coast to Monterey."

"The little inn in Monterey, where we stayed on our honeymoon. You lit a fire in that dinky fireplace and we had a bottle of sparkling burgundy—neither of us had ever had sparkling burgundy before—and apples and Gouda. The sparkling burgundy was redder than red wine and prettier than it tasted. It was too sweet, but we loved it. We didn't know any better. We sat on the floor in front of the fire, and you poured, and we watched it bubble, and we ate the apple and Gouda and drank wine and held our glasses up to the fire. The flame shined through the wine and made our faces red."

"It was wine perfect for pirate movies and honeymoons," Joe said.

"Nothing has ever matched it," Grace said.

"I'd like to return to that inn."

"The rooms were small. The fireplace smoked. God, it was romantic."

"It might disappoint us to go back," Joe said. "We're used to better things now."

"That night we dreamed of the future. We had discovered the West—the ocean, the mountains, the desert, the skies. The magnificent skies and gorgeous sunsets. We wanted only to find a place big enough for you to build a practice and small enough to feel like a small town."

"We found it."

Grace put her nose in the snifter of gin and savored the coriander and juniper. "I'll never forget the first time we met. I was scrubbed for 'Wild Bill' Clanahan, remember? A thoracotomy. You were the pup, and it was your first case with him. I'll never forget your big brown eyes peering at me between your cap and mask. You did a fine job on me with those eyes. I was a shapeless blob in full nursing regalia—paper cap, a neck wrapper, surgical gown, gloves. You didn't say a word when I gowned and gloved you. But you undressed me with those brown eyes. Stripped me bare-assed right there in the OR. I knew it, and I was mortified."

"You gave me the come-on," Joe said.

"Not so," Grace stated indignantly. "I was mortified. I blushed. Clanahan noticed."

"We were just a couple of hired hands to him."

"He did notice. He mentioned it later."

"You never told me that. What did he say?"

"He said you looked me over pretty good."

"I don't believe you."

"Eyes tell every story in the operating room—joy, sadness, fear, anger, panic, tragedy, a broken heart, lust."

"And a come-on," Joe said.

Grace's speech had thickened. She sipped her gin and stared at Joe. "Do you still do it?"

"Do what?"

"Strip girls with your eyes, like you did me, bare-assed."

He grinned. "Only in the operating room, my love."

"Bullshit!"

Joe pretended arrogance. "The operating room is one of the last strongholds of absolute power on this earth. In the OR the surgeon is God. He can strip girls all he wants, especially sexy nurses on the make. These days it works both ways. We have girl surgeons going after boy nurses with tight asses. God help us."

"Double bullshit!"

"Look. You're mine to strip whenever I please and leave nothing to the imagination. I want nothing else."

"Come on," Grace teased. "You're hot-blooded. You love to strip nurses. Admit it."

"Well, occasionally."

"Do you strip Muriel?"

"Sometimes." Suddenly Joe felt the need to be wary.

"Every day? In the OR? That crucible of life and death, of drama, of sex, and pain, and pathos?"

"Not every day." It didn't sound like he intended.

"You like her black tits, don't you? You wanna suck 'em, don't you? You love chocolate milk. What about her black ass? Her sweet, firm, black, bubble ass. It turns you on, doesn't it?"

"For God's sake, Grace."

"What about Carnation McGillicuddy?"

"You know Carnation?"

"Everyone knows Carnation," Grace said. "Miss Tits and Ass Universe."

"Ah, Carnation McGillicuddy," Joe said, going along. "Like a belly-dancer in a bubble-bath. Every surgeon's fantasy. She happens to be a damn good nurse."

"You love to stand behind her and watch her ass jiggle when she preps, don't you? She's an easy strip. She wears a skintight little OR dress, no bulky gown like I wore. It all hangs out."

"You've been talking to Muriel."

Grace bored in. "So now we have Kate. Something new. Hot flesh. Young stuff. Do you prefer her to Muriel? To Carnation? Did you fuck her in New York?"

Joe angrily pulled the snifter out of Grace's hands. "That's enough."

"Did you?" Grace demanded.

"No, I didn't fuck her."

"Kate must be a goodie two-shoes."

"You're drunk. You're trying to provoke me, and you're succeeding. What the hell is the matter with you? I come home with big news and you pick a fight."

Grace suddenly buried her face in his shoulder. "Why do you have to be president of anything?" she whispered. "Why can't you just be my husband?"

"It's important," he replied gently.

"Important to you."

"Important to both of us. It's worth doing."

"We're on the edge, you and I. We have everything, yet we have nothing."

"You're exaggerating," Joe said.

"I'm so damn lonely."

"You have no reason to be lonely."

"You're slipping away from me."

"I"m not slipping away. We both have a lot on our minds. God knows, the kids are a big job for you."

"I know. But I'm unhappy."

"You don't mean that."

"You're unhappy too. I know you. You've hit a plateau, and you're restless. Stagnation eats you alive. You have to break out. It's an obsession. It blinds you. That's why you quit school to join the marines, never thinking what it might do to your mother and Janie. It took a big dose of combat to settle you down. Vietnam was hell, but you thrived on it. Then you got shot and came home, half dead and crazy. The Sergeant Cobb thing demonized you. Your family saved your ass. Now you're God Almighty, a big fucking chest surgeon. You have the ultimate status, but the challenge is gone. You're floundering. You're brilliant and successful and completely miserable. You need a fresh go at something, a new war, a new exhilaration. That's why you did that goddamn speech. That's why you mess with that goddamn Kate, and that goddamn Duke, and that whole goddamn crowd. You crave combat. You're obsessed with combat, any combat—war, surgery, politics, anything."

"You don't know what in the hell you're talking about," Joe said angrily.

"I know you."

"Look, I admit I'm restless."

"Three years out of our lives now will destroy us," Grace said.

"I won't let anything destroy us."

"God, I hope not."

"If I don't go for it, we'll both wish I had."

"You're going to go for it. What I think doesn't matter."

"I want your approval."

"You know I always give in. Jesus! I'm so goddamn reliable. I may be a little drunk, but I know what I'm saying."

"You're more than a little drunk."

"So what?"

"When we go to bed, you'll conk out."

"You know the signal, doctor. Just tap me on the butt. You don't have to say a word. Day or night, rain or shine, sleet or snow. Tap old Grace on the butt. She'll deliver."

"It doesn't work when you're drunk."

"What you mean is," she punched his crotch with her finger, "*it* doesn't work when *you're* drunk."

Joe flinched. "How about some soft music?" He got up and shuffled through the cassettes in the music cabinet. "Soft music is good for the nerves." He slipped a cassette into the tape deck.

Grace followed him and when he turned she tipped her face up to his. "Dance with me, doctor."

They embraced and kissed and swayed to the dulcet music of the Harmonicats' "Peg of My Heart," and their bodies fused and they danced.

"Oh doctor," Grace said.

"Yes, nurse."

"This is heavenly."

"The old tunes are the best."

"I apologize," she murmured.

"For what?"

"For being a bitch."

"I hadn't noticed."

"I didn't mean what I said about Kate. You can't help lusting. I understand why you like tits and asses. You wouldn't be worth much if you didn't. I'm really only jealous of your obsession. I understand this AMA thing, and I want you to go for it. I love you, and I am very proud to be your wife."

"And I love you," Joe said.

"I wouldn't want you any other way."

He squeezed her. "This is a nice way to make love."

"So respectable," she said.

"Civilized."

"No commotion."

"No hollering."

"No sweating."

Shadows from the firelight danced on the adobe wall.

Then Joe said, "Let's talk about your drinking."

"Why?"

"You drink too much. That's why."

"I don't agree."

"You had a snifter full of gin when I came home. You filled it twice that I know of."

"I like gin."

"Do you drink every afternoon?"

"Maybe. So what?"

"You've taken cabs home from the club."

"I wasn't drunk. It was just a precaution. You know how cops are."

"Grace, I love you. Please listen to me."

"I'm not an alcoholic, if that's what you're trying to say."

"Denial is a cardinal sign."

"It's simply not so. I enjoy a cocktail in the afternoon. So do my friends. I happen to prefer gin. Sometimes I drink a little more when I get lonely. Alcoholics drink in the morning. I don't drink in the morning. If I start drinking in the morning, I'll let you know. In the meantime, doctor, I don't have a problem. Nothing is going to happen."

"I want you to see someone."

"Why? I'll deal with it."

"You can't deal with it."

"I can quit anytime I want."

"You're in classic denial."

"Can we stop arguing and dance?"

"I called Pete Malone at the Rehab Center. He'll be glad to see you."

"How could you?" Grace demanded, angrily.

"Look, if Pete says I'm wrong, fine. I'd love to be wrong. But don't take a chance. Please see him."

"Oh, Joe. Do I have to?" She clung to him.

"Promise me," Joe insisted.

"All right. I promise. Now, can we dance?"

[11]

JOE TELEPHONED Kate from his office. "Do you have a minute?"

"Of course. I just got home, and I'm curled up on the sofa with my Chablis, reading my *Tribune*. I would love to chat."

"Duke Rodansky came through Phoenix last night. He wants me to run for president of the AMA."

"Do it," she said.

"That was quick. Did you know?"

"No, but I'm not surprised. It's a great idea."

"Duke says a coalition will back me—California, Texas, Illinois, maybe some others."

"I hear rumors that some of the heavy hitters in the house of delegates want you to run. It has the makings of a ground swell."

"I've only made one speech, otherwise I'm an unknown."

"But what a speech. They see you as a man who'll stand up to the power barons."

"The president of the AMA is only a figurehead," Joe said.

"They want to change that. The relationship between the chairman of the board and the president of the AMA is a stupid paradox."

"What could I do about that?"

"You could change the balance of power."

"That's what Duke said."

"A strong president can wield enormous influence."

"Bully pulpit?"

"Exactly. The president is the voice of the AMA. You could make interesting things happen."

"For example?"

"A bylaw change shifting certain authority from the chairman to the president. That would dilute the EVP's power to control the board through the chairman."

"Does Letitia know I might run?"

"I don't know, but she'll take it as a personal threat. She knows she can't control you."

"The AMA is a public trust. We all have the same mission."

"She thinks you're a loose cannon."

"Loose cannon my ass," Joe snorted.

Kate giggled. "Interesting thought."

❦

"Did you decide?" The gruff voice was unmistakably that of Duke Rodansky.

"You said I had forty-eight hours," Joe replied.

"I lied."

"Okay, I'll do it," Joe said, laughing. "What now?"

"I'm still in Los Angeles. If you invite me nicely, I'll stop in Phoenix on my way home and show you how to organize a campaign. I might even stay the night and regale you and your bride with lofty oratory."

"Damn it, Duke. I have a busy schedule."

"I take that as inviting me nicely. See you tomorrow."

❦

They carried their cocktails to the oak table outside on the whitewashed patio. It was a cool evening and the sweaters felt good. The moon was but a thin crescent in the west near Venus, and a million stars burned in the clear black sky above the mountain, beyond the aurora of city lights. Beef filets were cooking on the grill, and the drippings flamed and crackled deliciously on the smoldering mesquite, and the aroma made them awfully hungry.

"I'm glad you're staying the night with us," Grace said. "We can have a leisurely dinner, get drunk if we want, and not rush to the airport."

"I invited myself," Duke said. "I should have been more mannerly."

Grace smiled. "I'm glad you're here."

"It worked out well," Joe said. "My schedule was lighter than I expected."

"The steaks are almost ready," Grace said. Plates with baked potatoes and a basket of sourdough buns were on the hearth next to the fire, and a giant bowl of salad waited on the table. "Joe uncorked an interesting red Bordeaux."

"Wonderful," Duke said.

Joe poured a taste of the Bordeaux into a goblet and swirled it under his nose. "She called it 'interesting,' as though we're connoisseurs. Actually, we buy our wine cheap at the grocery, unless we're in some romantic place, like Antibes."

Grace scolded him. "You're destroying the continental ambience I was trying to create for Duke."

"The ambience is perfect," Duke said.

Joe sampled the Bordeaux. "Excellent. Very dry."

"I like dry red," Duke said.

Joe poured and the others tasted with approval.

"I love it here in the foothill," Joe said. He pointed to a gentle sprawl of mountains in the distance silhouetted against the fading afterglow of the sunset. "Those are the White Tanks. Sunsets over the White Tanks are always beautiful. The Harquahala Plain is just beyond, along the road to Los Angeles. It's great country out there—miles and miles of pristine desert and rambling mountains."

"Joe is enamored with the West," Grace explained.

"I enjoy our little niche in the foothill," Joe said. "The quail are plentiful. We put food out for them. They forage for water, whistling their little da-dee'-da, da-dee'-da. Gambel quail. They have the perky topknots, arrogant little devils. They strut like they own the world." He tasted his filet. "The steak is perfect, sweetie."

"Excellent," Duke said.

"I'm glad they're good," Grace said. "Joe usually cooks the steaks."

"I can see why you like it here," Duke said.

"Phoenix is wonderful to come home to," Joe said, "especially from Chicago in the winter."

Grace turned to Duke. "You persuaded my husband to do something crazy."

"Did you hear his famous Garden speech?" Duke asked.

"Of course," Grace said.

"Then you understand."

"There must be others who can do the job."

"Not like Joe."

"He says you would be a great president."

Duke laughed. "Right now, we need Joe."

"To be perfectly honest, I have misgivings," Grace said. "I think you're both crazy. I suppose that's why you get along so well. Anyway, what happens next?"

"We have to get organized," Duke replied. "The election is only three months off."

"I'm ready," Joe said.

"You're running against Mike Devlin, chairman of the board and heir apparent to the presidency. Mike is ruthless. He owns a fistful of markers. But when you climb the ladder, as he has, you also make enemies.

"You're a proven television performer. You'll have a good shot at the new delegates. Most of them know you from TV. However, the house is a sophisticated crowd. One good night on the tube won't hack it. They want substance.

"You also have the advantage of surprise. Mike's been coasting. The minute your announcement goes out, I guarantee, he'll panic. With only three months to go, he'll fall all over himself organizing a campaign.

"Mike has powerful backers—Letitia Jordan for one. They'll fight like hell. They need Mike's vote to control the board.

However, you'll have a strong coalition of your own—California, Texas, Illinois, the Rocky Mountain caucus. They know how to deliver votes. Board members have a lot of influence, no doubt about it, but Mike has enemies on the board too—the bastards at the foot of the table, remember.

"Is running out of a small state a problem?" Joe asked.

"It depends on the candidate," Duke said. "Small staters do well if they have balls—excuse me, Grace."

"I like balls," Grace said demurely.

"Then balls it is." Duke raised his glass of Bordeaux. "Sometimes the big states have a helluva time sticking together. Take California. It's hard to figure if California is a microcosm of the AMA, or the AMA is a microcosm of California. They've got city docs, country docs, San Francisco docs, L.A. docs, university docs, mountain docs, desert docs, ocean docs, movie star docs, hippie docs, everything. They never agree.

"Sometimes, when they run a campaign for one of their own, it's like, fabulous parties, a ton of money, and half the delegation may vote for the other guy. The secret ballot hides a lot of broken promises. However, you're from a neighboring state. If they decide to go for you, they'll likely be unanimous.

"Big states spend more money, but you can't buy this election. You have to be a good candidate."

"I don't want to be a flash in the pan," Joe said.

"You won't be. You already know the issues. More important, you're a mainstreamer."

They finished the steaks and Grace said, "I have coffee and apple pie and cheddar."

"I can't say no to that," Duke said.

"I'll have my customary sliver," Joe said.

"Of course," Grace said. "Your customary sliver, then your customary second sliver, and another customary sliver at bedtime. You might as well have a big piece now and get it over with."

"Thank you, darling," Joe said acidly.

"The lady's point is well taken," Duke said. "I'll have all mine now, if I may."

"You may," Grace said and arose from the table.

"Be yourself," Duke said. "That's the first golden rule of campaigning. If you don't know the answer, say so. This AMA crowd picks off a phony like a CAT scan picks off flies.

"The second rule, get personal. You have over four hundred delegates to deal with. Invite each of them, personally, to consider your candidacy."

"How do I do that?" Joe asked.

"Use your telephone. If you start now and make calls every day, you can get it done."

"That's a tall order."

"A personal call identifies you. It puts you on a first name basis. Mike Devlin won't make those calls. He won't bother. He thinks they owe him the presidency."

"There goes my phone bill," Grace said.

"The last rule," Duke continued, "ten hits on every delegate."

"Hits?" Joe said.

"Contacts. Announcements, personal letters, brochures, calls, from you and your state delegation. Go for ten. Keep a score-card."

"You're serious."

"Absolutely. Lots of hits. The harder you campaign, the better." He turned to Grace. "The pie is damn good."

She brought snifters of cognac and they moved to the den and Joe and Duke settled into the leather chairs and talked. When Grace finished in the kitchen, she replenished their cognac and curled up in her favorite corner of the sofa.

"Bring Grace to Chicago," Duke said.

"I plan to," Joe said.

"Excellent. The delegates will want to see her. You're lucky to have Grace. She's extraordinary."

"Will I have an opportunity to solicit?" Grace inquired sleepily.

"In a manner of speaking," Duke said.

"I was once a great hooker. Expensive though."

"That's good," Duke said. "We need class."

"If Joe wins, will he travel a lot?"

"Of course."

"I hate that."

"You can travel with him."

"And leave the children?"

"We can work something out," Joe said.

"The presidency of the American Medical Association takes a lot of time, but it's worth it," Duke said.

"I don't care," Grace said, suddenly angry. "It will tear us apart. I hate that."

"Grace, please," Joe said.

"What kind of a neurosurgeon are you?" Grace asked. She teetered unsteadily on the sofa.

"I win a few, lose a few," Duke answered.

"You're an incorrigible bastard," Grace said. "You're both incorrigible bastards."

AMA speaker Dr. John clowe announced CJ's victory

[12]

THE SPEAKER of the house stepped to the podium and pounded the gavel. "For president-elect, you have chosen Dr. Joseph Hawkins of Arizona." A great cheer arose.

Kate was waiting in the corridor when Joe emerged from the convention hall. People gathered to congratulate him, then she caught his eye and waved and worked her way through the crowd until they locked hands. He pulled her to him, and she smiled and kissed his cheek.

"Congratulations, Joe," she whispered. "I knew you could do it."

"Thank you for being here," he said. "I've missed you. I see you're as beautiful as ever."

"Thank you. I've missed you too. But, we'll be working together now."

"I'm looking forward to that."

127

Duke was gleeful. "That, my friend, was a piece of cake."

"Quit talking and crack the champagne," Joe said.

On the table a bottle of Schramsberg was immersed in a bucket of crushed ice. Duke popped the cork and patiently topped three flutes with the foaming bubbly. "It was a lot of work, but you won and won big."

"I'm exhausted," Grace said. "My feet hurt." She sank into one of Mrs. Marriott's orange chairs.

"You pulled three hundred seven votes out of a possible four-hundred twenty-six," Duke said. "That's an impressive repudiation of the status quo."

"Now I have to deliver," Joe said.

"I'll bet all four hundred twenty-six told you afterwards they voted for you."

"More like four thousand twenty-six."

"Ah. The virtues of the secret ballot."

"I'm very proud of you," Grace said. "Salute!" And they drank.

"Grace, you were magnificent," Joe said. "The Beautiful Blond from Buxom Bend."

"I delivered two dozen votes and only had to fuck half of them. I hardly mussed my hair."

"Grace!" Joe protested.

She moaned. "Joe, baby. Please rub my poor feet."

Joe settled cross-legged on the floor in front of her chair, eased her shoes off, and began massaging—toes, arch, then ankles. "White stockings," he noted. "A nurse on her day off."

"Shut up," she said, then moaned again. "Oh, doctor. That feels so good."

"What happens tomorrow?" Joe asked Duke.

"The house should adjourn by noon. We have a private luncheon for the board and the wives, then we elect new officers and take care of routine matters. You can make the dinner flight home."

"I'm going home tonight," Grace said.

"I'm sorry," Duke said. "I wanted to watch the wives size you up, and vice versa."

"That will have to wait," Grace said. "I promised to be there for the kids tomorrow."

"By the way," Duke said, "I've decided to run for vice-chairman."

"You have my vote," Joe said.

"Good. Maybe I'll get lucky." He finished his champagne. "I think I'll head for my room while I can still navigate."

Grace stood on her tiptoes to kiss the big man. "I like you," she said.

"I hope so. You'll be seeing a lot of me." Duke hit Joe with a high five and departed.

Then Grace poured the last of the champagne. "Well, lieutenant, you survived another firefight. I'm glad you won. I'm a jealous wench, but I promise I won't complain. Now I have the whole summer to put things in order. Come fall, I'll help you make this the greatest adventure of your life."

"You're wonderful," Joe said.

She touched her forehead to his chin, then kissed his lips. "I love you."

"I love you too. I'm also a touch drunk."

"So am I."

"This is the last drink," Joe said. "We'll make it a dry summer."

"I have an appointment to see Dr. Malone day after tomorrow. I promise to do exactly what he says."

Joe embraced her. "I know you will," he said.

"And next month we'll take the kids to Monument Valley, like we promised."

"You bet."

"I have a couple of hours," Grace said. "Please make love to me."

❧

According to plan, the new board of trustees elected Bob Maxwell chairman. "Thank you for your confidence, gentlemen," he said. "I am keenly aware of the importance of this chair, and I pledge to uphold the tradition established by the distinguished physicians who have preceded me. Now, I would like to welcome our new president-elect, Dr. Joe Hawkins."

"Thank you, Mr. Chairman," Joe replied, surprised. "It is a

great honor to join this distinguished board. I will do everything in my power to deserve your respect."

Duke winked, as if to say, "Christ, Hawkins, the shit is getting awfully deep in here." Then Duke was elected vice-chairman and Joe returned the wink.

After the elections Letitia announced, "Mr. Chairman, you have before you the proposed calendar of meetings for the year."

"Without objection," Bob Maxwell declared, pausing slightly, "the calendar is approved."

Letitia continued. "Mr. Chairman, next is approval for foreign travel. The speaker of the house, the president, yourself, your EVP, and appropriate staff—the World Medical Committee on International Resources, in Tokyo, next month."

"Without objection, the Tokyo meeting is approved."

And so it went. "Without objection, the motion is approved." —well oiled—"Without objection, the motion is approved."

Finally Letitia announced, "Mr. Chairman, I have nothing else."

Then Bob Maxwell inquired, "Is there other business to come before the board?"

Cleve Randall, a youthful internist from Detroit, spoke up. "Mr. Chairman, I have a matter for executive session."

"We are in executive session. Proceed."

"As the board knows, the College of Surgeons has long been harping about unnecessary surgery. Now they've launched a campaign to inform the public that surgery should be performed only by board-certified surgeons or members of the college. To get to the point, Letitia recently debated the issue of unnecessary surgery on public television with a professor of gynecology named Roger Harper. I watched the debate and, frankly, I was appalled. Roger argued that pelvic congestion syndrome is a fiction concocted by unscrupulous practitioners to justify the removal of normal uteri from emotionally disturbed women. He went on to say that some practitioners perform hysterectomies simply on request. Then Letitia piped up. 'Just like a patronizing, sexist, male gynecologist. If a woman has pain in her pelvis and wants a hysterectomy, by God she ought to have it.'

"Roger Harper hit the ceiling. 'This is a travesty. A hysterectomy, like all surgery, should be performed only for valid indications, not at the whim of the patient,' and so on. The debate got pretty testy, to no one's credit, I might add. It doesn't help the image of medicine for two leading docs to square off in a shouting match on national television. Unfortunately Roger succeeded in putting the AMA on trial for shielding incompetent surgery, and the whole point of the debate was lost."

"I take strong exception," Letitia argued. "The AMA was not put on trial. The debate was not lost. Roger Harper came on like Dr. Purity in his goddamn ivory tower. He needed straightening out. Cleve, you simply failed to comprehend the nuances of the discussion."

"I know a bungled performance when I see it," Cleve Randall replied. "Mr. Chairman. It's time we recognize that Letitia, for all of her ability, cannot represent us carte blanche. We have a gynecologist and a whole goddamn platoon of surgeons on this board. Someone else should have debated Roger Harper."

"I performed dozens of hysterectomies when I was in practice," Letitia fumed. "I had a lot of black ladies come in with pelvic pain, begging for relief. They liked a woman doctor. I removed the uterus, and it cured 'em. I know what I'm talking about."

"Goddammit Letitia," Cleve Randall snapped. "That's the trouble. You think you know it all, but you don't. You're a politician, not a surgeon. You have no business debating complex surgical issues."

Bob Maxwell tapped his gavel. "Just a moment, gentlemen. Cleve, I was there. I thought Letitia did a good job."

"Letitia is a superb debater," Cleve Randall said. "But she's a GP from Bolton, Mississippi, the prototype of what the college is squawking about—the sweet little country doc who goes quietly about her business getting rich on unnecessary surgery. Roger Harper is a professor of gynecology. It was no contest."

"I can tell you one thing," Letitia growled. "I've never tied off a ureter, and I know for a fact that Roger Harper has."

"Mr. Chairman." Duke Rodansky raised his hand. "I also saw the debate. I agree with Cleve, but that's not to fault Letitia. It was an awkward circumstance. The point is, we should always send the person with the top credentials for the situation at hand. It's plain, common sense. Letitia should take no offense."

"Letitia is still our best spokesman," Bob Maxwell said. "I have full confidence in her ability to handle whatever comes along."

"I submit, Mr. Chairman," Duke answered, "that our president-elect is also an outstanding spokesman, as he recently demonstrated. I hope you will place the same confidence in him."

Joe glared at Duke, thinking, "You turkey, don't drag me into this."

"Indeed, I welcome Dr. Hawkins to our stable of talent," Bob Maxwell replied. "Now, gentlemen, and lady. We have all had a say, and I see no reason to belabor this discussion. I will heed your concerns when making my assignments."

"Fair enough," Cleve Randall said.

"Is there further business to come before the board?" Bob Maxwell inquired.

Joe raised his hand. "Mr. Chairman. I would appreciate a briefing on the Leonard Breslow matter."

"Of course," Bob Maxwell said, turning to Letitia.

"Yes, Mr. Chairman," Letitia said. "Leonard Breslow died from a broken neck when he fell down a stairway in his condo last February. It was a fluke. The authorities are still investigating. As is customary upon the unexplained departure of a senior financial officer, we conducted an immediate audit. This was completed four weeks after the accident. No irregularities were found. We were, of course, shocked and deeply saddened by Len's death. He was a valued member of our team. A search is underway for a new CFO."

"Very well," Bob Maxwell said. "If there is no further business, we stand adjourned. Have a good summer. Joe, can you join Letitia and me for a moment?"

The three of them huddled around the head of the table. "I thought we might clarify a few matters," Letitia said.

Then Bob Maxwell said, "I hope you don't get the wrong impression from that little exchange you just witnessed between Letitia and Cleve. We have no shrinking violets on the board. Sometimes it gets lively."

Joe laughed. "I enjoyed it."

"Cleve is a good internist who knows little about surgical matters," Letitia said. "He was out of line."

"He made a good point," Joe said. "Send the right person for the job."

"We always try to send a person with proper credentials," Letitia replied, "but some things arise on short notice. I'm readily available. It's my job, and as a former GP I have broad clinical experience and can effectively handle most situations."

"Letitia is an able spokesman," Bob Maxwell said.

"She addressed my state association last year," Joe said. "I've also seen her on Newsline and MacNeil-Lehrer. She's a superb spokesman."

"Well, thank you, Joe," Letitia said.

Bob Maxwell smiled. "I felt certain you would agree, Joe."

"Since Joe is new to the board," Letitia said, "it would be appropriate to explain the working relationship between the president and the chairman."

"I would appreciate that," Joe said.

Letitia continued. "The chairman's authority flows from the power the house of delegates vests in the board of trustees. The board sets its own rules of operation, elects the chairman, and authorizes him to conduct its affairs. In short, the chairman, who serves at the pleasure of the board, is the controlling elected official of the AMA."

"Of course," Bob Maxwell said, "the president is regarded as the principal spokesman for the AMA."

"We try to collaborate on important matters," Letitia said. "It would be to your advantage to become a member of the team."

Joe smiled. They had come right to the point. "I thought my election put me on the team," he said.

"I mean the first team," Letitia replied.

Then Bob Maxwell said, "You see, Joe, we have various levels of cooperation within the board itself. To function effectively, we must have a reliable core willing to work together."

"Those who work together share in the benefits," Letitia added.

"We realize," Bob Maxwell said, "that your success in Madison Square Garden, and your speaking ability, led to your election. And you know that we had expected Mike Devlin to become president-elect. However, that's history, and it's time to move on. We hope you will close ranks with us for the good of the AMA."

"I intend to work for the good of the AMA," Joe said.

"Good," Letitia said. "I am sure you will have some interesting assignments. Customarily the president-elect is one of the AMA representatives to the World Medical Association. The next meeting of the assembly is in Madrid next spring. Perhaps that would interest you."

"I know very little about the World Medical Association," Joe said, "but I'd be willing to give it a try."

"Consider it done," Bob Maxwell said.

"We'll provide the necessary briefings," Letitia said. "It's important to understand AMA policy. Obviously you prepared well for your campaign. You have an excellent grasp of the issues."

"I found out how little I know," Joe said.

"That always happens," Bob Maxwell said.

"Kate is an excellent PR gal," Letitia said. "She has good speechwriters and knows how to use them. When you get a speaking assignment, she'll brief you and prepare the speech. I noticed that in the Garden speech you discarded the text we had agreed upon. We hope that in the future you will adhere to the material we provide, subject of course to your own personal editing."

"I don't like canned speeches," Joe said.

"You'll get the hang of it," Letitia said.

"I prefer to prepare my own material," Joe said.

"Of course," Letitia replied, an edge creeping into her voice. "Certainly you should edit the speeches to fit your own style. But it's important to represent our policies accurately."

"From time to time it may be necessary to improvise," Bob Maxwell said.

"I expect to participate in those decisions," Joe said.

"Fair enough," Bob Maxwell said. "Welcome to the team. You'll have ample say in the affairs of the AMA."

"Agreed?" Letitia asked.

Joe smiled. The message was plain: Go along to get along—right out of the Lyndon Johnson–Sam Rayburn playbook. All political bodies work the same way. The AMA is no exception. "Relax, guys," he said. "I've been a team player all my life."

❧

The phone rang as Joe entered his room. "Dr. Hawkins. My name is Gihachi Myoshi. Perhaps you remember me as George. I am calling from Tokyo on behalf of Dr. Kajimoto, president of the Japan Medical Association."

"Yes, George," Joe replied. "I recognize your voice. How are you?"

"Ah. Very well, sir. Can you speak with Dr. Kajimoto at this time?"

"Of course."

"Thank you, sir."

The phone crackled with Kajimoto's familiar staccato: "Greetings, Dr. Hawkins."

"Greetings, sir. How are you?"

"I am well, but for the infirmities of old age."

"You sound quite spirited," Joe said. As in their first conversation, George's skillful translation quickly fell unnoticed.

"Unfortunately my body is not so spirited," Kajimoto replied.

"I find that hard to believe," Joe said.

"I congratulate you on your election," Kajimoto said. "You have attained the highest honor of the American Medical Association."

"Thank you very much, sir," Joe said.

"I followed your campaign with pleasure," Kajimoto said. "Like your father, you faced overwhelming odds with courage. You will be an excellent president."

"Many friends helped," Joe said.

"You alone commanded the votes."

"I am very pleased and very honored."

"How did Dr. Jordan respond to your victory?"

"She wanted Dr. Devlin to win."

"Dr. Jordan does not like interference."

"So I have been told."

"When we talked previously, I predicted you would become a spokesman for the AMA."

"I did not take your prediction seriously," Joe said.

"I regret that we did not wager," Kajimoto said. The gruff staccato softened. "I would have won some American dollars."

Joe laughed. "I would never bet against you, sir."

"Have you given further consideration to visiting me in Tokyo?"

"I think about it often. Now that the election is over, I hope to make definite plans."

"Will you attend the meeting of the World Medical Association Assembly in Madrid next spring?"

"Yes, I expect to attend."

"Unfortunately my infirmities will not permit travel to Madrid. Perhaps you can arrange to visit Tokyo upon conclusion of the meeting."

"That sounds promising. Madrid to Tokyo would be a long journey, but I am most anxious to meet with you."

"An appropriate invitation will be issued." Then Kajimoto said, "I now wish to discuss a delicate matter."

"Of course."

"I have reason to believe Dr. Jordan performs services for the tobacco cartel that are not consistent with the mission of the AMA."

"I don't understand," Joe said.

"Allow me to explain," Kajimoto said. "The tobacco cartel is composed of American and British tobacco companies and a silent partner known as the Tora Society. The Tora Society is a Japanese crime syndicate. The cartel controls one-third of the world cigarette market. The Tora Society controls the cartel."

"I know nothing of the Tora Society," Joe said.

"Tora is Japanese for tiger. In Japan the tiger symbolizes power and stealth. The Toras originated among survivors of the wealthy elite of Japan who had opposed the war with the United States because they feared destruction of their assets. In the decade before the war, samurai militarists assassinated leaders of the elite and seized control of the Japanese government. The militarists invaded Manchuria and attacked Pearl Harbor. When Japan surrendered to the United States, the militarists fell from power. Some committed suicide, some were executed for war crimes, others withdrew into seclusion. The Tora Society arose during the American occupation of Japan. It professed to work for the good of Japan and was recognized by General MacArthur. Unfortunately, when Japan regained independence the Toras fell prey to criminal elements led by former militarists.

"My father was a founder of the Tora Society. I am a physician, but a Tora by birthright. I know their ways. However, I and many Toras deplore criminal acts.

"The Toras acquired great power after the war. They own banks and legitimate businesses in Japan and the United States. They also deal in narcotics, prostitution, and gambling and conceal their assets in the banks. The tobacco cartel is their most profitable enterprise. This is because nicotine, like opium, is highly addictive."

"We've known that for years, sir," Joe said.

"The cartel manipulates nicotine levels in cigarettes to increase addiction. Your term for this practice is 'spiking.' Spiking sustains the American cigarette market. The Toras are utilizing spiked cigarettes to develop new markets in China, notably among women. At this time fewer than one of ten Chinese women smoke.

"For many years the cartel has employed a successful strategy to challenge the harmful effects of smoking. The strategy prevented political and legal results unfavorable to the cartel. However, evidence about the health charge is mounting. For this reason the Toras solicited the services of Dr. Jordan."

Joe was stunned. Unmistakably, Kajimoto was saying that Letitia Jordan was on the take. "Do you have proof?" Joe asked.

"I have observed notable omissions by the AMA that benefit the cartel," Kajimoto replied. "The AMA rarely makes public statements against smoking. Also, the AMA does not challenge the tobacco subsidy provided by your government or testify against tobacco companies in lawsuits asserting that smoking causes cancer and other fatal diseases."

"And you attribute these 'notable omissions,' as you call them, to Dr. Jordan?"

"No other plausible explanation exists. Dr. Jordan administers the AMA. Only she can cause omissions of such great importance."

"Frankly, sir, I hadn't noticed. If true, why would Letitia Jordan of all people do such a thing?"

"She is handsomely compensated," Kajimoto replied.

"You mean, the cartel actually pays her?"

"That is correct. Very substantial sums."

"You're suggesting bribery. With all due respect, sir, I find that hard to believe."

"Your reaction is understandable," Kajimoto said. "I ask only that you retain my information for future assessment of its authenticity."

"Fair enough," Joe said.

"A final point: as president of the AMA, you can stop Dr. Jordan. That would anger the Toras, and they are capable of extreme measures."

"Are you warning me?" Joe asked.

"I believe you would say, 'heads-up.'"

"You have a way with the metaphor."

"I learn from George," Kajimoto replied.

"I grew up in Denver," George said.

"That makes you a fellow Westerner," Joe said.

"George is proud of his American education," Kajimoto said.

"And rightfully so," Joe said. "George is a brilliant translator."

"George conveys my thoughts in English with greater eloquence than I speak them in Japanese," Kajimoto said.

"Thank you, Dr. Hawkins. Thank you, Dr. Kajimoto," George said, hissing softly, Japanese style. Joe envisioned him as a little guy with big teeth, smiling and bowing.

Joe then asked, "Dr. Kajimoto, why do you bring these things to me?"

"I was a samurai. Your father spared my life. Hence, I am indebted to you. It is a debt of honor. That is samurai custom."

"I see. Well, once again you have given me a lot to think

about." The old Jap had told a crazy tale, still Joe liked and wanted to trust him. "I'm glad you called, sir."

"Thank you," Kajimoto said.

"I look forward to meeting you in Tokyo," Joe said. "I will make arrangements as soon as possible."

"I also look forward to our meeting," Kajimoto said. "Good luck."

❦

Moments later the phone rang again. "Joe. This is Muriel. There's been an accident. . . . Grace is dead."

[13]

LETITIA JORDAN was curled up in a chair staring at her husband, her diminutive body all but lost in the ponderous billows of a white cotton morning robe. They were sitting at the marble table in front of the big window in the alcove of their penthouse in Chicago, and on the table was a stately Gorham coffee pot and a fresh bouquet of yellow roses in a blue vase. Luther Agostelli had dressed for the day and was nursing the last of his breakfast coffee while watching the morning sunbeams knife through the layers of gray stratus low in the east over Lake Michigan. They had not conversed since arising and she had administered his morning orgasm.

The penthouse was on the fortieth floor of the prestigious Crystal on North Michigan Avenue, near the old Water Tower. The old Navy Pier with its ungainly towers at the far end, a giant Ferris wheel in the middle, and sightseers' boats moored at the sides sprawled a half-mile into the lake in front of them. When abandoned by the navy after World War II, the aging brick and wood pier became a university campus dubbed by Illinoisans, "Harvard on the Rocks." In the east beneath the clouds, the blue horizon line, like that of an ocean, stretched to infinity. A dingy cargo ship trailing black smoke trudged through the water a couple of miles out, and a scattering of sailboats and motor cruisers with feathery wakes cruised beyond the breakwater and the lighthouse. The lake was deep blue with patches of gray where scuddy stratus reflected in the water, and near the horizon the colors melded and the lake appeared mottled and drab.

Letitia and Luther lived comfortably in the penthouse. They had transformed a double suite into a lavish home. The great room in the center had a magnificent panorama—Lake Michigan, the city towers, airliners searching for O'Hare, little planes flying in and out of Meigs Field on the lake, the shoreline curving to the steel furnaces of Gary to the south, the outer drive running north along the beach, and in the distance the condos of the Gold Coast looking like toy buildings. It was fun to show off the penthouse and the furnishings and paintings and knickknacks and the Italian marble, and the view, and it was nice to have breakfasts and quiet suppers in the alcove and gaze at the lake.

They had married ten years ago, but had not been well-to-do until Letitia landed her job with the AMA. She remembered how angry Luther became in their early days in Mississippi when they had to scrimp to send alimony checks to his first wife in Jackson. Now they had plenty of money. Luther took care of his alimony and personal expenses from the small psychiatric practice he conducted in Chicago, and Letitia's income paid for everything else. They traveled handsomely and spent thousands of dollars on china and crystal and paintings in foreign countries.

The AMA had purchased the penthouse in the Crystal and leased it to them. "Standard corporate practice," Letitia had explained, and they would be required to entertain.

Indeed, they welcomed a succession of politicians, businessmen, and assorted brethren of the AMA. Letitia had only to select the menus—the caterers did the rest—and remember names and look elegant and hone the small-talk she had learned from the masters in London. Otherwise, the penthouse and its panorama were theirs.

Luther sipped his coffee and squinted against the growing brightness of the sun. He turned to Letitia. "You're morose this morning."

"Yes."

"Devlin lost. So what?" He had never liked Mike Devlin.

"It was a fluke."

"Presidents come and presidents go. That's what you always say."

"That's what I always say," Letitia repeated.

"You always say you can deal any deck they hand you. In the final analysis, you're the AMA. That's what you always say. You should be pleased about Bob Maxwell. He's one of your cronies."

"Bob will be an adequate chairman."

"It was a set up, wasn't it? Like always."

"Yes. Like always," Letitia conceded.

"The slate."

"That's right, the slate."

"Bob Maxwell is bullheaded and stupid."

"He feeds on adulation. He'll do what I say."

"You don't love him, do you?"

"No."

"You don't even like him."

"No."

"You use him, and he uses you. That's it."

"That's it."

"Bob Maxwell is an asshole. Frankly, I like Joe Hawkins a lot better than either Mike Devlin or Bob Maxwell."

"Just keep it to yourself, Luther."

"It was terrible about Grace Hawkins."

"Of course it was."

"Do you know what happened?"

"Only that she was driving home and ran off the road. The car rolled. She died instantly."

"Was she alone?"

"Yes."

"Was she drunk?"

"I understand she had a drinking problem."

"What a pity. She was a beautiful woman."

"Indeed she was."

"Grace Hawkins would have added panache to the board wives. God knows, they could use some panache." Luther poured a final splash of coffee for himself. "Have you heard from Dr. Hawkins?"

"No. The funeral is today. Perhaps I'll hear something by the end of the week."

"What do you think he'll do?"

"He'll resign."

"How can you be sure?"

"I have a feeling. It's too bad she didn't kill herself before the election. That would have cinched it."

"What a terrible thing to say."

"I mean, if she had to die anyway."

"That's disgusting."

Letitia glared at him. "Goddammit Luther! Don't fuck with me this morning. I'm in no mood."

Luther ignored the unwifely reprimand. "Joe Hawkins is a nice man. Maybe, after he's had a chance to think things out, he'll return. He would be a fine president." Luther gazed at the distant clouds. "The sun's having its problems this morning."

"Yes, the sun's having its problems," Letitia said. "We're all having our problems. I'm sorry I snapped at you. I didn't mean it."

"You're having trouble?"

"It's building up."

"Building up." That's what she had said when they first met ten years ago in Jackson. She had driven from Bolton desperately seeking help, a raging paranoiac tormented by delusions of persecution, deeply depressed and in serious trouble. He had hospitalized her, and within a week she had improved dramatically and returned to her practice in Bolton with no one the wiser. He became her therapist and, within the year, they married.

"You know," he had teased, "it's considered unprofessional for the psychiatrist to fall in love with the patient."

"So what?" she had replied.

"How long?" Luther asked.

"Couple of weeks."

"This is the first since that time in New York with Kate Murphy, isn't it?"

"Yes."

"You've been under a lot of pressure."

"They're ganging up on me."

"I know. The election was rough."

"It was rough."

"Been taking your Thorazine?"

"Yes."

"Noncompliance is the usual cause of relapse."

"I know. I've been taking it faithfully."

"Then you should increase the dose. Go back to t.i.d."

"Whatever you say. You always take good care of me."

"We take good care of each other."

"I don't know what I'd do without you, Luther. I mean that."

"Are you going to work today?"

"No. I'm taking off through the weekend."

"I see my last patient at eleven."

She brightened up. "Wonderful. Come home for lunch. I'll fix that crab salad you like. Then we'll have the afternoon to ourselves. We can talk, and relax, and I'll love you just the way you like it, I promise."

"That's a deal." Luther finished his coffee. "Time to go." He turned to the big window for a last look, standing stiff-necked and ramrod straight, and in the morning light his round cheeks glowed rosy red.

Then Letitia giggled. "Luther, you're as bad as I am. When you stand in front of the window like that, it's like you're getting ready to rear back and beat your chest and yodel, like a goddamn, fucking, little Tarzan. And I love you."

❧

"Good morning Dr. Hawkins. I'm Sergeant Melrose." The sergeant was a tall man dressed in the conventional summer garb of Phoenix—cotton slacks, short-sleeve shirt, no tie, no jacket. A .38-caliber Smith and Wesson snub-nose in a leather holster hung from his belt, and he held a manilla envelope. "Thank you for seeing me."

Joe escorted Sergeant Melrose into the kitchen and they sat at the breakfast table. "Coffee?" Joe inquired.

"No thank you, sir. I'll be brief. I'd like to update you on our investigation of the accident involving Mrs. Hawkins. I also want to extend the condolences of the department. You have many friends in the department, Dr. Hawkins. You've taken care of us when we needed you, on some occasions saved our lives. We were saddened to hear of your loss."

"Please thank everyone for me," Joe said.

Sergeant Melrose opened the clasp on the manilla envelope and withdrew some papers and photographs. "I know this is difficult, sir. I would like for you to examine some photographs."

Joe nodded and the sergeant handed him three eight-by-tens. "These were taken at the crash site after the body was removed. The car rolled two-and-a-half turns down the slope. There was no fire. Her seat belt was fastened, and she stayed with the car. The top was down. We found blood on a rock near the road, where she apparently hit her head on the first roll."

The photographs were painful to behold. Joe's beautiful red Jaguar lay wheels up amidst rocks in the desert, like a toy car broken and discarded by a child, doors and fenders battered and windshield flattened, the open cockpit flush on the sand.

"They had to pick the car up to get her out," Sergeant Melrose said. He produced another photograph. "This shows the blood on the rock."

Joe shook his head sadly. "She must have taken one helluva lick."

"Yes sir, she did," Sergeant Melrose said. The last of the photographs showed the Jaguar right-side-up on a cement floor inside a building. "These were taken in the impound garage. You can see the extensive roll damage to the body, fenders, hood, and the smashed windshield. The chassis was intact. Actually the car was drivable."

Joe grimaced. "You're right, sergeant," he said. "This is difficult."

Sergeant Melrose handed Joe the papers. "This is the medical examiner's report. There were minor abrasions and a midshaft fracture of the left humerus. Apparently her arm caught under the door when the car rolled. There were no internal injuries. The fatal blow was a depressed skull fracture."

"Was she dead when they found her?"

"Yes, sir. Death was practically instantaneous."

"She never knew what happened," Joe said.

"It was a freak accident, sir. Without the rock, she would have survived with only a broken arm."

"What a tragedy," Joe said.

"I understand that Mrs. Hawkins returned from Chicago the evening before the accident and spent the next morning at home. That afternoon she drove alone to the Safeway for cookies and soda pop."

"She loved to drive my Jag," Joe said.

"The accident happened when she was on her way home, on the second switchback going up the hill."

"I know," Joe said. "I drive that road every day."

Sergeant Melrose continued. "She was in the outside lane and ran off the road about halfway to the turn. There was no guard-rail. The car went off the asphalt and rolled. The slope was fairly steep at that point. The time was approximately 2 P.M."

Joe leaned back and closed his eyes. "Grace never drove fast, even in the Jag. She liked to mosey along that road with the top down and enjoy the view."

"She was a good driver?"

"Absolutely," Joe replied. "I always gunned the Jag and double-clutched and all the rest. She did none of that. She was a safe driver, if something of a slowpoke. I kidded her about lugging the engine."

"She was going slow when she ran off the road. She was only in third gear."

"Twenty-five, maybe thirty," Joe said.

"Doc, I understand Mrs. Hawkins had a drinking problem. For what it's worth, she hadn't been drinking when she died. All the tests were normal. No drugs, no blood alcohol."

"I'm grateful for that," Joe said.

"However, we don't know what caused the accident."

"Didn't she simply run off the road?"

Sergeant Melrose selected one of the photographs. "This is a blowup of the driver's side of the car, taken in the impound garage." He pointed to the front fender. "Those linear scratches on the fender came from another vehicle, with a brown paint job. Do you recognize them?"

Joe examined the photograph. "No. They weren't there when we left for Chicago."

"Did Mrs. Hawkins drive the car earlier in the day of the crash?"

"The kids said she used the Suburban."

"The scratches could have been picked up on her way to or from the store. Or they could have been picked up in the parking lot. However, they are also consistent with a heavy sideswipe by an overtaking vehicle on the driver's side, suggesting she was run off the road."

"You mean someone bumped her?"

"It's possible. Unfortunately there were no witnesses. If that's what happened, it was a hit-and-run thing. We'll know when we find the other vehicle. We've posted advisories to all repair shops, and we're checking the paint with the manufacturers."

"I can't believe this," Joe said.

Sergeant Melrose returned the photographs to the manilla envelope. "That's all I have for now, Doc. I'll contact you when I have something to report. Again, sir, my condolences."

[14]

A BEAUTIFUL little girl of ten with blond hair and long legs, toting a yellow rucksack, stepped into the warm morning sunlight. Her younger sister, sturdy and brunette, a towheaded

little brother, and Joe, tallish and tan with good shoulders and a
crop of tousled brown hair, lugging a Coleman Cooler, followed.
They were all dressed alike in jeans, T-shirts, and sneakers and Joe
wore aviator sunglasses.

The motel was in the old Indian village of Kayenta on the
Navajo Reservation in northern Arizona. They crawled into a blue
and white Suburban—the older girl, Tracy, in back and the other
two in front with Joe—drove past the Navajo trading post on the
highway, the filling station, and the ramshackle shanties; then
turned north on the road to Mexican Hat and picked up speed.
Traffic was light and the shanties of Kayenta soon fell behind.

It was a pretty July morning. Cumulus clouds, harbingers of
the towering thunderheads that build in the summer afternoons
over the high country, were already forming and there was a light
breeze. It was cooler in Kayenta than in the valley to the south
where they lived, where the summer sun blistered everything, and
the air on the reservation was clear and clean.

On the sunrise side of the road, a splintery volcanic peak
known as Agathla loomed a thousand feet above the flat, and
along the highway to Shiprock, the sandstone serrations of Comb
Ridge were turning orange in the fresh sunlight. Across the road
the layered edge of Tyende Mesa, a long ribbon of a cliff ragged
and crumbling like a broken piecrust, where years ago a great
sandstone plateau had cracked along miles of subterranean fault,
meandered lazily north. The Suburban crossed the long, morning
shadow of Agathla then came to something in the cliff so bizarre
it must have been sculptured by Gods: the likeness of an owl's
head with a great hooked beak and haunting eyes. The eyes
appeared to track them as they drove by.

"The Navajos call that 'Owl Rock'," Joe announced. "They say
that ugly old owl remembers every traveler to come along this
trail for the last thousand years."

Then the road veered from Tyende Mesa and moved into barren range with scattered sage and patches of gramma and an
occasional mesquite or juniper. Only the serpentine patterns of
dry washes carved in the sand bore witness that water had ever
touched this arid piece of earth.

The sun ascended as they traveled, and the range changed from sand to reddish brown, and giant monoliths of red sandstone with flat tops and cracked and eroded cliffs loomed into view. A half-mile from the road, on the edge of a wash, stood a hut made of logs and mud. The hut was six-sided, and the corners bristled with the interlocking tips of the logs. The roof was layered with asphalt shingles stained garish green, and a wisp of gray smoke curled from a stovepipe chimney. In front was an empty farm wagon, and in a nearby log corral a horse stood motionless in the spotted shade under a juniper.

"That's a ho-gan," Joe said, accenting the first syllable and shorting the "a" as the Indians do. He pulled off the road. "Many of the reservation Navajos still live in hogans."

"The roof sucks," Tracy said in a matter-of-fact way.

"Indians like gaudy colors," their father explained. "The government provides free asphalt shingles for them. They can have a whole house of asphalt shingles if they want, any color they want, free. This family must have preferred logs and mud, except for the roof. Asphalt shingles make a good roof that doesn't leak in the winter when the snow piles on top."

"Do they have lights?" Tracy asked.

"Only lanterns."

"Where do they get water?"

"They haul it on wagons. Some have wells."

"Are they inside now?"

"Yes."

"Why don't they come out?"

"Indians don't come out until they have something to do. If we wait, someone will come out."

"Where's the door?"

"On the other side, facing the sunrise, so they can see the first light of day."

They studied the hogan and the horse in the corral, then Joe started the Suburban and returned to the road. "Navajos like their hogans," he said. "They've lived that way for centuries."

They saw other hogans as they drove. Most were made of mud and logs, some had shingle roofs, usually blue, green, or red, some had one or two horses outside or a few head of cattle. Now and then they saw a Navajo man or woman, or children playing. They drove leisurely and after a few miles came to a crossroad and turned east toward a distant ridge of flat-topped sandstone.

Joe pointed ahead. "See those funny shaped rocks on the left? The far one is called the King. He's sitting on a throne. Follow the ridge to the right. The long, boxy rock is the Stagecoach. Next is the Bear. He's a little hard to make out. See the Rabbit, to the right of the Bear? See the nose and the ears? He's looking at the Bear." He pointed to the stone profiles as he drove.

The road led to a pass in the sandstone wall, and beyond the pass lay a vast flatland. "This is Monument Valley," Joe announced. They stopped at the tribal station and Joe paid the fee and obtained a map, then they drove across the pass and along a narrow road of volcanic shale. Monument Valley sprawled before them, miles of raw desert dotted with sage, sand, red rocks, patches of orange and yellow, and great mountainous monuments, gargantuan remnants of an ancient volcanic explosion, stark, isolated, hallowed ground, the cemetery of the Gods.

"We're still in Arizona. The northern half of Monument Valley is in Utah."

The monuments were giant buttes of red sandstone. Some towered a thousand feet or more above the valley and were formed in many shapes—flat-topped, box-like, slender, squat, cylindrical—with sheer, vertical walls and sloping taluses of shale and sand that had accumulated over eons of erosion.

Joe pointed to the two tallest. "Those are called the Mittens. They look like the mittens you wear on your hands in winter." Each of the giant buttes had a thumb-like appendage on the side. "The thumbs are sticking out. Use your imagination."

He pulled off the road and they got out. It was noon and the sun was hot where it streamed through the cumuli beginning to fill the sky.

"Left hand, right hand. You can tell by the thumbs. They look more like real mittens at night when they're silhouetted against the moonlight. The big fellow in the middle with no thumb is Merrick's Butte."

They studied the majestic buttes, and the valley was still but for a whisper of breeze. Nothing moved.

"Do Indians live here?" Rosie asked in a whisper.

"A few," her father replied. "They're tucked away, out of the sun, where you can't see them. They tend sheep, goats, and cattle."

"What's a monument?" she asked.

Joe thought, then replied, "A monument is something that reminds us of a special person or a special thing, like the Washington Monument that reminds us of George Washington, or the Punchbowl in Honolulu, where my father is buried with other men who died in the war. These monuments are for the gods of the Navajos. The Navajos believe Monument Valley was made a place of great beauty so their Gods can live here forever in happiness."

"Are the Gods here now?"

"The Navajos believe they are."

"I don't see anyone," Tracy said, her hair reflecting the sunlight like polished gold.

"We seem to be all alone," Joe said.

"I like it all alone," she said.

"So do I," her father replied.

"I'm hungry," Jake said.

"It's time for lunch," Joe announced. "I know a great place that mom really liked."

They crawled into the Suburban and drove along the shale road past Merrick's Butte and the Mittens and into the red dunes of the south valley, where the slender monoliths of the Ye Be Chai, a cluster of towering stone columns, rose from the sand. The father explained the tallest of the Ye Be Chai was named Totem Pole because its craggy shaft appeared to have been carved with the faces of Indians.

Beyond Totem Pole they came to a fork and drove up a gentle slope to a hidden ravine and a promontory. Joe parked the Suburban, and they carried the Coleman Cooler and the rucksack to the edge of the promontory and looked down on the Mittens and the sprawl of giant buttes and red rocks in the valley. The breeze was steady and stronger, and cooler.

"This is Artist's Point," he said. "Painters and photographers like to come here. You can see all of Monument Valley."

They sat on flat rocks while Joe extracted bread and peanut butter and paper plates from the rucksack. "Every one make their own sandwiches," he said. "We have jelly, mayonnaise, mustard, pickles, lettuce, and ham and cheese, and cokes and water in the cooler."

The wind picked up and they weighted the paper plates with jars. Thankfully it was too windy for flies. They ate hungrily and got seconds on soda pop from the cooler. Finally Joe produced a bag of Hershey Nuggets. "I know you like these," he explained.

"*You* like them," Tracy teased.

Then they rested against the rocks. "It's nice here," she said.

"I thought you would like it," Joe said.

"Did Mom like Monument Valley?"

"She loved Monument Valley. It was one of her favorite places. She wanted us all to come this summer. She loved to have lunch here and look at the valley. Once, a few years ago, she and I came in the winter, and the snow was so deep we almost didn't make it up the road. We were all alone and cold and wanted to build a fire, but there was no wood. All we had to warm us was a thermos of hot chocolate. It tasted so good. The valley was beautiful that day, covered with fresh snow."

"It's pretty today, too," Tracy said.

"It's too bad Grandma and Aunt Janie couldn't come," Rosie said.

"I wanted us to come alone. We'll bring them next time. Anyway, they were tired and had to unpack."

"I miss Mom," Jake said softly.

"So do I," Joe replied. "I can't believe she's gone."

"Why did she go off the road?" Tracy asked.

"I don't know, she was such a good driver."

The wind picked up steadily and their full stomachs made them sleepy. The three children lay down and dozed. Joe rested against the rock, and the wind grew stronger and a giant thunderhead rose over the valley. It cast a dark shadow on the Mittens.

Then Joe roused them. "We're going to have a storm," he announced.

They watched the majestic thunderhead tower and swell. The crest was billowy and white and tinged with pink sunlight. It cavorted like the head of foam on a pot of slow-boiling milk. The flanks were gray and ragged, and a shaft of blue rain slanted to the valley floor beneath. Undaunted by heavenly powers, the Mittens stood firm, as they had for millions of years, enveloped by the rain.

A jagged streak of lightning struck the earth beneath the thunderhead, and moments later they heard the muffled crash of distant thunder.

"If you count the seconds between the lightning and the thunder, you can tell how far away it is," Joe said.

At the next flash they counted aloud together: "One thousand one, one thousand two, one thousand three . . . one thousand nine," waiting for the thunder.

"Almost two miles," Joe announced. "Sound travels about one mile in five seconds."

The thunderhead darkened and moved ominously toward the promontory. Again they counted, trying to time the loudest with the brightest because now the flashes overlapped the sound. "It's coming in," Joe noted. "The wind is stronger. We'd better load up and get out of here. A desert storm is beautiful to watch, but dangerous."

They packed their things and drove cautiously down the slope. "Lightning is bad in high places," Joe said. "We'll be safe in the valley."

It was raining torrents when they got to the bottom, and pellets of hail hammered the steel roof of the Suburban. The wipers were thrashing at top speed, but they could barely see out the windshield. Lightning struck at the high rocks, and they caught glimpses of rainwater streaming along the flattened shale on the roadbed. Thunder exploded around them, and each shattering crash overpowered the clacking wipers and the pounding rain and hail.

Joe cautiously guided the big vehicle along the highest ridges in the road. "See what I mean about desert storms?" he shouted.

Jake and Rosie in front inched closer to their father, and Tracy in back rested her chin on the seatback. Joe glanced down at their serious young faces, then smiled and winked, and they felt safe and smiled back trustingly and snuggled against his shoulder.

As quickly as it had come, the storm moved behind them and Joe pulled off the road near the Mittens. They got out and studied the washed sandstone buttes and the clearing sky and the father hugged the children to his side. The wet shale was slippery, and thin rivulets of water still trickled down the slopes and puddled in the ruts. Then the storm moved beyond the Ye Be Chai, and the lightning and thunder faded. The breeze softened, and the air felt damp, clean, and fresh, and the sunbeams nosed through the broken clouds and warmed them.

[15]

IN THE FALL, Joe flew to Chicago for the yearly budget meeting of the board of trustees. It was his first time away from home since Grace's death. The other trustees were milling around and greeting each other when he entered the big board room and Bob Maxwell was patiently coaxing them to sit down. "Let's get going, gentlemen. We have a long session today."

Joe piled a briefcase and an armload of notebooks on the long table, then Duke Rodansky's gruff voice overpowered the chatter. "Hey Joe. You gotta buy a bigger briefcase."

"And a luggage cart," Cleve Randall called out.

Joe grinned and Duke sided up to him and gripped his hand. "How are you doing, old buddy?"

"It's been a rotten summer," Joe replied.

"I know," Duke said.

"I appreciated your calls," Joe said.

"It's good to see you," Duke said.

"Same here," Joe said.

The trustees finally settled into their chairs and Bob Maxwell rapped the gavel. "Thank you, gentlemen, and good morning.

The meeting is called to order." He turned to Joe. "Before we take up the agenda, I want to welcome our president-elect and express condolences for the tragic death of Mrs. Hawkins. Joe, you have our deepest sympathy. We're delighted to have you with us again."

"Thank you, Mr. Chairman," Joe replied, rather surprised. "Your wonderful calls and letters were a great comfort." His voice softened. "Grace's death devastated my family. But I have three wonderful children to live for—Tracy, Rosie, and Jake—and we had the summer to regroup. My mother and sister have joined us. We have a big house in the foothills with plenty of room for six Hawkinses, a fire in the hearth and the smell of good cooking in the kitchen, and we have a home again. Life goes on. I am back at work, busy, and I intend to fulfill my responsibilities."

"Very good," Bob Maxwell said. "Gentlemen, as you know, it's time to approve the budget for next year. Letitia advises me we have an interesting day ahead, so with that, I'll turn the meeting over to her."

"Thank you, Mr. Chairman," Letitia Jordan said. "Good morning, gentlemen. As you know, preparation of the AMA budget is a continual, year-round process culminating in the recommendations you will receive today. Last year the AMA converted to a mission budget. This format enables you to focus solely on relevant information and will simplify finalization of the budget."

She stepped to the podium and picked up the electric pointer. "Environmental analysis is the foundation of the mission budget. The environment of medicine defines the issues that threaten the practice of medicine. Of course we are always careful about the context in which we discuss physician incomes, but we understand what our members expect of the AMA."

The lights dimmed and the first slide illuminated the screen. "These are the primary environmental factors that impact the budget. The 'skyrocketing' cost of health care, as our critics like to say, is still number one. Cost in turn generates other factors—competition, federal budget cuts, erosion of professionalism, and public health anxieties, not the least of which is AIDS.

Cost is putting pressure on physicians to provide more service for less compensation, which is unfair."

She brought up the next slide. "We have allocated revenues to the nine missions that define the range of AMA activities. The total constitutes our entire expense budget—one hundred seventy-five million dollars. With mission budgeting you need only to approve the allocations. You are not required to review line-item budget detail. We have performed that odious task for you."

Cleve Randall interrupted. "I would like to see the line-item schedules."

"I'll be happy to provide those schedules to the finance committee," Letitia replied. "However, I hope to confine our present discussion to principles. The time of this board is too valuable to spend on minutiae. That's what your staff is for—to help you focus on the global perspectives of the AMA."

Cleve persisted. "I would like to see the schedules myself. I don't regard them as minutiae."

Bob Maxwell intervened. "You may see any schedules you want, Cleve. Letitia was merely suggesting that the finance committee is the appropriate body to review budget detail, and I concur. But tell us what you need, and you shall have it." He looked about the room and smiled. "As you all know, gentlemen, you are the nine-hundred-pound gorillas. You can have anything you want, anytime you want it."

Letitia turned to the next slide. "Representation of the profession is our number one mission, gentlemen. The allocation is fifty million dollars.

"Representation involves a multitude of activities—the house of delegates, medical staff affairs, policy development, lobbying, campaigning, international medicine, and many others. Representation is what our members demand and need. Some see us as a labor union, but unfortunately we don't enjoy the antitrust exemptions that protect labor."

The next slide appeared. "The second mission is scientific information—journals, the library, and the computer network. We publish ten journals, some in as many as six languages. Our journals reach a million readers around the world. The AMA library fills thousands of requests every year and is the primary international source for researchers. Any physician with a computer can access our network. This mission is the backbone of the AMA. Preeminence in science assures our credibility as a professional organization. Credibility, in turn, is essential to good representation. The allocation—forty million dollars."

Letitia continued to the final slide. "Our ninth and last mission is the contingency fund—one million dollars. While not exactly a mission, the contingency fund is a critical part of the budget. You might call it a discretionary fund."

Joe raised his hand. "What is the budget for the board of trustees?"

"Four million," Letitia replied.

"Where is that allocated in the mission list?"

"In administration."

"Administration shows only four million total," Joe said.

"Correct. We allocate the bulk of administrative costs to the other missions."

Joe persisted. "Then, what is the actual cost of administration?"

"Fifty-five million," Letitia replied.

"Where does that appear in the budget?"

"Administrative costs are summarized in the supporting schedules and the analysis of revenues and expenses. These will be covered in the next part of our presentation."

"What is the procedure for transferring money out of the contingency fund?" Joe asked.

"Those transfers are done at my discretion," Letitia replied. "If the amount is substantial, or the purpose unusual, I of course inform the chairman, and he decides whether to inform the finance committee and the full board."

"One other point, Mr. Chairman, if I may," Joe said. "I have a special interest in the smoking problem, and I don't believe the AMA is doing enough to fight smoking."

Letitia replied, "The council on scientific affairs has issued a number of reports laying out the facts."

"What about the addiction question?" Joe said. "What about spiking? What about the subsidy?"

"The experts still argue about addiction," Letitia replied. "Spiking and the subsidy are political matters. We must tread carefully lest we offend our friends in Congress. The board approved that policy three years ago."

"Then I respectfully disagree with the policy," Joe said. "Physicians have long known that nicotine is addictive. The facts are clear. Smoking kills more people every year than anything else, largely because of addiction. Regardless of political considerations, the AMA must take the lead in this fight."

"We do have other priorities," Letitia said impatiently. "Socialized medicine for one. Our members would not be pleased if we fought the battle against smoking and lost the war against socialized medicine."

Joe softened his tone. "Good point, Letitia. I want us to win both the battle and the war, and I hope we can devise a strategy to do so. Obviously this a complex issue that we can't resolve today."

With that Bob Maxwell intervened. "I suggest we postpone discussion of our tobacco policy to the meeting with AMPAC and the legislative council. We'll give it a thorough airing at that time."

"That's agreeable with me, Mr. Chairman," Joe replied. "I simply wanted to raise my concerns."

Cleve Randall spoke. "I concur. A full discussion of the smoking problem is needed. Now I have a question. Where do you account for foreign travel?"

"Foreign travel is assigned to international medicine—under representation," Letitia replied.

Cleve then asked, "Is foreign travel for administration also assigned to international medicine?"

"With possible exceptions, yes," Letitia replied.

"Might those 'exceptions' be paid out of the contingency fund?"

"Under certain circumstances, yes."

"For example?"

"An unexpected problem with one of our foreign publishers. An issue involving the World Medical Association that required face-to-face discussion."

"According to our rules, the board approves foreign travel for board members," Cleve said. "Who approves foreign travel for administration?"

"I do," Letitia replied.

"Not the board?"

"Board approval for administrative travel, foreign or otherwise, is implicit with approval of the budget," Letitia said. "Of course I advise the chairman of special circumstances."

"I would like to see a schedule of all foreign travel and expense accounts, irrespective of allocation, and the total cost," Cleve said. "I would also like to see a full cost analysis of our involvement with the World Medical Association."

Letitia bristled. "You realize, Cleve, you're asking for quite a lot of information."

"I still want to see those schedules."

"Then you shall have them," Letitia said, obviously irritated.

"Of course," Bob Maxwell said.

Letitia then said, "I'll now turn the balance of the presentation over to my staff."

A series of well-rehearsed dissertations on accounting came next, and Joe watched with fascination the adroit unfolding of the AMA's vast financial empire. A cast of Letitia Jordan's senior staff, all seasoned performers, trooped to the podium and explained the complexities of balance sheets, surplus and loss, revenue and expense, the real estate portfolio, retirement funds, subsidiary corporations, and membership statistics. For the finale Letitia gave an eloquent oration describing the association's rise, under her personal leadership, from financial ruin to wealth. All in all, it was a remarkable show.

When the afternoon session convened, Bob Maxwell announced, "I've asked Letitia to bring us up to date on the Breslow matter."

"Thank you, Mr. Chairman," Letitia said. "Unfortunately I have little to add to our previous reports. In the conference call last July, I advised you that investigators are looking into the possibility of homicide because of the extraordinary nature of the cervical fracture that killed Len. They think the fracture, which the coroner described as a 'hangman's fracture' with severance of the cervical cord, was too severe to have been caused by the fall. The detectives gave me a personal demonstration of how it could have been inflicted by someone trained in barehand killing. I saw the X rays and agree that it was a terrible fracture. Len also took a blow to the lower rib cage that fractured the tenth rib and punctured the lung, producing a pneumothorax. And he had a smashed nose, which was caused by the fall but did not bleed, suggesting that death preceded the fracture. They also found a strand of wool snagged under one of his fingernails, possibly from the clothing of an assailant.

"They have no motive, but because Len was the chief financial officer, our financial records are being examined for possible clues.

"The police also found one of Len's letterheads with the word "LEDGER" written on it. They believe it might be a code. Frankly, this seems pretty flimsy, like the wool under the finger nail.

"I telephoned Detective Caliano yesterday for an update. He told me only that the matter is still under investigation."

"I believe this will prove to be a false alarm," Bob Maxwell said.

"They have a point about the 'hangman's fracture,'" Duke said. "You don't get that kind of injury from a fall down the stairs."

❦

Kate was waiting in the foyer outside the boardroom. "Hello, Dr. Hawkins." She smiled and was as pretty as he remembered.

"Hello, Kate." They shook hands.

"How are you?"

"I'm okay. How about you?"

"I'm fine," she replied. "You look wonderful. Great tan."

"You look damn good yourself," Joe said.

She beamed. "I go to the beach. Lake Michigan is not the ocean, but it's the only beach I have."

"I've been looking forward to seeing you."

"Same here."

"Thank you for the call, and the note."

"I'm afraid I was miserably awkward."

Joe smiled. "Not at all. You were perfect."

"I'm awfully glad you didn't resign."

"I thought about it, but not for long. I should have let you known sooner. It was a difficult summer—the funeral, the kids, the investigation. I'm sorry."

"I understand," she said. "How are the kids?"

"They're okay. Grace and I had promised to take them to Monument Valley and the Indian reservations, one of our favorite places. So I took them, and we did some other things together. My mother retired, and she and my sister Janie moved into the house with us. It's a home again, and things are stable. The kids really miss Grace, but they love Mom and Janie."

"Do you know what caused the accident?"

"Not for certain. The investigation is still open. Grace had gone to get cookies and Cokes for the kids and was returning from the grocery store. She ran off the road and rolled down the slope. She was in my Jaguar. The top was down, and her head hit a rock. She died instantly. They found some unexplained scratch marks on the side of the Jaguar, like another vehicle forced her off the road. They're considering hit-and-run. She wasn't speeding. Her blood alcohol was normal."

"They don't know who did it?"

"They're looking for the other vehicle, if there was one."

"How awful."

Joe then said, "Well, on a happier note, I see you're still running PR for this raunchy outfit."

"Indeed I am, and I have fabulous news. The White House called an hour ago. The President wants to meet with you."

"The President of the United States?"

"Himself."

"You're kidding."

"He is pleased that you are resuming your presidency and asked that you see him next month when he's in Los Angeles. He also invited me. It'll be just the two of us."

"What's it all about?"

"He'll advise us when we meet."

"Does Letitia know?"

"Yes, and she's pissed."

"Trouble for you?"

"So what?" she said.

"Every time you turn up in my life, something happens."

"Do you mind?"

"Of course not."

"You'll be seeing quite a lot of me, you know."

"That will be nice."

"I'll be setting up some briefings." Joe nodded and she smiled enthusiastically.

"Listen," Joe said. "Duke Rodansky and I are having dinner tonight. He knows a place up north with good soft-shell crab. Can you join us, eight o'clock?"

"That would be Mario's," she said. "It's one of Dr. Rodansky's favorites. It has a piano bar, and the crab is wonderful. Just the three of us?"

"Yes."

"Mario's, then, at eight," Kate said.

"You have really blue eyes," Joe said.

[16]

MARIO'S IS a cozy little restaurant in the basement of an old brownstone on Goethe Street in the heart of Chicago's Old Town, a ten-minute cab ride from the Water Tower on North Michigan. It has a following of well-to-do north-siders who like intimacy, three-ounce martinis, and a simple menu. A young man in a dinner jacket plays ballads on the piano in the alcove bar and on the wall, under a warm light, hangs a print of Gauguin's *Young Girl*, the one with the dark, bewitching eyes. The maître d' is a comical fellow named Reuben who wears a slicked-down hairpiece, embarrassingly obvious, always askew, and he kisses the hands of the ladies.

Kate was sitting alone in the alcove bar when Joe arrived. She had changed to a stylish evening dress of white silk and had a delicate gold chain around her neck. The young pianist was playing a dreamy "Amapola."

"Been waiting long?" Joe asked.

"Just long enough for Reuben to kiss my hand."

"The maître d', I take it."

"Yes. The funny little man."

"I like the piano. That's my kind of music."

"I thought you would like it."

"Something to drink?"

"Chardonnay."

"Perfect." Joe signaled the bartender.

"Where's Dr. Rodansky?"

"He'll be along soon. I'm glad we have a moment alone." He studied her face. "You're very beautiful."

"You're embarrassing me."

"Don't be embarrassed."

"I'll try not."

"By the way, remember my telling you that Dr. Kajimoto called after the Garden speech?"

"Of course. I was impressed."

"He called again last June right after the election, by chance, only minutes before I got the call about Grace. He told me an incredible story about Letitia Jordan. I simply forgot about it until I saw you today."

The bartender brought two glasses of Chardonnay, and they took a moment to sample the chilled wine.

"The long and short of it is," Joe continued, "Kajimoto said that American and British tobacco companies are involved in a cartel that controls one-third of the world cigarette market, that a Japanese crime syndicate known as the Tora Society controls the cartel, and they're spiking cigarettes with nicotine. He also said that Letitia Jordan is working for the cartel, which is why the AMA laid off the fight against smoking and the tobacco subsidy."

"Do you believe him?"

"I don't know. It's a lot to think about. He warned me about the Toras. The tobacco cartel is their big enchilada. He says they wouldn't like it if I interfered with Letitia."

"Does this mean you're in some kind of danger?"

"He didn't go that far."

"What was his reason for telling you?"

"It has to do with the debt of honor he incurred when my father spared his life on Tarawa."

"I remember."

Joe took a swallow of wine. "Well, what do you think?"

"Putting it mildly, I'm shocked."

"He also invited me to visit him in Tokyo."

"Wow!"

"I've told no one but you, not even Duke. Let's keep it that way until I find out what's going on. In the meantime, keep your eyes open."

"Certainly."

Joe looked up. "Here he is now."

Duke Rodansky entered the bar and sauntered up to the table. "Sorry I'm late. Had a couple of calls to make. What are you drinking?"

"Chardonnay," Joe replied.

"Ugh," Duke said. He called to the bartender. "Black Label on the rocks."

"Neurosurgeons need hard liquor," Joe said.

"That they do," Duke said.

"I hope you don't object to my sitting in," Kate said.

"I'm sincerely delighted," Duke replied. "I know you won't rat on us."

The bartender brought their drinks and Reuben appeared with the menu. They quickly decided on the soft-shell crab.

"That makes it simple," Duke said. He lifted his glass and turned to Joe. "Well, Mr. President-elect, what do you think of your first board meeting?"

"Letitia Jordan is a megalomaniac," Joe replied flatly.

"You don't mince words," Duke said.

"She gave a masterful performance," Joe said. "But it was a dog-and-pony show, a fucking charade."

"Do you say that because you've been listening to me?"

"Listening to you had nothing to do with it," Joe replied. "It was obvious. The environmental analysis, the mission budget, how she pulled the AMA from the brink of ruin and built it into a great empire, her goddamn empire. You can hide anything behind pretty slides and hyperbole. The whole day was an exercise in self-aggrandizement."

"I take it you're pissed off," Duke said, grinning.

"What really rankles me is this business of protecting the doctors' incomes," Joe continued. "The hidden agenda—the secret union—things we whisper in the boardroom but never mention in public. Bullshit! Medicine is a calling. I refuse to believe the American Medical Association is obligated to become a trade union. That would be rank hypocrisy. Politics is a reality. You have to deal with politics to survive. I understand that. But our goal should be to make medicine better for patients."

"Our members tell us they want representation," Duke argued. "In recent years some have pushed for collective bargaining and union tactics. They're under a lot of pressure, and they're restless. We also have a new breed out there who don't know and care less about tradition."

"I'll bet Letitia manipulates the surveys to say what she wants them to say," Joe said. "I will never believe doctors want unionism to dominate the practice of medicine. The doctors I know want the AMA to represent patient interests even above their own. We have a public trust, for God's sake. Our job is taking care of sick people. The income will take care of itself."

"That may be naive," Duke said.

"I'm convinced the mainstream docs agree with me. Letitia thinks appealing to the hell-raisers is the key to power. Christ! Letitia would kill for power. The representation thing is a play for power."

"Okay, okay," Duke said, holding his hands up in surrender. "Why didn't you say so at the meeting?"

"I'm the new boy on the block. I talked enough as it was. My turn will come."

"You did ask some interesting questions," Duke said. "The tobacco thing drew blood."

"I wanted to get it on the table."

"Cleve Randall was trying to help you along," Duke said. "He likes to needle Letitia."

"He succeeded admirably," Joe said.

"Cleve is convinced Letitia is playing games with the subsidiaries."

"Is that why he asked for the schedules?"

"Right. But he won't find anything. It would take a full-scale audit to uncover something like that."

"What about the contingency fund?"

"You can hide a lot in a million dollar account."

"Does Letitia pocket any of that?" Joe asked.

"I doubt it. But she sure likes having a million dollars at her disposal."

"Money is power," Joe said, "and power is . . ."

". . . the ultimate aphrodisiac," Kate said.

"I was about to say corruption," Joe said, surprised.

"I like Kate's perspective," Duke said.

"What about the World Medical Association?" Joe asked.

"Good question," Duke answered. "The World Medical was organized in the fifties by a Swiss doctor named Pierre Globa, a remarkable man who fought in the French underground during the war. The Germans tortured him. Somehow he survived and after the war went to medical school. Eventually he became the wealthiest physician in Switzerland. He owns a two hundred bed hospital in Geneva and is said to have other real estate holdings in Geneva and Zurich. He also owns the World Medical headquarters in Ferney-Voltaire, a little town across the French border, near Geneva.

"Pierre Globa is an idealist. Some say he's a zealot. He passionately believes medicine can transcend political boundaries, that if doctors from different nations unite to address health issues of common interest, it will promote peace.

"Pierre Globa is also a man of enormous drive and compelling personality. The World Medical is his legacy. But it's had tough sledding. More than a hundred countries are on the roster. However, many provide only token participation, primarily the third world countries. They have no money. And there's no representation out of Scandanavia or the communist bloc."

"So much for transcending political boundaries," Joe said.

"Exactly," Duke replied. "We quit the World Medical about ten years ago. That was a deathblow to them. Pierre was ready to give up. Then Letitia became EVP. She pursuaded Pierre to hang on. When the AMA began to recover from its financial problems, Letitia convinced the board that it had an obligation to salvage the World Medical and become a major player in international medicine."

"That seems appropriate," Joe said.

"Very appropriate, I agree. The problem was control. Under the old rules each member organization had an equal vote, regardless of size or what it paid in dues. If we were to bankroll the World Medical, Letitia wanted a bigger say in things. She approached Pierre, and he engineered the necessary organizational changes. Now we foot over half the bill for the entire organization, and we control the general assembly. As you might expect, some of the smaller countries resent the AMA."

"Pierre Globa sounds like a man who wouldn't easily relinquish control."

"True, but he'd reached his limits. He saw the AMA as a savior. We're talking subsidy of a million dollars a year, plus incidentals, plus the prestige of the AMA. Pierre knew what he was doing—he protected his legacy. He still wields power through the force of his personality."

"So Letitia, in effect, bought the WMA."

"Exactly." Duke upended his whiskey and signaled for another. "The World Medical is doing nicely now. It meets in exotic places around the world, the general assembly issues learned proclamations, and everyone has a grand time. But when you get right down to it, the World Medical is nothing but a travel club. It does nothing for our membership."

"A nice perk for the brass," Joe said.

"Right," Duke said and smiled and lowered his voice. "It's basically Letitia's plaything."

"Is Letitia screwing Pierre?" Joe asked.

"Oh hell no," Duke said. "They have plenty of opportunity. Letitia goes to Ferney-Voltaire two or three times a year, and she attends all the WMA meetings, but she's no more Pierre's mistress than I am. Luther always travels with her, rarely lets her out of his sight. Pierre is married to a beautiful woman of his own, Françoise, who would cut the heart out of any woman who dared fool with her man, then castrate the man."

"I've met Françoise," Kate said. "She's a beautiful lady, and Dr. Globa is justifiably very proud of her."

"Pierre and Letitia have an interesting alliance," Duke said. "Both believe the end justifies the means, but they have different goals. Pierre pursues ideology. Letitia craves power."

Joe leaned back and folded his arms. "The whole thing is bizarre."

"Incidentally," Duke said, "Japan is a major player in the World Medical."

"Kajimoto?" Joe said.

"Absolutely. Kajimoto is thick with Pierre Globa. On Pierre's behalf he backed Letitia's takeover of the general assembly. Japan Medical also foots a big piece of the bill."

"That's true," Kate said.

"Have you heard from him lately?" Duke asked Joe.

Joe glanced at Kate, then replied, "He called to congratulate me last June when I was elected."

For a moment no one spoke. "I hope the soft-shell crab is good," Kate ventured.

Reuben approached and signaled for a fresh round of drinks, then escorted them into the dining room. The waiter appeared with salads and chilled forks and a basket of bread, and the bartender brought the Black Label and Chardonnay.

"Have you told Duke about the call from the White House?" Kate asked Joe.

"I saved it for you."

"What call from the White House?" Duke asked.

"We have exciting news," Kate said. "The White House called this afternoon. The President wants to meet with Joe. He invited me too."

"Jesus Christ!" Duke said. "That is exciting. What's it all about?"

"The President's secretary said he would advise us when we meet."

"When?" Duke asked.

"Next month," Kate replied, "in Los Angeles."

"Does Letitia know?"

"I told her," Kate said.

"She'll take it as an affront," Duke said. "Which it is. Chamberlain has no love for Letitia Jordan."

"Dr. Jordan was not happy," Kate said.

"Here's why," Duke said. "The AMA tries to wangle an audience with the President once a year or so, depending on the political climate. The entourage always includes Letitia, one or two deputies, the chairman of the board, our president, and sometimes the executive committee. We set up briefings, press releases, and pictures, a big fucking deal. Now, out of the blue, you and Kate get a personal invitation that pointedly excludes Letitia. You're damn right it's an affront."

"We have to go," Kate said.

"Of course you have to go," Duke said. "What do you think Chamberlain wants?"

"I replayed the tape of the phone call," Kate replied. "He promised to correct the record on the 'fatcats,' which he did, and he promised to talk to Joe about the national health policy. He distrusts the leadership of the AMA. And he likes Joe."

"I remember he had a nice word for you too," Joe added. "The empty Garden idea impressed him."

"Well, he backed down on his national health policy," Duke said.

"Maybe he just wants to meet Joe," Kate said.

"Why the mystery?" Duke said.

"We'll know in two weeks," Kate said.

"Shit!" Duke said. "He's not calling you in to talk about a goddamn health policy."

The waiter arrived with a sizzling platter of soft-shell crabs and warned them of hot plates.

"What is the Chardonnay?" Joe asked the waiter.

"Mondavi, 1983," the man replied.

"We should have ordered a bottle to begin with. Well, bring another round, and another Black Label."

"The crab is excellent," Duke said, tasting a sample.

"What do you know about the Breslow matter?" Joe asked Kate.

"Very little," she replied. "Leonard Breslow came on last year as chief financial officer. I saw him at staff meetings, but I didn't know him very well. He was a quiet man, well groomed, rather meticulous, something of a fitness nut, made good presentations, seemed content to stay in the background most of the time. I was shocked when he died. We were told it was an accident, a weird fall on the stairs that broke his neck. Later we heard a rumor about homicide. Then they told us that investigators would be reviewing files and financial records. I was instructed to refer press inquiries to Dr. Jordan's office."

"It was a hangman's fracture," Duke said. "Severed the spinal cord. It's hard to believe a fall down the stairs did that."

"That's gruesome," Kate said.

"The police think someone may have killed him with a choke hold," Duke said. "He also had a broken rib and a pneumo-thorax."

"It was no ordinary fall," Joe said.

"Do they have a suspect?" Kate asked.

"Possibly a professional killer. They're checking the records for financial irregularities, looking for a lead."

"You're talking stolen money?" Kate asked.

"If Len manipulated the accounts, the money trail might lead to the culprit," Duke replied.

"The killer, if there was one, knew what he was doing," Joe said.

"The police found a mysterious piece of paper with the word 'LEDGER' printed on it," Duke said.

"No explanation?" Kate asked.

"Possibly a code."

"I've heard nothing about that," Kate said.

"Letitia told us in a conference call last summer. You missed that call, Joe. There was nothing new today. The investigation is still on."

Joe thought for a moment. "The choke hold interests me. A man capable of breaking another man's neck with his bare hands probably had special training. The injuries you describe fit a known pattern. A blow to the flank strong enough to break ribs momentarily paralyzes the victim and causes hyperextension of the neck. The attacker can apply the choke hold and snap the spine before the victim can defend himself. Death is almost instantaneous. It's difficult to imagine an injury like that resulting from a fall down some stairs."

"Evidently the police agree with you," Duke said.

❧

Duke Rodansky entered the room and slipped off his trenchcoat. A stunningly beautiful black woman lay on the bed reading a magazine, her head propped on fluffy pillows and a white sheet pulled up to her nipples. She had sable hair and eyes resembling black pearls, and when she smiled her teeth gleamed like polished porcelain.

Duke leaned down and kissed her, and she tasted the Scotch in his mouth. He pulled away and hung the trenchcoat in the closet, then smiled and began to disrobe.

"I'm glad to see you," she said. "What took so long? I'm going crazy."

"I couldn't rush the dinner. They might have wondered."

"I'm glad you like them. Sometimes I don't think you like anyone at these meetings."

"I know. Did you eat something?"

"Yes, and you're my dessert."

"Of course."

He sat on the bed beside her. "It's nice and warm in here."

"Poor baby. You mustn't have a chill."

"Not likely."

She slipped her arms around his muscular chest and pulled him on top of her, then they kissed and she ran her hand over the warm skin of his flank.

"You feel good," she said.

"I like your perfume," he said.

"Obsession."

"I noticed it when I opened the door."

"You want to talk first?" she asked.

"We argued about the usual things. Nothing new. Remember Breslow, the man who was found dead last February? The cops are still investigating."

"Why, for heaven's sake?" she asked.

"He may have been murdered."

"Are you serious?"

"Yes."

"That's frightening." She snuggled closer. "What else?"

"The President of the United States invited Joe and Kate to meet with him in Los Angeles next month. That'll blow the tits off of Letitia Jordan."

"You won't mind that, will you?"

"I won't mind. It may cause trouble for Joe."

"I hope someday you can put all of that behind you. Maybe loosen up a bit."

He pulled the sheet down. Her breasts sprawled and her waist tapered like an hourglass. "I love you," he whispered.

"I love you."

"Black on white." He ran his hands over her breasts and firm belly, and she squirmed under his touch. "Your skin is so beautiful. So black and beautiful." He kissed her nipples and turned off the light and pulled the sheet away, revealing a stark, ebony contour. He stroked her legs and turned her on her belly and kneaded the firm muscles in her buttocks. "Smooth . . . tight . . . black . . . so beautiful. I love your skin."

"I know what you love. You love my sweet, black, bubble ass.

You like my tits, but you love my sweet, black, bubble ass. God, that feels good. Do it harder."

"Black bottom pie."

"Harder . . . harder."

"You first," he said.

"I don't care."

"You first. I always get it back, in spades."

"Oh God! . . . Oh God!"

He rolled her.

"Please . . . please," she murmured.

"Please what?" he teased.

"Please, baby . . . I have to have it now. Please baby. . . . Oh God!"

[17]

INSIDE, THE LEARJET smelled like new leather.

Bob Maxwell eased his bulky frame down the narrow aisle, and the leather creaked as he sank into the seat and squirmed to find the safety belt. Letitia Jordan settled across the aisle. At a foot shorter and a hundred pounds lighter, Letitia had a decided advantage in the snug cabin of the private jet.

Letitia grinned. "Well, how do you like it?"

"Damn! It sure smells new."

"It's brand new."

"If my ass was any bigger, I wouldn't fit."

"The seats are comfortable."

"Very comfortable," Bob Maxwell replied as he stretched. "Better than regular airline seats, once you're in."

"Plenty of room to work or sleep. There's a minikitchen up front. The john is in back," and Letitia pointed over her shoulder.

"You said you had a surprise. I didn't expect a Learjet."

"We've had a rough week. I didn't think either of us relished another airline ride to Washington."

A leggy young woman in a tight miniskirt climbed on board. She was followed by the pilot, a man with short brown hair and a moustache, in dark slacks, a white shirt, and aviator sunglasses. He secured the cabin door. "We're ready to go, Dr. Jordan."

"Fine, Chuck. This is Dr. Bob Maxwell, chairman of the board of the American Medical Association."

"Glad to have you aboard, sir."

"Thank you."

"Peggy is your hostess today."

The leggy young woman smiled.

"Hello, Peggy," Letitia said.

Chuck turned and crawled through the cockpit door. The copilot was already in the right seat examining papers fastened on a clipboard.

"Fasten your seat belts," Peggy said, and took her place in the seat in front of Letitia.

"You've flown with Chuck before?" Bob Maxwell inquired.

"A few times," Letitia replied. "I've been testing the concept."

Bob Maxwell nodded, amused.

Soon they heard the whisper of the Garrett turbofans and felt a soft vibration. The Learjet rolled out of the parking area and trundled down the taxiway along the row of airplanes parked in the tiedown strip. The little jet rocked gently as it taxied, and the cabin creaked as the Oleo struts in the landing gear flexed on the ripples in the taxiway.

Chuck's cheery voice came over the cabin loudspeaker. "We're cleared for immediate takeoff, folks. Check your belts. We fly runway heading south to an altitude of two-thousand feet, then turn east and climb on course to our cruising altitude of thirty-three thousand. It's a clear morning. Dr. Maxwell, you'll have a fine view of Gary and the south shore of Lake Michigan from your side."

Through the cockpit door they could see Chuck and the copilot checking switches and instruments. The plane turned onto the runway, and the whisper of the jet engines rose to a muffled scream. The Learjet trembled for a moment, held by its tether, gathering strength, then leaped ahead, pushing them back in their seats. In seconds the nose pitched up, the Learjet pulled off the runway in a steep climb, the gear motors whined, and the wheels thumped into the belly. The noise of the jet engines fell behind.

"How 'bout that?" Letitia said, grinning.

They climbed on the runway heading then heeled into a steep left turn and, when the nose was on the morning sun, rolled level and settled into a shallow climb. From his seat on the starboard side Bob Maxwell saw the lakeshore, the steel mills of Gary, and the Ogden sand dunes. Thin haze partially obscured the shore, and gray smoke trailed west from the steel mills over the southern reaches of Chicago.

"We're cleared to our cruising altitude," Chuck announced. "The air this morning is stable. We should have a smooth ride. Feel free to move about, but please keep the belts fastened when you're seated. Center reports good tailwinds—about seventy knots. That should put us into National in about sixty-five minutes."

"We're not quite as fast as airliners," Letitia said, "but we save a lot of time using Meigs instead of O'Hare. Door-to-door we beat the airliners by an hour, not to mention the convenience of setting your own schedule. We make dozens of trips to Washington every month. A plane like this could be a real advantage."

"The takeoff was a blast," Bob Maxwell said.

"It's unusual to have a delay operating out of Meigs," Letitia replied.

"I mean, it was like a roller coaster."

"Yes," Letitia agreed. "More fun."

"It's a quiet little airplane."

"Very quiet. Easy to converse. This model 31 is a big improvement over earlier models. For one thing, it's safer. The first Learjets had a bad reputation. This one cruises at 445 knots and, believe it or not, can go to fifty-one thousand feet. That can take you over a lot of bad weather. The damn Concorde only goes to sixty-five thousand."

"Your enthusiasm is contagious."

"I hope so," Letitia said.

Peggy approached them. "Bloody Marys this morning, folks?"

"Perfect," Letitia replied.

"Coffee and a Danish?"

"Of course."

"Coming up." She turned away.

Letitia leaned closer to Bob Maxwell and lowered her voice. "She's a pretty girl. They hire 'em that way."

Bob Maxwell nodded agreement and smiled.

"You did very well with your first meeting, Mr. Chairman," Letitia said.

"Thank you."

"Chairing the board isn't easy. You handled it smoothly."

Peggy returned with the Bloody Marys, coffee, sweet rolls, and a bottle of Tabasco. "Enjoy," she said as she arranged the things on their lap tables.

As Chuck had predicted, the air was smooth and within minutes they reached cruising altitude. The whistle of the slipstream grew louder as he trimmed the Learjet on its step and made top speed.

Bob Maxwell shook Tabasco into his Bloody Mary, stirred it with a celery stalk, and tasted the result. "That hits the spot," he said, and passed the Tabasco to Letitia. "I thought the meeting, in general, went well. Some of the troops are restive about the budget."

"Always a few complainers," Letitia said.

"We mustn't take them too lightly."

"This is a good Bloody Mary."

"Cleve Randall called last night. He was not satisfied with the information you presented to the finance committee."

"I thought we produced a reasonable package of schedules, given the short notice."

"I know, but he wants specific answers to specific questions. He thinks you're stiffing him."

"Not true," Letitia retorted.

"He's not going to back off. And, he has support."

"What kind of support?"

"Rodansky for sure. Probably others."

"What about Hawkins?"

"A wild card," Bob Maxwell replied. "Rodansky can probably influence him."

"Well, perhaps we can sweeten Hawkins up with a nice, first-class trip to Madrid."

"I wouldn't count on it. He strikes me as being independent."

"We'll see."

"They're going to push for an independent audit," Bob Maxwell said. "They may swing the votes."

"Fuck 'em," Letitia snapped.

Her characteristic reply annoyed Bob Maxwell. "I don't want that audit anymore than you," he said.

"Then fuck 'em."

"Dammit, Letitia, it's not that simple." He wished she were not so crude.

"They don't have the votes to fire me."

"They don't want to fire you. They want to back you down."

"What are you saying?"

"If Randall brings the audit matter to a vote and wins, you'll be faced with a direct order to comply. I want to defuse Randall."

"What do you suggest?"

"Get the Martin Ross crowd to put on a dog-and-pony show. Preempt the complainers. Dazzle 'em. You know what I mean."

"When?"

"At the next board meeting. Randall's only argument is cover-up. Neutralize that and he's done. I've talked to our people. They'll back you, but they don't want a showdown."

Letitia sipped her Bloody Mary and seemed to calm down. "All right. I'll set it up."

Peggy emerged from the minikitchen with fresh coffee. "Another Bloody Mary?" she asked.

"Absolutely," Letitia replied, and Bob Maxwell agreed, vainly hoping the coffee would neutralize the vodka by the time they arrived in Washington.

"Is there anything more I should know about the Breslow matter?" Bob Maxwell then asked.

"I've covered it all," Letitia replied.

"Why is it taking so long? They should have wrapped it up last summer."

"I don't know. Presumably they're still looking for an under-world connection."

"You're sure they found nothing in our computer files?"

"If they did, they haven't told me."

"Have they explained the LEDGER thing?"

"Not yet. It was probably a doodle."

"I don't know."

Letitia shook her head. "Len Breslow was incapable of under-world dealings."

"Still, it smells bad. They must be on to something."

"So far, all I've heard is speculation," Letitia said. "How do you like the ride?"

"Great," Bob Maxwell replied. "This is quite a toy."

"I want to buy one."

Bob Maxwell stared at her. "You're kidding."

"I'm not kidding. It would be a good investment."

"My God. What does one of these damn things cost?"

"About four million, but don't think of it in terms of cost."

"How should I think of it?"

"As a profit center. We can justify the cost, perhaps make a little money."

Bob Maxwell laughed. "You've got my attention."

Letitia continued. "Figure an average passenger load of 3.5. That's conservative. It costs two thousand dollars an hour to operate."

"How much to fly Chicago to Washington?"

"Four grand, including the Bloody Marys."

"You can buy a lot of airline tickets for that."

"True, but when you factor in the value of convenience, execu-tive time saved through scheduling, and conducting business on the plane enroute, it pays off."

Bob Maxwell thought for a moment. "At that rate you and I are worth two grand an hour."

"We're a bargain," Letitia replied.

"C'mon, Letitia."

She was undaunted. "It would give us flexibility. We could haul board members around. A flying board room. That would be a nice perk. We could pick up our congressional friends and special guests. As chairman, you would have this little baby at your full disposal. The prestige factor would be enormous."

"Look," Bob Maxwell said, "I'm sure the accountants can figure out a way to justify an airplane. But it would be goddamn ostentatious for the American Medical Association to own a business jet. We have doctors out there smothering under the cost of malpractice and inflation. They're not likely to cheer when the AMA jet flies over."

"The AMA is the most prestigious organization of its kind in the world," Letitia replied. "Some may think it ostentatious to own a business jet, but if used efficiently and wisely, it would be an appropriate symbol of power. It would open doors and opportunities heretofore beyond our reach."

"You're getting a bit carried away."

"I know I'm coming on strong, but I believe you'll agree after you think about it."

"How would you proceed?"

"I could simply make an administrative decision."

"That would be unwise," Bob Maxwell said.

"Agreed," Letitia said. "We want board approval. I have a plan to finesse that. We set up a lease for the hours we expect to fly. Then we build operating experience and do a cost analysis. We might decide we need a bigger plane, like a Falcon or a Gulfstream, or more hours. Of course all board members would have nice trips and ample opportunity to buy into the idea. When the time is ripe, six months or a year, we talk about purchase. If it doesn't pan out, we quietly forget it."

"The lease would be a trial."

"Exactly."

"That might work."

"Will you back me?"

Bob Maxwell hesitated. "I want to get past the Cleve Randall thing first."

"Fair enough," Letitia said. "Now, I have another proposition. This one is easy."

"And what might that be?"

"I want you to go around the world."

"Trying to get rid of me?" Bob Maxwell grinned.

"This is a legitimate business trip. We conduct international affairs that require the personal attention of the chairman of the board. Here's the itinerary: You travel west. First stop, Sydney, Australia. You'll like Sydney. It has a magnificent harbor and good restaurants. I want you to spend an afternoon with Larry Oswald. Larry is CEO of the Australian Medical. He's a good friend. We need his vote in the World Medical.

"Then Tokyo. Meet Kajimoto. Visit the publishing house that prints our journal in Japanese. Perhaps a side trip to Fuji View, or Kyoto on the bullet train.

"Singapore. Lay over a couple of days to rest and check out the convention possibilities. A clean, pretty city, great hotels, great food, great shopping.

"New Delhi. The next International Congress of the World Medical will be in New Delhi. That's unfortunate, but we're stuck with it. Check out the hotels. Watch out for the cobras."

"Jeez!" Bob Maxwell murmured.

"Paris. Our French publisher needs a hands-on visit. They're butchering JAMA. Your visit will impress them.

"On the way to Paris, you might spend a couple of days at Nice, check out the girls on the beaches. The casino in Monte Carlo is worth an evening.

"After Paris, London. Talk to our friends at the British Medical. Get Sir Tony to see things our way. That son of a bitch argues just to hear himself talk.

"Then London to New York on the Concorde. That's a treat. The damn thing is three times faster than this little bird. It gives you a real kick in the ass when you take off."

"You've flown the Concorde?"

"Of course," Letitia replied. "It saves time. But that's not why you fly the Concorde. You fly the Concorde because it's the *Concorde*."

"That's quite an itinerary," Bob Maxwell said.

"Four weeks," Letitia said. "You'll take Marietta, of course. I'll send someone along to smooth the way."

"It sounds like a public relations tour."

"A visit from the chairman of the board and his wife carries a lot of weight."

"When do we go?"

"In the spring. We should settle the dates this month."

"It'll be exciting," Bob Maxwell said. "I'll talk to Marietta as soon as we return."

Letitia settled back in the leather seat and closed her eyes, satisfied. Soon the sound and vibration of the turbofans softened, and they could feel the little jet slow and the nose drop. "We'll be landing in fifteen minutes," Chuck announced. "Fasten your seat belts and stow the trays. The weather's good. Should be no delays."

"Incidentally," Letitia said in a subdued voice, "Duke Rodansky has himself a little poon tang stashed in Chicago."

"What the hell are you talking about?"

"A black chick," Letitia replied. "She lives in an apartment on the North Side."

"How do you know that?"

"It's been going around."

"Who is she?"

"Name's Shirley Raymond. She's a paralegal."

"Are you sure?"

"Absolutely."

"Jesus Christ!"

"It might be worth knowing someday."

"Yes, it might."

"I'll keep my eyes open."

"Keep me informed. This could be dynamite."

"And another thing," Letitia said. "I'm furious about Hawkins and Kate seeing Chamberlain."

"Chamberlain invited them, didn't he?"

"Damn right he did."

"They can't decline."

"I want to know what the hell is going on. Chamberlain called Hawkins after that goddamn Garden speech. I've never been able to find out exactly what he said."

"Relax. He's playing games."

"Why would he waste time on us?"

"His way of putting us down. Remember, you burned him during the campaign."

"I don't like it."

"You can't stop Hawkins, and sure as hell you can't fire Kate."

"Hawkins is a troublemaker," Letitia said. "In his first meeting he questions the contingency fund and the tobacco policy, then he wangles a private audience with the President of the United States."

"Don't let your marbles get out of hand."

"I'll get the son of a bitch," Letitia said.

[18]

A PORTLY GENTLEMAN with fat jowls and curly hair greeted Joe and Kate when they stepped off the elevator in the Century Plaza Hotel in Los Angeles. "Good afternoon, folks. My name is Carter," he announced with a jovial smile. "I'll be taking you to see the President."

Near the elevator a pair of fit-looking young men in dark business suits stood guard. Each displayed a gold stickpin in the lapel of his jacket identifying the elite Secret Service, sworn to die if necessary to save the life of the President of the United States. Each remained inscrutable.

"The President is looking forward to your visit," Carter said.

"We're delighted to be here," Joe said.

"Please follow me," Carter said.

"Only two guards?" Joe inquired as they proceeded down the corridor.

"The place is full of them," Carter replied, still smiling. "They know how to be inconspicuous."

Carter led them through a double door to the foyer of a pent-house, then to a formal dining room furnished with George II in dark mahogany and a massive chandelier laden with diamond-like prisms. The sun beaming through a great window facing the Pacific caught the prisms and reflected assorted rainbows on the wall.

"Wait here," Carter said, and disappeared. In ten minutes he returned followed by the familiar, lanky figure of President David Chamberlain. Both Joe and Kate momentarily suffered an embarrassing compulsion to stare when the President entered. Until then they had seen him only on television and in photographs.

"Mr. President," said Carter, "this is Dr. Hawkins and Miss Murphy."

David Chamberlain wore dark slacks, a white polo shirt, and a camel cashmere jacket. His thick hair was chestnut brown streaked with gray, and his face was pleasingly tan and angular. Beneath heavy brows, the eyes were dark and stern and perhaps a little tired.

He smiled and the eyes softened reassuringly, then he shook their hands firmly. "Joe and Kate. Thank you for coming." A man of Joe's vintage holding a leather portfolio accompanied him. "This is Scott Ragan, my assistant."

They sat around the dinner table, and Carter brought a tray of iced tea, lemon slices, and packets of sugar, then disappeared.

"Well," David Chamberlain said. "I've been looking forward to this meeting." His voice filled the room.

"So have we, Mr. President," Joe said.

"I apologize for the mystery. It was impractical to explain in advance what I wanted to talk about."

"Yes, sir," Joe said.

"First, let me express my deepest sympathy for the loss of Mrs. Hawkins."

"Thank you Mr. President. I was grateful for your letter."

"Some years ago my son died in an unexpected manner. I understand that kind of grief."

"I'm sorry to hear that, Mr. President," Joe said. "I didn't know about your son."

"I was a freshman senator then." David Chamberlain's face

darkened and for a moment he appeared on the verge of explaining, then he squeezed a lemon slice into his iced tea and turned to Kate and the famous smile reappeared. "Young lady, I've been waiting for months to find out how you came up with the idea to stage this man's speech in an empty stadium?"

Kate instantly flushed. "It was a lucky thought, Mr. President. You are a formidable adversary. We needed something spectacular."

"It was a damn fine idea."

"Thank you, Mr. President. Of course, it was Dr. Hawkins' speech."

"Nicely said. By the way, I know about the 'book' you have on me. I also know you supplied my people with a few, shall we say, questionable tidbits of your own, like in sandbagging?"

"Mr. President, I'm embarrassed," Kate said.

David Chamberlain laughed. "Don't be. Everyone in Washington plays those games."

"You're very gracious, sir," Kate said.

"I hope you don't still regard me as a vindictive son of a bitch," he chided.

"No, sir," they replied simultaneously.

David Chamberlain appeared pleased. "Joe, your military training is evident."

"Thank you, sir."

"Well, you are now president-elect of the American Medical Association."

"That's correct, sir."

"A high honor, indeed. When is the inauguration?"

"Next June, sir."

"What then?"

"The term is one year. Other than continuing my surgical practice, I have no special plans after that."

"Ah, maybe you would like to become my surgeon general."

"I don't know, Mr. President," Joe said uneasily. "I love my practice."

"Surgeon general sounds great to me, Mr. President," Kate said, flashing a presumptuous grin.

The President laughed. "Incidentally, will your presidential duties include the World Medical Association?"

"Yes, sir. I plan to attend the meeting in Madrid next spring."

"Very good. The architect of the World Medical is an old friend of mine, a Swiss doctor named Pierre Globa. I would consider it a special favor if you would convey my warmest personal regards to Pierre and to his beautiful wife, Françoise. Tell them I miss the good times. They'll understand. Perhaps Pierre will regale you with some of our adventures."

"I'll be honored to convey your message, Mr. President."

"Excellent. Excellent." David Chamberlain paused to sip his iced tea. "Tell me, my young friends, why do you think I've had it in for the AMA?"

"I understand you were angered by personal remarks Letitia Jordan made during your campaign," Joe replied.

"Letitia Jordan did irritate me. The truth is, I believed the entire medical profession was irresponsible. I was wrong. You're a real doctor, Joe, the kind I'd like to have take care of me or my family, and your superb rebuttal made me appreciate the stupidity of bashing dedicated rank-and-file physicians of the country when the real villain is the top dog. So I decided to change tactics. In the meantime, certain matters have come to my attention." He again sipped the iced tea. "What I am about to say must remain confidential."

"Of course, Mr. President."

"Very well. We have a tobacco cartel operating in the United States. The cartel controls a third of the world tobacco market. It includes American tobacco companies, English tobacco companies, and certain Japanese investors. And, it's connected with the AMA."

"Our Washington office cooperates with congressmen from the tobacco states, Mr. President," Kate responded. "We practice normal coalition politics. Is that what you mean?"

"The connection I'm talking about goes much deeper than 'normal coalition politics,'" David Chamberlain said. "Letitia Jordan is the connection. The tobacco cartel pays her to suppress antismoking efforts by the AMA."

Joe glanced at Kate, wondering if she remembered what Kajimoto had said.

David Chamberlain continued. "The AMA has done precious little to inform the public about the hazards of smoking. I realize you've issued the standard scientific reports, but that's tokenism. Never has the AMA testified on smoking before a congressional committee, led an antismoking crusade, or, God forbid, taken a hard stand against the tobacco subsidies. As far as the public is concerned, the AMA is silent on tobacco.

"I don't fault the AMA or the doctors out there in the trenches doing their job. I fault Letitia Jordan. Failure to confront the subsidy issue cannot be dismissed simply as a dereliction. It was self-serving."

Kate defended her boss. "Dr. Jordan believes the AMA should confine its statements to medical facts and leave the tobacco subsidy to Congress."

"That's hardly credible in view of your other political activities," David Chamberlain growled.

"She feels it serves our greater interest not to offend the tobacco delegation," Kate said.

"You mean Senator Ridge."

Kate persisted. "Senator Ridge is very powerful. If the AMA were to attack his subsidies, he would fight us on every front."

"Jonathan Ridge is a contemptible bastard," David Chamberlain said.

"Unfortunately, Mr. President, we have no choice but to deal with him," Kate said.

"That's a cop-out. Assuredly, it gives the appearance of politics as usual. Scratch my back, and I'll scratch yours." David Chamberlain rested his arms on the table. "Does 'politics as usual' strike you as reason enough for the American Medical Association, the most important medical organization in the world, to waffle on an issue as important as smoking, the leading killer of all time?"

"No, sir," Joe replied.

"Why, for example, have you not informed the public about the addictive properties of nicotine?"

"We have," Joe said. "Doctors have known for decades that

nicotine is addictive, and that the cigarette industry depends upon nicotine addiction for survival. Perhaps we haven't said enough."

"Exactly," David Chamberlain said. "The fact is, Letitia Jordan sold out the AMA. Under the guise of 'politics as usual,' she makes certain things not happen. The woman is central to a massive conspiracy organized by the tobacco cartel to deliberately mislead the public about the hazards of smoking."

He turned to Scott Ragan. "Let's have that file." Scott Ragan slid some papers out of his portfolio. "This is a memo," David Chamberlain said, "recently introduced as evidence in a federal district court by a man suing three cigarette companies for negligence in the death of his wife who died of lung cancer from smoking. It's 'tobacco's smoking gun,' pardon the irony."

He handed copies to Joe and Kate.

"The memo was written by a vice-president of the Tobacco Institute." David Chamberlain then read aloud: "'For nearly twenty years, this industry has employed a single strategy to defend itself on three major fronts: litigation, politics, and public opinion.

"'While the strategy was brilliantly conceived and executed over the years, helping us win important battles, it has always been a holding strategy, consisting of creating doubt about the health charge without actually denying it.

"'On the litigation front, for which the strategy was designed, it has been successful.

"'On the political front, the strategy helped make possible an orderly retreat.

"'But we must increase the effort. Our plans should include influencing important scientific organizations to downplay their antismoking policies. In this regard, the support of tobacco state congressmen can be enlisted.'"

David Chamberlain waited for his guests to peruse the memo, then added, "A single strategy . . . creating doubt about the health charge . . . making sweetheart deals with scientific organizations . . . enlisting the support of tobacco state congressmen. It smacks of a full-blown conspiracy.

"We also know that over the last three years a large amount of money—three million dollars, in fact—has been deposited to a single bank account in the Cayman Islands registered jointly to Letitia Jordan and her husband, Luther Agostelli. The tobacco people pay the money to a law firm in Chicago that arranges the deposits."

"My God! What are they buying?" Joe asked.

"Time," the President replied. "Time for the cartel to pull its chestnuts out of the fire. Consider the stakes. Half a million Americans have lung cancer. So far, not a single lawsuit against tobacco companies on the cancer connection has succeeded. But,"—he pointed a finger at Joe—"if a court should hold a cigarette company liable for a single case, it could open the floodgates and bankrupt the industry. We're talking billions."

David Chamberlain read from the memorandum. "'On the litigation front, for which it was designed, the strategy has been successful.'

"They deliberately created," he read, "'doubt about the health charge without actually denying it,' and by God, it's worked. I know something about litigation. As long as the AMA, the premier medical organization in the world and a major player in the health affairs of our country, declines to take an unqualified legal stand against smoking, it will be difficult to overcome that doubt in a court of law."

"Is the AMA that influential?" Joe asked.

"The AMA is damn influential. Of course the conspiracy represents advertising interests, state governments, and a whole range of those who profit one way or another from the sale of tobacco. But make no mistake, the AMA, that is, Letitia Jordan, is key to the cartel's litigation strategy.

"Eventually the scientific facts will prevail. But remember, it's a holding strategy. They only need a few more years. Most of the poor souls alive today with lung cancer will then be dead or beyond the statute of limitations. That piece of liability will simply go away. In the meantime, warning labels have come along. If you smoke and get cancer, the tobacco companies say, 'Too damn bad. You can't sue us. You've had fair warning.' The damn warning labels let the bastards off the hook. It's one helluva paradox. Of course the warning labels will eventually have their own day in court."

David Chamberlain sipped his iced tea and leaned back and smiled. "There's something remarkable about iced tea when one gets exercised." He inspected the condensate on the cold glass. "Clearly the antismoking campaign is taking its toll. Cigarette sales have dropped. But the time they're buying is letting them reorganize. Tobacco is diversifying and creating foreign markets to offset domestic losses. I understand now they're targeting Chinese women, very few of whom smoke."

Scott Ragan then spoke. He had an odd, crackling voice. "Notwithstanding, the tobacco industry believes it's imperative to contain the liability problem as long as possible."

Joe again looked at Kate, then said, "Mr. President, the president of the Japan Medical Association has already told me some of these things."

"Old Doc Kajimoto?"

"Yes, sir," Joe replied.

"That's a surprise. So much for confidentiality."

"You know Kajimoto, Mr. President?" Joe inquired.

"I met him in Switzerland fifteen years ago when Pierre Globa and I were with the CIA. We called him Doc Kajimoto."

"You seem to know everyone, Mr. President."

"That happens when you hang around long enough. What exactly did Kajimoto have to say?"

"I've talked to him only on the phone," Joe replied. "He called after the Garden speech. He was an Imperial Japanese Marine in the war and a survivor of Tarawa, where my father died. He claims my father spared his life. He made the connection when he heard my speech. He was friendly and seemed to know a lot about the AMA. He called again, last June, when I was elected president. At that time he told me Letitia Jordan was in the service of the tobacco cartel, just as you said. He mentioned the lawsuits and the subsidy and the marketing in the Orient. He said the manufacturers are spiking cigarettes with nicotine to make them more addictive, and that a Japanese crime syndicate known as the Tora Society controls the cartel. He said the Toras started as good guys after the war, then turned bad. Kajimoto's father was a founder of the Tora Society. Kajimoto himself is a Tora by birthright, but disavows their criminal activities. He also said the Toras wouldn't like it if I interfered with Letitia Jordan."

"The Tora Society is for real," David Chamberlain said. "We know about them. What's Kajimoto's stake in all of this?"

"He wanted to warn me. Said he owes me a 'debt of honor' on account of my father. Apparently it's an old samurai custom."

"That's quite a story. Do you believe him?"

"He sounded believable."

"It might be worth checking out," David Chamberlain said. "Scott, see what you can find out."

"He even invited me to visit Tokyo," Joe said.

"By all means, go. I hear he's a great host."

"Perhaps next spring, after the meeting in Madrid."

"Kajimoto is one of Pierre Globa's more interesting sidekicks. He's an impressive guy, richer than God, and knows everyone and everything. Years ago he came to Switzerland to help us resolve a problem. Then he gave Pierre a hand with the World Medical." David Chamberlain chuckled. "Those two old pelicans are vintage rascals."

"Dr. Kajimoto and Dr. Globa have always been good friends of the AMA," Kate said.

"This is getting interesting," David Chamberlain said. "And Scott has more. Fill us in, will you Scott."

Scott Ragan extracted a file from the portfolio. "One of your top executives, Leonard Breslow, was murdered last February. Breslow was the chief financial officer of the AMA. On the evening of February 20, he was found dead at the foot of a staircase in his condo building on Lake Shore Drive in Chicago. Initially it was thought to be a case of accidental death, but upon further investigation the police concluded he was killed by an assailant who snapped his neck barehanded and threw the body down the stairs to make it look like an accident. Interestingly, the tip-off was a four-centimeter strand of navy blue wool snagged in one of the victim's fingernails. The police believe it came from a sweater worn by the assailant and got caught in the fingernail during the struggle. Otherwise, the killing was a thoroughly professional job."

"Did you know about this?" David Chamberlain asked.

"We've heard speculation about foul play," Joe replied. "Nothing more."

Scott Ragan continued. "In the course of the investigation, one of Breslow's letterheads with the word 'LEDGER' handprinted on it was found in his personal lock box. This proved to be the entrée to a basic code known as the Vigenere Table, which in turn disclosed a six-digit number that accessed a secret file in the AMA computer—the 'LEDGER FILE.' The file contained information about Letitia Jordan that Breslow had assembled for the purpose of blackmailing her.

"Breslow had access to all salaries, bonuses, and expense accounts in the AMA computers. He prepared joint tax returns for Dr. Jordan and her husband. Incidentally, the three million dollars of tobacco money was not reported as income. We have of course, as the President has indicated, verified that this money is in a Cayman Island bank. We have no indication that Breslow was aware of its existence.

"The file also contained details of Dr. Jordan's salary, benefits, deferred compensation, expense accounts, stipends, and a memorandum from Breslow."

"What stipends?" Joe asked.

"The AMA owns a holding company and seven subsidiary corporations. Dr. Jordan receives annual stipends from each totaling some three hundred thousand dollars."

"I don't recall hearing about stipends," Joe said.

"These particular stipends are not normally called out in routine reports to the board of trustees."

"The board is not informed?"

"They're informed," Scott Ragan said. "But some of the information is hard to find."

"Who authorized the stipends?"

"Dr. Jordan is the chief executive officer," Scott Ragan replied. "She has the legal authority to authorize the stipends and did so."

"Do you have Letitia Jordan's total compensation?"

Scott Ragan perused his notes. "Salary and benefits come to four hundred thousand dollars, her deferred compensation plan—the golden parachute—is three hundred thousand, the penthouse in the Crystal is two hundred thousand, and the expense account and limousine and other perks average two hundred thousand. Annual compensation from the AMA, including the stipends, totals about one million four. The tobacco payments have averaged a million dollars a year on top of that. Of course, these figures are rounded off."

"Wow," Joe said in a low voice. "I assume the information is accurate."

"Much of it came to light in our investigation of the tobacco conspiracy," Scott Ragan replied. "It's been verified."

"The President of the United States has certain intelligence capabilities at his personal disposal," David Chamberlain said, smiling.

Scott Ragan then said, "Leonard Breslow had AIDS."

"My God," Joe whispered.

"They found HIV at the autopsy. His private physician told the police that Breslow had known about the HIV for six months and was making plans to die."

"How did he get it?" Joe asked.

"He was gay," Scott Ragan replied. "They ruled out accidental inoculation. According to his physician Breslow had been having sporadic homosexual contacts for years. Incidentally, Mrs. Breslow knows nothing about this. Breslow assured his physician he had not had recent sexual relations with Mrs. Breslow and instructed him not to inform her."

"I've heard rumors he was gay," Kate said.

"Poor devil," Joe said.

"Breslow planned the blackmail to obtain money for his family before dying," Scott Ragan said. "He made his initial approach to Dr. Jordan about four weeks before the killing. He told her he was having personal problems and asked for two hundred thousand dollars. She exploded and actually threatened to kill him. This frightened Breslow, and he decided to set up LEDGER for insurance. He left the codeword in his personal lockbox, where it would be found and deciphered in case something happened to him. He planned to confront Dr. Jordan again, tell her about LEDGER, and demand the money. Unfortunately that didn't happen. The last entry to LEDGER was made at six-fifteen, the evening of February 20, an hour before Breslow was killed. He had an appointment to see Dr. Jordan the next morning."

"She's the only one who had motive," David Chamberlain said.

"The police believe Dr. Jordan hired a hit-man to do the job," Scott Ragan said. "All they have is motive, but the investigation is continuing."

"Who knows this?" Joe asked.

"Only the four of us and the authorities," Scott Ragan said. "Dr. Jordan is aware an investigation is underway. But she has not been told about LEDGER or its contents, and she has not been informed that she is a suspect."

Joe Hawkins slumped in his chair and exchanged looks with Kate. "Mr. President, I would have great difficulty believing this if I were not hearing it from the President of the United States."

"One more thing," Scott Ragan said. "This is the last entry on the Breslow memorandum." He handed a slip of paper to Joe. "Can you enlighten us?"

Joe read from the paper. "'Y–1—BRAZIL—JENO—CHECK IT OUT.'" He handed the paper to Kate, then replied, "Maybe something about a chromosome."

"It means nothing to me," Kate said.

"Let's wrap this up," David Chamberlain said. "Letitia Jordan conspired with the tobacco cartel to dupe the public, for which she was paid a cool three million dollars. She also draws a lavish salary and perks from the AMA. Breslow was her financial confidant and a closet gay. He got unlucky, contracted AIDS, and knowing about Letitia's wealth, appealed to her for money. She threatened to kill Breslow. Breslow then set up a secret computer file with incriminating information about her. He planned to approach her again, tell her about the file, and renew his appeal for money, but he was killed before he could get to her. Letitia Jordan had motive, ergo, the police believe she hired someone to kill Breslow. And now we have the Kajimoto factor. The old boy apparently knows all about the cartel, the Tora Society, and the meanderings of Letitia Jordan, and God knows what else."

David Chamberlain settled back in his chair. "Joe, I invited you here today because I need your help. The breach between government and medicine is unacceptable. I intend to fix it. The Letitia Jordan investigation is proceeding. She's going down, big time, and when she does we'll have an unparalleled opportunity to forge an alliance between my administration and the AMA. You're the one, my friend. The responsibility for righting the house of medicine will fall squarely on you.

"I'm prepared to make substantial commitments. I intend to ask Congress to create a separate department of health with cabinet rank. In the meantime, I want you to serve as my personal advisor on health matters."

"What about your health policy, sir?" Joe asked.

"Consider it on the shelf, provided you agree to develop an alternative. No one in this country should go without health care. You know that. I know that. We should be able to do something about it."

"That's a compelling challenge, Mr. President."

"Look, Joe, I want to close ranks. The pay is lousy. The aggravation is worse. Will you help me?"

Joe smiled. "When you put it like that, Mr. President, it's impossible to refuse."

"The cartel is a criminal matter for the justice department to deal with. I assure you, they're on top of it. Senator Ridge and others will be indicted. RICO is a great law.

"However, I don't know what to make of Kajimoto. His calling you was a total surprise to me. Is he legitimate, or is something else going on? For what it's worth, I'm inclined to trust the old bastard."

"So am I," Joe said.

David Chamberlain turned to Kate and flashed the famous smile. "Young lady, you're a feisty one. I want you on board too. Will you give us a hand."

"Yes, sir," Kate said, blushing.

"Of course, all of this must remain confidential."

"Yes, sir," Joe said.

"Excellent," David Chamberlain said. "Excellent. We have a deal. Now, it's important for me to know what's happening in the AMA. I want you to advise Scott of anything you consider relevant to our discussion. I'm not asking you to snitch. Just keep your eyes open and give me the benefit of your counsel. Agreed?"

"Agreed, Mr. President," Joe replied.

"Good. In the meantime, remember, this is a high-stakes game. There's enough in that damn file to blow the conspiracy out of the water. Everything these people have is on the line—personal fortunes, power, political careers, the cartel itself. They're desperate. Kajimoto offered good advice. Proceed with caution."

"I understand, Mr. President," Joe said.

"Letitia Jordan is a charlatan, but she's only a pawn. Jonathan Ridge is the bastard I want. I guarantee you, I'm going to nail him."

The door opened and Carter waddled into the room, signaling it was time for the President to move on.

"I see my man Carter is here to whisk me off," David Chamberlain said, again smiling. They stood and shook hands. "Thanks for coming. I've found two new friends. That doesn't happen every day. Take care." Then he departed and the room seemed empty without him.

"He likes you," Scott Ragan said.

"I'm glad," Kate said.

"No love for Senator Ridge," Joe said.

"That's an understatement," Scott Ragan said.

"What happens now?" Joe asked.

"The police will continue the murder investigation. I'll be monitoring the process, and I'll keep you informed. It'll take time. You know what the President expects. Otherwise, it's business as usual.

"I'd also like to add my admonition about Letitia Jordan. She arranged the Breslow killing, she can arrange another."

"What do we say about this meeting?" Joe asked.

"Simply that you and the President discussed a broad range of health issues with emphasis on providing care to the underserved. Elaborate as you see fit."

Scott Ragan handed them his card. "You can always reach me at this number. Don't hesitate to call. You're family now. One more thing: when the President instructed you to hold this matter in strict confidence, he ordained you with a security clearance. If you breech the confidence, you will be subject to prosecution." Scott Ragan smiled dryly. "Thought you might want to know the rules."

❦

"I don't get it," Joe said when they stepped out of the elevator. "The President of the United States must have better things to do than take on Letitia Jordan."

"I could use a drink," Kate said.

"I wonder what he's really after," Joe said. They walked across the lobby of the Century Plaza.

[19]

THE NEXT AFTERNOON Sergeant Melrose came to Joe's office. "It was definitely a collision, Doc. We have the other vehicle, a Chevy half-ton pickup. A quail hunter found it twenty miles south of Phoenix on the Gila Indian Reservation."

He handed Joe a packet of photographs and settled into a chair. "The photograph on top is the one I showed you before with collision marks on the left front fender of the Jaguar. The other photographs show matching collision marks on the right front fender of the pickup. The laboratory confirmed the cross-match on the paint."

Joe examined the photographs as the sergeant spoke.

"It appears the driver of the pickup overtook Mrs. Hawkins and pulled alongside, like he was attempting to pass, then side-swiped her. She lost control and ran off the road, and he took off.

Ultimately, he proceeded south on I–10, took the road to Maricopa across the Gila Indian Reservation, then split for the desert. He concealed the pickup in a thicket of mesquite way the hell off the Maricopa road. We were lucky to find it. The only people who go there are hunters."

"I know the area," Joe said. "I've hunted quail on the reservation many times."

"A used car dealership in Phoenix sold the pickup three days prior to the incident. The buyer was a white male about thirty years old, clean shaven, dark hair, wearing a white shirt and jeans. He paid with cash—folding money—and used a phony driver's license. He was covering his tracks, so we don't have an ID. We're sure, though, he had at least one accomplice with another vehicle. Someone had to haul him out of the desert when he stashed the pickup. Otherwise it was a helluva walk."

The sergeant leaned back in his chair. "It's likely these guys were up to something completely unrelated to Mrs. Hawkins, like a heist of some sort. Maybe they were casing the neighborhood, or joyriding, or maybe they were high. If that was the case, the collision was simply an unfortunate accident, and they panicked and ran."

"Bastards!"

"However, we have some inconsistencies. The pickup has a brown paint job that made good desert camouflauge. And that mesquite thicket in the middle of nowhere was a little too perfect. It may be pure coincidence, but the way they got rid of the pickup more resembles a carefully planned getaway than an act of panic."

"What are you getting at?"

"It's possible they were after Mrs. Hawkins."

"I don't understand."

"Hired guns, out to terrorize, not kill, but it got out of hand. Had they intended to kill her, they would have used more certain means."

Joe was incredulous. "I can't believe this."

"It's pure conjecture. If they were hired guns, they were pretty amateurish."

Joe could only shake his head in disbelief.

"Did Mrs. Hawkins have any serious enemies?"

"Of course not."

"Perhaps someone was trying to get to you through her. Does that ring any bells?"

"No," Joe replied.

"A political or business enemy? A disgruntled patient, a crazy?"

"Not really, not that I know of."

"'Not really?'" the sergeant queried.

"I suppose everyone has enemies. It doesn't mean they're violent."

"Yes, I suppose so. Have you or Mrs. Hawkins received any threatening calls or messages?"

"No," Joe said, deciding not to mention his conversations with Kajimoto and the President.

The sergeant persisted. "Are you sure?"

"I'm sure," Joe replied, impatiently. "Jesus Christ! Does this sort of thing happen in Phoenix?"

"I'm afraid it does, Doc. No longer is Phoenix a lonesome little cow town."

"I guess you're right," Joe said. "I'm sorry. I know you're doing your job."

"At this point we're treating Mrs. Hawkins' death as coincident to the commission of a crime by parties unknown. Legally, that's murder. We've put out a nationwide alert."

"Poor Grace," Joe said.

"Doc, I want you to know, the entire department is out to nail the sons of bitches who did this."

"Can you find them?"

"We have a good shot." Then Sergeant Melrose gathered the photographs and rose to leave. "That's all I have for now."

"Thank you for everything, sergeant."

They shook hands. "In the meantime, if anything comes to mind, anything at all, call me." The sergeant then smiled. "That includes fixing tickets. If you need a ticket fixed, I'm your man, Doc."

Joe returned the smile. "I'll remember that."

197

❦

Joe immediately called Scott Ragan. "You were right not to tell him about Kajimoto or the President," Scott said. "We're not ready to break security, and you haven't significantly compromised the sergeant's investigation."

"The sergeant is a nice guy. I'd like to level with him."

"Let it run its course. When the time comes, I'll personally explain matters. He'll understand. In the meantime, I'll see what I can turn up at this end."

"Fair enough," Joe said.

❦

Then Joe called Kate. She was in her apartment nursing a glass of Chardonnay. "Good trip home?" he inquired.

"Smooth, all the way from LAX. Except I was a nervous wreck over what the President said. I've been hoping you would call."

"Along those lines, something else has come up. The officer investigating Grace's accident just paid me a visit. Remember, they thought another vehicle may have run her off the road? They found the vehicle, a Chevy pickup, abandoned in the desert. It was hit-and-run, possibly deliberate—someone trying to get at me through Grace." Joe then recounted his conversation with Sergeant Melrose.

"Oh, Joe," Kate said, sorrowfully, then asked, "Did you tell him about Kajimoto and the tobacco cartel and the Tora Society, and what the President said?"

"No. But I called Scott Ragan. He said I was right to keep quiet. He'll square it with the sergeant."

"Then you're covered."

"The sergeant made it clear he was only speculating. I have to believe the whole thing was a fluke. God knows, that's bad enough."

"I'm sorry you have to relive it. I wish there was something I could do."

"You're there when I need you."

"And you for me," she replied.

"Did you report to Letitia on LA?"

"This morning. She grilled me of course. She's paranoid as hell about you and the President. She was polite, though. No rough stuff like in New York."

"What did you tell her?"

"Just what Scott Ragan said. I embellished it some."

"Good. I dictated a note to Maxwell along those lines."

"Did you operate today?"

"Two thoracotomies this morning, and a busy office. I'm pooped. This is the first quiet moment."

Kate sighed. "I wish we could be together."

"So do I. We'll catch up, soon."

"When are you coming in?"

"The board meeting next month."

"Call me in the meantime?"

"Damn right I will."

❧

At the next meeting of the board of trustees, a silky-voiced auditor from the firm of Martin Ross, expensively dressed in a pinstripe suit and armed with color slides and an electronic projector, presented the financial audit of the American Medical Association. This was the dog-and-pony show Bob Maxwell had ordered, and the auditor was a skilled patronizer.

At the conclusion Cleve Randall bored in. "Is Doctor Jordan paid stipends by the holding company and the subsidiaries?"

"Yes, sir," the auditor replied.

"Do AMA senior executives receive stipends from the holding company and the subsidiaries?"

"Yes, sir."

"What about expense accounts?"

"Those accounts are minimal. They're included in the general expense categories."

"What do you mean by minimal?"

"Not material to the fiscal outcome."

"Where do you show the details of the stipends and the expense accounts?"

"Normally we don't break out that detail."

"Dammit!" Cleve barked. "Why do I feel like I'm chasing my tail?"

"Our report was prepared in accordance with generally accepted accounting procedures," the silky-voiced auditor droned. "Compensation to Dr. Jordan and other senior executives was paid in accordance with their employment contracts, as approved by the board, and is included in various summarizing accounts."

"You mean, buried," Cleve said.

"Our intent was to simplify the report," the man replied. He was becoming nervous.

"Do you have the exact numbers?" Cleve asked.

"Yes, sir." The auditor opened a file. "Dr. Jordan receives an annual stipend of $90,000 from the holding company and $30,000 from each of the seven subsidiaries, for a grand total of $300,000. The senior executives receive lesser amounts consistent with their duties. Expense reimbursements to Dr. Jordan average $25,000 per year total for the holding company and subsidiaries. Lesser amounts go to the other executives. These of course are in addition to salaries paid by the AMA."

After a moment of awkward silence, Bob Maxwell said, "Cleve, this is all on the up and up. Letitia is paid handsomely, and she should be. The executive committee reviewed the contracts, and they were approved by the board last year. The same thing will happen when they come up for renewal next year. Paying senior staff out of the subsidiaries enables us to provide adequate compensation without having to take it all from the parent organization. It's done all the time."

"Why the cloak and dagger?"

"There's no cloak and dagger," Bob Maxwell replied. "You had your questions answered."

Shaking his head, Cleve Randall then said, "Letitia, your staff has again dazzled us with a brilliant, if not disingenuous, production. I'm certain the AMA is in excellent financial condition. But frankly, I question the candor of Martin Ross, and I am mindful they run a seven-figure account with you."

"Are you implying that an accounting firm of the stature of

Martin Ross would prostitute itself for a client?" Letitia asked.

"Absolutely," Cleve replied. "Accounting firms do it all the time."

The silky-voiced auditor bristled. "I take offense at that remark, sir."

"I'm glad you do," Cleve said. "I want your full attention. I'm not going to back off. I want supporting data—specific balances in the retirement accounts of our executive staff, details on the cost of Dr. Jordan's condominium in the Omni, the special improvements, the Italian marble, the furnishings, the goddamn art collection, the rent and how it was established. I want expense account chits, foreign travel chits, and I want to see complete books on the subsidiaries, not just summarizing statements."

"Now wait a minute, Cleve," Bob Maxwell said. "We've already produced a great deal of material. Surely you've seen enough to be satisfied."

Then Duke Rodansky, who had listened quietly, interrupted. "I'm not satisfied!"

"What more, in God's name, would it take, Duke?" Bob Maxwell demanded.

"The personal tax returns of our senior execs," Duke replied.

"That's absurd," Bob Maxwell said. "The nine-nineties are public knowledge. Isn't that enough?"

"No way. Nine-nineties contain limited information and only from the nonprofit side. I want to see what's going on in the subsidiaries. I want, by God, to see everything."

"Dammit Duke, that's out of line," Bob Maxwell retorted. "We can't order our executives to show us their personal tax returns."

"We can order them to show us anything we want," Duke shot back. "They comply or get the hell out."

"No!" Bob Maxwell shouted. "That's going too far."

Duke then settled back and lowered his voice. "Mr. Chairman. It's been a long morning. We're all frazzled. I suggest we postpone the tax return matter to the next meeting of the board."

"Well taken," Bob Maxwell replied, obviously relieved at Duke's apparent change of heart. "We need to cool off. I hope that on the eve of the holiday season we can resolve our differences amicably."

"However, gentlemen," Duke said, "if you remain unwilling to produce the tax returns, be advised: I will move for a full-scale, independent, internal audit."

That evening Joe and Duke slipped out of the hotel and taxied to Gene and Georgetti's over by the river. They slid into a quiet booth in back and Joe asked, "Are you drinking Black Label tonight?"

"Of course."

"I think I'll join you."

"Good man."

"Two double Black Labels, on the rocks," Joe said to the waiter.

"Doubles!" Duke laughed. "That's a fine start. By the way, where's Kate?"

"She couldn't make it. I'm having dinner with her tomorrow night. Would you care to join us."

"Sorry. I'm leaving when we adjourn."

The waiter brought their drinks and Joe sipped the heavy whiskey and frowned. "Alligator piss."

"It grows on you," Duke said.

"Are you hungry?" Joe inquired.

"Definitely," Duke replied. He turned to the waiter. "I'll go with a filet, medium rare, baked potato, and a big chunk of iceberg with Thousand Island."

"That sounds about right," Joe said. "Make it two, and some Dijon, please."

"And Durkee," Duke said.

"Durkee!" Joe said. "With steak?"

"I eat Durkee on everything," Duke replied. "When I was a resident, the food in my hospital was inedible, so I smothered it with Durkee. I became Durkee-dependent. Fortunately we had unlimited supplies."

"You didn't ask for Durkee at my house."

"I didn't want to insult Grace on my first visit."

Duke settled back in the booth and sipped his Scotch. "Well,

Dr. Hawkins, what do you think of our organization now?"

"The same I thought the last time you asked," Joe replied. "I must say, though, the stipends from the subsidiaries, while perhaps excessive are perfectly legal. I take it Cleve thought there was a cover-up."

"He still thinks that."

"The only impropriety was that the stipends were not prominently displayed in the report so they could be easily noticed."

"Cleve regards that as intentionally deceptive."

"I think he was jolted by the money Letitia makes."

"True. However, it's a high-paying job."

"You threw them one helluva curve with that tax thing."

"That was my intention."

"You laid back. Then, wham!"

"I got fed up with the doublespeak."

"What's your next move?"

"The tax thing was a hip shot. Unfortunately I got ahead of myself. I didn't have the votes. For all I know, it may be illegal to demand tax returns. That's why I backed off. I'll see how it lines up by the next board meeting."

"What's a nine-ninety?"

The waiter served the icebergs and a bowl of Thousand Island. Duke jiggled the ice cubes in his drink. "The nine-ninety is an informational return that nonprofit corporations are required to file with the IRS. It reports the income and certain benefits of the five highest paid executives. It was just another obscure tax form until the courts ordered disclosure. These days investigative reporters have orgasms over nine-nineties." He took a bite of crispy iceberg. "This is really cold."

"Have our nine-nineties been publicized?"

"Sure have. Letitia made the *Wall Street Journal* last spring. Over seven hundred grand."

"And you still want the tax returns?"

"Damn right. You don't get the full story with nine-nineties. Expense accounts, certain perks, and pay from the subsidiaries are excluded, and only the top five execs are covered. I want the whole fucking picture."

Joe grinned at his burly friend. "You love to shake her up, don't you?"

"You think I'm rat-fucking her?"

"I know you are."

"I only want my audit."

"That qualifies as rat-fucking."

"Maybe you're right," Duke said. "What the hell. I'm getting drunk."

"Suppose you get the audit. Suppose you turn up a little hanky-panky, but nothing illegal. What then?"

"Good question. Probably a reprimand for Letitia. She would regale us with one of her all-time great sackcloth and ashes speeches. Then we would fire Martin Ross, hire a new auditor, set up tighter controls, and go about our business. The usual drill."

"What would it take to fire Letitia?"

"Major corruption. I'm talking world-class. The board is too implicated to fire her over anything less. And we don't want to piss off the feminists."

The waiter brought their steaks and the Durkee and Dijon, and also a bottle of Worcestershire. "Just in case," the man ventured as he placed the collection of bottles on the table. "Can I bring anything else? Another Black Label?"

"Why not?" Joe replied.

"Jesus Christ!" Duke said. "You're really going for it."

Joe grinned. "You're the only neurosurgeon I've ever tried to drink with."

"Big fucking honor."

"I must have acquired suicidal tendencies."

Duke spooned a load of Durkee onto his steak and cut through the center. "As I told you before, if we fire Letitia we have to find another son of a bitch just like her. That would be a lot of trouble."

"It may come to that," Joe said.

"It may."

"What about the Breslow investigation?"

"I've heard nothing since the last board meeting."

The waiter returned with fresh drinks, and Joe ogled the sizable

pourings of Scotch in the highball glasses. "Chew your steak
well," he admonished. "You're too damn big for me to do a
Heimlich."

"You could handle it, my friend, if anyone could."

"He knew what he was doing," Joe said.

"Heimlich?"

"No. The man who killed Breslow."

"The mysterious hired killer?"

"If he really did kill Breslow with his bare hands, he was a pro,"
Joe said.

"I agree," Duke said.

"Tell me about the Italian marble."

"That I know something about," Duke said. "Last year Letitia
imported a giant slab of marble from Italy for the table top in the
board room in the Washington headquarters. Supposedly it cost
half a mill. The damn thing was so big—you'll see when you go
to Washington—they had to haul it up the outside of the building with a crane and cut a hole in the wall to get it in. She put a
small piece of the same marble on the dining room table in her
condo. I don't know what that cost."

"And the art collection?"

"It's really something. The centerpiece is a sculpture over the
entrance to the Washington building, a crazy thing, sort of a three
dimensional montage of toilet seats and pots and pans and junk.
They commissioned a sculptress to do it, Josephine somebody, a
crazy lady, at a handsome fee. There's a bunch of paintings,
etchings, and the like scattered through the building, 'part of the
decor,' and Letitia keeps a few paintings in her condo. She hired
an art dealer to make the purchases. We knew nothing about it
until the grand opening of the building. Rumor is, the damn
collection cost three million." Duke paused for a swallow of
Scotch. "You know, except for that thing over the entrance, most
of us like the art collection. It has class. Letitia didn't have to
sneak it in the back door."

The waiter interrupted. He was holding a small cardboard box
tied with a black ribbon. "Dr. Rodansky?"

"I'm Dr. Rodansky," Duke replied.

"A man delivered this for you."

"Who was he?" Duke inquired.

"I don't know, sir. He left immediately."

Duke grinned. "There's no card. It must be a Christmas present from one of my secret admirers. Not a pretty wrapping, though."

"Are you expecting a bomb?" Joe asked.

"Not that I know of." Duke shook the box and turned it over in his hands. "There's something inside." He slipped off the ribbon and opened the box. "Christ!"

"What is it?" Joe asked.

They stared. In the bottom of the box was a black feathered creature, smaller than the hand of an infant, skewered on a long hatpin with a red bead on the end.

Duke lifted the repugnant thing from the box and cradled it in his palm. It had a tiny, balding head and pointed beak, spindly legs, a pair of winglets, and wispy black feathers. Dried blood matted the down where the hatpin had pinned the winglets to the fragile body.

Joe touched it. "A baby chicken."

"Killed with a hatpin," Duke said.

"Freshly dead."

"A black chick."

"What the hell is it, voodoo?"

"No," Duke replied grimly. "It's some asshole's idea of a joke."

"Joke?"

The big man dropped it back in the box. He drained his Black Label and signaled the waiter for another. "You'll need one too."

"What's this all about?" Joe asked.

I don't know if I'm ready to tell you."

"Why not?"

"You may not understand."

"Try me."

"It involves my personal life."

"It's up to you," Joe said.

Duke shrugged. "What the hell," he said. "I might as well tell you. I've been married twenty years to Barbara. She's a wonderful lady. We have a nice home and two good kids. I work hard, make a ton of money, enjoy the kids. Barbara is a good wife, keeps a good house, takes good care of us, plays golf, does volunteer work, has a bunch of friends. It's your standard, perfect, midwestern, successful situation. She doesn't cotton much to the AMA, though. Thinks we're a bunch of old farts playing games."

"Grace would have liked her," Joe said.

"I have a girlfriend in Chicago. Her name is Shirley Raymond. She's a paralegal. Lives in Old Town. She makes me feel good. I'm not proud of it. But, I keep seeing her."

"Shirley is your business," Joe said.

"Shirley is black."

Joe said nothing.

"Understand? My girlfriend is a black chick. I have a black chick stashed in Chicago. That's what this fucking caper is all about."

After a long moment, Joe said, "Duke, it may not be a joke."

"What do you mean?"

"It may be a threat."

"Naw. Some asshole is jerking my chain about Shirley."

"A death threat."

"What the fuck are you talking about?"

"Look. I know some things you don't. I can't explain, so don't ask questions. Trust me. Letitia may be trying to scare you into backing off."

"What do you mean?"

"The tax return thing."

Duke was stunned. "That's heavy stuff, Joe."

"Letitia is crazy."

"You're serious."

"Very serious. Call Shirley. Get her out of Chicago. Tonight if possible."

"Christ! She can't just up and leave town."

"Duke, Letitia might kill her."

"I can't believe that."

"Believe it. Get her out. Hide her somewhere. Work out the details later."

"You don't fuck around, do you?"

"This is no time to fuck around, Duke. Get her the hell out of there. Do it now!"

"It's a bluff."

"Maybe, but don't take that chance."

"If she touches Shirley . . ."

"Call Maxwell now, from the restaurant. Tell him you've thought it over, you got carried away, you're not going to demand the tax returns, you don't want an independent audit, you're satisfied with our auditor. Be apologetic. Make it sincere. He'll tell Letitia. If anything is on, that should stop it."

"You mean, cave in?" Duke was disbelieving.

"Give her what she wants, for now."

"She'll think she owns me."

"That's what you want her to think."

"What about Cleve?"

"He'll understand when you explain."

Duke shook his head. "Cleve won't back off."

"It won't matter. Cleve can't nail Letitia by himself, and Letitia knows it."

"What if you're wrong?"

"I buy dinner next time."

"This isn't right," Duke said.

"Of course it isn't," Joe replied.

"That fucking bitch. I really will rat-fuck her."

"Your time will come."

"What does that mean?"

"Letitia Jordan is going down, Duke. Take my word for it."

Then Duke asked. "Does this have anything to do with the President?"

Joe said nothing.

Duke grinned. "I understand." Then, "My friend, I'm sure glad we got you elected to this outfit."

"I hope so," Joe said.

"Do you suppose Letitia killed that damn chick herself and put it in the box?"

"I doubt it. One of the local 'sick joke' services probably did it. We'll never be able to trace it."

"Harpooned it with a hatpin. I wonder how long it took the poor critter to die."

Joe downed the last of his drink. "Let's get back to the hotel. You've got some calling to do."

"Should we notify the police?"

"No use."

"What'll I say to Shirley? I can't tell her about this." He looked at the box. "What'll we do with the damn thing?"

"Shut the box and tell the waiter to throw it out."

"Shirley will think I'm drunk. I'm not drunk. I don't feel drunk. I'm damn mad, maybe scared. I should be drunk. I've had enough Scotch. Shit! I am drunk."

"That's bizarre," Scott Ragan said. "You did the right thing. Letitia Jordan is dangerous. Who knows what's in those tax returns? Furthermore, if it goes to a vote and she loses, it would seriously undermine her power."

"Remember the mysterious stipends you and the President told us about?" Joe asked.

"I remember."

"All legal and proper, although not broken out in the routine reports given to the board. They were in her contract. The chairman of the board defended her."

"I wonder what he would say if he knew about the black chick."

"She must be loony. Jeez! A black chick."

"The mark of death," Scott said.

"Can I tell Duke what's going on? He's pretty upset."

"Not yet. It may be another three or four months."

"I can't keep a lid on that long."

"You have to. In the meantime, Letitia Jordan may get careless. Maybe you can apply a little pressure."

"I'll try."

"Better alert Kate."

"Will do."

"Incidentally, are you drunk?"

"Rodansky put me under the table."

"Thanks for calling," Scott said.

[20]

MARIO'S HAD a new piano player, a blond kid with a baby face who looked young enough to be a high schooler. He was doing a stylish "Deep Purple" reminiscent of Eddie Duchin when Joe arrived.

Kate was waiting in the alcove bar and Joe leaned down and kissed her forehead. "You always manage to arrive early," he said.

"That's part of my job."

"I like the kid on the piano. He plays like he was around when they wrote that song."

"He played 'Amapola' before you arrived. It was just as romantic as the last time we were here."

"He'll do fine. Have you ordered?"

"No."

"What say we have champagne?"

"I'd like that."

Joe conferred with the bartender, who then produced a pair of crystal flutes and a silver bucket containing a bottle of champagne packed in ice. The bartender deftly popped the cork and poured a splash into one of the flutes. "Schramsberg Blanc de Noir, 1983," Joe read off the label. "Napa Valley." He tasted the champagne.

"Excellent." The bartender filled the slender flutes and returned the bottle to the ice.

"You're looking fit," Kate said. "How do you stay so tan?"

"Remember, I live in Arizona."

"I hate you." She peered at her champagne. "Is it flat? I see only one little string of bubbles." She sipped the champagne. "It's not flat."

"These are diamond-cut flutes. They're ground to a fine point inside the hollow stem. Champagne bubbles form only on the bottom. Since the bottom of the flute is a point, ergo, a single strand of bubbles, and the champagne retains its bite. True connoisseurs drink their champagne only out of diamond cut flutes. You get lots of bubbles in a widemouth, but the champagne goes flat that much quicker."

"I'm impressed." She picked up her flute and contemplated the steady trail of bubbles rising in the stem. "They're like a chain of tiny diamonds."

"Genuine champagne comes from the Champagne district of France. Other champagnes, technically speaking, should be called sparkling wines. I learned that in a lecture on wine when I was in France. Unfortunately I remember little else."

"I'm still impressed," Kate said. She sipped her champagne and smiled. "It's good to see you, Joe." She was in a tastefully revealing black dress, a silk scarf of crimson and gold, and black alligator cowboy boots with flared heels.

"It's good to see you," he replied. "I invited Duke, but he couldn't make it."

"I like Dr. Rodansky, but I'm glad we're alone."

"Me too."

"We should drink a toast."

"A toast." Joe tapped his flute against hers and they drank. "I like your Luchesse's. They surprised me."

"You must be an expert on boots."

"Luchesse's are famous where I come from."

"They're famous where I come from too. However, I found these at Marshall Field. I told the guy who sold them to me—he's probably never been west of Peoria—that I have a friend from the Old West. He assured me you would approve."

"I approve."

"They're wonderful in the winter."

"It's a shame they hide your ankles."

Reuben appeared and Joe announced, "We don't need menus. We'll have a Caesar salad with lots of anchovies and the soft-shell crab. And we'll sit here and enjoy the piano until you're ready for us."

"Excellent choices, doctor," Reuben replied in his squeaky voice and departed.

"How do you know what I want?" Kate inquired.

"You like what I like."

"And that's that?"

"That's that," Joe said with finality.

"Fair enough, I suppose," she said. "Well, have you been busy?"

"Very busy. That's good. When I have time to think, the reality of Grace's death hits me, and the guilt. And, of course, the nightmares."

"Nightmares?"

"They started after Vietnam. I was always trying to run in deep mud; I was slipping, falling down, flailing, and they were shooting at me. I would wake up terrified. I hated going to bed. Now they're different, but all I remember is that something terrible happened, and someone died. Last week I had a new one. I couldn't breathe, and I was pleading for penicillin. I was just as terrified."

"Why the guilt?"

"Grace was an alcoholic, and I let it happen. She had the kids to take care of. I worked long hours, often at night. Somewhere along the line she started drinking. I was in denial—a cardinal symptom in alcoholics and their spouses—but I finally realized what was happening, and we had a serious talk before my election. She agreed to do something and had an appointment with a counselor. She wasn't drunk when she crashed, but maybe it wouldn't have happened if I'd been more attentive."

Kate touched his hand. "It wasn't your fault."

"Guilt is normal. The question is, how you handle it. I get tense, restless, short tempered, sometimes I explode."

"I can't imagine that."

"My kids were great. God, how I love 'em. They handled their own grief and made over me. My mother and my sister made over me. My friends made over me. They kept me occupied. I'm okay if I stay occupied."

I wanted to call you," Kate said, "but I didn't want to intrude."

"You could never intrude." Joe smiled affectionately. "You're very good for me."

"That's nice." She sipped her Schramsberg. "This is wonderful."

"Eighty-three was a good year. I don't actually know that," he added. "I'm trying to act sophisticated."

Reuben then escorted them into the dining room, and Joe watched the black dress cling deliciously to Kate's shapely bottom as she walked. El rumpo magnifico, he thought. Christ, Hawkins. You're a horny bastard. But then, how could one not admire such elegance. The Caesars were on the table, and the waiter presented chilled forks on a napkin and a basket of hot bread, then filled the champagne flutes and departed.

Kate tasted the salad. "I hope you like anchovies. This is loaded."

"I love anchovies. You look quite smart tonight, by the way."

"Thank you."

"Your ensemble makes me think of a cadence I used to know."

"I don't understand."

"A marching cadence, from my former life, about a girl in alligator boots and a red bandana. After dinner I'll demonstrate."

"Fair enough. This isn't your everyday red bandana, though." Kate tossed her head and adjusted the scarf and sounded smug. "It's an Hermès."

"I'll pretend it's a cowboy bandana," Joe said.

The waiter appeared with their entrées. "Soft shells sautéed in lemon butter," he said. "Extremely hot." The little crabs sizzled in their baths of boiling butter, and the waiter served string beans and new potatoes and parsley and poured the last of the champagne.

"Careful," Joe said. He cut a sliver of hot crab and gingerly touched it to his tongue.

"Tell me about the board meeting," Kate said.

"We had a big row." Joe outlined the events of the meeting and his dinner conversation with Duke.

"I'm flabbergasted," Kate said.

"I was flabbergasted myself."

"I've heard rumors about a black girl."

"You didn't tell me."

"I didn't think it bore repeating."

"Her name is Shirley," Joe said.

"The black chick. Have you talked to Scott?"

"I called him last evening. He agrees that Letitia would do anything to force Duke to capitulate, and that we did the right thing."

"I heard about the row," Kate said. "The jungle drums worked overtime today."

Joe smiled. "I can imagine."

"What happens now?" Kate asked.

"We bide our time. The investigations are proceeding, but it may take months."

"Have you thought about the President's proposal?"

"Yes. It would help the cause if he announced the new cabinet position immediately. I'm going to ask him to do that. The Letitia problem must be resolved, of course. I'm impatient, but in the meantime, we have a full schedule, the leadership conference, speeches, board meeting in April, the World Medical."

"Guess what! I'm going to the World Medical in Madrid."

"That's wonderful," Joe exclaimed.

"I've never traveled overseas."

"You'll love it. I'll take you to a bullfight. The premier bullring of the world, Las Ventas, is in Madrid. All the great matadors fight there."

"I'll have to think about that."

"The bullfight is intoxicating," Joe said.

"Are you an aficionado?"

"Of a sort. I've been to bullfights in Mexico City, Tijuana, Nogales, Madrid. Not many, actually. I've read some about bullfighting."

"I'm surprised. I thought you would hate all forms of violence and killing. You've known so much of it."

"I don't fully understand it myself. The bullfight casts a powerful spell. You get hooked. It's quite a scene—tradition, color, music, drama. God, what drama."

"We'll see Pierre Globa in Madrid," Kate said.

"I want to convey President Chamberlain's message. Perhaps we can corner Pierre for a drink and ask him about the 'good times.'"

"The President suggested we do that."

"Look," Joe said. "Let's fly to Madrid together."

"That would be fun."

"I'll come to Chicago, and we can go from here."

She beamed. "Splendid."

"Done. Now, why are you going?"

"Apartheid. The South African Medical Society wants in, but the black African bloc won't have it. They've threatened to walk out. South African Medical argues that apartheid is a government policy, which they disavow. They point out that other countries in the World Medical bear crosses—an obvious reference to Germany, Japan, and Italy; that the goal of the World Medical is peace through the common bond of medicine; that medicine should, as Pierre Globa says, transcend political boundaries; that admitting South Africa is what the World Medical is all about. The AMA agrees. Under the new voting rules, the AMA can overturn the black African bloc."

"And bear the brunt of their wrath."

"Right. It will be a delicate situation. My job is to deal with the media. You should also know there's a hidden agenda. My boss has a personal stake in South Africa. She likes to visit Capetown on company business, hopes to do some consulting down there when she retires from the AMA. She expects to come out of this on the good side of the South Africans."

"Let's change the subject," Joe said.

"You're tired of Letitia Jordan?"

"Right now I want to finish this delicious crab and ponder your extraordinary anatomy."

Kate instantly blushed. "That's fresh. You've never been fresh before."

"You've never looked so inviting. Please don't be offended."

"I can't help it if my boobs are big. I'm not fat, am I?"

"You don't look fat."

"My brothers say I'm stocky."

"You're beautifully proportioned—not fat, not stocky, just right."

She put her hand to her bosom. "Truthfully, is it too revealing?"

"Of course not. It's a pretty dress in good taste. It displays your backside nicely, too."

"You know that embarrasses me," she scolded.

"You've got it, flaunt it," Joe said, grinning.

"I bought the damn dress to please you."

"You do please me. You look wonderful. You'd look good in a gunny sack."

"I can live with that. But you're still fresh."

"Perhaps we'd better attend to the crab."

"Perhaps we had," Kate said.

❦

The cold air stung their cheeks when they stepped out of the foyer at Mario's, and their breath turned to white vapor. A light snow was falling. They were warm in their trenchcoats, and Kate clutched Joe's arm and snuggled to his side.

"Let's walk to my place. It's only a few blocks."

"You got it," he answered.

She led him across the driveway and along the sidewalk, leaving tracks in the fresh snow. "This is Goethe Street." She used the German pronunciation. "If you want to get here in a cab, you may have to say, 'Goath,' like goat with a lithp."

Joe smiled. "I found that out." They walked briskly, and wet snowflakes floated against their cheeks and into their eyes. "Let's try the cadence," he said. "Get in step, like this. Left . . . left . . . left . . . left . . . left, right, left, right, left. A little faster. That's good.

I left' my girl' in Butte,' Montan'a
Al'ligator boots' and a red' bandan'a
Loved' her like' a man' gone cra'zy
She' gave me' a yel'low dai'sy
I prom'ised to' return' whenev'er
Told' me she' would wait' for'ever
Cried' when I' marched off' to glo'ry
Kept' my heart' and that's' the sto'ry
I left' my girl' in Butte', Montan'a
Al'ligator boots' and a red' bandan'a
Al'ligator boots' and a red' bandan'a
Al'ligator boots' and a red' bandan'a.

They slowed to a stroll.

"Did you just make it up?" Kate asked.

"Not entirely. It's an old cadence. It had 'In-di-an-a' in place of 'Butte-Mon-tan-a,' the same syllables, and 'alligator shoes' and 'a hot fan-dan-go.'"

"Write it out for me when we get to my apartment so I can learn it."

The streetlamps on Goethe cast a yellow glow around the shadows on the sidewalk, and a light wind caused the snowflakes to dance in the light. Occasionally a car drove by with its wipers clack, clack, clacking on the windshield.

A man suddenly stepped in front of them. He was medium build and wore a wool cap pulled over his ears and a shapeless jacket. They stopped, surprised, and the man fidgeted nervously. Nothing of his face was visible except heavy eyebrows and a dark moustache.

They heard a metallic click, and suddenly the man brandished a switchblade knife. The blade was long and tapered, and it shined in the dim light.

"My God!" Kate whispered. She gripped Joe and felt the muscles tighten in his arm.

The man pointed the switchblade.

Imperceptibly Joe loosened Kate's grip on his arm and set his feet. He stared coldly at the man's eyes.

217

The man waved the switchblade menacingly.

"Please, don't," Kate cried out. She slipped the purse from her shoulder and let it fall to the sidewalk.

The man dropped his eyes and in that instant Joe threw a rapier kick, too quick to see. The knife ripped loose and rattled on the sidewalk. Then a kick in the groin, and the man screamed and doubled over. Joe stepped in, as if choreographed, and brought his locked fists up to crush the man's face, and the man straightened and screamed and blood spurted from his nose. A knee in the groin doubled him again, and Joe drove the locked fists down on the base of the man's skull with the force of a sledgehammer. The man fell prone and Joe brutally twisted his arm in a hammer lock and the bone snapped with a sickening crack. He grabbed a handful of hair and jerked the man's head back then smashed the face into the sidewalk. The man twisted, helpless in Joe's grip, and screamed. Joe jerked his head back and forth, smashing his face again, and again, and the man screamed. Blood spattered over the sidewalk and soaked the wet snow.

"Joe!" Kate screamed. "Stop! You're killing him." She pulled at Joe's trenchcoat. "You're killing him. Please stop. Please, please stop."

The man ceased struggling, and Joe released him and got to his feet. Now the man lay face down, sobbing with gurgling noises. Joe turned him over. Blood smeared the face and matted the moustache. His breath came in jerks, and he rolled his tongue and shut his eyes. The broken arm bent grotesquely above the elbow.

"He's lucky," Joe said. "He only has a bloody nose and a fractured humerus. It's going to hurt. He'll think twice before he tries to mug somebody again."

Kate stared at the man's broken arm and the wreckage of a face. He tried to sit up.

"Help him, Joe," she said.

Joe hoisted the man to a sitting position. The man winced and opened his eyes and clutched the arm. He looked at Joe, dazed and fearful. Kate knelt and took a handkerchief from her purse and daubed blood from the man's smashed nose. The breathing came easier.

She turned to Joe. "Is he all right?"

"I think so."

"He's very young."

"A kid."

"I thought you were going to kill him."

"I nearly did."

"Can we help you?" Kate asked the man. He shook his head and said nothing and, cradling the arm, turned and struggled to his feet. He waited, as if wondering what Joe might do, then loped off into the darkness.

"Should we call the police?" Kate asked.

"Let the poor son of a bitch go."

Joe picked up the switchblade, closed it, and dropped it in his pocket. "I'll throw this damn thing in the river." He looked at the blood on the snow.

Kate slipped her arm around him. "Are you all right? You're trembling."

"I'm all right."

"That was awesome. I hardly saw what happened until you had him down."

"I lost control," Joe said. "A long time ago I was what they called, 'a killing machine.'"

"You frightened me."

"I would have killed him. You stopped me."

"Have you ever killed anyone like that? I mean, with your bare hands."

"Yes."

"You're still trembling."

"I know."

"Oh, Joe."

"I'd like a drink"

"I have Scotch at home."

"You've just seen the dark side of Joe Hawkins."

"It was understandable. You were awfully good, that's all."

They walked in silence in the snow and stopped in front of an apartment building.

"This is it," Kate said.

Joe tipped her face up. "Before we ran into that poor kid, I was thinking we might make love."

She wrapped her arms around his neck and kissed him long on the mouth.

❦

It was deliciously warm inside Kate's apartment. She hung their trenchcoats in a closet and helped Joe out of his jacket and tie. He sat down and she stood behind him and massaged his shoulders. Then she poured some Glenlivet. "This should make us feel better."

"Thank you," Joe said. "It hits the spot."

"Are you sure you're all right?"

"Yes. I'm just a little surprised at myself."

"I sure hope you never get pissed off at me."

Joe smiled. "Not likely."

"I turned up my heat before going to Mario's," she said. "I wanted us to be comfortable with our clothes off, in case things worked out that way."

"That was very thoughtful," he said, smiling.

They finished the Glenlivet, and she led him to her bed and pulled the spread down. She pulled his shoes and socks off, then carefully removed his clothes and hung them neatly over a chair and he stood in the warm room, naked. She embraced him and rubbed her hands up and down his back until the heavy torso muscles relaxed. Then he sat on the edge of the bed and watched her undress.

"You're beautiful," he said.

"Thank you." She pulled him close and buried his face between her breasts. "You're still tense."

"I feel much better now," Joe said.

"Good. You know, when you kissed me a moment ago, that was our first real kiss."

"And this will be the first time we make love." He dropped his hands to her buttocks. "Your skin is warm and smooth. The muscles are firm."

He lay back on the bed and she fluffed the pillow and lay down beside him. He cradled her head in his arm and she gently rubbed his belly with the flat of her hand. He kissed her and she teased his lips with her tongue as she stroked his chest and shoulders and his thighs.

"My God!" she exclaimed. She had found the jagged scar along the inside of his thigh.

"That's where I got hit," he said.

"It's terrible." She was astounded.

"It was terrible at the time. It's okay now."

She touched the heavy scar tissue. "Is it sensitive?"

"No. I hardly know it's there."

"You almost lost your leg?"

"Almost. I was lucky, and I had a good surgeon."

She ran her fingers along the scar up to his groin and hesitated. "Joe, it's so close."

"Yes. That was nice when the nurses changed the dressings."

"I'll bet they waited in line." She kissed him. "Joe. Please make love to me."

[21]

IT WAS THEIR FIRST Christmas after Grace's death, and they had the big dinner on Christmas Eve. Joe's mother cooked a monstrous platter of fried chicken, her specialty, which Tracy, Rosie, and little Jake wanted instead of turkey, and Janie did hot rolls and mashed potatoes and gravy and the rest. But they longed for Grace and despite brave faces, the children cried when Joe said the blessing. Then everyone cried. After dinner the children helped with the dishes and Joe lit the fire in the family room and they watched the *Nutcracker* and remembered happier Christmases. Finally, they went to bed, and when the house was quiet, Joe put gifts from Santa under the tree.

At midnight his bedside phone rang. "Merry Christmas," Kate said cheerily.

"Merry Christmas," Joe answered, delighted.

"Did I wake you?"

"No. I just crawled into bed. I was thinking about you."

"I'm in bed too. My folks are asleep. It's a good time to talk."

"Is it cold in Butte?"

"It's frigging cold, like twenty below right now, colder than Chicago. I went for a sleigh ride with my father this evening and froze, but the snow was so beautiful in the moonlight I didn't care."

"It was balmy here all day. I hardly needed a sweater."

"You dog! I remember how nice it was in Phoenix the first time I met you."

"And I remember your blue eyes and having a spritzer in the bar in the hotel and you telling me company secrets about the AMA."

"We had fun," she said.

"Do you do Christmas in the morning?"

"Always," she replied.

"So do we."

"My mom will have a scrumptious turkey dinner tomorrow afternoon."

"We've always had turkey on Christmas, but the kids conned my mom into frying chicken tonight. They decided they didn't want turkey. Maybe they just wanted to change the routine. Anyway, they're planning on eating leftovers tomorrow and the rest of the week, and she certainly fixed enough."

"Sounds great to me."

"Actually, it was a pretty sad evening. Everyone cried—the kids, Mom, Janie, me. I hope we feel better tomorrow."

"I wish I could do something to help."

"You're doing it," Joe said. "I love talking to you with the lights out and the phone on the pillow. It's almost as good as having you next to me."

"Pillow talk," Kate said.

"Let's talk every night."

"You got it."

❦

After the holidays Joe took his turn on the roster of medical society meetings and every week or so would journey to the likes of Memphis, Biloxi, Portland, Oke City, or Grand Rapids. The doctors had rejoiced in his Madison Square Garden speech and ascendancy to leadership in the American Medical Association, for he was one of them, a mainstream doc. Now he was their elected leader, and when he came to visit, they exercised their rights as constituents and questioned him mercilessly about the future of medicine and the villains trying to destroy freedom and what was the AMA doing about it. It was challenging, and a hectic schedule, but he was rarely away from home more than a night or two and between assignments he tended faithfully to his family and his practice. He liked traveling and making new friends and, all in all, it felt good to be wanted.

Of course he saw Kate as often as possible. Sometimes she met him at O'Hare when he was passing through and they would have lunch, maybe a cup of coffee, or only a brief hello. When he stayed in Chicago, they dined discreetly in secluded restaurants with good wines, or ordered room service, and they made love.

The fight with the mugger troubled him. God knows, someone who comes at you with a switchblade deserves no quarter. But Joe had lost control. Kate argued that he only did what anyone else would have done, had they been able, and she was damn glad things turned out the way they did.

"I know I tried to stop you," she said. "The poor devil looked helpless, and I reacted. After thinking about it, I wouldn't have cared if you had killed him. He might have killed us. He was probably on cocaine or something, another addict trying to steal money. It would have been good riddance."

"He was just a kid," Joe said.

"You handled him easily."

"I'm glad you stopped me. I wouldn't want another killing on my conscience."

❦

Duke Rodansky announced that he was withdrawing his demand for the personal tax returns of the executive staff. "After sober reflection," he explained, "I decided we should get on with the important business and quit bickering over petty details."

"Something's rotten here," Cleve Randall later confided to Joe. "Duke doesn't back down, and he doesn't sell out."

"He changed his mind, that's all," Joe said. "It wouldn't have been worth the bloodshed."

Cleve shook his head. "I don't care. Something is rotten."

Privately Joe complimented Duke. "That was a good move. Letitia should be placated."

"Did you see the look on Cleve's face?" Duke said. "I feel like a fucking turncoat."

"He'll forgive you when he understands."

"I hope so."

"How's Shirley doing?"

"She's confused."

"What do you tell her?"

"That her life is in danger. She has to do what I say, and don't ask questions. It's not easy."

"I can imagine."

"When this is over I'm thinking I won't see Shirley anymore. There's no use kidding myself. The least I can do is see that she gets on with her life."

❦

At the spring meeting of the board of trustees, Letitia Jordan unveiled a proposal to increase membership dues.

"Gentlemen, I fully understand the sensitivity of this issue," she said. "The bottom line is, no choice. We require a twenty dollar dues increase next year to maintain programs and build reserves."

Something about Letitia's take-it-or-leave-it demeanor angered Joe. "Members won't quibble over twenty dollars if they get their money's worth," he growled. "Unfortunately many doctors see no tangible benefit to AMA membership. They're under tremendous pressure to maintain high standards in the face of rising costs. They don't believe the AMA is helping. That's why membership is falling off. It's not a question of twenty dollars, or a thousand dollars. It's a question of value. A dues increase at this time will seriously erode membership."

"Notwithstanding anticipated losses, we project the twenty

dollar increase will net enough to meet our needs," Letitia responded.

"You'll have to convince the house of delegates," Cleve Randall said. "They're looking for a 'no increase' recommendation."

"They have to understand fiscal responsibility," Letitia said.

"They do understand fiscal responsibility," Joe said. "And they expect the same of us. They want a strong AMA, and they want to have confidence in the leadership. But they're restless, Letitia. We shouldn't hit them with a dues increase we can do without."

"It's imperative," Letitia said.

"It's not imperative," Cleve Randall said. "Fade out the less conspicuous programs and cut your overhead. You know the drill."

"What about the reserves?" demanded Letitia.

"What about them?" answered Joe.

"We're obligated to increase reserves," Letitia said.

"We're in a crisis," Cleve Randall said.

"This is what reserves are for," Joe said.

Bob Maxwell tapped his gavel. "It's obvious we have two points of view. Both have merit. It's also obvious we have an impasse. I'm going to terminate the discussion and ask staff to prepare alternate recommendations along the lines discussed by Joe and Cleve. We'll take it up at the next session."

"That's agreeable, Mr. Chairman," Joe said.

"Fine," Bob Maxwell said. "Now gentlemen, Letitia has a final item that wasn't on your agenda."

"Thank you, Mr. Chairman," Letitia said. "Gentlemen, all of us travel a great deal for the AMA. We use commercial air carriers, which are satisfactory in most instances. However, airline travel is congested and sometimes the schedules are inconvenient. Special demands are placed on the chairman of the board. Some of you live in communities not well served by airlines. We also have daily staff travel between Chicago and Washington and, on occasion, to other cities. The value of time squandered by inefficiency is considerable. I've studied this matter for two years and have concluded that the AMA would benefit from an alternate means of air travel.

"Last fall the chairman and I flew roundtrip Chicago to Washington in a Learjet. We departed from Meigs and landed at National. It took us less than three hours to go from the door of this building to the door of the Washington headquarters. We had four good hours in Washington and returned to Chicago for dinner. On the trip home two members of the Washington staff briefed us on legislative activities. It was a productive day.

"Staff members have been flying between Chicago and Washington to evaluate the concept of corporate jet travel. The Learjet 31 is configured to seat four, facing each other, like a miniature conference room. Our people conducted business profitably on these flights."

She passed out folders. "This is an analysis of the travel needs of the association. It shows how a Learjet can save money and produce the most efficient use of travel time."

Joe had decided to keep quiet after the dues debacle, but this was too much. "Just a minute, Letitia. Are you telling us you want the AMA to buy a Learjet?"

"I'm talking about a lease."

"What kind of lease?" Joe asked.

"We've negotiated with a company called AirExec. They maintain a fleet of corporate jets and contract to sell blocks of flying time. The price is based on an hourly rate. The bigger the block, the cheaper the rate. If we guarantee six hundred hours, which I anticipate will meet our current need, we get the cheapest rate. If we guarantee, say, four hundred hours, the hourly rate is proportionately higher. AirExec supplies the planes, crews, maintenance, and handles all arrangements. In other words, they deal with the headaches, while we enjoy convenience and the economies of scale. We simply schedule our flights. The details are in your folders—rates, cost of layover time, and so on. I think you'll find it an attractive proposition."

"I can attest to the convenience," Bob Maxwell said. "The trip I made with Letitia was most impressive. The plane was comfortable, and we had a very attractive young lady taking care of us."

Joe leafed through the folder. "What will six hundred hours cost?"

"Two thousand dollars an hour. With incidentals, figure a million and a half a year."

"You say that's cheaper than airline travel?"

"It's cheaper than airline travel when you consider the value of time saved. Assuming an average load factor of 3.5, the estimated annual offset in first class airline tickets and hotel accommodations will be four hundred thousand dollars. The balance of a million-one is made up by allocating executive time at an average of four hundred dollars per hour. The principal users will be board members and senior execs who go at a much higher rate. The prestige factor should also be considered. A company jet will make an impressive statement for the AMA."

"C'mon, Letitia!" Joe said. "Anyway you slice it, you cannot fly a Learjet, or any other goddamn airplane, including a Piper Cub, from here to Washington for the price of four airline tickets."

"I'm not saying you can," Letitia replied. "But your point is not valid. No analysis is credible unless it takes into account the value of executive time."

"Your accountants can justify a rocket ship with spangles if you tell them to," Joe said.

"You're being facetious," Letitia said.

"And you're absurd," Joe said.

"I resent that, Joe," Letitia retorted.

Bob Maxwell intervened. "Everyone. Calm down."

Joe was unyielding. "This is a travesty," he said. "We spent the last hour discussing why a twenty dollar dues increase will enrage our members, and now you want to buy a goddamn company jet. Nothing could be more ill-advised."

"I'm not proposing to buy a jet," Letitia insisted. "I'm only proposing to lease one. We'll have no capital outlay. I guarantee it will be cost-effective."

"Bullshit!"

"Please," Bob Maxwell pled.

"This attack is unwarranted," Letitia said, flushed and angry.

"If anything, it's overdue," Joe snapped. "Membership is eroding. We mustn't isolate ourselves from the rank-and-file membership and become a coldhearted financial empire. We need caring

227

and compassion. If you go tooling around the country in a private jet, it'll make a statement all right—about the abdication of responsibility."

Letitia turned livid. "You have no right to say that, Joe. I know my responsibilities. You're the one who's out of touch. We're in a war, goddammit. If you want to survive, you play the game."

"This has nothing to do with playing the game," Joe said. "It's plain stupid."

"You're offensive," Letitia shouted.

"For God's sake, Letitia, this is another of your goddamn ego trips. The docs will see through it in a minute, to say nothing of Washington and the barracudas in the press. I can hear it now: The AMA, in a cavalier display of garish opulence, flies around the country in the company jet, jacking up the cost of health care."

"That's preposterous," Letitia said.

Joe, boiling mad, leaned forward and glared at the stubborn little woman who was so effectively enraging him. "Letitia, you can take the goddamn jet and stick it. If you pursue this blatant idiocy, I'll do everything in my power to break you."

Silence befell the boardroom. Finally Bob Maxwell said, "That appears to be an ultimatum."

"That's exactly what it is," Joe growled.

"We don't do business that way on this board," Bob Maxwell said. "We operate on consensus."

"I'm with Joe," Cleve Randall announced quietly.

"Well," Bob Maxwell said. He surveyed the troubled faces around the table. It was obvious that Joe had won supporters. "I believe we should adjourn. This discussion was, of course, informal. Nothing will appear in the minutes."

Letitia slumped sullenly in her chair, struggling for composure.

Bob Maxwell turned to Joe. "You've made some harsh allegations, Joe. I trust they reflected the heat of argument."

Joe thought for a moment. "Mr. Chairman, if I have been unduly abrasive, I hope you will understand the intensity of my feelings and accept my apology. However, I fear we are in danger of forsaking the traditional values that make medicine a noble profession. I would like to be wrong."

❦

Scott Ragan's metallic voice crackled on the telephone. "Good evening, Joe. Where are you calling from?"

"Chicago. As a matter of fact, I'm in Miss Murphy's cozy apartment, sitting in her one and only comfortable chair, getting drunk on a Bloody Mary laced with Tabasco."

Scott laughed. "And where is the ever-glamorous Miss Murphy?"

"In the kitchen cooking hamburgers, like the good Irish homemaker she is. I wish you could join us."

"How do you know I can't?"

"You're in Washington, aren't you?"

"No, but you're safe. I'm in San Francisco. They put my calls through, wherever I am. You'd better mean it next time you ask me over. I might be just down the street."

"I'll keep that in mind. I really do wish you were here. What I'm calling about should be discussed in person."

"That sounds serious."

Joe took a swig of his drink and stirred the icy red liquid with a celery stalk. "I had a helluva row with Letitia Jordan this afternoon. I'm afraid I got mad."

Kate interrupted from the kitchen doorway. "The hamburgers are almost ready. If that's Scott Ragan, you have five minutes."

"Kate said we have five minutes."

"I heard," Scott said.

Kate took the phone. "Scott?"

"Good evening, Kate."

"Our president-elect outdid himself today. I wasn't there, but I heard he put up a great fight."

"I'm waiting," Scott said.

Joe retrieved the phone and related what had happened. "It was bad enough when Letitia wanted to raise the dues. We rejected that, then she trotted out this hairy-assed scheme to lease a jet. I told her to stick it."

"I would love to have heard that," Scott said.

"Cleve Randall and some of the others were also unhappy. The chairman got the message. He adjourned the meeting to prevent a vote."

"So, you backed Letitia Jordan down."

"I've been trying to stay out of her way, but she was so goddamn arrogant, I simply got pissed. I thought you should know."

"Did Duke Rodansky get involved?"

"He stayed out of it."

"Good."

"When can I tell Duke what's going on? He's pretty restless."

"Not yet. Keep him in line."

"Any progress?" Joe asked.

"The investigators are still looking for a break in the Breslow case," Scott replied. "They're not ready to make an arrest."

"What do they need?"

"A link between Letitia Jordan and the suspected killer. They're hoping for another contact. She may have a new job for him."

"Meaning?"

"I told you, Letitia Jordan is dangerous. Now that you have humiliated her, she may go after you."

"Does that make me a decoy?"

"You might call it that. If she does something stupid, we'll take advantage of it."

"You'll let this pigeon know, I hope," Joe said.

Scott laughed. "We'll let you know."

"And if there is no contact?"

"We'll go with what we have. We can indict Letitia on the other matters. The President will honor his commitment. He still intends, with your help, to form an alliance with the AMA and ultimately create a new department of health. He also intends to bring down Jonathan Ridge and the tobacco cartel. The pieces are falling into place."

"Would he commit up front to the department of health? It would strengthen my hand."

"I'll ask him. By the way, he told me to express his complete confidence in you and Kate. In other words, he likes you both, a lot."

Joe paused. "This whole thing is crazy. Why is the President so personally involved."

"That's his style," Scott replied.

❦

They finished the hamburgers and attacked chocolate ice cream and expresso. "How do you like the Häagen-Dazs?" Kate asked.

"It's the best," Joe replied.

"Fitting for the most demanding chocolaholic?"

"Absolutely."

"Good. I hope it's making you pliable. I have news, and a proposition."

Joe smiled. "Proceed, vixen."

"We received your formal invitation today to visit Dr. Kajimoto in Tokyo after the World Medical."

"Why didn't you tell me sooner?"

"I'm more persuasive at bedtime."

"Can't argue that."

"Here's the proposition. When you go to Madrid for the World Medical next month, return by way of Tokyo."

"You mean, go around the world, like Kajimoto suggested?"

"You love to travel. It would be fun."

"I suppose it would."

"Madrid, maybe Monaco, Singapore, Manila, then Tokyo and home. Wouldn't that be exciting?"

"I'd like to visit Tarawa."

"You can do that."

"Maybe I could divert to Tarawa from Manila. It would be a long, hard trip."

She poured two snifters of Courvoisier and kissed him. "I know a way to make it bearable."

"And how is that?"

"Take me with you."

❦

Letitia had called her husband on the car phone, and he had her Tanqueray waiting when she entered their condo.

"What happened?"

231

"That goddamn Hawkins got to me." She took a big swallow of the gin and appeared to be on the verge of hyperventilating.

"About the airplane?"

"About everything. The airplane was the last straw. He threatened me." She was nearly incoherent.

Luther Agostelli had on a silk dressing robe. He put his arms around Letitia and kissed her on the mouth, then began to undo her clothes.

"He declared war," Letitia said. "I know he wants to take me out."

Luther quietly finished undressing her and dropped his robe, and they stood together on the soft carpet in the great room. Letitia was trembling. She downed her gin and began to breathe more comfortably. He embraced her and kissed her again on the mouth and rubbed the small of her back with his palm. Her muscles started to relax.

"Hawkins was only baiting you," he said gently. "You can handle him any day of the week."

"There's a conspiracy. I can feel it."

"There's no conspiracy. It was a normal boardroom flareup." He walked her to the bedroom and they lay down and he held her in his arms.

"What shall I do?" she asked.

"Maybe it's time to take care of Hawkins."

"What do you mean?"

"Nothing in particular," he said.

"Don't play games. You know how that upsets me."

"I'm not playing games."

"I can trust you, can't I?"

"Of course."

"Mean it?"

"I mean it."

"I'll feel better when we make love."

[22]

IT WAS DAWN when their plane landed in Madrid. They had flown all night and the crossing was smooth, but sleep had come fitfully and they were tired. From the gate it was a long walk through a sealed corridor to the international concourse in the Barajas terminal. Luggage was spewing onto the carousel when they arrived, and they quickly found their bags and made their way through customs and to the queue of taxicabs waiting outside. The sky was overcast and the air, hot and steamy, and when they drove from the airport to the city, the empty streets were still covered with puddles from an early rain. In the gray light the pastel Spanish buildings seemed dreary and very old.

The clerk at the Hotel Melia yawned, handed them registration cards, and took their passports, saying they would be returned in the afternoon, then summoned a bellman to escort them to their rooms.

"We're on the fifth floor," Joe said.

"I wonder where the others are," Kate said.

They stepped off the elevator and came to Kate's room. "The thing to do now is crash," Joe said. "This evening we'll go for a walk, have dinner, then crash again. That should restore the circadian rhythm."

"Your place or mine?" Kate asked.

"We'd better sleep in our own rooms for now." He kissed her and patted her rump. "Right now, baby, we need sleep."

"You're right," she whispered. "Call me the minute you wake up."

The rooms were cool and the beds spacious and comfortable and they slept soundly. Late in the afternoon they awakened, showered, and dressed in loose cottons and sandals. They met in the lobby and after ascertaining that none of the AMA delegation had seen them, walked along the Gran Via to the Puerta del

233

Sol and held hands and mingled with the Madrilenos in the evening promenade. They perspired in the dank, lingering heat and found a small bar off the Puerta with a ceiling fan and swigged Spanish beer, ate tapas, and cooled down. Then it was dark, and they walked back to the Hotel Melia under the streetlamps with the dwindling promenaders and stopped to browse the quaint leathers and ceramics in the shop windows. In the café in the hotel they ordered scallops and a bottle of chilled Fino, and when they had finished eating and drinking, the tiredness again weighed on them and they returned to the welcome coolness of their rooms and slept out the night.

At noon the next day the members of the World Medical Association and their entourages gathered in the palatial ballroom of the Hotel Melia for the traditional welcoming reception. When Joe entered the crowded room, he found Kate inside the door. "That's Pierre Globa," she said, nodding toward a leathery-faced, sinewy man with thin gray hair. He was engaged in animated conversation with two black men.

They made their way across the room, and Pierre Globa immediately recognized Joe. He smiled and excused himself from the two black men. "Dr. Hawkins," he said extending his hand. "I am Pierre Globa."

"How do you do, Dr. Globa," Joe said. "This is Kate Murphy."

Pierre Globa bowed slightly. "Ah, Miss Murphy. My pleasure. I was informed that you would be in attendance to assist with our press relations." He spoke fluent English with a pleasing accent.

"How do you do, Dr. Globa," Kate said.

"I had a recent communication from an old friend, your President, David Chamberlain," Pierre Globa said. "He mentioned both of you, quite favorably."

"President Chamberlain asked me to convey his warmest personal regards, Dr. Globa," Joe said.

"How good of you."

"It's my great honor."

Pierre Globa grinned and his face wrinkled profusely. "He has become a very important man. But please, call me Pierre, and I will call you Joe and Kate."

"We would like that," Joe said.

"What are your plans for the afternoon?" Pierre Globa then asked.

"I have a busy schedule," Kate replied. "After the opening ceremonies I'm going to touch base with Dr. Jordan and Dr. Maxwell to firm up our position on South Africa. Then I've called a meeting with the PR people from the other countries to plan strategy and hammer out press releases. Then your secretary has kindly arranged a meeting with the media representatives. I understand the South Africans are quite distraught. It appears they intend to make a cause célèbre of their situation. I hope that whatever they do, we can spin it into something positive—close ranks for the greater good, that sort of thing."

"You have your hands full," Pierre Globa said.

"I'm also going to the opening ceremonies," Joe said. "No special plans after that, except to touch base with our delegation."

Pierre Globa then asked, "Can the two of you join me for a quiet dinner this evening after things have settled down? I know a nice place where we can dine leisurely and talk for as long as we desire."

"I would be delighted," Joe said.

"I'd love to," Kate said, "provided I'm clear with Dr. Jordan."

"Good. Let us meet in the lobby at eight. My wife, Françoise, will accompany me."

"Splendid," Joe said.

Pierre Globa glanced across the room at the two black men waiting for him. They seemed impatient. "I must get back to our South African colleagues. I'm afraid they want to do something stupid."

Joe nodded. "See you at eight."

As Pierre Globa walked away, Kate said, "He exudes charisma."

"That he does."

"Incidentally, Françoise Globa is the woman talking to Letitia and her husband, and the Maxwells."

"She's very beautiful," Joe said.

"They've been watching us. We'd better get over there."

"Do you suppose Letitia knows we're lovers?"

"No way," Kate replied.

"She sees us together."

"That's true, but we've been discreet. I spend time with all the AMA officers. Besides, she expects me to keep an eye on you."

"That's one thing. Sleeping together is quite another."

"We'll be careful, at least until they're gone."

"If she finds out, it'll be trouble for you."

"So what?" Kate answered.

❦

"I recommend the sea bass," Pierre Globa announced.

He had taken them to Zalacaine, nestled in an old villa in Madrid. The waiter had recited the fresh catch for the evening, sea bass and monkfish.

"And a good wine from the Marques de Murrieta Bordega, perhaps a Blanco Ygay," Pierre Globa continued. He looked at the waiter.

"Blanco Ygay," the waiter repeated.

"Excellent. And a simple salad—romaine, tomato, a few Spanish shrimp for body, sweet vinegar?"

"Please order for me," Joe said.

"And for me," Kate said.

"And me," Françoise echoed. "That happens anyway when one dines with Pierre." Her smooth white skin seemed ageless.

Pierre Globa seemed delighted. He instructed the waiter and turned to Kate. "I'm so glad you found it possible to dine with us."

"Thank you," she replied, smiling. "Dr. Jordan was pleased that we could become better acquainted."

"Did you accomplish your mission this afternoon?" Pierre Globa asked. "It sounded complicated."

"I think so. It rather depends on what the black South African countries decide to do. At the moment they're being coy with us."

"Perhaps they don't know what to do," Pierre Globa said. "Perhaps they've come to realize the consequences of walking out."

"That's entirely possible," Kate said. "In any event, I pulled together a meeting with my counterparts from England, Australia, France, Germany, Japan, Spain, Portugal, Brazil, the Philippines, Belgium, Italy—practically everyone. We drafted media material in various languages to cover every contingency. Then I personally contacted the media reps here in Madrid. They plan to cover the session with television when the vote is taken tomorrow afternoon, and they hope to interview key people to get reaction. That of course includes you two gentlemen. I'll have a briefing packet for you by noon tomorrow. I'll also have wire service stories ready to go, various languages of course."

"Very good," Pierre Globa said, admiringly. "Do you like working for Letitia Jordan?"

"I have a wonderful job."

"A discreet answer."

"I try to be discreet."

"I am told it was your idea for Joe Hawkins to make that dramatic speech in Madison Square Garden with no audience."

"Yes, sir."

"It made a great impression on David Chamberlain," Pierre Globa said. "He would trade ten of his staff for one like you."

"Dr. Hawkins delivered the speech," Kate said. "He deserves the credit."

"Ah, but David knows it was your idea. He likes daring ideas."

"David Chamberlain is a man of daring himself," Kate said.

"I can see why Letitia Jordan is so high on you. She told me how you started with the AMA as an intern, and she came to hire you when your predecessor resigned. You are young for such an important job, but evidently your age is of no consequence. Letitia says you have proven yourself many times over."

"You're most gracious," Kate replied. "Dr. Jordan has given me a wonderful opportunity. It also helps that I love my job."

"You are a beautiful woman. Your eyes of blue are most fetching. And you are definitely, shall I say, of healthy stock."

"He means," Françoise said, "that you have a beautiful body. Pierre has an eye for female bodies."

Kate flushed deeply.

237

"Please don't be embarrassed," Pierre Globa said. "When a woman is beautiful, she should rejoice in her beauty. Everyone should rejoice in her beauty."

"Thank you," Kate said simply.

"Now, I am anxious to hear about my old friend, David Chamberlain?"

"Kate and I met with him last November," Joe said. "He looked well. We've seen him many times on television. He seems to be on top of things."

"Is he a popular President?"

"A very popular President."

"That is good. I knew him many years ago. He was a young lawyer then with your CIA in Geneva. We were comrades. A fine young man he was. I am not surprised that he became your President. I am glad he is my friend. I would not want him for an enemy."

"He said he misses the good times, and that you might tell us about them," Joe said.

"Yes," Pierre Globa replied contentedly. "We had some very good times."

The waiter brought two bottles of Blanco Ygay in a chrome bucket of ice, drew the cork of one, and poured a splash for tasting. "Excellent," Pierre Globa announced after sniffing the cork and sipping the almond-colored wine. The waiter filled their glasses and they drank. The wine was drier than the Fino in the hotel, and Joe liked the delicate, oak-tinged bouquet.

"I was what you Americans call a retread," Pierre Globa said. "It was twenty years after the war that I met David Chamberlain. I had become a physician and owned a hospital in Geneva. Another war was going on then, a different war, with the Communists. Because of my experience in the underground, your government thought I would be useful. David was my contact. My duties were to listen and report and occasionally perform a special assignment. We were comrades for five years. Those were the good times."

"Pierre is modest," Françoise said. "His work for the CIA was like his years in the underground."

"An exaggeration, my dear. What I did for the CIA was not dangerous."

"Sometimes it was."

"Sometimes, but not often. I knew many people and heard many things. I reported what I heard to David, that's all. The CIA works like that. Bits of information are collected from thousands of sources all over the world and transmitted to Washington. Now and then an important pattern develops. The collectors know only the meaningless bits they collect, never the complete picture. It's very unromantic.

"I lived in Geneva and had many friends in France. David and I visited France together—Lyon, Beaulieu, St. Tropez. Once, in Beaulieu, we got very drunk in the bar at La Réserve. It was after an assignment. We were drunk for three days. That was one of the good times."

"I've not been to Lyon," Joe said. "I've been to Beaulieu, however, and dined at La Réserve. It was wonderful."

"It is always wonderful," Pierre Globa said.

"I've been to Nice and Cannes, and I've stayed on Le Cap d'Antibes," Joe said. "I like to walk the streets of St. Tropez. It's beautiful there. All of the Côte d'Azur is beautiful."

"Ah, we have much in common."

"It is rumored that Pierre killed a Communist agent in France," Françoise said. "Perhaps that was when he got drunk with David Chamberlain."

"Always, there are rumors," Pierre Globa said.

Françoise looked at him, and her eyes brightened affectionately. "He does not deny it."

Pierre Globa smiled wisely. "Many things happen," he said. "This part of the world is peaceful now. I am old and rich and a little tired. I don't worry about things as I used to." He looked at Joe. "You were a marine officer, wounded in Vietnam, awarded the Silver Star. Now you are a fine surgeon with three young children. Your wife died last year in an automobile accident. Your father was a marine officer killed fighting Japs in the battle of Tarawa. He was a great hero awarded the Congressional Medal of Honor. Even in the underground in France, I heard about

Tarawa. I wonder how many people know today what happened a half-century ago on Tarawa."

"You are well informed," Joe said. "I plan to travel from Madrid to Tarawa, then on to Tokyo. All I have of my father are his medals and some letters and pictures, a few personal things, and my mother's wonderful memories. I've never been to Tarawa. Colonel Shoup, my father's commanding officer, wrote my mother and sent a map. My father died next to a pier on an island named Betio. I know the exact spot."

Pierre Globa spoke softly. "I understand. I return to Lyon from time to time, to the wall where friends died. It's the least one can do."

The waiter arrived with heaping salads of romaine and tomato and huge Spanish shrimp, a cruet of red vinegar, and a basket of hot bread. "I like a simple salad and good bread," Pierre Globa said.

"Fortunately we all like what Pierre likes," Françoise teased.

Pierre Globa ignored her. "It's a long way from Madrid to the Pacific," he said.

"Indeed it is," Joe replied. "Dr. Kajimoto invited me to Tokyo. I plan to go around the world. From here I fly to Nice, Singapore, Manila—near Vietnam, but not to stop—then the island hopper to Tarawa. After Tarawa, north to Tokyo, then home."

"That is an ambitious journey," Pierre Globa said.

"It will be an adventure," Joe said. "Something I've always wanted to do."

"Will you feel uncomfortable, visiting Kajimoto?"

"Perhaps."

"Because you think of him as a Jap?"

"Not exactly. He fought on Tarawa. He was an imperial marine, and he actually fought my father. He says my father spared his life, and that he owes me a debt of honor. I may be uncomfortable about that."

"I know the story," Pierre Globa said. "Kajimoto recently informed me. He said he had spoken to you on two occasions. He holds you in very high regard."

"Do you know of his relationship with the Tora Society?" Joe inquired.

Pierre Globa thought for a moment, then answered, "Only that he is a Tora by birthright, and that he is very powerful and can be ruthless. I do not fully understand his connection with the Tora Society."

"Nor do I," Joe said.

"I believe you will like Kajimoto. I met him in Switzerland some fifteen years ago when David Chamberlain and I were working for the CIA." He chuckled softly. "We called him Doc Kajimoto. He helped us perform a difficult task, and we became friends. Before his health failed he attended World Medical meetings and made significant contributions. He has the way of a wise man. He makes you forget unpleasant past events."

The waiter came with platters of sea bass. "One can find better sea bass along the Côte d'Azur, or in Geneva where I live, for that matter," Pierre Globa said, "but in Spain it is quite acceptable, and much better than monkfish."

"It's excellent," Kate said, tasting the succulent meat. "I'm glad you ordered for us."

"Merci," Pierre Globa said.

"David told me of your meeting in California. He hoped that you and I would talk in Madrid. He thinks you will make a fine president for the AMA, that you are a much better leader than Letitia Jordan. Of course, you know David Chamberlain does not like Letitia Jordan."

"Yes," Joe said. "He made that quite clear."

"Did David mention his son?" Pierre Globa asked.

"He said he lost a son years ago," Joe replied.

"Nothing more," Kate added.

"I will tell you about his son. It will help you understand your President."

"We would like that," Joe said.

"Would you care for some raspberries and cognac?" Pierre Globa inquired.

"Of course," Françoise replied, smiling.

"I prefer Martell, but it is not available," Pierre Globa said. "However, they have Cognac Bouron, very good." He instructed the waiter.

"We are in your hands," Joe said.

"David's son was named Bryce," Pierre Globa began. "He was a vigorous, energetic, bright young man. When Bryce graduated from law school, like David, he worked for one of your state attorneys. Then he was accepted by the CIA and assigned to Geneva. David was a senator. When Bryce came to Geneva, David asked me to look after him. It hardly seemed necessary. On occasion we invited Bryce for dinner. He seemed very happy and in no need of looking after.

"A year passed, then I was informed that Bryce had been discovered engaging in a homosexual act with a young man from the Russian embassy. I was shocked. I tried to contact Bryce. He was under house arrest in CIA headquarters and incommunicado. I called David. He had not been notified and, of course, was devastated. He had no inkling that Bryce was homosexual and was certain it was a mistake.

"David tried to contact Bryce. Though David was a United States senator, they would not let him talk to his son. David appealed to Jonathan Ridge. Senator Ridge was chairman of the committee responsible for the CIA. Admiral Busey, director of the CIA, reported to Senator Ridge. David was convinced that Bryce was innocent. He pled with Senator Ridge to have Admiral Busey release Bryce to David's personal custody. Senator Ridge refused. He told David that Bryce was a homosexual and a security risk and must be dealt with severely. He would not even let David communicate with his son. Senator Ridge demeaned Bryce. David was hurt and became very angry."

"Were you connected with the CIA then?" Joe asked.

"No. My information came from friends. Admiral Busey was outraged when he found that I had learned about Bryce and called David, but he could not identify my sources. Of course Admiral Busey was a peacetime admiral and incapable of understanding the camaraderie that exists between old warriors."

"There was nothing you could do?" Joe asked.

"Nothing. David immediately flew to Geneva. He stayed in my home. We continued our efforts to contact Bryce, without success. A week passed. We learned nothing. David became extremely agitated. One evening, as we dined, Admiral Busey called. Bryce had committed suicide."

"My God!" Joe whispered.

"I had endured some difficult times with my friend, who is now your President, but that was the worst. We both cried like babies."

"What happened?" Joe asked.

"We were told only that Bryce had hanged himself. They said the matter was classified and refused to tell us more. Although David was a United States senator, he was never told if his son was a homosexual, or a traitor. He was given only his dead body to take home."

"That's unbelievable," Joe said.

"Not until David Chamberlain was elected President did he find the truth. He ordered the new director of the CIA—Admiral Busey was dead by then—to show him the complete file on Bryce.

"A hotel maid was said to have found Bryce engaging in sodomy with the young Russian. She reported the incident, and Bryce was immediately placed in solitary confinement in CIA headquarters and allowed to see no one other than his detainers. They interrogated him for seven days, accusing him of sodomy and treason. He steadfastly denied the charges. He asked for his father and was told the senator had renounced him. This of course was a lie. The file indicated that he became increasingly depressed, which the interrogators described as, 'approaching the breaking point,' and a sign that he would 'soon tell the truth.' On the eighth day he was described as 'severely depressed,' 'almost ready to talk,' and 'responding satisfactorily to interrogation.' It was a very hard interrogation. Finally, he leaned his cot on end against the wall and hung himself with a trouser leg. He made a poor job of it and strangled to death slowly. Bryce died thinking his father had forsaken him. He did not know that David had come to Geneva to help."

"That's a horror story," Joe said.

"The maid died mysteriously two weeks after the incident. The Russian was never seen again. The investigation revealed no evidence of breach of security. The CIA eventually concluded that the affair was staged by the Russians to embarrass the United States. In your parlance, Bryce was framed. The plan failed when he died. Bryce was not homosexual. He was certainly not a traitor. Jonathan Ridge explained none of this to David. He offered neither sympathy nor apology. David was unaware of the conclusions until he saw the file, ten years later."

"I didn't know things like this happened," Joe said.

"Bryce was a victim of gestapo tactics," Pierre Globa replied. "His death was an avoidable tragedy. The matter is not finished, of course. David Chamberlain holds undying hatred for Jonathan Ridge. Take my word, it is not good to have David for your enemy. No, the matter is not finished. Ultimately David Chamberlain will destroy Jonathan Ridge. He would prefer to kill him with his bare hands."

"The President told us of his dislike for Senator Ridge. We assumed it was a political matter."

"You believed it was the tobacco affair," Pierre Globa said.

"Yes, the tobacco affair."

"David is sincere about the tobacco affair."

"He is very persuasive," Joe said.

"Why was the story about Bryce never disclosed?" Kate asked.

"It was announced that Bryce died of pneumonia," Pierre Globa replied. "And the matter was forgotten. The CIA has that power. You must keep the secret. It would hurt your President to reveal it."

"We will keep the secret."

Pierre Globa seemed content and leaned back in his chair. "Tell me," he said, "what is happening these days to our great medical profession?"

It was midnight when they returned to the Melia Madrid, and Joe and Kate said goodnight to Pierre Globa and Françoise. "I'll stay with you tonight," Joe said upon getting off the elevator. "That goddamn Letitia might have one of her paranoid fits in the middle of the night and decide to call you." Kate unlocked her door and they entered. The maid had turned on a small bedside lamp, fluffed the bed, and left a chocolate mint on each pillow. "I wonder who she thinks I'm sleeping with."

Joe sank into the settee. "This room is big enough to be a suite."

"It's a wonderful old hotel. Big rooms, high ceilings. Charm and elegance. Would you like another cognac?"

"If you join me."

Kate found two miniatures of Courvoisier in the minibar, then sat next to Joe and slipped off her shoes. They touched glasses and tasted the Courvoisier, which seemed very strong.

"Well, what do you think?" she asked.

"I feel the cognac already."

"About the President's son."

"I'm shocked," Joe said.

"Me too."

"You heard none of it before tonight?"

"Only what the President told us in California," Kate replied.

"I'm getting the drift. This is a vendetta. The President is using us to get Jonathan Ridge. That stuff about Letitia and the AMA is the means to the end." Joe leaned his head against the back of the chair. "He's using us . . . God! He's using us, and I'm tired."

"I don't know what to think," Kate said. Maybe tomorrow it'll make sense. Anyway, I feel grubby. Let's take a shower and go to bed."

She rose and began to disrobe. Joe watched admiringly as she removed her dress and hung it neatly in the closet, then slipped off her underthings and dropped them into a laundry basket. Her skin was smooth and tan except for the triangular white patches where a scanty swimsuit had covered her nipples and bits of her bottom and belly when she sunbathed. In the mellow light of the bedside lamp, her body appeared flawless. She seemed unmindful of his presence and when she was naked, swished indecently past him into the bathroom. He heard sounds of her brushing her teeth and then the blast of shower water, and in a moment she appeared at the bathroom door with a towel around her waist, still brushing her teeth.

"The shower is wonderful. Big jets of hot water." Her breasts jiggled invitingly above the towel as she brushed.

"Great."

"I have a spare toothbrush and a razor."

"You think of everything."

"I want you naked, now."

"Patience, woman."

"I'm getting in the shower." She disappeared.

Joe undressed and entered the bathroom. It was steamy, and the mirrors had fogged. Kate stuck her wet head out the shower door and pointed to a toothbrush and a tube of Colgate on the sink.

He brushed his teeth and watched the movements of her body through the frosted glass of the shower door as she bathed. He rinsed out the Colgate, opened the shower door, plunged into the pounding hot water alongside her, and they embraced. Her skin was flushed and hot from the shower, and she turned her face up and kissed him firmly on the mouth. Then she kissed him again and plunged her tongue through his lips.

She soaped his face with a bar of castile and handed him a safety razor. Obediently he shaved his whisker shadow with short strokes under the shower. She soaped his back, buttocks, and thighs and leaned him over and soaped between his buttocks and spread them to let the streaming water wash the soap away. She soaped his armpits, chest, belly, his legs, and his genitals, leaving ringlets of matted hair in the layers of lather. She stood on her tiptoes and shampooed his hair with the castile, then held his face in her hands and pressed against him and again kissed deep into his mouth. The torrent of hot water cascaded over their heads and washed the soap and lather off their locked bodies and down their legs, and the thick suds floated to the drain in the white tile floor of the shower.

"I have an erection," he murmured.

"That was the general idea."

"It's a sin to waste a perfectly good erection."

"I have no intention of wasting it."

She turned off the water and they stood in the shower stall and buffed each other with the Melia's giant turkish towels until the skin glowed. She playfully draped her towel over his erect penis, then they went to the bed and stretched out on the cool, cotton sheets. His freshly shaved face was smooth against her cheeks, and she smelled the fresh scent of castile and lightly stroked the terrible scar on his thigh. They made love, slowly, deliciously.

Then Joe held Kate in his arms. It was minutes before he spoke. "Do you suppose Pierre knows more about Kajimoto and the Toras than he let on?"

"I have no idea."

"Do you suppose he knows we're lovers?"

"Probably. Will he tell Letitia?"

"I really don't give a damn," Joe said.

"You don't care if I get fired?"

"Something like that. Don't worry. Pierre won't tell. Neither will Françoise. She understands."

"I've never been fired," Kate said.

"Pierre was anxious to talk about Bryce Chamberlain. He must have been instructed by the President."

"Why didn't the President tell us himself?"

"Too painful," Joe said. "That's why he asked his old comrade to tell us."

"Do you think he's using us?"

"Yes, but I think he means to keep his commitments."

"I have no doubt about that," Kate said.

"He can make a powerful political move and nail Jonathan Ridge at the same time."

"I feel like I'm in over my head."

"You're a delicious lady. I love you."

"And I love you."

"Will the fucking South Africans walk out tomorrow? Does anybody care?"

"If they do, I'm ready for them."

[23]

O N SUNDAY AFTERNOON Joe and Kate went to the Plaza
de Las Ventas in Madrid to see the bullfights. They purchased seat
cushions and cold beer from a vendor on the crowded ramp
inside the plaza and a program with color photographs of bulls
and bullfighters. Their seats were in the very first row on the
shaded side of the bullring, and they were fortunate to have them,
for thousands of people had come to the bullfights that day and
many had to stand where the ramps entered the arena. Some had
to stand in the sun and the sun was very hot.

The bullring in the Plaza de Las Ventas is a great circle of spot-
less, beach-white sand enclosed by the *barrera*, a sturdy, plank
fence, shoulder high, painted red with a yellow stripe rimming the
top and the bottom. Separating the *barrera* from the wall
guarding the spectator seats is a narrow runway, the *callejon*.
Bullfighters stand in the *callejon* while waiting to enter the ring,
and the lucky people in the first row are very close, can talk to the
bullfighters and shake their hands, and smell the sweat and the
bulls.

"What did these seats cost?" asked Kate.

"I don't know," Joe replied. "Pierre got them."

"They're good seats."

"The best."

"I'm plenty close enough," she said, nervously.

Joe laughed. "You're quite safe. I understand bulls rarely jump
into the seats."

"Very comforting."

"Spring is the time of the San Isidro Festival," Joe said, "the
beginning of the season, a time to see good bullfights. The bulls
are better fed, and the matadors are fresh and still unhurt and will
try to be extra heroic so they can win fat contracts for later in the
year. Fuentes is fighting today. He is highly regarded for his
capework."

Whistles came from the crowd. "They're a minute late starting," Joe explained. "Bullfight crowds are very impatient." Then trumpets sounded and the crowd cheered. A gate across the ring swung open and a pair of richly costumed riders on white horses rode majestically forward and lifted their hats to the *Presidente* in his box high above the ring. The *Presidente* signaled to begin the fights, and the riders retired to the gate. The trumpets sounded again, and the crowd cheered, and the riders reappeared, followed by the bullfighters who paraded across the ring single file, in three columns, while the band, composed mainly of trumpets, blasted the stadium with bullfight music.

"The grand entrance is the *paseo*. The guys out front are the matadors. Fuentes is on your left. The ranking matador always enters in that position. The guys behind the matador are his *cuadrilla*. The first three are *banderilleros* and the last two are *picadores*. All are *toreros*. Anyone who participates in the ring is a *torero*. In Spain it's a great thing to be a *torero*."

The *toreros* wore skin-tight costumes of brightly colored silk and gold brocade and little boat-shaped black hats. Several had a pigtail. The matadors were the most elegantly dressed and carried heavy parade capes of red silk and jewel and gold brocade.

"Look how they strut," Joe said.

"The costumes are beautiful," Kate said.

When the processional had crossed the ring, the two riders cantered their horses back to the gate and disappeared, and the *toreros* entered the *callejon* and prepared for the fights. The matadors spread their parade capes over the wall in front of the seats and began stretching their muscles and searching for pretty girls, and the crowd settled and became expectant.

Fuentes would fight the first bull. He stood a scant twenty yards away from Joe and Kate, his arms folded on the top plank of the *barrera*, and gazed soberly across the ring at the gate where the bulls would enter. He was flat-bellied and long-legged and costumed in crimson. He had doffed his hat, revealing dark hair slicked back and fastened with a cloth button at the nape of the neck. He turned to the crowd—his face thin, handsome, bronze, and perhaps a little sad.

Attendants hurriedly raked the sand to smooth the tracks of the processional, then disappeared. It was momentarily quiet, and the ring was empty but for two *banderilleros* stationed with their capes at opposite sides.

"The *banderilleros'* job is to run the bull around the ring and get him to hook at the cape to show which horn he favors," Joe said. "They drag the cape and make the bull chase it, but they never pass the bull with the cape because he might get wise and be spoiled for the matador."

The trumpets sounded, prompting a loud cheer from the crowd, and the gate opened. The first bull trotted smartly into the ring.

"My God! He's ferocious," whispered Kate in wonderment.

The bull was a black Miura, a breed known to bullfighters as killer bulls, with polished horns and a massive head and shoulders and grotesquely trim in the haunch. One of the *banderilleros* advanced and shook his cape to get the bull's attention, and the bull promptly charged. The *banderillero* retreated, zigzagging across the sand, dragging the cape, and the bull came full speed. At the last moment the *banderillero* broke and scrambled to safety behind one of the *burladeros*, shields of thick wood mounted around the inside of the *barrera*, and wide enough for three men. The bull caromed off the heavy planks and slowed to a trot, boiling mad, looking for a fight. He spotted the bullfighters behind the *barrera* near Fuentes and made for them. The other *banderillero* shouted and swirled his cape, vainly trying to draw him away, but the Miura was unswerving. He rammed the thick wall at full speed, split a huge splinter off the top, and tumbled over the top on his back, thrashing and snorting, legs kicking in the air like a giant bug.

The bullfighters in the *callejon* wanted no part of a half-ton, enraged black Miura and fled. He had landed at the feet of Joe and Kate, close enough for them to smell him and hear him snort and see the foam bubbling in his nostrils. His great shoulders filled the corridor, and Kate clutched Joe's arm with both hands and held on.

The bull struggled to his feet then ran amuck in the narrow

passageway, hooking at the capes and paraphernalia, smashing the water cooler, and the bullfighters bolted and hopped over the *barrera* into the ring like a gaggle of puppets. It was comical to watch, but anyone caught by the bull would surely be trampled and gored to death.

A *banderillero* opened a gate and shunted the bull back into the ring, and the bullfighters then hopped the fence again. The crowd hooted and whistled contemptuously, and the bull, with nothing in sight to charge, trotted briskly across the sand and considered his next move.

"Jesus Christ!" Joe cried. "How's that for starters?"

"He was in my lap," Kate said.

"He'll be a good bull if he doesn't kill himself. He's fearless."

Meanwhile Fuentes stayed clear of the melee and calmly studied the bull to see how he ran. When the bull came back in the ring, Fuentes signaled the other *banderillero* who shouted and waved his cape, and the bull wheeled and again charged. Like his comrade, this *banderillero* ran ahead of the bull, zigzagging and dragging the cape to make the bull drop his head and give Fuentes a good look at his charateristics—which horn he favored and how he would charge and if he could see with both eyes. The *banderillero* was fast, but the bull was faster and soon had the man sprinting for his life to the nearest *burladero*. This time the bull pulled up short, having learned about planks of strong wood, and surveyed the empty ring.

When the crowd grew quiet, Fuentes stepped out with his fighting cape.

"Look at Fuentes," Joe said. "He's pleased. This is a brave bull—a clean, straight charger, no tendency to cut for the man, a decent horn span, determined. Fuentes will probably work him alone. That's his prerogative."

All eyes riveted on Fuentes. He reared back and tucked in his chin and the sad face hardened. He unfurled the cape and moved catlike toward the bull, who eyed him from across the ring. Fuentes stopped. The bull, now twenty yards away, stared. Fuentes shook the cape, and the bull glowered and pawed the sand. Fuentes took three quick steps, stopped, shook the cape, shook the cape again, and stomped his foot. The bull charged. Fuentes stood firm and spread the cape to his side, and the bull thundered in—straight, head down—and Fuentes, an unflinching ramrod, passed the bull with a graceful, flowing *verónica* that drew the first appreciative *olé* from the crowd.

The bull turned and Fuentes shook the cape. The bull charged and Fuentes passed him with another *verónica*, and another, and another. This was truly a great bull. Fuentes took him across the ring with *verónicas*, drawing him always closer, shifting from side to side. He led the bull into the sun, swirled the cape in a stunning *mariposa*, the butterfly wing, amidst thunderous *olés*, and the crowd stood and cheered. On the final pass Fuentes reversed so abruptly that the bull fell to his knees and Fuentes turned his back in triumph—the great animal subdued and breathless—and strutted away. Fuentes raised a hand to the delirious crowd, grateful witness to the match of a brilliant matador with generations of noble bull breeding.

The trumpets signaled and Joe explained: "The *picador* carries a spear called the *pic*. It has a steel lance mounted on the business end. He rides a horse so he can get on top of the bull when he charges and drive the lance into the heavy muscle hump behind the neck. It has a collar flange to keep it from penetrating too deep. The idea is to chew up the neck muscles but avoid internal injury. Properly done, picing makes the bull drop his head and takes the quickness out of his horns.

"The horses are worthless old nags. They're blindfolded and wear a heavy pad on the side turned to the bull. In the old days horses didn't wear pads, and they always got killed. Public sentiment stopped that. Still, horses have the worst of it. They seldom survive more than one or two bulls. They get knocked around pretty bad. Sometimes the horse breaks a leg. Sometimes the bull gets under the pad and gores the horse and disembowels him on the sand."

"Ugh," Kate grunted in disgust.

"See the steel boot the *picador* wears on the leg nearest the bull? That's his only protection. *Picadores* are seldom seriously hurt because if they get in trouble, tne matadors draw the bulls away. But they get knocked around a lot.

"There are two *picadores*. Each will try to pic the bull two, maybe three times. If they do a bad job they can overdamage the muscle or maybe stab the chest or the spine and spoil the bull. The matador watches pretty closely. He'll stop the picing if it gets out of hand. A *picador* must never spoil a good bull."

The first *picador* entered the ring and stationed his horse close to the fence, and the *banderilleros* led the bull to him with their capes. The *picador* spurred the horse to take a step, which provoked the bull. The bull charged, and the *picador* buried the lance in the muscle hump and churned it to morcellate the fibers. The infuriated bull dug his horns into the pad under the horse and nearly upset him, then the *banderilleros* darted in and drew the bull away.

When the *picador* was ready, they let the bull attack again and the *picador* made good stabs into the muscle hump, which was now bleeding profusely, but the bull upended the hapless horse and dumped the *picador* on the sand. The determined bull, oblivious to Fuentes and the *banderilleros* who frantically tried to draw him off, rooted his horns under the pad and brutally ripped the horse's belly. The horse screamed and blood gushed out the belly wound onto the sand, which meant the aorta had been punctured and the horse would quickly bleed to death. The *picador* fought to get free, and Fuentes finally maneuvered the bull away with some risky cape work that drew *olés* and cheers. When the bull was out of range, the *picador* extricated himself and appeared unhurt. The poor horse was bled out by then, and a team of attendants dragged his carcass away with a team of mules. Then they shoveled up the bloody sand and raked the surface smooth again while the bull was diverted by the *banderilleros*.

Kate could only say, "That was terrible."

The bull could have stood more of the pic, but Fuentes signaled to stop and the crowd applauded, for they wanted this fine bull to be at his best for the kill. The trumpets sounded for the *banderillas*.

"The *banderilla* is a two-foot stick with a barbed steel point on one end," Joe said. "It's wrapped in colored paper with ruffles. 'Placing the *banderillas*' means sticking them in pairs in the muscle hump where the pics were stuck. The barbs hold them in the muscle hump, and they flounce around and irritate the bull and wear him down for his final scene with the matador. Three pairs are placed. This is a job for the *banderilleros*. (Don't confuse *banderilla* with *banderillero*.) Sometimes the matador, if he is good with *banderillas*, and the bull is good, will place a pair to demonstrate his superior skill. The placing of *banderillas* is tricky business. It's the favorite thing of many aficionados."

The first *banderillero* entered the ring and began stalking the bull with a catlike strut. His arms stretched out and each hand gripped the blunt end of a *banderilla* with the steel tip pointed at the bull. The bull watched warily from across the ring, not as menacing as when he was fresh, and the *banderillero* crept closer with little stutter steps until the bull decided to charge. The *banderillero* raised his arms and ran to meet the bull. When the bull tried to hook him, the *banderillero* danced nimbly in front of the horns, seemed to glide as he reached in, his belly millimeters from disaster, and drove the pair of *banderillas* down firmly into the center of the muscle hump. The bull, tormented by the sting of the steel barbs, pranced and tossed his head trying vainly to shake them off. But they were elegantly placed and held fast as the *banderillero* spun nimbly away. The crowd cheered both man and bull, for it was a classic and daring placement.

"It takes a quick, flat-bellied guy to do that without taking a horn in the gut," Joe said. "Even then he has to suck it to the backbone."

The second *banderillero* entered and began to stalk. He was shorter than the first, bandy-legged and funny, and looked as if he would never make it over the bull's horns. The bull watched, then charged, and the bandy-legged *banderillero* soared incredibly and found the mark and escaped. The crowd cheered. This first bull of the afternoon was becoming a feast.

Fuentes decided to place the third pair of *banderillas* himself. The crowd egged him to surpass his underlings, and he did not disappoint them. Few bullfighters can stalk more suspensefully than Fuentes, and the crowd watched in awesome silence. When the bull charged and Fuentes met him in the sun, the long, pencil-thin legs of the matador lofted the razor-thin body to an impossible height and the *banderillas* descended in a flashing arc to bite squarely into the thickest part of the muscle. There was an instant of silence, of disbelief, then hysterical cheering, and Fuentes haughtily turned his back on the bull and strutted away.

The trumpets signaled. "Last act, coming up," Joe said. "The *faena*. Now the matador goes it alone."

Suddenly the ring was empty but for the bleeding bull standing near the center, and wary, with a cluster of *banderillas* dangling from his shoulders. Fuentes returned carrying his hat, a little red cape, and the killing sword. He stood for a moment like a ramrod, tragic, feet together, the hat raised in salute to the crowd. He turned, dedicating the bull to all, then tossed the hat over the *barrera* and prepared for the kill.

"The little red cape is a *muleta*," Joe explained. "It's fastened to a stick so he can hold it away from his body."

Fuentes approached the bull with the *muleta* in one hand and the sword in the other. He stopped, shook the *muleta*, and stepped forward. The bull waited. His breathing was labored now, the nostrils were flaring, and he seemed tired. The bull hesitated, then charged. Fuentes stood like a sapling bowed in the wind and led him with the *muleta*, holding it low to drop the head and lifting it at the last second as he rumbled past, trying to hook the fluttering cloth. The bull turned and Fuentes led him again, closer, and again, still closer, and after a series of passes, each more daring and followed by thunderous cries of *olé*, Fuentes turned his back and strutted away. In a moment he returned for more passes—right, left, in front, behind, so close the shoulders of the bull smeared blood on his costume. Fuentes then dropped for the knee passes—the *rodillas*, the most danger-ous of all—and mesmerized the bull. Still on his knees, he turned his back, and the crowd exploded in frenzy and the trumpets blew in tribute.

"This is it," Joe said. The bull is ready for the kill. He's tired but still very dangerous. Knowing when to kill is part of the art of bullfighting. When he has a fine bull, the matador is tempted to work him and show off, but the bull can be driven to exhaustion and spoiled. Sometimes a matador who is afraid will try to run the bull down to make him easy to kill. This never fools aficionados. The kill should come when the bull still has the strength and will to test the matador."

Fuentes stalked the bull head-on, holding the *muleta* to the side. He enticed another short pass, and another, then held the *muleta* low in front of the frustrated bull to bring the head down. Fuentes sighted with the sword. Neither man nor animal moved. It was the classic "moment of truth." Then Fuentes moved in and the bull lunged at the *muleta*. At precisely the right instant Fuentes leaped over the horns and drove the sword to its hilt between the shoulder blades. The thrust was so quick it was almost impossible to follow.

The great black Miura staggered and turned and stared at his tormentor, who faced him waiting to be certain the sword had found a fatal mark. The *banderilleros* ran into the ring, but Fuentes waved them back. In seconds the legs of the bull turned wobbly and blood streamed from the mouth. The gallant bull staggered and fought death with all his heart, then majestically sat down and rolled on his side and lay still on the blood-soaked sand.

The crowd cheered deliriously, and the *Presidente* promptly awarded Fuentes both ears and the tail. Fuentes smiled and no longer looked sad. He walked around the ring and the people tossed hats, furs, purses, and bouquets of flowers.

"A magnificent kill," Joe said. "One in a hundred. You saw the very best in your very first fight."

Kate had watched, speechless, spellbound. "That was awesome," she said through clenched teeth. She held tightly to Joe's arm, put her lips to his ear and whispered, "I want you, now."

"We have five bulls to go."

"I can't wait."

"You must wait."

The remainder of the *corrida* was fairly routine. The second matador earned one ear from each of his bulls, and Fuentes fought well enough with his other bull to earn both ears. But the matador Guerra, who once was great and now had a fat belly and was afraid, lost the *muleta* on the horns of his second bull, a very bad bull, and took six tries to make the kill. He dropped the sword on one try and all-in-all looked silly. The crowd whistled and peppered him with seat cushions, fruit, and beer bottles. It wasn't entirely his fault because matadors past prime are mainly program fillers and never draw good bulls. Poor Guerra was stoic. He had suffered many gorings and in his declining years preferred ignominy to death on the horns.

It was dusk and a light rain was falling when they returned to the Melia Madrid. They walked to a small café down the street and sat at a table with a candle and ordered beer and Ropa Vieja. The waiter offered a plate of crackers and a thick wedge of cheese with the beer. He told them, in fair English, that the cheese was Queso Cabrales, the best of Spanish blue and a great delicacy.

Kate drank long of the beer. "I was thirsty," she explained.

"It was hot out there," Joe replied. He studied the catch-light of candle flame in her eyes.

"Do you think he's spoofing about the cheese?"

"Probably."

"It is good, and I'm not a blue-cheese fan."

"I'm glad you have an appetite," Joe said. "I thought the bullfight might disturb you."

"The horse killing did."

"That's understandable. It disturbs me too."

"After the first bull, I wanted you."

Joe smiled and leaned over and kissed her.

"It really was intoxicating."

"Yes, it really was."

When the waiter brought the Ropa Vieja in big bowls, they ordered more beer and ate hungrily and finished with lime ice and expresso.

Kate sucked on a spoonful of lime ice. "I'm glad the meeting is over. The Africans were a hassle, weren't they?"

"They sure as hell walked out," Joe said.

"Even Pierre couldn't talk them out of it."

"You handled it magnificently," Joe said. "The television coverage, the press releases, the interviews, were coordinated and persuasive. You succeeded admirably in blunting the inflammatory rhetoric."

"You're sweet to say that," Kate replied. "However, we also got lucky. It turned out the agitators were a relatively small but vocal dissident group. Their allies backed off when it became apparent they were losing the public relations battle. The concept of closing ranks for the greater good worked out well."

"Still, you orchestrated the whole thing. It was a difficult task, and you handled it well. You are a fantastic young woman. I truly admire you, and I love you."

Kate touched his hand and smiled happily.

"I enjoyed the banquet," Joe said. "In spite of what we know about her, Letitia is tremendously entertaining."

"She charms people," Kate said. "She certainly charmed me. That's one of the reasons I came to work for her. I was a disciple."

"Did Letitia and the others go home this morning?"

"Yes. They're gone. They think I'm on my way to Butte for a vacation, and they know you're heading on to Tokyo. We're alone, at last."

"I like being alone with you. You stabilize me, put me at ease. I feel totally uninhibited. Say anything. Do anything. Ask anything. No restrictions. It's a good feeling." Joe touched her hand. "I love you."

"And I love you."

"From here on baby, it's just you and me."

"Okay, Mr. Bogart, let's go back to the hotel. I'd like a cognac, and you. Your room. I've checked out of mine."

They returned to the Melia Madrid and Kate poured the cognac. "Have you noticed—danger is one of my aphrodisiacs."

Joe grinned. "Is that what it is. I thought you were just out to lay a rich doctor."

"You bastard!"

"Such language."

"I'm trying to be serious. Your speech in the Garden—that was dangerous, and I wanted you. Of course, it was only momentary lust."

"You're telling me I missed an opportunity?"

"No. You were married, and I wasn't prepared to become a scarlet woman. I may have wanted to, but I wouldn't have. We had no foundation. Know what I mean?" She looked up. "By any chance, did you lust for me?"

"Of course," Joe replied.

She stood up and began to undress.

Joe groaned. "Can I finish my cognac?"

"I'll be in the shower."

It was midnight in Madrid when the phone rang. The metallic voice of Scott Ragan crackled in the earpiece. "Sorry to call so late."

"It's okay," Joe replied. "What's up?"

"The Chicago police found a man who was hired to kill Leonard Breslow."

"No kidding," Joe said, instantly awake.

"Luther Agostelli, Letitia's husband, hired him."

"Jeez!"

"There's only one problem. He didn't do it."

"What do you mean?"

"He didn't kill Breslow. It was a scam. Agostelli paid him thirty grand for the job, and he took the money and disappeared. The police picked him up on a tip. He sang like a canary when they told him he was under arrest for murder. Identified Agostelli from a photograph. Never saw Letitia."

"How do they know he didn't do it?"

"He had a solid alibi. Furthermore, he's a known, two-bit con man, not a killer."

Joe was speechless.

"Agostelli set it up. He hung out a couple of times in a known crime bar in Chicago, pretending to be in his cups. He made it known what he wanted, and somebody put this guy in touch with him. The police tell me it goes on all the time."

"Does Agostelli know?"

"No. He thinks his man did it."

"You're telling me that Letitia's husband paid a guy thirty thousand dollars to kill Leonard Breslow, and the guy took the money and walked. Meantime, somebody else killed Breslow."

"That's right. The police had the damn murder solved, and now they've got nothing—no suspect, no motive, no leads. It's almost funny."

"They're still convinced Breslow was murdered?"

"Absolutely."

"This is bizarre. What happens now?"

"The police start over. The killer is still out there. Agostelli, and presumably Letitia, will be charged with attempted murder."

"When?"

"Later. The police will hold off for now in deference to the President."

"I'll be home in a couple of weeks," Joe said. "I'm flying out tomorrow for Monaco and Singapore, then on to the Gilbert Islands and Tokyo."

"I know," Scott said. "When you see Kajimoto, you might pick his brains. Remember the thing, 'Y–1—Brazil—Jeno,' in the Breslow memo? Your thought panned out. 'Y–1 is a new genetic breed of tobacco with super levels of nicotine and highly addictive. It was developed in Brazil and patented in the United States. 'Jeno' is an obscure Japanese company that apparently owns the patent. We can't seem to get a handle on 'Jeno.' Maybe Kajimoto can help. He knows everything."

"Okay. If I get a chance, I'll ask him. Incidentally, how did Breslow get wind of Y–1 in the first place?"

"It was on a loose scrap of paper in Luther's financial file. Luther knew about it, but apparently Letitia did not."

"Scott, who the hell did kill Breslow?"

"That, my friend, is a good question."

[24]

IT WAS A PRETTY flight to Nice that day. The plane took off at noon, and they had Bloody Marys and a pleasing basket lunch of crackers, Manchego cheese, and finger sandwiches. From Madrid they flew over the Iberian mountains and the coast of Spain at Barcelona, then across the northern lip of the Mediterranean. Except for thin cirrus and a little haze, the sky was clear. They were on the port side of the plane and could see the rambling Pyrenees in the distance and the rugged Costa Brava and the great Golfe du Lion lapping into the south of France, then Marseille, Toulon, and all of the Côte d'Azur. The Mediterranean was cobalt blue. On the approach to Nice they saw many sails on the water and the white wakes of motor yachts, and as the water shallowed near the beach, the blue paled to turquoise, then shades of brilliant green.

From the airport at Nice a minibus carried them along the narrow coast road to Monte Carlo. The traffic was awful, and in some stretches the minibus could manage only a few yards at a time, but they were lovers in no hurry. They held hands and enjoyed the Mediterranean under the afternoon sun, the lazy villages, the beaches covered with near-naked bathers, the homes tucked into green cliffs.

At the Hôtel de Paris, gardens and bright flowers and Rolls Royces seemed to be everywhere. Beside the fountain were sculptures of nude mermaids, and about the lobby were great slabs of pink and white marble and thick carpets. The clerk at the reception desk wore a dress jacket. Their room faced the Mediterranean and had a wide balcony with French doors, a billowing silken curtain, a pair of chaise lounges, and a coffee table and chairs. The French doors lay open and the silken curtain flapped in the warm breeze. Outside, the sun painted a blinding swath of flame across the blue water.

"This is fabulous," Kate sighed.

"Enjoy it. We'll have nothing as pretty as the Mediterranean on the rest of the trip."

She wrapped her arms around his neck and kissed him hungrily. "You're going to be damn glad you brought me."

"I already am."

"What's the plan?"

"We unpack, then walk around the harbor. The richest people in the world keep the biggest yachts in the world in the Monte Carlo harbor."

The sign on the street above the harbor said, "John F. Kennedy Avenue." "It feels strange to see his name on a street in Monte Carlo," Kate said. She and Joe locked hands and strolled along the harbor and looked at the boats. One very long boat was porcelain white, and the name on the bow was printed in bold Greek letters. It was grander than a baby ocean liner, and they stopped to see if anyone famous might be on deck. "It looks deserted," Kate said. "How could someone own a yacht that beautiful and ever want to go ashore?" They watched and rested for a spell, but no one appeared on the handsome vessel and they moved on.

They walked to the far corner of the harbor. Nearly two hours had passed when they returned, and they were hot and thirsty. They found chairs by a marble column in the hotel lobby and could see the oval flower garden in front and, across the terrace, the lavish, Parisian facade of the casino and people strolling in and out. When the waiter appeared, Joe ordered Beefeater and tonic and lime slices.

"I feel awfully British with one of these," Joe said when the waiter delivered their drinks. He touched his glass to Kate's. "At times nothing tastes better than Beefeater and tonic."

She squeezed some lime into her glass and sipped the icy drink. "I have a serious question. Am I brazen?"

"Definitely."

"I know I love you desperately and it shows."

"And I love you."

"This is happening awfully fast," she said.

"What's happening awfully fast?"

"Us."

"One can die awfully fast, too."

She frowned. "What a sad thought."

"Live every day as if it were the last," Joe said.

"Do you really feel that way?"

"Sometimes, when I'm very happy, like now, I feel that way. I guess I'm afraid it will end."

"Don't think about it ending. Promise me."

"All right. I promise."

She feasted on the elegance of the lobby and the people in expensive clothes and jewelry, rustling about and having cocktails and tête-à-têtes. "Who are they?" she wondered aloud.

"Oh, rich people, diplomats, spies, presidents, kings, rogues, vagabonds, of course, lovers."

"What a wonderful place for a honeymoon."

"When you've shacked up in Monte Carlo, you don't need a honeymoon."

She laughed. "No deal. I want a honeymoon at least once a year."

"I can live with that," Joe replied.

"I feel the gin."

"You're swilling it like lemonade."

"It goes down fast when you're thirsty." She settled back in her chair and smiled affectionately. "What do you plan to do, Dr. Hawkins, with the rest of your life?"

"I've been thinking about that lately."

"Your term with the AMA will consume another year."

"I know. I'm committed."

"How about EVP when Letitia Jordan goes?"

"No way."

"You would be a great EVP."

"I don't want to leave Arizona."

"The President may offer you something. Surgeon general? The first secretary of health? It would be awfully hard to say no."

He thought a moment. "Yes. But I want to go home. I have a

lot to go home to. I love my practice. I love my children. I really miss them when I'm gone."

"We have a lot in common," Kate said. "I love the West, and I love children. I'm lucky. I was raised in a small town, and I have a loving family. That's the best of all worlds."

"I'll bet you were fun to watch grow up," Joe said.

"I suppose I was. When I was a little girl, I was round and sturdy, and I had muscular legs, and the people in Butte always said I looked healthy. In high school my shape changed, and boys started hanging around my locker and walking me home after school. I was embarrassed at the way I looked."

"What do you mean?" Joe interrupted.

"I acquired boobs and a big butt. My mom dressed me in pleated skirts, sloppy joes, and cardigans, and loose blouses with long tails, to conceal my figure. And she taught me to slope-shoulder, to keep the buttons on my blouses from pulling, and to tuck my bottom in when I walked. Then she had me take ballet lessons to learn how to move properly. Actually, I became quite good because of my strong legs."

"You had a good mom."

"I had a good father too. And a pair of good little brothers—twins. They were a year younger than I. They gave me fits, but they watched over me, taught me how to fight, where to kick a boy if ever I was seriously attacked. That never happened, thank God. It was understood in Butte that you would have the Murphy twins to answer to if you messed with their sister.

"My dad backed me on everything. Well, almost. I got interested in drama, and I performed in school plays and gave readings. I won the state high school competition for dramatic reading with a piece from *Rebecca*. Naturally I came home quite inflated and in a brash moment announced my intention to quit school and go to Hollywood. That was a big mistake. My father squashed me pretty good. I'd never seen him so mad. But his wisdom proved sound. Then I got interested in journalism, made valedictorian, and won a scholarship to the University of Missouri."

"Any regrets?"

"No. I fantasize about Hollywood. Sometimes I wish I had given it a try."

"You have good parents," Joe said.

"I can't imagine growing up without a father, like you did, or a mother."

"It always bugged me. Mom was wonderful, and Janie worshiped me, but I wanted my father."

Kate sipped her drink. "I love my job, my career, but I want to have a home, a family, take care of my husband, fix breakfast in the morning, dinner in the evening, go to church on Sunday, do the PTA and Little League bit, be excruciatingly normal."

"The world is your oyster, Kate. You can have anything you want."

"Would you care to have more babies?" she asked.

"Very much."

"I'd like to have them for you."

"That's a beautiful thought," Joe said.

She downed the last of her drink. "How soon can I start?"

"You are definitely brazen," Joe said and kissed her.

The French doors still lay open when they returned to their room. The breeze had stiffened, and the silken curtain whipped like a pennant on the mast of a running sailboat. The sun was low, and the breeze was cooler and carried the fragrance of fresh flowers.

The maid had prepared the bed and turned on the radio. They decided she must have known they were Americans, because the station she had selected was playing the music of American big bands. They undressed and embraced in the center of the room and swayed with the music, and the breeze cooled them.

"I want you to know," Kate whispered, "my love for you is unconditional. I'll love you the rest of my life. I'll go anywhere with you, do anything you say, give you anything you want, anytime you want it."

He kissed the tip of her nose. "You're an incorrigible romantic."

"Look who's talking."

They danced to the dreamy music, and their bodies melded and traced a clover leaf on the floor.

"You're a wonderful dancer," Joe said.

"I love to dance."

"You're weightless."

"It's good when we're pressed close like this. I feel your moves before you make them."

"You have great tits, my dear." He loosened his arms and cupped his hands beneath her breasts. They were firm and heavy. He leaned down and gently sucked and nibbled the pink nipples and they swelled in his mouth, then he nestled them together and sucked both at once. "There," he said with satisfaction and pulled her close again. "Now the nipples feel like diamonds."

The announcer chattered in French, and they understood "Artie Shaw" and "Begin the Beguine."

"I must dance to that," Kate said. She pulled away, then draped the silken curtain across the front of her body and posed—a lovely bronze statue in the yellow, afternoon sunlight—and her nipples made peaks under the sheer fabric. The soaring, magical tones of the Shaw clarinet and the blend of saxophones and brass filled the room—Shaw's was the most memorable of all playings of "Begin the Beguine"—and Kate danced. Joe, plainly astonished, retreated to the bed. She undulated and pirouetted, teasing, flourishing the curtain, aping the graceful veronicas of the matadors, twisting, then dropped the curtain, baring her lithe, tan body. She danced recklessly across the room, langorous, impromptu choreography, a crazy concoction of pagan, African, and honky-tonk. She pirouetted to the bed where Joe lay watching, clasped her hands behind her head, arms back, undulating, then spun and thrust her rump into his face. Droplets of sweat from the small of her back trickled into the cleavage of her buttocks, and Joe touched the moist skin. She turned, pumping, undulating, and sweat moistened her navel and the skin between her breasts. The music softened, then soared, ended abruptly, and she shrieked "Olé!" and collapsed on top of him.

He lifted her head and kissed her on the mouth, and they lay still for a moment. Then she straddled him. He pulled her down hard, and she was delicious. She leaned on his shoulders and moaned and writhed, and he wondered if the rabid movements were painful, then, didn't care. "Oh God! Oh God! I can't wait," she screamed and exploded, and exploded, and exploded, and exploded.

Her perspiring body crumpled almost lifelessly by his side, and they were silent for a moment. Then Joe reached for the radio. "I'm turning this damn thing off before you fuck me to death."

"I certainly don't want to do that. We're not even halfway around the world."

He cradled her in his arms. "It's almost six," he said. "We have a dinner reservation at eight. Time for a short nap. After dinner I'll take you to the casino to play baccarat. I'll wear my tuxedo, you wear a pretty dress. We'll pretend it's the twenties."

"Perfect." She pulled the sheet over them.

In an hour they awakened and quickly showered and dressed. Joe donned a white dinner jacket and red tie, and Kate put on a swishy, off-the-shoulder dress of pink with a long waist that provocatively displayed her hips. "You look like a flapper," he said.

"I can't believe you hauled a tuxedo all the way over here," she said.

"I've always wanted to put on a tuxedo and go to the casino in Monte Carlo, like in the old movies."

"Just for the hell of it?"

"Just for the hell of it."

"You're gorgeous," she said.

They rode the elevator to the grill on the eighth floor of the hotel, and the maître d' seated them at the side where they could see everything. "Look up," Joe said. The roof was open, the sky was clear, and the stars twinkled prettily. "They're bright like the stars over the mountains at home. Soon we'll see the moon."

He leafed through the book of wines. "They have Chassagne-Montrachet. You like dry white. Chassagne-Montrachet is from a little town in Burgundy and considered one of the finest dry whites in France."

"How do you know that?"

"It says so right here. This is the tourist list. It has an English translation under the French. I must look like a tourist."

"You've come a long way from Jacksonville, Illinois."

"Let's break the rules and have our wine now." He instructed the waiter, and in a moment the man returned with a tall bottle packed in ice and a pair of frosted Bordeau glasses. He uncorked the wine and poured a sample. "Excellent," Joe declared, and the waiter precisely half-filled the glasses.

"This is delicious," Kate said.

"Full bodied," Joe said.

"The way you like it," she said, grinning.

"Of course. Now, what about dinner?"

"You decide."

"Very well, my dear." He perused the menu. "We'll have a salade niçoise and the canard à l'orange. That's mixed salad with tuna and anchovies, and roast duck basted with orange liqueur."

"It sounds delicious."

Joe gave the order to the waiter and looked up. "Now, we can see the moon," he said.

"You arranged the moon perfectly. You arranged everything perfectly. Madrid. The bullfights. Monte Carlo." She let her evening bag drop to the floor, then leaned down to retrieve it and deftly fondled his crotch."

"For God's sake, Kate. You were never like this in Chicago. You were more or less normal."

"You've unleashed the devil in me."

"Frankly, I can't keep up."

"Oooh," she said, feigning sympathy. "What did you say about living every day as if it were the last?"

"I wasn't contemplating sexual suicide."

"No sad stories, big boy. If anyone gets fucked to death on this trip, it'll be me."

Joe grinned, "By the way, the wine is truly magnificent."

The waiter served their salades niçoise and poured more wine.

"Your inauguration is just around the corner," Kate said. "You have an important speech to prepare."

"Yes, I've been thinking about it."

"How will all of this end?"

"The AMA is a great organization. It will cleanse itself and survive to become even stronger. Letitia Jordan will fall. The tobacco conspiracy will collapse. Public trust will return, and the Aesculapians will stand tall again."

"Dr. Jordan will not go quietly," Kate said.

"A lot depends on President Chamberlain. He hates Senator Ridge. He'll do anything to square that account. Letitia is a bit player on his agenda."

"David Chamberlain is an angry man."

"I don't blame him. If I'd lost a son the way he did, I'd feel the same way."

"It was a rotten business."

"Pierre was the messenger," Joe said. "The President didn't tell us himself because he couldn't bear to. It eats him alive, every minute, every day. Sleep is the only escape, and when he sleeps, he dreams. Sometimes he can't function. Hate is a powerful emotion. He's got to finish it with Jonathan Ridge. By chance, you and I came along. David Chamberlain is using us, but he's not Machiavellian. He's desperate. He truly needs help. He's reaching out. He craves understanding, approval. Pierre, his old comrade, is the only one he can trust. Pierre said just enough. He knew we would draw the proper conclusions."

"You have a lot of insight into the President."

"I know something of what he's going through. I understand demons. I feel sorry for him."

"Could he be stringing you along . . ."

". . . to get at Jonathan Ridge? Not entirely. Underneath the political veneer, I see an honorable man who wants to trust and be trusted. He'll get Ridge, but he'll fulfill his commitments to us."

"What will he do to Senator Ridge?"

"He'd like to rip his heart out. I don't know. Censure, impeachment, jail, disgrace. It will be as vengeful as David Chamberlain can make it."

Kate took his hand. "I wish we could forget all of it, just stay here forever and make love."

Joe looked at her. A lifetime in Monte Carlo with this beautiful, adoring woman with the dancing blue eyes and chestnut hair was delicious to contemplate. He squeezed her hand and whispered, "I love you."

The waiter interrupted with a platter of roast duck, and they attacked the food.

"I'm starving," Kate said.

❦

They walked from the Hôtel de Paris around the magnificent flowers of the oval garden to the casino. The casino had high ceilings, massive chandeliers, and thick carpets, and the croupiers wore tuxedos. A big room, the American Room, was filled with slot machines and the clamor of levers being pulled. Other rooms had only the soft sounds of croupiers calling the games and the curious strolling about. Joe and Kate entered a club room that was splendidly adorned with leather chairs and oak tables and paneled walls. There were men in tuxedos and women in expensive dresses, and roulette wheels and tables for craps and blackjack, a baccarat pit, and the muted murmur of elegant gambling. The baccarat pit was roped off, which gave it an aura of exclusivity. A handful of players sat around the table and others stood behind them and watched.

"Baccarat is the simplest of all the games to play," Joe said. "Four cards are dealt, two for the player, two for the banker. Another card may be drawn, depending on the total of the first two. The hand closest to nine wins. The rules are set. You have no choices. The croupier calls the game. The only thing to decide is whether to bet on the player or the banker, and how much. Roulette is the popular casino game in Europe, but sophisticated gamblers prefer baccarat. Baccarat has the glamour, the intrigue—James Bond, 'The Red Shoes.' One must play baccarat in Monte Carlo, as one must attend the bullfights in Madrid."

Joe took a seat at the baccarat table and exchanged a handful of francs for chips. Kate stationed herself behind him, pressing her belly against his back.

Baccarat is fast, and in half an hour Joe had won a thousand francs. Kate ordered cognac for them, and they played together. But their luck changed. In another half-hour only a handful of chips remained. Then they pulled even. They continued to play, but the tide turned again and the chips dwindled.

"We're down a thousand francs," Joe announced. "It's midnight. Lets call it quits."

"This gets in your blood," Kate said.

They walked back to the hotel holding hands, pausing to look at the flowers in the moonlight—carnations, roses, daffodils. The air was cool and moist and fragrant. The window of their room still lay open, and the silken curtain was blowing in the cool breeze. They undressed and crawled under the sheet, pulled the coverlet over them, and kissed and made love, tenderly, deliciously. Then Kate burrowed her rump against Joe's belly, and he cradled her in his arms. In moments they fell asleep.

[25]

IN THE MORNING Joe and Kate had breakfast on the balcony of their room. They rose early and huddled at the wash basin to brush their teeth and splash cold water on their faces, then donned thick, terry bathrobes and sunglasses and sat outside in the sun and watched fishing boats from the docks fan across the Mediterranean for the early catch. The waiter brought Bloody Marys and Tabasco, coffee, chilled Crenshaws, a basket of croissants, and English jellies. Kate poured coffee and opened the jelly jars. "Orange marmalade and raspberry," she announced. She squeezed a lime on the Crenshaw and sampled the watery melon. "Sweet," she said, "delicious," and they ate hungrily. The breeze was chilly, even under the warming sun, and the terry bathrobes felt good.

"The chauffeur will pick us up at ten," Joe said. "We'll drive to Nice, then Antibes and Cannes, lunch in Cannes, then on to Ste.-Maxime and take the ferry to Saint-Tropez. You'll enjoy Saint-Tropez. We'll shop and have a cold ale, then ferry back, drive to Beaulieu, and dine at La Réserve, one of Pierre Globa's favorite places, where he and David Chamberlain got drunk, remember. I'm taking a jacket and a fresh shirt for dinner. You can share my garment bag, if you care to bring a change?"

271

The chauffeur arrived on time in a comfortable Mercedes diesel sedan. They drove along the coastal road to Nice, and the chauffeur told stories about the Côte d'Azur, then they came to the village of Antibes and hiked the footpath around the Cap, looked at the pretty estates and flower gardens, and explored green terraces with glorious views of the coast. In Cannes they passed a very long beach blanketed with bathers. Then it was noon, and the streets of Cannes had become congested. The chauffeur picked his way along the Boulevard de la Croisette by the Carlton Hotel and finally dropped them at the Blue Bar.

They sat on the terrace of the Blue Bar, in sight of the beach, and ordered bouillabaisse and a carafe of Chardonnay. The steaming bouillabaisse came in deep bowls and was filled with slices of meat derived from ocean creatures of unknown identity. From its looks they didn't particularly want to know what the bouillabaisse contained and were surprised how good it tasted.

"Do you suppose there's octopus in this?" Kate asked.

"I hope not," Joe said.

"It's good." She swallowed more bouillabaisse. "Tell me, what do you think of the board wives?"

"They seem very nice," he answered.

"How about Marietta Maxwell?"

"Young, attractive, flaunts her charms around the older wives, makes no particular effort to fit in. Likes to carouse, drink, go her own way. Relishes being the wife of the chairman, but rather misses the big picture. Overall, I would classify her as a bimbo."

"She's Dr. Maxwell's third wife."

"So I understand."

"He wouldn't relish you calling Marietta a bimbo. She's his trophy. He thinks she attracts votes."

"That's doubtful."

"She's also the leader of the second-wife contingent, which in this case includes third wives. The other second wife is Mrs. Lattimer. Of course they lost Barbara Devlin when you defeated her husband. I suspect the first wives resent the second and third wives."

Joe grinned. "Not surprising."

"Marietta Maxwell thinks she's sexy, and she flirts. I've heard snide remarks from the first wives."

"Why are you telling me this?"

"She had an affair with Dr. Rodansky."

"How do you know that?"

"It was a rumor when I first started working for the AMA. Marietta put the move on Dr. Rodansky when he joined the board. They were quite an item. His wife rarely attended the meetings, so Marietta latched on, sat next to him at the dinners, played with him under the table, enticed him into late-night barhopping."

"What about her husband?"

"He didn't care. I'm not sure he had a choice. Marietta was his bauble, and she got her way. He didn't go for barhopping. He was glad someone looked after her. She mixed it up, flirted with others, passed her favors around, but Dr. Rodansky was the main event."

"Perhaps it was only flirting."

"It was more than flirting. Two years ago, when the board was in town, I had occasion one evening to deliver some papers to Dr. Jordan in the Drake. She was in Dr. Devlin's suite. Dr. Devlin, you remember, was then chairman of the board. I saw Marietta Maxwell at the door to another room down the corridor, and someone let her in. When I got to Dr. Devlin's suite, Dr. Maxwell was there, but no Marietta. I was curious, so I checked the room numbers and discovered that Marietta had entered Dr. Rodansky's room."

"You little snoop," Joe chided.

"She's had private dinners with Dr. Rodansky."

"Why haven't you told me before?"

"He's your friend. Anyway, it was old news, so I just didn't. Things have changed. Now that I officially love you, I tell you everything."

"Duke must be quite a swordsman."

"Something happened after that. The affair obviously cooled. No more barhopping or private dinners. Publicly they were cordial, and she was back, flirting with the field. That included you."

"I suppose it did."

"Later I heard rumors about Dr. Rodansky and other girls. That may explain why he and Marietta Maxwell are no longer an item."

"You don't like Marietta Maxwell, do you?"

"Frankly, no," Kate said.

"That's plain enough. Duke is my friend. Do his philanderings bother you?"

"If he's your friend, that's all that matters."

"I have raunchy friends you don't even know."

"I don't care."

"More wine?"

"I'm full. I can't finish the bouillabaisse."

"It's time to go." Joe paid the waiter, and they departed. The chauffeur eased the Mercedes through the jammed streets of Cannes and worked his way along the crowded coast road to Mandelieu–La Napoule. The name was hyphenated, he explained, because it began as two villages. They passed the beaches and shops of Mandelieu–La Napoule, then the road narrowed and meandered with the coast. Joe held her hand. "I'm glad you're here."

They came to a rugged cove and paused to watch the foaming seawater swirl across sand and rock. "You've been here before, haven't you?" Kate said.

"Three years ago, with Grace."

"Did you stay in the Hôtel de Paris?"

"No. We stayed on the Cap."

"Then the Hôtel de Paris is ours." She snuggled against his shoulder. "This is lovely. The Mediterranean, so beautiful, so serene."

"The color of your eyes."

"I wonder if it ever turns ferocious, like other seas."

"I don't see how it could."

"I love the romantic little bays and beaches, the coves, the villages."

"Imagine how it was when they were invaded."

"Invaded?"

"World War II. The invasion of France. The Anvil landings

along the Côte d'Azur. Our troops landed here two months after
D Day, drove north to Lyon, then Dijon, connected with Patton's Third Army from Normandy, trapped the Germans in the
Southwest of France. Patton was the hammer. These guys were
the anvil. Prince Aly Kahn landed in Cannes. He was an officer in
the British army. Before the war he vacationed every year at the
Carlton Hotel, and when he landed it fell his lot to liberate the
Carlton. The story goes that he led his troops into the lobby—
dirty, in combat gear, on the heels of the fleeing Germans—and
the bell captain, without batting an eye, greeted him with, 'Bon
matin, Prince Aly,' as if he had simply returned for his annual
visit."

"Who was Prince Aly Kahn?"

"A wealthy playboy, once married to Rita Hayworth."

"I can't envision bloodshed on a beach this beautiful," Kate
said.

"The worst of it was around Toulon and Marseille."

"How do you know these things?" she asked.

"I like to read about the war."

"It must have been a terrible war."

"It was worse than terrible. Yet it has an incredible fascination.
War is one of the great themes of mankind. That war was
compelling and horrible, but the greatest war of them all."

"You speak of it almost with reverence."

"I suppose I do. It killed my father, but it was his war. What I
know best about him—his letters, beliefs, feelings, where he was,
what he did, how much he loved us—centered around the war.
I was trying to emulate him when I joined the marines, but my
war wasn't his war. What he did stood for something. My war was
futility, pure shit."

"Isn't all war futility, pure shit?"

"Some wars involve principle."

"What kind of principle is worth killing millions of people for?"

"Saving the world from madmen."

"You win." She leaned over and kissed him, and they rode in
silence for a few moments. Then she asked, "Do you like being a
surgeon?"

"I can't imagine doing anything else. I love it. Of course, not everyone agrees with my viewpoint."

"Dr. Conlan is a surgeon, but he's not like you."

"Duke thinks Peter Conlan is gay."

"He may be right," Kate said, then asked, "How long does it take to become a surgeon?"

"It took me seven years after medical school. One year of internship, four years general surgery, two years thoracic surgery. That's changed some, but it's still a long time."

"Judgment. It's easy to learn how to cut and sew, and tie square knots. Judgment takes experience, and experience takes time. It's a lifelong process. Seven years barely scratches the surface. You never know enough. When you think you do, you get your eyes wiped."

"Are you a good surgeon?"

"I win a few, lose a few."

"Smart ass!"

"We're entering Ste.-Maxime," the chauffeur announced. "The ferries run every half-hour. They don't carry automobiles. I'll wait at the dock. Be careful of pickpockets," he added cheerily.

The ferry was at the dock when they arrived, and soon they were churning smoothly across the little bay. In half an hour they reached their destination.

Saint-Tropez is a mélange—an old harbor and boat yard and maze of meandering streets, shops, and opulent homes. Joe and Kate strolled, held hands, and browsed and purchased knick-knacks. It was sweltering along the narrow streets where there was no breeze, and they entered Dalolo's and ordered cold ale. The waiter brought big steins of Kronenbourg, icy cold and better than American beer, and they drank and watched the boats moving about the old harbor.

"So far, so good," Joe said. "No pickpockets."

After a second Kronenbourg they left Dololo's and strolled around the harbor to the dock and boarded the ferry. They sat in the bow, and when the ferry got underway they could see Ste.-Maxime across the bay. A young steward served demitasses of espresso, hot and strong, just right. They held hands, sipped espresso, and heard the shallow waves spanking the bow and felt the soft, lulling vibrations of the engines. Kate leaned her head on Joe's shoulder, and they watched the gently undulating blue water. The companion ferry passed on their port side on it's way to Saint-Tropez, and they waved. Its shallow wake bounced them a little.

Kate kissed him on the cheek. "A few months ago I was a hotshot career woman. Now, I can't get enough of you. I didn't know I could love someone this much."

"You're beautiful," Joe said, snuggling her.

"I want the trouble to end. I want us to go home and be normal people."

"We'll go home," he said, "and I'll show you Arizona. The north rim of the Canyon is only hours away, and the road through the Navajo Reservation and along the Vermilion Cliffs into the Kaibab is spectacular. Or we can go south to Aravaipa and Patagonia, and the Saguaros. You'll make a big hit in your alligator boots and your red bandana."

The chauffeur met them when the ferry pulled into Ste.-Maxime. They retraced the coast road to St. Raphael, then turned inland and picked up the motorway where the going was much faster. They looked down on Cannes, Cap d'Antibes, and Nice as they passed, turned off at Beaulieu and cruised along a boulevard lined with tall palm trees, then came to La Réserve.

La Réserve is a peaceful little hotel on the waterfront, steeped with the elegance of aristocracy—pale yellow and white shutters, secluded beach, palm trees, potted plants, white chairs, tables, and settees.

"You match the decor," Joe said. Kate had changed into a summery, yellow cotton and fastened a white carnation in her hair.

They sat on the terrace and watched the boats at the dock and the sun sinking into the Mediterranean. In the bar a young man in a white jacket at the piano was playing "San Francisco."

"You have a knack for finding romantic piano bars," Kate remarked.

Joe ordered De Venoge. "This is genuine champagne," he said when the waiter filled the flutes.

"Suddenly I'm hungry," Kate said.

"How about a Charolais tenderloin, medium rare? The Charolais are fine beef cattle." Joe instructed the waiter and they settled back with their De Venoge.

"I like La Réserve," Kate said.

"Grace and I came here once. We had lunch. She loved the Côte d'Azur. We talked about coming back."

"Will you tell me about her?"

He sipped his champagne. "I met Grace when I was the pup on the surgical service. She was a scrub nurse, a damn good one. She told me I looked her up and down in the OR. I did, but I didn't know it was so obvious. My boss was a man named Clanahan, 'Wild Bill' Clanahan. He was a professional curmudgeon and a helluva surgeon. My first case with him was a lobectomy. I let a retractor slip when he was ligating the pulmonary artery. It was clumsy. 'Sorry, sir,' I said. God, what a mistake. 'Son,' he said, 'I'll say you're sorry. You're the sorriest damn thing I ever saw.' I was mortified. Grace told me later he pulled the same line on every new resident. 'Don't say you're sorry around Wild Bill,' she said. Actually, the whole scene was pretty funny.

"When I did my first tracheotomy, the senior resident, a real son of a bitch, scrubbed in. He tried to take over. Grace was scrubbed. Every time the guy reached for an instrument, she passed it to me. We struggled through somehow, and the patient survived. There was nothing between Grace and me then. She just wanted me to have a chance.

"We got married in my second year of residency. She worked until I finished training, when she wasn't having babies. God knows, we needed the money. Tracy came first, then Rosie. Little Jake was born in Arizona. He's named for my father. They're all about two years apart. Grace was a terrific mother. I had a crazy schedule, but she always managed.

"We moved to Phoenix, and my practice took off. We bought a house, a car, a station wagon. She raised the kids, hauled them around in the station wagon, did the country club, the League, church, the whole bit. I got a Christmas card every year from a corpsman I had known in Vietnam named Olie. He signed it,

'Just a sailor doin' twenty.' I've thought about Olie many times. Grace and I were just a pair of sailors doin' twenty. We lived, loved, had great kids. But I was restless, and she became bored and lonely. She began meeting her friends in the afternoon for a drink. They drank a lot. None of them realized how much. It got to poor Grace. I should have known."

The maître d' summoned them to the dining room. "Now I really am hungry," Joe said.

"Me too," Kate said.

"Grace wanted me to do the AMA thing. Not at first, though. We had a row. She said I was obsessed with combat, that I thrived on it. I didn't want to hear that. She was more perceptive than I gave her credit for. But she pitched in, helped with the campaign, worked the crowd at the convention, hustled votes."

"I met her then," Kate said. "She was elegant."

"After the election she told me how happy she was. She planned on the summer to put our lives in order. She felt good. We made love, and she flew home. It was the last time I saw her. Sometimes . . ."

"You're doing fine," Kate said softly.

"I love Grace. I'll always love her. She gave me three wonderful children. We had a wonderful life. That will never change. She's a beautiful memory."

"You're very fortunate."

"That was then. This is now. I don't know how it was decided that you and I would connect, but I know I love you. I love you with all my heart. Nothing in the past diminishes that."

The waiter served the Charolais tenderloins, perfectly charred and lightly peppered and delicately pink in the center. The man at the piano played "Some Enchanted Evening."

"Tomorrow will be another long day," Joe said. "We fly all the way to Singapore, the other side of the world."

"I'm glad you let me come along," Kate said.

[26]

NEXT MORNING they again had breakfast on the balcony. Joe seemed distracted, and finally Kate inquired, "What's the matter?"

"Sorry, sweetie. I've been thinking about Scott Ragan's call."

"I know. I've been thinking about it too."

"If Letitia's hired gun didn't kill Breslow, who the hell did? And why?" He shrugged. "The cartel? It had the look of a professional killing. But as far as we know, the cartel had no interest in Breslow. Maybe it was a gay thing, a lover's quarrel. Breslow was a closet gay with only random contacts, nothing big time, hardly fertile ground for murder. No, the killer had to be an AMA insider close enough to Breslow to nurture a motive, someone who knew how to kill with his bare hands, or how to hire it done, most likely the latter. The question is, who?"

"I have no idea," Kate said.

"At this point," Joe said, "neither do I."

They checked out of the Hôtel de Paris, saddened to leave Monaco and the Mediterranean, and rode the minibus to the airport in Nice. It was an easy one-hour flight to Rome on Air France, across the Lugerian Sea—in the morning haze they could make out the shadows of Genoa on the distant coast to the north—then across the upper tip of Corsica and the Mediterranean and along the western beaches of Italy. In Rome they boarded the flight to Singapore.

Rome was muggy, and clusters of rain clouds hung over the airport. The 747 lumbered onto the apron at the end of the runway and turned to the wind. Its powerful turbofans spooled up, and the giant plane shuddered, then started down the runway, sluggishly at first, then accelerated rapidly, pressing them back in their seats. After what seemed an eternity, the nose lifted and suddenly, majestically, the plane flew. The landing gear thumped into the belly, and they heeled into a steep, climbing turn. Turbulence jostled them momentarily when they penetrated the rain clouds, but above the clouds the sun was bright and the air smooth as a millpond. Then the plane rolled out on a southeasterly heading and settled into a steady climb. The whisper of slipstream mounted as they gained speed.

"That was a long takeoff," Joe said. "We're heavy."

The captain announced the flying time would be twelve hours and they would land in Singapore shortly after sunrise; the initial cruising altitude would be thirty-one thousand feet and after burning off fuel, they would climb to thirty-seven thousand; they would fly over the eastern Mediterranean, Crete, Cairo, Riyadh, the Arabian Sea, Bombay, the Bay of Bengal, and into Singapore; there were good tailwinds; and he expected decent weather and a smooth trip.

The plane leveled off, and the flight attendant—a black-haired Oriental girl in a silk sheath slit to mid-thigh—brought Bloody Marys and a plate of egg rolls and water chestnuts. Her name was Lisa Lin.

"Steward make Bloody Marys with pepper vodka," Lisa Lin announced in halting English. "Very spicy. Tabasco not required. If you not like, will make with regular vodka. Soon will serve tiffin. Dinner this evening. Breakfast before landing."

Kate settled back and stretched her legs. "I could become accustomed to this."

"It grows on you."

After the Bloody Marys and tidbits, Lisa Lin brought the tiffin of baked chicken breast and curried rice and a sweet fruit she said was mangosteen from Malaysia. They ate appreciatively, then had crème de menthe frappés and coffee.

They flew over Messina on the eastern tip of Sicily and watched the tip of southern Italy slide slowly behind the plane. When they were over the open Mediterranean, Kate turned and looked lovingly at Joe. "Tell me more about your father."

"I don't remember him, but I know he was a great guy. He's always around. It's like he was never gone. He grew up in southern Illinois in a coal miner's family, in a tough little town called Benld. He was a good athlete. He won a basketball scholarship to the university."

"Was he tall?"

"Six-three. That was in the days when six-three was pretty good for basketball. My father met my mother at the university. They dated, then he graduated and joined the marines and went to Quantico. He proposed when he came home on his first leave. He was a proud new 'Brown Bar.' The second lieutenants are called 'Brown Bars.' They married the following spring after she graduated. War was starting in Europe. I was born the next year. Then came Pearl Harbor. My father shipped out a few months later. Mother was pregnant with Janie."

"That must have been heartbreaking."

"He wrote my mother almost every day—where he was, what he was doing, what he was thinking, his dreams, his fears, how much he loved and missed us, the new life we would have after the war. Dozens of letters. Mother saved them all. He comes to life in his letters. When I read them, it's like hearing him talk. I brought a few along. I thought you might like to read them." Joe pulled a brown envelope from his duffel. Inside was a thin packet of tissue-like letter papers crammed with lines of small handwriting. Strips had been cut from some and the folds were worn. "This is what they called 'V-Mail.' The censors snipped out things that might tip off the enemy. It seemed a little silly when the mail didn't make it home until months later." He handed one of the letters to Kate.

"I feel like an interloper."

"It's okay. My mother knows we're going to read them. I want you to know him."

She read aloud from the fragile paper: "'26 April 1942. 0900. Hello sweetheart. I am on a navy troopship loaded with marines. We have just pulled away from the Embarcadero in San Francisco heading across the Pacific. It's mid-morning and cold. I am on deck in front of the bridge with some other officers. It seems like a good time to write, although I don't know how or when the mail will get off this ship. No one knows where we're going, but I suppose we'll find out soon enough. I hope it's somewhere to kill Japs. That's what we want. We're coming up to the Golden Gate Bridge. The fog is burning off, but it is still a gray day. Now we are directly under the bridge. It's supposed to be red. From here it only looks rusty. Maybe it's the fog. It's a magnificent bridge, though. I wonder when I'll see it again. I know you and Joe and the little one would like to see it. Maybe we can come to San Francisco when the war is over and drive across together. God, I hope we can end it soon. We must never forsake freedom. That's why we are here on this ship. We have a big job to do. I feel good about it. I constantly think about you and Joe and the little one. I'm sorry I can't watch your tummy grow and feel the little one kick, pull your warm backside next to me at night, hold your hand in the hospital. I'll be praying for you. I love you with all my heart, Punkin, you can be sure of that. Our love is what I live for. Remember—somehow, someway, we'll always be together. Now the bridge is falling behind. The ship is riding the offshore swells. They say you get seasick here, but so far I'm okay. Am out of paper so will stop. I'll try to write every day. You will probably receive them all at once after we reach our destination. Ha! All my love, Jake.'"

"He always ran the sentences together like that," Joe said.

"It's a sweet, simple letter."

Joe handed her another. "This was written on the eve of Guadalcanal."

"'6 August 1942. 1800. Hello sweetheart. What happens in the next few days will be old news when you receive this. It is dusk and sticky hot. I am sitting on the deck of a ship headed for the channel between Guadalcanal and Tulagi in the Solomon Islands. Look on a map and you will find the Solomons northeast of Australia. Guadalcanal is big. Tulagi is little. It's part of the Floridas, no relation to the state. Tomorrow morning the First Marine Division will land on Guadalcanal. It will be the first attack initiated by the United States in this war. The whole world will be watching. My outfit is assigned to Tulagi, our first combat. We know Japs are there, but we don't know how many or what to expect. We're plenty scared, who wouldn't be, but we know what we have to do. I am looking at the picture of you and Joe

and me. I miss you so much, Punkin, sometimes I think I can't
stand it. Remember 'Memories of You' and the times we danced
naked. (Hope the censor enjoys this.) Knowing that you and Joe
and the new one will be waiting keeps me going. I can't wait to
see you again. You must be looking very pregnant by now. You're
especially beautiful when you're pregnant. What a crazy world it
is. Guadalcanal and Tulagi are terrible, stinking islands. No one
ever heard of them. Suddenly, they are important. I hate having
to be here, but am proud to be an American. I guess I wouldn't
miss this show for anything. All my love, Jake.'"

"The main force landed on Guadalcanal," Joe explained. "They
surprised the Japs and took the airstrip. It was tougher going for
a while on Tulagi, where my father landed, but they secured
Tulagi the next day. The Japs retaliated. There was a terrible sea
battle, the Battle of Savo Island. Our navy took an awful licking.
A few days later the Japs landed a whole army on Guadalcanal. Guadalcanal turned out to be one of the epic battles of all time. It took
six months to finish the job. My father fought on Bloody Ridge
with Colonel Edson. He came out that time without a scratch.
His outfit was relieved in December. They were pretty beat up.
Most of them had malaria. They went to New Zealand to recuper-
ate. The next summer they joined the Second Division to train for
Tarawa."

Joe selected a third letter. "This is the last one he wrote before
he died."

"'20 November 1943. 0100,'" Kate read. "'Hello sweetheart.
I am topside on a troopship named Zeilin. The code name is Blue
Fox, but when you receive this it won't matter. It's too hot to
sleep. The half-moon is pretty. I almost wish you could see it. In
a few hours we are going to hit a stinking little island named
Betio, part of Tarawa Atoll in the Gilbert Islands just above the
equator. Betio is ugly. On the map it looks like a dead bird lying
on its back with the beak sticking up. It covers only half a square
mile. They were telling us how stinking it is, and someone asked,
if it's that bad why don't we let the Japs keep it? It has an airstrip,
that's why, and we have to take it so they don't bomb us when we
hit the next stinking island. We'll hit a lot of stinking islands on

the way to Tokyo. We showed the Japs at Guadalcanal. Now we're on our way. The sooner we get it done, the sooner we get home. My outfit is ready. They're the greatest guys in the world. This war is the biggest thing that ever happened to mankind. I hate it but am proud to be here. I am looking at the picture. You are prettier than ever. Joe is a fine young man and little Janie is a dream. I would really hate having them grow up without me. I don't intend to let that happen. I miss you terribly—your love, your warm body, your kisses, your wonderful smile. I love you, I love you, I love you. Jake.'"

Kate wept softly. "What a sweet, loving man."

"My father loved and feared and suffered like anyone else. He wasn't looking to be a hero. He never questioned what had to be done. He simply did it. He hated the war, but it had a purpose. He believed in it. He was content with his belief. I went to Vietnam to experience what he experienced. It wasn't the same. There was no spirit in Vietnam, and no redemption."

"Joe, I love you so much."

They held hands and napped intermittently, had sirloin for dinner, then curled up under their blankets and slept until Lisa Lin awakened them at sunrise. They landed in Singapore on schedule. It was still early when they checked into their hotel, the elegant Shangri La, and they fell into the giant bed and slept until noon.

"Are you hungry?" Joe asked when they had showered and dressed."

"Not really. I have a mild headache."

"Same here. Probably the long flight and the drinks. The Singapore Sling is reputed to be an excellent remedy for hangovers."

They entered the lobby of the Shangri La and settled into a pair of lounge chairs near a massive, polygonal column. An Oriental girl resembling Lisa Lin placed a small bowl of almonds on the table and waited for their order. "Two Singapore Slings," Joe said with authority.

"I've never had a Singapore Sling," Kate said.

"It wouldn't be right to come to Singapore and not have a Singapore Sling."

Kate inspected the cavernous lobby. "You have a propensity for great hotels."

"I'm afraid this will be the last decent place between here and Tokyo. Tomorrow we fly to Manila, then change planes and fly all night to a little island named Nauru, with a stop in Guam. Nauru is on the equator a few thousand miles east of here. Tarawa is an hour beyond, but that flight goes only once a week. We have to lay over in Nauru."

The Oriental girl returned with their effervescing highballs. "What's in it?" Kate asked.

"Mostly fizz water and gin, I think. Goes better with almonds."

Kate munched an almond while she drank. "It does hit the spot."

"This is quite a place," Joe observed, glancing about. "Whites, blacks, Indians, Arabs, Orientals, Brits—turbans, trenchcoats, flowing robes."

"Spies?" Kate asked.

"Of course."

They sat quietly and watched the people in the lobby, then Kate said, "Joe, I have something to tell you. I've lived in sin."

"Damn!" Joe said. "A scarlet woman."

"Don't make fun. I'm serious."

"All right," he said. "Tell me."

"I had boyfriends in high school, but I was a virgin until my sophomore year in college. Then I fell in love with Marvin. That is, I thought I was in love. We shacked up for two years. We were both virgins when we met. We learned together. Then I realized I was no more than a sex partner. Marvin was a law student. He studied hard and expected me to service him. I wanted more. I tried to explain my feelings. I don't think he ever understood. Anyway, I felt used. I behaved abominably. I started nagging. One night we had a big fight. He slapped me—not hard, but a slap. It wasn't entirely his fault. I provoked him. But I walked out. I was looking for an excuse. I thought I loved Marvin. Now I know it was nothing like what I feel for you."

Joe took her hand. "Forget it. You and I love each other now. That's all that matters."

"You don't think I'm tainted?"

"I prefer women of experience," Joe said smiling.

"Joe, I totally, totally love you."

"Let's walk," Joe said. "The bellhop told me it's only ten minutes to good shopping."

From the hotel they strolled down a pretty street lined with green lawns and blooming African tulip trees and plumeria, then made their way along Orchard Road with the shops and stores of downtown Singapore. They came to a shopping cluster and joined the people browsing among the counters. There was everything from trinkets to furniture. One shop filled with leather pieces had rows of purses and handbags lined up on racks, and a young Chinaman addressed them in fairly understandable English. "We make all merchandise in own workshop," he proclaimed with a proud smile.

Kate was attracted to a rack labeled "Crocodile," and the young Chinaman eagerly began pulling handbags out. "Malaysian crocodile from Singapore crocodile farm," he said. "Like Chinese crocodile on Yangtze River. Very cheap. We cure skins, make bags, in own workshop. Very good price."

"Is he bullshitting us?" Joe whispered.

"Of course he is."

"Are they genuine?"

"Absolutely. I've never seen nicer." Kate selected a dressy black bag with a gold clasp and long shoulder strap. "This is stunning." She inspected the stitching and the pattern of the markings, then opened the bag and ran her fingers over the soft leather lining. "It's beautifully finished." She turned to the young Chinaman. "How much?"

"Nine hundred American dollar," he replied flatly with no change of face.

"A bag like this would go for at least three thousand in Marshall Field," she said to Joe.

"Do you really want it?"

"Can we afford it?"

Joe turned to the young Chinaman. "Four-fifty."

"Joe!" Kate whispered. "That's only half."

The young Chinaman frowned. "Ah. Seven hundred dollar. Best price."

"Sorry," Joe said. He shrugged and took Kate by the arm and started for the door of the shop.

The young Chinaman grinned. "Okay. Four hundred fifty American dollar." He hurried to the counter and slipped the bag into a chamois wrapper and began writing the sales slip. Still grinning, he said, "You make hard bargain."

"Damn!" Joe mumbled. "I didn't start low enough."

Kate was astonished. "I thought nine hundred was a steal."

"Now, if you feel up to it, we have time for a short tour. Singapore Harbor is one of the famous deepwater harbors of the world. The concierge can arrange for a driver."

"Joe, you and I are having the nicest love affaire in the whole world."

[27]

THEIR PLANE arrived over Manila at noon, and as it circled to land they had a fine view of Corregidor and the southern tip of Bataan across Manila Bay.

"Someday we'll return and visit Corregidor and 'Bloody Bataan,' Joe said. "That's a war story unto itself."

They had four hours to kill in Manila and found a place in the terminal that served decent American hamburgers. Then it was on to Nauru.

Air Nauru flew fat little Boeings crammed with cheap seats. Their plane was grubby inside and smelled like a sweaty locker-room, but they were grateful to discover they had an American pilot. Fortunately the plane was only half-filled, and they staked out a row of seats to themselves and managed to be comfortable with pillows. The only amenities were strange bottled beverages and strong coffee. After takeoff they tried something reputed to be fruit punch, then fell asleep. It was the middle of the night when they landed at Guam, about halfway to Nauru, and all they could see of the historic island was a shadowy blob and runway lights.

They slept on the second leg, and the sun was rising behind a distant scattering of low cumulus when the Boeing began its final approach to Nauru. This was a strange little island shaped like an oyster, four miles across the long way, encircled by an offshore coral reef, a ribbon beach of white sand, and a wreath of lush, tropical foliage and palm trees. The interior was rough, barren plateau that from the air resembled a floret of raw cauliflower with a parsley fringe—a jagged, gray waste of moonish desolation covered with serpentine scars where miners scavenged lime phosphate from the surface. Pinnacles of coral rose like stalagmites from the depths of the abandoned phosphate fields and cast long, jagged shadows in the morning crosslight.

Enroute they had read about the atoll known as "Birdshit Island." The plateau of crusted phosphate fields that dominated its topography rose some three hundred feet above the ocean. For centuries millions of seagoing birds, for reasons known only to them, had nested on Nauru and deposited untold tons of guano. The guano, rich in nitrogen and phosphoric acid, leached with the limey coral of the little atoll to synthesize high grade lime phosphate, a source of fine fertilizer that commanded good prices from the Aussies and Zealanders. Mining the phosphate brought wealth to the Nauruans but devastation to their island, for before the end of this century the supply of leached birdshit will exhaust and nothing will remain for the Nauruans but to find a new island home.

The Boeing landed hard, almost a crash, and the pilot blasted the plane to a shuddering stop at the very end of the runway with his thrust reversers. As they taxied to the ramp he came on the PA: "Welcome to the Republic of Nauru. I apologize for the bounce. These little islands have short runways. We have to plant the airplane on a dime, like a carrier landing. Sometimes we hit pretty hard." Kate wondered if any of the passengers comprehended English, let alone the metaphor, and if the pilot, who sounded Texan and probably was talking for the benefit of the two Americans aboard, cared.

They retrieved their bags, hired a taxi, and drove along the narrow, coastal road past the gateway to the president's palace, then to the Meneng Hotel, a whitewashed, two-story, cement block affair on the eastern beach. A Nauruan boy in a loose shirt, cutoffs, and sandals escorted them to their room on the upper floor and demonstrated how to operate the hot-water machine— at full production it fed little more than a rivulet to the shower. There was a double bed and a fan on the ceiling with big, white wood paddle-blades, a window facing the morning sun, and a porch with a splendid view of the blue-green water of Anibare Bay and the ocean. The tide was out and a shallow swath of calm demarcated the beach and the coral reef. Waves lapped evenly over the green coral and a steady, warm wind blew.

They were hungry and had steak and eggs and thick slabs of buttered toast in the hotel café, then the bone-tiredness of jet travel set in. They returned to their room and quickly fell asleep under the cooling breeze of the paddle-blade ceiling fan.

Joe awakened first. It was mid-afternoon, and he sat on the porch while Kate slept. The breeze had picked up, and puffy rain clouds painted great, blotchy shadows on the ocean. Whitecaps covered Anibare Bay, and breakers now tumbled over the coral reef. The clouds were forming anvils in the distance as a squallish cylinder of blue rain slanted to the ocean.

Then Kate eased up behind him and began massaging his shoulders. "Still thinking about it?"

Joe nodded. "It had to be an insider, maybe someone on the board. It's scary, where that might take us. Two people set out to kill the same man at the same time. One failed, the other succeeded. We solved the failure, but we're baffled by the success. The one that failed had a motive, which we know. The real killer must have had a motive, which we don't know? How does the cartel figure? Is there a connection with Grace?" He looked up. "It's bugging the hell out of me."

Kate massaged while they watched the gathering clouds. Then they bathed under the skimpy shower, dressed, and descended to the lobby.

From the clerk they purchased a map of Nauru's walking trails, a bottle of water with a shoulder strap, and a bag of sugar cookies. Behind the hotel, across the parking lot, began the trail to the central plateau and the phosphate fields. They penetrated the thick foliage of the coastal belt, the fringe of "parsley," then hiked up easy switchbacks on the coral cliff to the fields on top. The trail forked, and they headed into the heart of the plateau and along a road passing the field workshops. They followed the edges of the mined-out fields and peered into the mysterious, dark pits between the coral pinnacles where one might fall in and never be found. It was hot and dusty and difficult walking along some stretches of the plateau, and they munched on sugar cookies and were grateful for the water, although it tasted funny.

They followed the road to a working mine field and watched a sturdy crane lift loads of lime phosphate out of the coral pit and dump it into trucks that hauled it to the railway cars, which hauled it to the docks. They walked by stockpiles of lime phosphate and abandoned fields, then descended the switchbacks on the coral cliffs and trudged through the cool foliage, emerging on the northern tip of Anibare Bay. A mile or so across the shallow curve of the bay they saw the white shape of the Mening Hotel, which in the light of the descending sun gleamed like pink mother-of-pearl. They made their way along the sand beach, staying near the water, and on a knoll above the beach sighted a pair of coastal guns that had been abandoned by the Japanese after the war. One sat cockeyed because the side of its mount had sunk into the sand. Then a rainsquall blew in.

They took to the sidewalk by the coastal road where walking was easier, but soon the rain caught up, and the breeze quickened. The rain fell in sheets and soaked their clothing, and the wet cotton next to their skin cooled them. When they were halfway to the hotel, the rain stopped and the last of the sun came out. In their room they stripped and hung their wet things on the porch and showered and buffed each other to a pink glow with bath towels, then lay on the bed under the gentle breeze of the ceiling fan. It was twilight.

"Imagine living all your life in a place called 'Birdshit Island,'" Joe said.

Kate snuggled and rested her arm on his chest. "Did you ever do drugs?"

"I smoked a few joints in Vietnam. Didn't help much."

"Tell me what happened in Vietnam."

"That was a long time ago, sweetheart."

"Please tell me."

"Well, it was early in the game, a year before the Tet offensive. We'd been there six months. There's a place called Quang Ngai on the east coast of South Vietnam, at the lower end of the Tonkin Gulf. We were on patrol and got word that marines were in trouble. I took the patrol in and broke up the attack. We were coming out with our dead and wounded. Sergeant Cobb was on my flank, wading in a stream. A fire fight broke out. He took a round from an AK-47. It knocked him down, tore a hole in his chest bigger than my fist. He screamed. I saw him thrashing in the water. He looked at me. God! I'll never forget that look, pleading for help. I hesitated. They trained us, trained us hard, never to stop, never jeopardize the mission. But I went to him. He was bleeding and choking. The fucking muddy water was sucking into his chest. I held his head up and tried to stuff my fist in the hole. His eyes just stared. I don't know if he realized I was there. He didn't last long. I felt him die in my arms. I held him. I cried. Then I got hit. The slug smashed my leg, I went down, saw my own blood gush on the water, passed out. I remember getting plasma and riding in a basket under a chopper. They told me later that some crazy warrant officer flew through hell to pick me up. I never got to thank him. Next I remember it was a couple of days later in the hospital. I had a big cast. The doc was telling me to wiggle my toes. He was the guy who saved my life, and my leg. I came home. Cobb was dead. A lot of them were dead."

Kate listened in silence.

"I had terrible guilt. The psychiatrist said I thought I should have saved Cobb, but nothing could have saved Cobb. Anyway, I failed and got shot in the process. They gave me a medal. I'm surprised it wasn't a court martial."

"The bullet broke the bone in your thigh?"

"That's right," Joe replied. "By itself, that wouldn't have been a fatal wound. But it nicked the big artery. I damn near bled to death. Most battlefield deaths are from exsanguination—the guy bleeds out before anyone can help him. That's how my father died. I've seen the bodies, lined up, waiting for body bags—pale, waxy, bloodless. It's eerie. You never forget it."

"That's gruesome."

"A guy stuffed a bandage in my wound. It saved my life. You can control most bleeding with pressure, even major arterial bleeding. My surgeon was a slick operator. He repaired the artery, took a graft from the saphenous vein."

"Your leg is nice and straight."

"Femurs heal pretty good, especially in young guys. The muscle recovered well. I have a good quad, good hamstrings. No nerve damage, thank God. I had it made when the arterial repair worked."

Kate ran her fingers up and down the long scar on the inside of his thigh. "Wow! That's awfully close."

[28]

THE MORNING equatorial sun was ablaze when the little Boeing began its approach. Joe had asked the pilot to circle Tarawa, and he obliged them with a gentle three-sixty before turning on final. The lazy tropical atoll was stunningly beautiful. The water was pale green over the shallow fringes of the great coral reef, then ocean blue in the central lagoon. The chain of little islands, now lush with green palms, graced the triangular atoll like a giant emerald tiara. It seemed inconceivable that one of the bloodiest battles of all wars had been fought on this remote, peaceful paradise.

Joe easily recognized the island of Betio at the western tip of Tarawa. His father had written that Betio looked like a dead bird lying on its back with the beak sticking up. The description still fit. Little had changed except the once battered little island was peppered with palm trees and clusters of modest dwellings. Only a faint outline of the long abandoned airstrip was visible. Remnants of the coconut log pier extended north over the coral apron, and Joe quickly spotted Beach Red 2, west of the pier, and the seawall where his father had died. He watched in silence until they were too low to see.

The plane landed on Bonriki at the eastern tip of the atoll. They checked into the Otintai Hotel on Bikenibeu by the lagoon and decided to try the restaurant. The coffee was something of a jolt, but tolerable when taken in small sips, and the briny, smoked tuna and crackers were surprisingly tasty.

Joe unfolded a small map. "Here's what I want to do," he said. "This is the map Colonel Shoup sent my mother. It traces my father's movements during the battle. It shows the transport rendezvous and the route of the landing craft and where my father's landing craft—his amphtrack—was blown up." He pointed to pencil marks on the map. "I know where he joined up with the guys under the bridge and where they hid behind the seawall. I know where he took out the pillboxes and where he made his stand and the aid station on the beach where he died." He studied the map, then looked at Kate. "I've gone over it a thousand times. I want to retrace his steps. I want to feel as much of what he felt as I possibly can. I want to rent a boat and spend the night on the ocean where the Zeilin anchored, come in at dawn, the way they came, with the 'dodging' tide, wade over the coral like he did and crawl over the seawall and stalk the pillboxes —maybe the pillboxes will still be there. Then I want to sit on the beach where my father died. Will you go with me?"

"I wouldn't let you go alone."

"We'll take the bus to Betio today and look for a boat. I'd like to go out tomorrow in time to anchor before sunset."

"Joe, darling, do you have any idea how desperately I love you?"

They took a bus along the causeway road to Betio and walked the pathways around the perimeter of the now overcrowded little island. Battered coastal guns still stood at Takarongo Point and Temakin Point, and rows of concrete tetrahedrons stuck out of the coral reef along the ocean side where the Japs had planted them to trap invaders. The path led behind the beaches, the remnants of the coconut log pier, the seawall, and the rusting hulk of a Sherman tank in the shallow water off Red Beach 2. Joe stayed off the beaches; he wanted to save that for when he waded in from the reef. They stopped at a small park, once a temporary cemetery for marines, now a pretty lawn with palms, banana and breadfruit trees, and papaya plants, and with a stone memorial pitifully mutilated with graffiti. "My father was buried here until he was moved to Punchbowl," Joe said. The port was crowded with Gilbertese, many on Japanese motorbikes, who tendered only passing curiosity on the two Americans.

On a small dock near the old pier, they found a tuna fisherman with a twenty-foot wooden pram he agreed to rent for their over-night adventure. The sturdy pram had a square bow and wide transom and an outboard motor. The paint was flaking off the sides, but it was seaworthy and of shallow draft ideal for traversing the shallow coral apron in front of Red Beach.

Joe gave the tuna fisherman a deposit, and the man agreed to have the pram fueled and ready the next afternoon. He said it would take two hours to make it to the open water outside the boat channel, and they could moor at the marker buoy and be safe for the night. He was a sunburned, wiry little man with a graying beard and enthusiastic smile. He said that every year Americans came to Tarawa to visit the battleground.

They returned to the Otintai on the causeway bus and had whitefish and rice and Australian beer for dinner and sampled the fried breadfruit that looked inviting but tasted awful. After dinner they sat on the veranda of the hotel until sundown, then took a lazy swim in the warm lagoon and showered off the seawater and toweled to a pink glow. They crawled into bed, and Joe clung to Kate, as if fearful she might vanish, and they lay on the cool sheets, and she kissed him on the mouth and ran her tongue inside his lips and across his teeth and massaged the nape of his neck with her warm palm. Then she massaged his shoulders and the small of his back, and soon they both fell asleep. They rested well and slept out the night and most of the morning.

The next afternoon they returned to the dock on Betio, and the tuna fisherman proudly displayed the readied pram. He had done a fine job. He had stowed life jackets, a compass, a chart of the atoll, flashlights, a five-gallon jug of fresh water, a lantern, a tarpaulin for rain protection, cushions to sleep on, and spare gasoline, enough, he said, to take them out and back twice. Joe had a small duffel with a supply of corned beef, tuna, crackers, dried fruit, and chocolate.

The outboard caught with a single pull of the lanyard, and they waved to the tuna fisherman and headed north from the dock over the coral apron toward the open lagoon, Kate in the bow, Joe steering from the stern. They wore loose cottons and tennis shoes, sunglasses, and big-billed fishing hats with white havelocks they had purchased at the Otintai. The sturdy pram skimmed easily over the crystalline water, barely stirring a wake with its flat bottom. The "dodging" tide was out, and they watched the colored coral passing beneath, like a brilliant tapestry, almost close enough to touch. They came to the end of the old pier at the fringe of the coral apron, and the water suddenly deepened and changed from pale green to blue. Kate signaled, and Joe steered the pram to follow the underwater fringe that would lead them to the boat channel. They cruised northwesterly, tracking the curve of the apron. The breeze was light and the lagoon calm, and the sun burned down on them. Three miles out they came to a wafer of barren coral with a marker buoy in the center. Joe steered west and followed the row of marker buoys along the southern boundary of the boat channel to the deep water of the open Pacific. He dead reckoned another mile or so outside the reef to where he calculated the Zeilin and the other transport ships had launched their landing craft, then came about and returned to the marker buoy at the mouth of the channel.

"Along here is where the landing craft assembled for the run to the beaches," Joe said. "We'll tie up for the night." The bow of the pram nudged against the marker buoy while Kate secured a line to the mooring ring. Joe cut the motor and let the pram drift on its tether. Then he broke out the rations, and they ate hungrily and drank water from the jug. When it was time for the chocolate, he produced a flask from the duffel. "Cognac," he announced and passed the flask to Kate.

"I'm grateful for the cushions," she said. "At least you won't bruise my ass fucking me on the bottom of the boat."

They stripped down. Kate's tawny body was a golden hue under the late afternoon sun. They leaned over the side to rinse their clothes, then she and Joe wrung them out and spread them over the gunwales. Joe dropped a ladder over the side, and they jumped into the water. It was delightfully cool, and they clung to the ladder and scrubbed and shampooed each other, then swam a quick lap around the pram and scrambled out and wrapped up in the towels.

"That was great," Kate said. She curled up in his arms.

"The water was perfect," Joe said.

"I wonder if the sunset was this beautiful the night before the invasion."

Joe pulled her hair back and kissed her forehead and leaned down and kissed her breasts. "You're awfully good to come with me. I love you. I'm sorry for the inconveniences."

"I wouldn't have missed it for the world."

"Watch the sun now. When it sets in the Pacific, it seems to hang on the horizon, then suddenly drop into the ocean. Darkness comes in a hurry."

"It's happening," Kate said.

"Soon the moon will rise."

"Will there be ghosts?" She squeezed him.

"Yes, ghosts. Long shadows dwell in the Pacific."

They slept huddled together on the cushions in the bottom of the pram. During the night it rained but they stayed dry under the tarpaulin. At dawn they awakened and devoured the remainder of the food, then slipped into their damp clothes. Joe started the outboard and cast off from the buoy and headed back through the boat channel, and the sun rose and warmed them. They turned south at the wafer of coral that marked the line of departure of the amphtracks. Dead ahead was the north shore of Betio. When they came to green water at the fringe of the coral apron, they could see the white sand of Beach Red 2 by the old coconut log pier. The "dodging" tide was out, and barely three feet of water covered the coral, as it had when the marines invaded. A hundred yards from the beach, on the spot where Joe Hawkins' amphtrack met destruction, Joe idled the outboard and slid into the cool, waist-deep water. Kate stayed with the pram. A current gripped his legs, and he struggled to keep balance. It surprised him how tricky it was wading on coral in waterlogged tennis shoes, and he cringed at the thought of doing it in boondockers with combat regalia and an M-1. He made it to the old pier and followed the surviving stanchions to the beach. He slipped, and the coral cut a shallow gash in his wrist, and when he flopped down by the remnant of seawall, he was exhausted. Kate had run the pram onto the beach and was sitting on the warm sand with the jug of water, smiling patiently.

"You're out of breath," she noted.

"That was more than I bargained for," Joe replied. He drank from the water jug. "I only came a hundred yards, with no gear. Our guys waded all the way with full gear, under heavy fire. I don't know how they did it."

She noticed the blood on his wrist. "What happened?"

"Coral is vicious. It's only a scratch." He pulled out the map. "This is a good little map. The yardages are marked. We're on Beach Red 2. Red 1 is beyond that bend in the shoreline. Red 3 is on the other side of the pier."

A few yards out the tipped hulk of an old Sherman tank rusted in the water. Joe pointed to it. "I have photographs showing that very tank and dead marines on the beach. They were taken the day of the invasion." A little farther out were the wrecks of two amphtracks.

A warm zephyr carried the smell of dead fish across the white sand beach, and the sun, halfway to its zenith, was now very hot. The tide was low, and the ancient wreckage of amphtracks, field pieces, vehicles, and shapeless junk—unclaimed relics of war disintegrating in the sea—lay exposed in shallow water across the coral apron. Two young boys wearing short pants and sun-browned like berries waded to the Sherman tank and crawled on top of the battered gun turret. "It's not a very pretty beach now," Kate said.

Joe stood up. "This is all that's left of the seawall," he said.

"Some of these pockmarks were made by bullets. We're standing about where my father landed when he waded in. He went back to get two men under the pier, then he huddled here and saw what was happening to the guys on the reef." He pointed to the coral apron they had just traversed. At the outer edge they could see the abrupt change from green to dark blue, where the reef dropped away to the deep water of the lagoon. "Machine guns behind the seawall cut them to ribbons. The colonel died instantly. My father was the only surviving officer on Beach Red 2. The beachhead was a shambles. He scouted the seawall and corralled the few marines able to fight. Between them they had a flamethrower, their M-1's, and grenades. It was little enough for tackling pillboxes."

Joe and Kate walked along the beach next to the remnants of the seawall. "This is where they went over the top," Joe said, consulting the map. Beyond the seawall ran a broad stretch of sand with palm trees and scattered patches of grass, and at the far edge of the sand, a dirt road. Cars and motorcycles passed infrequently. "It looks peaceful enough now." Joe took Kate by the hand, and they climbed over the seawall and walked toward the road.

Fifty yards inland they came to a concrete slab obscured by weeds. "The first pillbox must have been on this slab," Joe said. "The Japs killed our flamethrower guy. My father was right beside him. He commandeered the flamethrower and somehow crawled up to grenade range. He threw a couple of grenades, doused the pillbox with fire, then ran up and tossed a grenade inside. Then he gave it another shot of fire through the gun slit. Anyone still alive got fried."

"That's gruesome," Kate said.

"The pillboxes were in a row parallel to the seawall. The next one was about fifty yards over there." They walked across the soft sand. "There's no slab, but it must have been about here," Joe said. "He took it out the same way."

Ahead was a thin cluster of palms. "I see a pillbox," Joe said, and they walked hurriedly through the palms. The pillbox was shoulder high—a squatty, gray, truncated, six-sided, flat-topped thing of heavy steel with a gun slit in front and a small doorway in back. It was in remarkably good condition. The steel plates were still solidly bolted, and the surface, though thinly corroded, had a few shiny patches where the natives on Betio must have had reason to polish it. The pillbox was anchored firmly to a concrete slab. With a little tidying up, it could be battle-ready again.

Joe stood in front of the pillbox staring at the gun slit. He was trembling. "My God. This has to be where my father made his stand. It's marked on the map." His heart raced, and he stepped closer to the pillbox and tapped one of the steel plates. He walked to the rear of the pillbox, looked in the doorway, recoiled from the stench. "They must use it as an outhouse," he said. He stepped inside and in a moment retreated. "That is really awful. I'm sorry. Don't go in. I had to see. The damn thing couldn't hold more than two or three Japs and a machine gun. Can you imagine being locked in there and having a flamethrower come at you through that gun slit? What a way to die."

"I can't imagine any of it," Kate said.

"He finished it off like the others," Joe said. "They shot him in the thigh. He leaned against the pillbox here"—Joe moved to the side of the gun slit—"and tied a kerchief around the wound. The Japs charged from over there." He pointed in the direction of the dirt road behind the pillbox. "When the Japs got close, he spun out and burned them with the flamethrower. They were twenty or thirty yards away. A swarm of Japs kept coming—crazy little bastards—he blasted them with the flamethrower until it was empty. They went down like tenpins. The flamethrower incinerated them. You could smell burned flesh. He threw the last of the grenades. Then he opened fire with his M-1. I don't know how many clips he fired. Dead Japs piled up in front of him. They couldn't hit him. His men crawled forward and screamed at him to get down, but he just stood there and fired, like a crazy man. He took a bullet in the chest. It knocked him to his knees. He continued firing, then a twenty millimeter caught him in the shoulder. It nearly took his arm off. He fell beside the pillbox, right here, bleeding to death. His men turned back what was left of the Japs. One stuffed a kerchief in the wound. A corpsman gave my father morphine."

Tears flooded Joe's cheeks. "Oh, Joe," Kate whispered.

He knelt and retrieved a small metallic object buried in the sandy soil by the pillbox. "This is a thirty-caliber shell casing," he said, wiping it clean, "from one of our M-1's." He handed the casing to Kate. "It may have been one of my father's. He fired a couple of hundred rounds right here by the pillbox." She returned the casing and he dropped it into his pocket.

"Over there twenty yards out is probably where old Kajimoto went down, where my father didn't finish him." Joe just stared and shook his head.

"They got a stretcher and somehow carried my father back to the seawall." Joe gripped Kate's hand and they walked in silence to the seawall and along the beach to the pier. The two little boys still sat on the Sherman tank.

"They took him to the aid station by the pier. The corpsman bandaged him. The medical boxes hadn't made it to the beaches, and they had no plasma. The doctor had been killed on the reef. My father's men stayed with him, shaded him from the sun."

Joe reached into his shirt pocket. "Remember this picture of mother and little Janie and me? My father had it tucked in the webbing inside his helmet. Someone got it back to us."

"I remember," Kate replied.

"He bled out. He died. There was nothing anyone could do."

Joe sat on the sand, and Kate kneeled beside him. "My father died on this very spot." Joe began sobbing. "I'm so proud. I don't know how he did what he did. He was a nice, regular sort of guy, but when he had to, he turned into a killing machine. They said he killed a hundred Japs." Joe buried his face in his hands and cried, softly at first, then with great wrenching spasms. Kate hugged him and they cried together.

"I guess wars are won by nice, regular guys," she said.

"I know he's here," Joe said.

The breeze stirred and cooled them a little, but now the sun blazed in the clear sky, and it was hot sitting on the sand. The tide was returning. Surf crept steadily closer and the waves broke with soft splashes. She massaged his neck and shoulders and gradually the sobbing lessened and he relaxed in her arms. In a few moments he kissed her and smiled. "I'm okay."

He fetched the cassette player from the duffel in the pram. "Stardust" came first, and he turned the sound as loud as it would go and beckoned to Kate. They kicked off their shoes, embraced, danced on the sand, and were something to behold in their billowy white cottons and sunglasses and big-billed fishing hats. They danced into the surf where the wet sand was firm and the cool, dulcet water streamed over their feet. They danced to the music Jake and Betty Hawkins loved, romantic music, music for lovers—"I'll Be Seeing You," "Melancholy Baby,"—danced elegantly and adoringly, then outrageously to a raucous, blaring, trumpety "Two O'Clock Jump," cavorting like dervishes, sweating and breathless. Then they collapsed in the surf, embraced, kissed longingly, and the waves washed over them and floated the fishing hats onto the sand. They lay motionless, their bodies entwined, savoring the caresses of foaming seawater, and finally struggled to their feet and waded to the pram, and the breeze from the lagoon cooled them down. They drank from the water jug and started the outboard and chugged out, waving to the brown young boys perched on the hulk of the rusted Sherman.

"In four days, we landed eighteen thousand marines, took a thousand dead, two thousand wounded, killed five thousand Japs, all on this miserable half-square-mile of sand and coral. They still argue about the necessity. We made mistakes, but we learned. Tarawa showed the way. It was worth it. I hate not having my father, but I will never believe he died in vain."

That evening they had dinner in the Otintai then strolled for an hour along the dark roads of Bikenibeu. They returned and lay on the bed, and the breeze from the lagoon wafted the curtain on the big window in their room and brought the rank smell of fishing boats.

He stared at the shadowy ceiling. "I've been thinking about my kids. It's been almost three weeks. That's not fair."

"I want to meet them," Kate said.

"That'll be the next order of business."

Kate snuggled closer. "I understand we can get a Big Mac in Tokyo," she said.

"And fries, I hope. I'm sick of rice."

"I wonder what those two little brown boys thought about us wallowing on the sand."

"A pair of beached whales in heat," Joe said.

[29]

THE JAL-747 out of Guam landed midmorning at the Narita Airport in Tokyo. A chauffeur bearing a sign with both their names in bold letters met them at the customs desk.

"How did they know I was coming?" Kate whispered.

"Damned if I know," Joe said.

The chauffeur drove them to the Palace Hotel, and a young Japanese man of athletic bearing, smartly attired in gray chalk stripe, greeted them in the lobby. He bowed gracefully. "Dr. Hawkins. Welcome to Tokyo. I am Gihachi Miyoshi, Dr. Kajimoto's assistant. Perhaps you remember me as George. We have spoken on occasion by telephone."

"George, of course," Joe said. "I recognize your voice and your flawless English."

They shook hands. "I trust you had a comfortable journey," George said.

"Long, but very comfortable, thank you," Joe replied. He introduced Kate. "This is Miss Murphy."

Another graceful bow. "How do you do, Miss Murphy. I am honored."

"Dr. Hawkins told me about you," Kate said.

"I've arranged your accommodations," George said. "I hope

they are satisfactory. The afternoon is unscheduled. Perhaps you would care to rest."

"We are a little tired," Joe said.

"Very well. Dr. Kajimoto hopes you will join him for dinner."

"Sounds good."

"The chauffeur will pick you up at eight." George produced a card. "You can reach me at this number. I am at your service. Don't hesitate to call."

In the elevator Kate said, "I take it that was the infamous George."

"That's him," Joe said. "A little sturdier than I envisioned. He might double as a bodyguard."

The bellman escorted them to a luxurious suite with an enormous double bed and a panorama of the emperor's Imperial Palace across the moat that circled the palace grounds. "I suppose the entire Far East knows I'm sleeping with you," Kate said when she saw the bed.

"I detect the fine hand of Pierre Globa."

"Well, let's make the most of it."

They snuggled and had a delicious nap, then strolled along the moat, found a McDonalds near the hotel and joyfully ate Big Macs—"Jap Macs," Joe called them—with fries and a Coke. Then they napped again, showered, and dressed.

While they waited in the lobby, Joe abruptly announced, "I think Mike Devlin killed Leonard Breslow."

"You can't be serious," Kate replied.

"Assuming it was an insider, Devlin was the only person besides Letitia who could have had a motive."

"Convince me."

"Remember the axiom from Watergate, 'Follow the money'? In this case that means expense accounts. One of Breslow's special duties was reimbursing Devlin for his AMA expenses. If Devlin was pulling shenanigans, Breslow would know it. That's a blackmail situation, plain and simple. Ergo, motive."

"Like, what shenanigans?"

"Cheating on expenses. Devlin undoubtedly spent a lot of AMA money—we just witnessed Maxwell's performance in Madrid—

and no one questions the chairman of the board. In a year Devlin could easily have run up enough pad to trigger a charge of tax evasion. A word to the IRS could have destroyed him."

"Wouldn't the IRS find out anyway?"

"Probably not without a tip-off. Breslow could have covered. Anyway, when Breslow discovered his HIV problem, I figure he panicked and tried to get money out of Devlin, like he did with Letitia."

"You think Devlin hired someone to kill him?"

"Of course. Mike Devlin is no barehanded killer."

"Was Devlin also involved with the cartel?"

"It's possible, but I doubt it. The cartel owns Letitia and didn't need Devlin. Furthermore, Breslow made no mention of Devlin in the memo he left in the LEDGER FILE."

"Could Breslow have blackmailed other board members?"

"He didn't handle their reimbursements, so he wouldn't have known they were cheating. He dealt only with Devlin and Letitia. The chief financial officer personally takes care of the chairman of the board and the executive vice-president. Subordinates do the rest of us. Besides, Letitia and Devlin were the only big spenders. No one else was worth blackmailing."

"Are you dismissing the gay thing completely?"

"I think so. If this was a gay thing, it still had to be an insider. Conlan is a possibility, but it's only rumor that he was gay. Nothing connects him with Breslow. And sure as hell there are no gays on the board. Furthermore, this had the earmarks of a planned, professional execution, not a crime of passion."

"Do you really believe Dr. Devlin had the balls for this?" Kate obviously had a hard time with Joe's theory.

"Good question. The answer is, yes, if sufficiently motivated. Look, someone killed Breslow. It wasn't Letitia, and we've excluded everyone else but Devlin. I say it's worth a shot."

The chauffeur arrived promptly at eight and drove them to a secluded street near the hotel. He parked in front of a heavy steel gate in a stone wall, where George waited.

George bowed. "Good evening. Did you have a restful afternoon?"

"We did, thank you," Joe replied.

"This is Kicho, Dr. Kajimoto's favorite teahouse. Dr. Kajimoto is expecting you."

Kajimoto, a wizened, squat little man with sallow skin and a dour expression, stood within the dimly lighted entry. His bullet-shaped head was completely bald, his neck stubby, his belly round like a gourd, he had banty legs, and he wore an ill-fitting black suit with the rumpled look of a well-traveled drip-dry. This guy is right out of central casting, Joe thought. In uniform, with a samurai sword at his side, he could have been Admiral Yamamoto, or a sadistic Jap prison camp commander in a John Wayne or Alec Guinness war movie.

The old Oriental bowed, then extended his hand and greeted them with a veritable explosion of teeth—faintly yellowed but for a solitary bicuspid of gold—in a face of wrinkled parchment. It was a smile of astonishing warmth, a touch of mischief, and a remarkable transformation. "Dr. Hawkins. Miss Murphy. Welcome to Tokyo," he said in halting English with his familiar staccato. Kate stared at the exquisite Mobe pearl stickpin on his tie.

"Good evening, Dr. Kajimoto," Joe replied. "It's a pleasure to meet you."

Kajimoto then spoke in Japanese and, as before, George translated the conversation and quickly became unnoticed. "I speak English poorly," Kajimoto said. "However, George, who I promised would translate upon your visit, is fluent."

"I remember your promise," Joe said. "Thank you for having George. I'm sure we'll get along very well."

George grinned and said, "Thank you, Dr. Hawkins."

Again, the explosion of teeth, and Kajimoto said, "I am honored by your visit."

"The honor is ours, sir," Joe said.

Then Kajimoto said, "I was saddened by your wife's tragic death last year."

"I appreciated your kind note," Joe replied.

"Ah. Tonight you will experience a traditional Japanese dinner. I hope you enjoy my geishas. They are among the best in Japan."

They removed their shoes and a Japanese woman in a blue silk kimona led them into the teahouse. The corridors were utterly quiet and laden with incense. Straw matting covered the floors and was slippery under their stocking feet, and along the walls hung murals of animals, mountains, and ancient Japanese figures in flowing robes. They proceeded to a room barren of furniture but for a black lacquered table set low in a shallow pit in the center of the floor. Mats and napkins of white linen brocade and a cluster of lighted candles on a silver dish adorned the table, and silken pillows lay around the pit. Kajimoto removed his jacket, unabashedly exposing the gourdlike belly, and settled on his haunches with a pillow wedged into the small of his back. He unfolded a small pocket fan, briskly flagellated the air before his face, and seemed altogether content.

"Please feel free to remove your jacket," George said. "It is warm in the teahouse. There are fans on the table. Those not accustomed to sitting in the Japanese manner often experience discomfort, especially in the knees. A visit to the toilet also serves to stretch the legs." He smiled. "Americans make many visits to the toilet when dining in Japanese teahouses." They removed their jackets and sat around the table and fanned.

The first geisha appeared. She was a stunning Japanese woman in red brocade, and she glided smoothly over the straw matting with a whispery shuffle. Her coal-black hair was styled like a giant gingko leaf, her face was pasty white with clown makeup, her eyes were dark with heavy shadow and mascara, and she carried a silver tray holding a flasklike porcelain bottle and four miniature cups. Three geishas quickly followed, similarly costumed, gliding with the same whispery shuffle. The first geisha poured straw-colored liquid from the bottle into the miniature cups, and the others placed the cups in front of Kajimoto and his guests. Then they all smiled and kneeled obediently on the straw matting.

"This is sake," Kajimoto said. "Rice wine. Sake is served very warm."

Joe sipped the warm sake. "It tastes a little like sweet sherry. I like it."

Kajimoto turned to Kate. "Do you like the sake, Miss Murphy?"

"Very much, Dr. Kajimoto." It was the first Kate had spoken since entering the teahouse.

Joe turned to George. "Where did you learn English, my friend?"

"I grew up in Denver," George said. "My father was a college teacher. We moved to Japan when I was in high school. I then returned to the University of Chicago."

"How did you acquire the name 'George'?"

"My fellow students in Chicago called me George because it was easier than Gihachi."

"A reasonable compromise," Kajimoto said.

"I would like to propose a toast," Joe said. He raised his sake cup. "To our host."

"Hear! Hear!" Kate said, and they upended their drinks. Kajimoto appeared pleased and the geishas, smiling and giggling, promptly replenished the cups.

"How much sake must one drink to become drunk?" Joe asked.

"Less than one might think," Kajimoto replied. "Sake is consumed in small amounts. The geishas continuously add hot sake to the little cups to replace that consumed, and to preserve the warmth. It is easy to lose track of the amount one is drinking."

The geishas chattered cheerfully and produced a hibachi with hot coals, then served noodle soup and abalone, to be eaten with porcelain spoons and ivory chopsticks.

"This is delicious," Kate said.

"I enjoy Kicho," Kajimoto said. "Last year I was ill and entered the hospital. The food was very bad. Bad food is a frequent complaint about hospitals, yes?" He smiled. "While convalescing I ordered meals prepared by Kicho and served in the hospital by geishas. This caused the director of the hospital to lose face."

"That's a funny story," Joe said.

"It is good for a hospital director to lose face," Kajimoto said.

"I agree," Joe replied. "I trust you're feeling well now."

"I am well for an old man with cancer of the prostate. I still enjoy sake in sizable amounts."

"That's a very good sign," Joe said, smiling.

"I received palliative irradiation. My cancer has invaded the pelvic bones and cannot be cured. However, I expect to live a long time."

"You will live many years," Joe said. "May your capacity for sake never diminish."

Kajimoto smiled and shifted on his haunches. "Now, tell me about Tarawa."

"I had a remarkable visit," Joe said. "I found my father's battleground, waded in the lagoon where he came ashore, found the pillbox where he was fatally wounded, and the beach where he died."

"I have never returned to Tarawa," Kajimoto said. "After the war I studied Japanese and American accounts of the battle. I prepared a map depicting my own movements and the action in which I was wounded. In those accounts I read of Captain Hawkins' bravery and determined it was he who spared my life. Your speech awakened my remembrance." George handed him the map.

"General Shoup sent a map to my mother," Joe said, reaching for his jacket.

They unfolded the maps, disregarding the food and sake and the coddling geishas. Before them, in stark, military cartography, lay the wretched little island of Betio—the central lagoon, the coral reef, and the pier.

"Our maps are similar," Kajimoto said. "These were my positions." He pointed to marks on his map.

"My father's movements are marked on General Shoup's map," Joe said. "This is the boat channel in the reef, north of Betio. The main attack force rendezvoused outside the channel—here." He pointed to the location. "The landing craft entered the lagoon after midnight . . . naval ships bombarded Betio . . . three hours of heavy shelling . . . carrier planes bombed and strafed the beaches at dawn . . . the landing craft started their run . . . amphtracks followed by Higgins boats . . . three miles to the beaches . . . the tide deserted them . . . the amphtracks made it . . . the Higgins boats stuck on the coral . . . the enemy opened fire . . . machine guns and heavy stuff . . . a massive enfilade . . . the men in the Higgins boats had to wade through the fire to the beach . . . seven hundred yards, chest deep in water, over coral."

Kajimoto listened attentively.

"Kate and I retraced the invasion. My father's amphtrack was blown up about here." Joe pointed to a mark on his map. "I waded in like he did. A few derelicts of the battle are still there—an old Sherman tank, remnants of amphtracks and Higgins boats, a few field pieces. The pier and the seawall still stand. He landed on Beach Red 2, next to the pier. His colonel was killed going in, as were most of his men."

Kajimoto studied the maps, then said, "I was entrenched here, behind the seawall." He pointed to the location. "I believed Betio to be invincible. We had five thousand imperial marines. Only our large coastal guns and a few troops had been lost to the bombardment. I believed the Americans would all die in defeat. Yet, when I saw them wade across the reef and take the beaches, against terrible fire, I believed they would be victorious. They attacked in waves. Many fell, still they advanced. They were indomitable. I and my fellow marines lost heart. We had never witnessed courage of such magnitude."

"My father gathered his remaining men and crossed the seawall, here," Joe said, again pointing to the maps. "He took out a pillbox here, and here, and a third pillbox here. This is where he made his last stand."

"I was one hundred meters from the last pillbox," Kajimoto said, also pointing to the map. "I witnessed your father's attack and believed him to be a madman. My platoon charged his position. He killed those ahead of me with a flamethrower. I expected to be burned alive, but the flamethrower exhausted its fuel. I ran forward, firing at your father. Nothing seemed to touch him. He fired at me. I was hit in the chest and fell. I lay there helpless. He raised his rifle to kill me. Our eyes engaged, and he lowered the rifle. As I watched, he was hit and dropped to his knees. He continued firing, then suffered a mortal wound. He bled profusely."

"The pillbox still stands," Joe said. "It's rusty, but intact." He reached into his pocket. "I found this thirty-caliber casing. It could have been from my father's M-1."

Kajimoto examined the casing and smiled. "Perhaps it is the one used to shoot me."

"Perhaps," Joe said.

"Your father's bullet fractured my ribs and scapula and penetrated my lung. I coughed up blood. I was picked up by your navy corpsmen and treated on board a ship. A doctor inserted chest tubes and administered plasma. I regained consciousness. Later a surgeon drained an abscess and removed a segment of lung. When my condition improved I was interrogated, then taken to Australia. When Japan surrendered, I was repatriated."

"Thoracic surgery is my line of work," Joe said. "You were treated correctly and had a fine recovery."

"To my surprise I was not allowed to die. American doctors did not neglect prisoners."

"In their eyes you were a patient," Joe explained.

"Your father was a great hero," Kajimoto said. I admired his bravery. He fought courageously and killed many imperial marines, yet, he spared my life."

"It's a miracle that our paths cross after all these years," Joe said, stretching his legs beneath the table.

"Let us finish our dinner," Kajimoto said. After they folded the maps, the geishas poured fresh, hot sake, then served a succession of delicacies from the hibachi—sesame tofu, duck, sashimi, shrimp, beef, vegetables, rice—in tidy portions, each with ivory chopsticks.

"Did the visit to Tarawa kindle your hatred for Japanese?" Kajimoto asked.

"I no longer hate Japanese," Joe replied. "Tarawa was a long time ago. Many young men died there, Americans and Japanese. I was saddened, but I found solace, not hatred."

"That is good," Kajimoto said. "Hatred in war is inevitable. I hated my enemy. Now I am too old to hate."

"I am curious, sir," Joe said. "You told me your father opposed the war. Why, then, did you become an imperial marine?"

"Ah. You remember our previous conversation. As a young man I rebelled. Contrary to my father's wishes, I became a samurai militarist and favored the attack on Pearl Harbor. Many samurai became imperial marines. The crushing defeat of Japan caused me to renounce our military leaders. Fortunately my father forgave my militarism. After the war he encouraged me to study medicine and provided resources for me to organize the Japan Medical Association."

"We both had strong fathers," Joe said.

"For thirty-five years I have been president of the Japan Medical Association. I enjoy friendships with the AMA and other health organizations of the world. I hope those friendships will endure. There is much unrest in the world. Doctors must pursue peace through the common bond of medicine. In that regard I share the dream of my friend, the wise old warrior, Pierre Globa."

"Pierre Globa is a man of vision," Joe said.

"With the assistance of Pierre Globa, I organized a committee of the World Health Organization to study medical needs of the elderly. It is a tragic paradox that doctors will some day be overwhelmed by the fruits of their success. Soon the elderly of the world will exceed the resources needed to care for them."

"Kate told me of your work," Joe said. "I understand the 'Kajimoto Principle.' American politicians also understand. The ranks of the elderly in my country are expanding so rapidly, due to improved medical care, that our Medicare program will soon face bankruptcy. Your brilliant analysis clarified this important issue."

Kajimoto appeared pleased. "Perhaps you and Miss Murphy will attend the next meeting of my committee. We convene in the fall, in Kyoto. You would enjoy riding the bullet train to Kyoto."

"Your enduring presidency of Japan Medical is a remarkable achievement," Joe said.

"Ah," replied Kajimoto. "I am a realist, Dr. Hawkins. I endure because I provide a great deal of money to the Japan Medical Association."

Joe laughed. "Nevertheless, you are an important world leader in medicine."

"Some regard me as ruthless and uncompromising. I work to improve our profession. At times a firm hand is required."

Then Joe said, "You knew Kate would accompany me to Tokyo?"

"Ah. Pierre Globa telephoned me."

"We are very pleased with our accommodations," Joe said.

A twinkle brightened the eyes of the old Oriental. "Pierre Globa informed me that you and Miss Murphy are very close friends. I am an old man, but I remember romance. I am very happy for my two young colleagues."

He removed the Mobe pearl from his tie and handed it to Kate. "You admired my pearl," Miss Murphy. Please enjoy it, as I have for many years, and think of me when you wear it."

Kate was astonished. "It's beautiful, Dr. Kajimoto." She fastened the pearl to her dress. "I don't know how to thank you."

"Your presence is sufficient. Now, I propose a toast." Kajimoto raised his cup of sake. "To my young colleagues: May the sun warm your path through life together."

"That's a beautiful thought, Dr. Kajimoto," Kate said. She leaned over and kissed him.

Kajimoto beamed. "I like American customs." He turned to Joe. "I am very pleased you will become president of the American Medical Association. A new face is needed. You are an accomplished surgeon. You represent the best in our profession. I am confident you will become a distinguished leader."

"I will do my best," Joe said.

"Letitia Jordan said you were elected by accident. That is not true. You are admired and trusted. Your speech in Madison Square Garden was brilliant. Letitia Jordan believes she knows everything. She is not correct."

"You know Letitia well," Joe said.

"She incurred the displeasure of President Chamberlain. That is unfortunate for her. One is foolish to trifle with David Chamberlain."

"Extremely foolish," Joe said.

Kajimoto continued. "The current chairman of your board of trustees, Dr. Maxwell, will visit Japan next month. Letitia Jordan advised me that Dr. Maxwell will officially represent the AMA. I would prefer that you represented the AMA. Dr. Maxwell obeys Letitia Jordan."

Joe smiled, amused at Kajimoto's frankness. "Well, sir, I do not obey Letitia Jordan."

"Ah, quite true." Kajimoto sipped his sake. "What do you plan for your presidency?"

Joe thought for a moment, then replied, "Bottom line, I intend to restore fundamental integrity."

"Will you resolve differences with your government?"

"I hope so. President Chamberlain wants to forge an alliance with the AMA. He promised to create a separate department of health with cabinet rank. He also agreed to withdraw his proposal for a national health policy and collaborate with us on a suitable alternative." Kate winked her approval. Joe had not breached the President's confidence.

Then Kajimoto asked, "What will be the fate of Letitia Jordan?"

"She will be forced to resign."

"Ah. That will displease the tobacco cartel."

"Exactly," Joe said. He sipped his sake. "Regarding the cartel, Dr. Kajimoto, are you familiar with 'Y–1—Brazil—Jeno'?"

Kajimoto appeared momentarily startled. He frowned, then said, "I am aware that 'Y–1' is a genetically engineered strain of tobacco developed in Brazil. It contains a higher level of nicotine and is more addictive than conventional strains. Recently 'Y–1' has drawn the attention of the cartel."

"Bingo!" Joe said. "What about 'Jeno'?"

"'Jeno' is a Japanese electronics corporation."

"What does 'Jeno' have to do with 'Y–1'?"

"I am not aware of a connection between 'Y–1' and 'Jeno,'" Kajimoto replied. "Why do you inquire?"

"Curiosity," Joe replied. "Last year the chief financial officer of the AMA, a man named Leonard Breslow, died under mysterious circumstances. He knew about some of Letitia Jordan's dealings. The police think Breslow was murdered. They found mention of 'Y–1—Brazil—Jeno' in his files and believe it may be a clue. With your knowledge of the cartel, I thought you might know the meaning."

"I regret I cannot be of greater assistance." Then Kajimoto gestured and the geishas instantly retired. "Dr. Hawkins, I bring disturbing information." The spirited guttural softened. "I believe that you and Miss Murphy are in imminent danger to your lives."

Joe was stunned. "What do you mean?"

"Allow me to explain. As you know, the Tora Society of Japan controls the tobacco cartel. You also know that I am a Tora by birthright, although I do not condone criminal acts. From time to time I receive information about the Toras. Recently I learned that the death of Mrs. Hawkins resulted from a bungled attempt to frighten her, ordered by the Tora Society to intimidate you. Hoodlums were assigned to the task. They did not intend physical harm. They collided with her automobile by accident. For this grievous error they were executed."

Joe turned ashen and Kate gasped and reached for his hand. "Oh, Joe," she whispered.

Then Kajimoto said, "Luther Agostelli, the husband of Letitia Jordan, instigated the ill-fated attack."

"My God!" Joe said.

"At the direction of Letitia Jordan, he advised Jonathan Ridge that you posed a serious threat to the performance of her duties on behalf of the tobacco cartel, and that she wanted something done about it. Senator Ridge informed the cartel."

"Then, Letitia Jordan killed Grace!" Joe said.

"That is essentially correct," Kajimoto replied.

"Bitch!"

"Luther Agostelli also informed Senator Ridge that he had personally arranged the intimidation of Dr. Rodansky, who in a display of anger had demanded disclosure of the tax returns of senior AMA officials. According to Agostelli, forcing disclosure in this manner would have seriously undermined Letitia Jordan's authority in AMA affairs, upon which the cartel relies. I understand that a freshly killed infant chicken with black feathers symbolizing Dr. Rodansky's negro mistress—a 'black chick' in American vernacular, if you will—was delivered anonymously to Dr. Rodansky as a warning, and that Dr. Rodansky withdrew his demand. This incident was the work of Luther Agostelli."

Joe struggled to remain calm. "I was with Dr. Rodansky when he received the 'warning.'"

"Letitia Jordan had hoped the accidental death of Mrs.

Hawkins would cause you to resign your presidency. Since you did not resign, her husband has now asked Senator Ridge to have you removed."

"Let 'em try," Joe said, seething.

"Miss Murphy is also in danger."

Kate tightened her grip on Joe's hand.

"Dr. Hawkins, I can guarantee that neither of you will suffer harm provided you cease your opposition to Letitia Jordan and the cartel."

"I see," Joe said. "And if I don't agree?"

"The Toras will order your assassinations."

There it was, a bloody nightmare. In simple terms, it was back off or die. Joe, enraged and heartsick, looked at Kate, saw the trust in her eyes, the adoring love. God! If anything happened. He had lost Grace. He couldn't lose Kate. Would they try something in Tokyo? Doubtful. Too obvious. He would contact Scott, get the hell out of here. In the meantime, stay cool, shake 'em up, give 'em something to think about. You can't reason with a rattlesnake.

Joe lashed out. "Frankly, Dr. Kajimoto, I am shocked and angered. It is reprehensible that you would invite me to Tokyo, honor us with a delightful dinner and charming conversation, then threaten us. With all due respect, sir, I fail to understand your intentions."

"I sincerely regret the distress I bring to you and Miss Murphy," Kajimoto replied. "Please understand that I am fulfilling my duty."

"Duty?"

"Remember that I am a samurai. Like the American marine, once a samurai, always a samurai. By tradition, a samurai is beholden to one who saves his life. Upon death of the benefactor, the samurai is beholden to the first-born son. Therefore, I am beholden to you, Dr. Hawkins, the first-born son of Captain Jake Hawkins. I am obligated to preserve your life. That is what I am attempting to do. It is a debt of honor."

Joe reflected on Kajimoto's words, then replied calmly. "You make a compelling argument, sir. All right, tell your Tora friends to call off the assassinations. I will cease my opposition to Letitia

Jordan and the cartel." He again glanced at Kate and saw the look of disbelief. "However, be advised this may not have the effect they desire. President Chamberlain has already ordered the Department of Justice, the Federal Drug Authority, and the surgeon general of the United States to destroy the cartel. Letitia Jordan and other key figures will soon be indicted for criminal violations. I am powerless to influence these events."

Kajimoto paused, then said, "That is unfortunate. However, I will explain the circumstances and urge the Toras to accept your explanation."

Joe stared at the old man. Maybe you can reason with a rattlesnake. "I also advise you, sir, that Kate and I are acting under instructions of our President. If harm befalls either of us, those responsible will incur the undiluted wrath of David Chamberlain."

Kajimoto pondered Joe's words, then said, "So be it." His voice had weakened. He beckoned and the geishas promptly reappeared. "Now, some brandy."

"Dr. Kajimoto is tiring," George said.

The geishas served the spirit in small, crystalline glasses the shape of sake cups. "Apricot brandy from Hokkaido," George said, "Dr. Kajimoto's favorite."

Then Kajimoto said, "Aesculapius was the Greek god of healing. His symbol, the staff entwined with a serpent, denotes excellence and is the honored badge of your great American Medical Association. You, Dr. Hawkins, are a true Aesculapian."

"You honor me, sir," Joe said.

They sipped the brandy, and the flame of the candles cast a soft blush of cathedral light on Kajimoto's weathered face. "You are blessed with Miss Murphy, my friend. I pray for your eternal happiness."

"Thank you," Kate said.

"The brandy is strong," Joe said.

"Very strong," Kate said.

"Ah," Kajimoto said. "Very strong."

[30]

THEY RETURNED to the hotel without discussing Kajimoto, fearing the chauffeur had been assigned to eavesdrop. When they were alone Kate rushed to Joe's arms. "I don't understand the man," she said. "We were having a beautiful evening, then he dropped this . . . bomb."

"I suppose we should be grateful," Joe said.

"Honey." She trembled in his arms. "You didn't sell out, did you?"

"No, but I want him to think I did."

"You convinced me."

"I lied. I hope I convinced him."

"I'm sorry about everything. If I hadn't talked you into that stupid speech in the first place, none of this would have happened—Letitia Jordan, Kajimoto, the cartel, the whole mess. Your children would have their mother. No one would be threatening to kill us." Finally she relaxed. "I feel so damn guilty."

"You mustn't. It's not your fault."

"I can't help it."

"I know, but you mustn't." Tenderly he kissed her forehead. "We can't undo what's happened. I love you, Kate Murphy, here, now, and forever, with all my heart and soul. That will never change."

"Mean it?"

"You know I do."

"I'm scared. Are you scared?"

"Yes, but I don't think they'll try anything here in Tokyo."

"Right now I could use something stronger than sake."

"So could I."

He released her and she inspected the contents of the bar. "We have plenty of Courvoisier."

"That will do."

They poured doubles and curled up on the sofa. "This hits the spot," Joe said.

"I hate Letitia Jordan and Luther Agostelli," Kate said. "What a diabolical team."

"They're slime. I'd like to kill them both with my bare hands."

"God, how I admired Letitia."

"A lot of people have admired and believed in her. Now her phony empire is crashing."

"We had to learn how truly evil she is from an old samurai in a posh teahouse in Tokyo."

"All because my old man didn't pull the trigger when he had that same samurai in his sights a half-century ago. That's incredible."

"What do you make of Kajimoto?"

"He had to have been on Tarawa; he knows all the right details. The map was authentic—it matched the one General Shoup gave Mom. As for the rest, he's a Tora, but I believe he sincerely wants to help us out of this mess. The 'debt of honor' thing is fascinating."

"'Once a samurai, always a samurai,'" she said.

❦

"This is Scott Ragan." The metallic voice was unmistakable.

"And this is Joe Hawkins."

"Joe. I'm glad you called. How are things in Tokyo?"

"How do you know I'm in Tokyo?"

"The operator told me. Besides, I have your itinerary. I also know Kate is with you."

"Damn! You know everything."

"Part of my job."

"Did I call at a bad time?"

"Not at all. It's 10 A.M. here. It must be midnight in Tokyo. I've never understood that dateline thing."

"I'm in the hotel. Can you secure the line?"

"Of course. Hold on." There was a pause and a click, then Scott said, "We're scrambled. What's up?"

Joe took a deep breath. "Kate and I just had dinner with

319

Kajimoto. He said the Tora Society will kill us if I don't lay off Letitia Jordan and the tobacco thing."

"Jeez!"

"Kajimoto said Letitia and her husband instigated Grace's death. Jonathan Ridge is Letitia's contact with the cartel, and Luther Agostelli is the messenger. He informed Ridge that I was a threat to Letitia's operation. The Toras then tried to scare me off by terrorizing Grace. According to Kajimoto, they didn't intend to kill Grace. Small consolation. Anyway, Letitia expected me to resign. Now she wants the Toras to get rid of me."

"I can corroborate the connection between Letitia's husband, Jonathan Ridge, and the Toras," Scott Ragan said. "Since we last talked, the FBI picked up a Tora mobster in a drug bust who turned over in return for a shot at witness protection. The guy was a fountainhead of information. He knew about the Toras and the tobacco cartel, that Luther Agostelli is the contact between Letitia and Jonathan Ridge, and the contract to terrorize your wife. As Kajimoto told you, they only intended to frighten her but got careless. The mob has already executed the thugs who were responsible. He gave up enough to indict Letitia, Luther, and Ridge for murder one on the basis of being accomplices. He confirmed that the Toras had nothing to do with the Breslow murder."

"Kajimoto said Luther Agostelli also instigated the caper about Duke Rodansky and the black chick," Joe said.

"They're sick people!"

"I'd like to kill 'em."

"Don't blame you."

"Kajimoto says he can guarantee a deal: I back off, they back off."

"What did you say?"

"I said I'd take it, but they should understand the President has already declared his intention to destroy the cartel, and Letitia Jordan is going to be indicted on criminal charges. So it's out of my hands."

"Good move," Scott replied without hesitation. "String 'em

along. You didn't give anything away. Letitia is a dead duck, and the situation with the cartel is beyond your control."

"Exactly," Joe said. "I also told him that anyone who tries to harm Kate or me will answer to the President. Kajimoto respects David Chamberlain."

"Fair enough. How did Kajimoto react?"

"He believes the Toras will be satisfied. I assume that means they'll leave us alone."

"I agree. Incidentally, I asked our Japan expert about the 'debt of honor.' It's real. If your father saved Kajimoto's life, and your father is dead, Kajimoto is required to save your life. Period. No debt is more sacred to a Japanese man, especially a samurai. Failure to honor the debt means loss of face, which is the worst thing that can happen to a samurai."

"Well, the old guy has been telling the truth."

"Come to think of it," Scott said, "you've set up Letitia and her husband. They're no use to the cartel now, and they know too much. When they get arrested, they'll rat to save themselves. The Toras can't have that. Joe! You're a genius."

"I hope the bastards see it your way."

"You're scheduled out of Tokyo tomorrow evening. Two nights in Phoenix, then your executive committee meets in Chicago, right?"

"Right."

"Okay. Be prepared to lay out the whole case on Letitia and Luther—the Breslow affair, the murder of your wife, the bribes, the tobacco conspiracy, 'Ledger'—as you heard it from the President and me. We'll have agents there to make the arrests when you finish."

"Isn't that a bit melodramatic?" Joe asked. "Why don't you arrest them now?"

"The President wants you to confront Letitia in front of the executive committee. That will validate the President's commitment to the AMA and his faith in you. He expects you to emerge as the leader of the AMA."

"That's a tall order."

"The President is confident you can handle it. So am I."

"I presume Jonathan Ridge will also come tumbling down."

"That's correct. And several others. By the way, how's Kate?"

"She's scared, like me, but otherwise okay. How did you find out she's with me?"

"As you know, the President has extraordinary intelligence resources. Actually, it was a guess, and not a very difficult one."

"I might have figured you would catch us."

"Incidentally," Scott said, "the confidentiality is lifted. You can call Duke now. I know he's getting restless."

"I'll call as soon as we hang up."

"Let's meet for dinner in Chicago the night before the meeting —you, Kate, Duke, and me. We'll go over everything then."

"Mario's at eight?" Joe said. "You pay?"

"Fair enough."

"I'll tell Duke."

"By the way, did you ask Kajimoto about 'Y–1'?"

"I did. He knows 'Y–1' is a tobacco from Brazil with high nicotine content. He says the cartel is interested. He says Jeno is a Japanese electronics corporation, but claims he doesn't know of a connection. He seemed surprised when I asked."

"My people are looking into Jeno. We'll know something soon."

"One more thing," Joe said. "I've been thinking about the Breslow murder. If it wasn't Letitia, it had to be someone else inside the AMA, probably someone Breslow tried to blackmail over expense accounts. Breslow handled the Jordan and Devlin expense accounts. With Letitia ruled out, that leaves Devlin. Maybe Devlin was padding his expenses. Maybe Breslow knew it and hit him up, and Devlin did what Letitia tried to do—hired a guy to kill Breslow."

"Do you really believe that?" Scott said.

"I think it's worth a look."

"I'll pass the word."

"Fair enough."

"Listen Joe, is Kajimoto on the level?" Scott sounded worried.

"I hope so. At the moment he's all we've got."

"We should never have let you go to Tokyo."

"On the other hand, maybe we've turned it around."

"The Toras would kill their own mothers."

Then Kate took the phone. "Hello, Scott."

"Hello, Kate."

"What have you been telling Joe? He looks ferocious."

"I told him it's time to make our move. He'll give you the details."

"I hope it works out."

"It will. Don't worry, we're not going to let anything happen to you guys."

❦

"We leave Tokyo tomorrow evening," Joe said, "fly all night, land in San Francisco at noon. Then I go to Phoenix, and you're scheduled to go to Butte. Let's change the plan. I want you to come to Phoenix with me. It's time you meet my family. We'll have a couple of days in Phoenix, then go on to Chicago together."

Kate was delighted. "Joe, I want more than anything to meet your family."

"It'll be okay with your folks?"

"They'll be fine. I'll fix it."

"Great. I'll take care of the tickets."

"I hope your kids like me."

"They'll love you, just as I do."

"I already love them."

Joe then called Duke. Kate listened quietly until they finished talking, then asked, "How did he take it?"

"Calmly," Joe said. "He'd figured out a few things, but he was surprised at the extent of Letitia's transgressions."

"What did he say about us?"

"He was surprised, but he already suspected we were an item. He said I was 'one lucky s.o.b.' Sends his love. He's looking forward to the dinner in Chicago."

"You realize," she said, with a long sigh, "we've been together every minute for the last two weeks?"

"We'll have separate rooms in Phoenix."

"I'll leave my door unlocked."

He laughed. "I'll have to get by my mother."

"To think, it all started when I came to Phoenix to hear you speak at Rotary."

"It's been quite a year."

[31]

BETTY HAWKINS was a patrician lady handsomely endowed with long slender legs, tailored gray hair, and a spectacular smile. This evening she had enhanced her elegance by duding up in a red polka-dotted chef's apron with a giant bib. "It's beautiful outside," she observed. "It'll be nice dining on the patio."

"We're having champagne," Joe announced. "From California, but I'm calling it champagne anyway." He produced a silver bucket containing a bottle of Paul Masson packed in ice and popped the cork. "Mom, I know you want some of this. Anyone else?"

"Me," Kate said. "If I had to live with one drink, I'd pick champagne."

"A lady with class," Janie Hawkins said. "Me too."

"Mom's the world's greatest barbecuer of steaks and hamburgers, for that matter, anything," Janie said. She spoke with an odd flatness to her voice characteristic of a repaired cleft palate. "And she loves it. It takes a dedicated cook to satisfy this household."

Betty laughed. "There are more mouths to feed now. We were only three in Illinois."

"She's a beautiful grandmother," Joe said.

"The children love her," Janie said.

"She has great legs," Joe said.

"That's Joe's lascivious side," Janie explained.

"We're having hamburgers and cherry pop," Tracy announced. She was playing on the floor with Rosie and little Jake. "Baba always fixes what we want."

"The kids call her 'Baba,'" Joe explained.

"You're growing up, Tracy," Kate said. "How old are you?"

"Eleven," Tracy replied. "Rosie is eight. Little Jake is six."

"That's very good," Kate said.

"I didn't do all the cooking," Betty said. "Janie baked the potatoes. Tracy tossed the salad. Joe did procure the ice cream, I believe."

"Strawberry," Janie said. "His favorite."

"We set the table," Rosie said, all puffed up. "After dinner we're going to help with the dishes."

"Some people think I have it made," Joe said. "Actually, supervising is an awesome responsibility."

"Surgeons are all alike," Kate said.

When dinner was ready they sat around the long table on the patio. "Look at those beautiful steaks," Kate said.

"Mom learned to cook over a Bunsen burner," Janie said with a giggle. "She's come a long way, for a chemistry professor."

"I remember she used to come home from the lab smelling like rotten eggs," Joe said.

"Joe!" Betty scolded. "I taught you to say hydrogen sulfide."

"As far as I'm concerned, it was rotten eggs," Janie said.

Betty pretended exasperation. "I'm glad your children are more understanding of you, Joe, than you and Janie are of me."

"A toast," Joe said, ignoring Betty's protest and raising his glass. "To the greatest kids in the world."

"To the greatest grandkids," Betty responded.

"To the greatest nieces and the greatest nephew," Janie said.

"May each of you enjoy a lifetime of hickory barbecued hamburgers," Joe said.

"And cherry pop," Tracy chimed in.

"It's wonderful to hear joy in this house again," Betty said.

Then Tracy said, "Dad, do you have to go to Chicago tomorrow? We want you to stay."

Joe looked at the three little faces smiling irresistibly. "I have to finish something. But I'll be back in a few days and stay a long time."

"Promise?" Tracy persisted.

"Promise," Joe said.

"We love you," Tracy said.

"You know I love you," Joe said.

"I want to hear about your trip," Janie said. "I understand you went around the world."

"We did," Joe said. "First stop was Madrid for the World Medical Association. It was an interesting situation. The black African nations staged a walkout because the World Medical voted to admit the South African Medical Association, which at one time had supported apartheid. They had quite a row. Kate coordinated the public relations. It was her job to protect the AMA and put the best face possible on what happened, and she succeeded admirably. For all her beauty, she's quite talented."

"Joe took me to a bullfight in Madrid," Kate said.

"Did you hate it?" Janie asked.

"Only the horse killing. The first bull jumped over the fence, almost into my lap. That was exciting. Joe liked the whole thing. He's an aficionado."

"How can you possibly like bullfights, Joe," Janie scolded, "after all the bloody things you've seen?"

"There's more to bullfights than killing bulls," Joe said.

"Like what?" Janie demanded.

Betty intervened. "Let's postpone the bullfight discussion to another time. I want to hear about the rest of the trip."

"From Madrid we flew to Nice," Joe said. "It was a beautiful flight across the Mediterranean and along the south coast of France. We stayed in Monaco, in the Hôtel de Paris. We strolled around the harbor and fawned over the big yachts and drank gin and tonic. That evening we had dinner under the stars and played baccarat in the Casino. Next day we drove along the Côte d'Azur to Nice and Antibes and had lunch in Cannes. Then we drove the coast and took the ferry to Saint-Tropez. On the way back we had dinner in a little hotel on the waterfront. We had real champagne and watched the sun set in the Mediterranean."

"How utterly romantic," Betty said.

"I love the Mediterranean," Kate said.

"Then," Joe continued, "we flew to Singapore. We stayed at

the Shangri La, one of the great hotels of the world, and shopped and visited the harbor. From Singapore we flew by way of Manila and Guam all the way to a little island in the Pacific named Nauru, on the way to Tarawa. Nauru is usually called something else, which I won't mention now, related to the fact that over the centuries, birds nesting there deposited tons of guano. We had to lay over a couple of days. Flights between those little islands are crazy."

"You made it to Tarawa?" Janie asked.

"Finally," Joe said.

"Did you find what you were looking for?"

"Yes," Joe said. "I found it. Tarawa is a worthless nub of coral and sand. It's hard to believe that a great battle was fought on a piece of world so completely worthless."

"What did you do?" Janie asked.

"Retraced the invasion," Joe replied. "We rented a pram and spent the night on the ocean outside the coral reef where the troop ships rendezvoused. At dawn we followed the route of the landing craft to the beach. I waded in from where Dad's amph-track was blown up, like he did. We found the pillbox where he stopped the Japs and the place on the beach where he died. I had the map Colonel Shoup sent Mom."

"Joe told me about Tarawa," Kate said. "We sat on the sand by the old pier where Joe's father died. We cried. You could feel the ghosts. Joe had his tape player, and we played wonderful music and danced on the sand, in the surf, in the hot morning sun. It seemed natural. Joe's father was there. They were all there. I felt like I knew them."

Betty's eyes filled with tears. "I've never wanted to see Tara-wa," she said. "I visit Jake's grave in the Punchbowl. I know he's happy there. It's so beautiful, so peaceful. The headstones are simple—all the same—and the grass is green. Jake is buried near Ernie Pyle. By the chapel they have stone panoramas of the Pacific campaigns, including Tarawa, and rows of marble tablets en-graved with the names of the dead."

"The beach was timeless," Joe said. "I saw the same young

faces I saw in Quang Ngai, faces you might have seen at Bastogne, Chosen, Verdun, Gettysburg. It was sad, a little spooky, but somehow, exhilarating."

"You're beautiful, big brother," Janie said, and for a moment the room fell silent.

"Then we flew to Tokyo," Joe said. "We stayed in a swanky hotel across from the emperor's Imperial Palace. We had a special evening with Dr. Kajimoto—he's president of the Japan Medical Association—dinner by candlelight in a magnificent Japanese teahouse, complete with beautiful geishas." Joe omitted the frightening part.

"In some ways it was a wonderful evening," Kate said.

After dinner they sat on the patio with their coffee and strawberry ice cream. The dishes were done and the children were busy unto themselves.

"The children love you, Kate," Betty said. "We all love you."

"They're wonderful children," Kate said.

"They'll want to do things with you," Betty said.

"You'll have fun with them," Janie said.

"It's obvious that Joe is happy," Betty said. "We thank you for returning joy to his life."

"Oh, Betty," Kate said. Tears filled her eyes.

"After Jake died I was bitter, confused, full of hate. Fortunately I had wonderful memories and wonderful children. Without my children, I don't know what would have happened. They made me realize I had so much to live for. I still think of Jake every day. We have a beautiful love affair. We always will. The kids and I moved to a small town, a college town, a wonderful place. We had our ups and downs, like every family, but we had a good, loving home. It could have been better. The kids needed a father. I stopped hating a long time ago. Hate destroys. I tried to instill that in my children." She smiled. "Joe, bless his heart, had some incorrigible moments. He lost his way for a while. He needed his dad. Then he joined the marines. I was terrifed I might lose him and almost did. For a time I agonized over his inconsideration for

Janie and me. Then I realized he had to do it. It worked out for the best. I'm very proud of Joe and Janie. We love each other. Many parents are not so fortunate."

"You're a helluva woman, Mom," Janie said. "You made a wonderful home for us, cared for us, nurtured us, fathered us. Through all that you earned a Ph.D. and became a college professor, and you nursed me through my cleft palate. Somehow you got me to Chicago on the train all those times to see the doctor and have the operations."

"I remember," Joe said, "you always fixed a good breakfast for us and had us come home for lunch every day. You were magnificent on homework—there wasn't anything you didn't know. You saw me through my incorrigible moments, as well as Vietnam and the horrible time afterward. Then you inspired me to go to medical school. And when Grace died, you and Janie unhesitatingly uprooted your lives and came to take care of me and the kids. You're the greatest."

"It's all about love," Betty said.

"I remember well your favorite quotation, Mom," Joe said.

"'There is only one happiness in life, to love and be loved,'" Betty recited. "George Sand."

"I propose a toast," Janie said. "To the greatest mom in the world."

"Hear, hear," they all said.

Joe, I'm delighted you found Kate," Betty said.

"Me too, big brother," Janie said. "I propose another toast, to you and Kate."

After midnight Joe slipped into Kate's room and closed the door. The bedside lamp was on, and she was in the bathroom brushing her teeth. In a moment she emerged wrapped in a white towel and padded across the carpet. She dropped the towel and kissed Joe, and her kiss tasted like mint toothpaste. She loosened his robe and let it slide to the floor. They embraced and she kissed his nose and ran her minty tongue inside his lips. Her skin smelled of verbena. He touched her hair, damp from the shower, dropped his hands to her waist, pressed against her, sucked her tongue into his mouth.

"I thought you would never get here," she said when he released her.

"I wanted Mom to be asleep."

"She knows we're lovers."

"I know, but I don't want to flaunt it."

Kate rubbed against him. "You're coming alive." Then she led him to the bed.

"We must be quiet," Joe whispered.

❧

They rested in silence, and Kate said, "Why do I always have to do all the work?"

"You're the young and agile one, that's why."

She smirked, then said, "I'm glad you invited me. Your family is wonderful. I feel at home."

"I wish we could stay," Joe said.

"So do I," Kate said. "I hope our lives settle down soon. We're just back from a trip around the world. Tomorrow we fly to Chicago, have dinner with Duke and Scott, and plot the demise of Letitia Jordan and Luther Agostelli. That's a lot of action."

"Letitia won't surrender quietly."

"Did you call Maxwell?"

"Yes. This afternoon. I told him only that I had a matter concerning Letitia to discuss in executive session. He wanted to know more, and he was miffed when I wouldn't tell him, but he was gracious.

She stroked his belly. "I see my friend is still alert."

"You have the hot hand."

"Want to go again?"

"It's worth a try."

[32]

"SENATOR RIDGE calling," Sarah Mason announced on the intercom. "He sounds upset."

Letitia Jordan picked up the phone and pressed the privacy switch and activated the recorder. "Good afternoon, Jonathan . . . Yes, we're secure. What's up? . . . What are you talking about?" Alarmed, she straightened in her chair and listened intently. "The Tora Society? Never heard of it . . . Luther? . . . That's hard to believe. . . . Three million? . . . Impossible. . . . I know nothing about it." Suddenly she exploded, "What's happening here?" then settled back, scowling. "I know about RICO. . . . This is a terrible mistake. . . . I'm shocked, and I'm angry. . . . I'm sorry, Jonathan. . . . All right. . . . Thank you for calling."

She took a moment to regroup, then called Sarah Mason into the office. Do you have tomorrow's agenda?"

"It's in your briefcase."

"How about Maxwell's number?"

"In the briefcase. He's landing at O'Hare about now. He should be at the Marriott within an hour."

"Leave word that I'll call this evening. What about Hawkins?"

"He checked into the hotel at three. His number is in the briefcase."

"And the others?"

"Dr. Rodansky was scheduled to arrive an hour ago. The rest are due later this evening."

"The vultures are gathering," Letitia said with metallic sarcasm. "Thanks, Sarah. You can go now. I'm going to call home, then I'm out of here."

❦

Joe answered the door to his room at the Marriott and found a tight-lipped Letitia Jordan standing in the corridor. She was, as always, immaculate and beautiful, and he wanted to smash her pretty face.

"I swear, I did not kill Grace," she announced, emphatically, as if reading his mind, her voice trembling. "I had nothing to do with the killing of Leonard Breslow. I had nothing to do with that chicken episode and Duke Rodansky. I know nothing about the Tora Society. I did not sell out the AMA. And I did not, by God, put three million dollars into a Cayman Island bank."

Joe hesitated, then said, "Come in."

"I could use a big Tanqueray."

He opened the bar and poured a double. "Thank you." She downed a swallow, sat down, then downed another and seemed to relax. "It was Luther Agostelli."

"Your Luther?"

She nodded. "My Luther. He did it all, or at least arranged it. Jonathan Ridge just told me. That's why I'm here."

"The senator?"

"Yes."

"For God's sake, Letitia, what the hell are you talking about?"

"About Luther and me, and Jonathan Ridge."

"Okay. Enlighten me."

She faltered. "Bear with me. This is embarrassing. In plain terms, I'm a certified psychotic, an honest-to-God paranoid, delusions of persecution and bipolar disorder—the whole nine yards. Luther has been treating me for nine years. That's why I married him. Psychotherapy and medication. Currently I'm on Thorazine. I just popped one in the office before coming over here. I hope it kicks in soon. At this very moment I'm almost out of control, and I'm trying like hell not to implode in front of you."

"Gin on Thorazine; be careful."

"I understand," she said. "I'm also alcohol dependent, my own diagnosis. But I know my limits." Joe believed it. He'd seen her consume sizable amounts of gin without apparent effect.

She continued. "Psychiatrists are not supposed to fall in love with their patients, let alone marry them, but it worked for us. Ten years ago I moved to Bolton, Mississippi, a small town near Jackson. I put in long hours, built a big practice, and struggled with my problem. The harder I worked, the worse it got. I thought everyone was after me. I even heard voices in the shadows. I'll spare

332

the details, but finally I flamed out. That's when I hooked up with Luther. He diagnosed me, resurrected me, became my therapist, and eventually, my husband. He tends to my special needs, and I tend to his. Interestingly, Luther has his own problems. He doesn't look the part, but he's an insatiable satyr—sometimes five, six times a day, without fail." She smiled at the look on Joe's face. "I rather like taking care of him. The poor guy can't live without me any more than I can live without him. If ever a man and woman were hopelessly interdependent, we're it. A sex fiend and a psychotic. How 'bout that?"

"Do you love him?"

"Desperately. And he loves me. When the opportunity with the AMA came along, he encouraged me, then cheerfully closed his practice in Jackson and came with me to Chicago. As a matter of fact, he's been quite content here. Does a little psychiatry on the side—has a small office in the Pittsfield Building—and spends the rest of his time looking after me."

Her disclosures were making Joe uneasy.

"As you probably know," she went on, "the successful treatment of paranoia requires absolute trust between the patient and the doctor. That's how Luther managed me. He burrowed into my psyche until I trusted him implicitly. It's a complicated process, but he literally melded our personalities. We share our most intimate thoughts. I tell him everything, including all about the AMA, and vice versa. He restored my confidence and ultimately inspired me to function at a level far beyond my wildest dreams. I was fortunate."

"Indeed you were," Joe agreed. "But what does this have to do with Jonathan Ridge?"

"I'm coming to that. Jonathan Ridge controls the congressional tobacco caucus. We cooperate with those guys when we need their votes. I know you don't like it, and neither do I, but we do what we have to do. Some time ago Jonathan asked me to designate a confidant to convey messages on those occasions when utmost discretion was necessary. That's what you do in Washington when you don't want to leave tracks. I, of course, chose Luther. He was unknown on the political scene, he was the only person I trusted. He was my willing, my perfect 'secret agent.'"

"Frankly, Letitia, I think Jonathan Ridge is a murderous son of a bitch."

"From what I learned this afternoon, you're right. Jonathan called less than an hour ago. I knew something was wrong when I answered the phone. He'd heard that indictments would be coming down, including a murder indictment for him, and for Luther and me, for Grace's death. Then he launched into a tirade, saying he never realized she would be killed. He was totally surprised when I didn't know what he meant. Then he told me, and it was terrible. It seems that last year when you were just starting your campaign, Luther, completely unknown to me, told Jonathan that I thought you would screw things up for us, and that I wanted to get rid of you. That was an outright lie. I was rooting for Devlin—hell, I had to root for the son of a bitch—but getting rid of you was strictly Luther's idea. Actually, I like your style. I even liked you. Jonathan, however, had no reason to question Luther, and he told the tobacco cartel. Then things got out of hand. The cartel told the Tora Society, which I now know from Jonathan is a Japanese crime syndicate that controls the cartel. Jonathan said the Tora Society sent a couple of goons to terrorize your wife, thinking you would get the message and back off. For what it's worth, they botched it. They intended only to frighten, not kill. Nevertheless, Jonathan, Luther, and I are about to be indicted for murder."

Joe could hardly believe what he was hearing. "You really had nothing to do with Grace's death? Today was the first you knew she was murdered?"

"That's right. I was shocked. I always thought Grace had an unfortunate accident. I never dreamed that Luther, or Jonathan, for that matter, would do such a thing. And, I had never heard of the Tora Society."

"If that's true, I've been badly misinformed."

"It's true," said Letitia.

"The Tora Society is very powerful."

334

"So Jonathan told me."

"Kajimoto is a Tora."

"Kajimoto, our old Japanese friend?"

Joe nodded. "He's a legacy. His father was a Tora. However, he assures me he's a Tora in name only and has no part of their criminal activities."

"Good Lord. I certainly knew nothing about that."

"So, you say Luther was the instigator, and Jonathan the messenger."

"There's more. According to Jonathan, Luther, on his own, paid a man thirty grand to kill poor Len Breslow and make it look like an accident."

"You didn't tell him to do it?"

"Of course not. Len tried to shake me down for two hundred thou. He said he needed the money for personal reasons, and if I didn't pay, he would disclose embarrassing information about me and the AMA. Embarrassing? No way. I have a big income, which I earn honestly and without shame, and nothing to hide. I threw the s.o.b. out of my office. I was irate, but I don't kill people. Naturally I told Luther about it. He must have feared Len more than I realized. Unbeknownst to me he went out and hired a killer to get rid of him. I can't believe it. Jeez! If Len had asked for the money in a reasonable manner, I might have worked something out, and this wouldn't have happened."

"The police located the man Luther hired," Joe said. "He was a phony. He didn't kill anybody. Took the thirty grand and walked. He scammed Luther."

"Then Len's death was an accident after all?"

"No. Someone else killed him and tried to make it look like an accident."

"I'll be damned," Letitia said. "Does Luther know?"

"No. He still thinks his man did it."

"Who's the real killer, for God's sake?"

"That's a good question. Maybe someone in the AMA. By the way, the police discovered that Breslow was a closet gay and HIV positive. He left a note in the computer—remember the LEDGER file? That told it all. He was covering his ass. The man was desperate. He expected to die and wanted money for his family."

"Poor devil," Letitia whispered.

"What do you know about Duke Rodansky and the dead black chick in the box?" Joe asked.

"Only that it happened. I presume that was also Luther's doing. He has a good imagination."

"I was there," Joe said. "Duke thought someone had made a sick joke, but I believed it was a death threat from you against his girlfriend to make him drop the tax return thing. I persuaded him to notify Maxwell immediately that he'd changed his mind, and to get the girl out of town that night."

"Maxwell called me right after Duke called him," Letitia said, then added, "You really thought I was capable of doing such a thing?"

"I'm afraid I did. Remember when Kate and I met with the President in Los Angeles?"

"I certainly do. I was damn mad about it at the time."

Joe smiled. "He had been informed that you were a bad guy; that you had hooked up with Jonathan Ridge and taken money from the tobacco cartel; that when Breslow threatened to blow the whistle, you had him killed; and that you would kill again without hesitation. He even thought you might try to kill me."

"My God!" Letitia said, stunned.

"When Breslow died the police discovered his blackmail attempt. They assumed you were the perpetrator because they thought you had the sole motive. Under the circumstances it was logical to conclude the chick was a death threat."

"I've always wondered why Duke backed down. It wasn't like him. By the way, I've known about his black girlfriend for some time."

"Would you have given up the tax returns?"

"Absolutely not! I have nothing to hide, but Duke had no right. I'd have gone to the mat on that."

For the first time in the conversation, Joe started to feel better about Letitia. "Yes, I suppose you would have." He got up and fixed another Tanqueray and she accepted it gratefully. "Now, tell me what you know about the three million."

"That was another shocker. Jonathan asked if I had received all my money from the tobacco cartel. Again, I didn't know what the hell he was talking about. He then informed me that over the last three years the cartel had conveyed three million dollars to a Chicago law firm on my behalf, which in turn deposited the money to a joint bank account in Luther's and my name in the Cayman Islands. The arrangements were made through Luther, and Jonathan assumed I knew. Well, I didn't. Today was the first I heard that I had three mill in a bank account anywhere."

"How in the world did Luther work that?"

"Three years ago Jonathan proposed to Luther that I curtail the AMA's antismoking activity in exchange for tobacco support against socialized medicine. He also offered a personal retainer, meaning a bribe. Luther saw his chance. Remember, he was inside my head. He knew the feds had our backs to the wall and that I was in a froth, but he also knew I'd never take a bribe. So he relayed Jonathan's proposal, conveniently omitting the bribe. I ran it by the board, they bought it, and Luther finessed the retainer for himself. Luther actually sold out the AMA for three million—in my name, without my knowing it—and stashed the money. Until this very afternoon, Jonathan thought I was on the take."

"Still, you did what he wanted," Joe said. "You went soft on smoking, and you laid off the subsidies."

"Of course I did, but not for pay. I did it because I needed the tobacco votes in the worst way. It's ironic. He didn't know it, but he had me for nothing."

"It sure smells like a sellout."

"Well, it wasn't," Letitia said. "It was a trade, pure and simple, the kind that's done every day in Washington. Political necessity breeds strange bedfellows. And it worked. So far, we've held the line."

"You don't think it was wrong?"

"Absolutely not. Look, Joe, the tobacco people are phonies. They lie about nicotine and all the rest. But right now holding off the feds is our controlling priority. We mustn't lose sight of that. We'll take on smoking another day, and I promise we'll win. But if we do it now and lose on socialized medicine in the process, organized medicine will be finished. We won't have the muscle to fight anything, much less smoking."

"Believe it or not, I agree," Joe said.

"Having said that, I feel whorey about the whole thing. I'd like to find another way."

"Fair enough," Joe said. "How did you get a joint bank account in the Caymans without knowing it?"

"Maybe Luther forged my name. Or maybe I signed without knowing what it was. I never read anything Luther gave me to sign."

"How do I know you're not making all this up?"

"Good question. I called Luther immediately after talking to Jonathan. I had to hammer him, but he admitted everything. I have both Luther and Jonathan on tape."

"Did Luther say why?"

"He passionately believed he was protecting me. He was afraid that you, or Len, or Duke would bring me down, and that my precarious mental situation would not survive. He must have succumbed to a little paranoia himself. As for the three mill, the aroma was irresistible. He figured in the final analysis, I'd want the money and love him enough to forgive him. Actually I think he's crazy."

She fished a small Sony from her bag, and in a moment they heard Luther's unmistakable drawl fending off Letitia's angry interrogation and telling her he loved her. The tape confirmed everything.

"I'm absolutely shattered," Letitia said. "Until an hour ago I would have trusted that man with my life."

God! Joe thought. This is bizarre. For months he had believed this remarkable woman baring her soul was an utter villain, upon whom he would have gladly visited a violent death. Now Letitia was only a fragile, frightened, misunderstood little girl in the clutch of demons, on the verge of disintegration.

"Why did you come to me?" he asked.

She dabbed her eyes with a tissue. "When I discovered the truth about Luther, I could not let another minute go by having you think I had somehow brought harm to your wife and done all those other terrible things. I'm not that way. I believe in the AMA, and I give it my all. I know I push the envelope, sometimes over the line. I know you think I'm tough and ruthless, and I admit I love power, and I know I'm paranoid as hell. But I don't lie, I don't cheat, and I don't kill."

"I believe you," he said softly.

She smiled gratefully. "You and I had a couple of splendid arguments. I was wrong about the airplane. It was stupid, and I know it."

"I lost my temper," Joe said.

"You're feisty. You told me off. I liked that."

"I wasn't proud of it." He thought for a moment, then said, "Listen, I think I know a way out of this. If we side with the President against the tobacco crowd, he'll kill socialized medicine for us, quid pro quo, and we can forget the goddamn tobacco caucus."

Letitia was skeptical. "Are you sure?"

"I'm positive. He'll also establish a formal alliance with the AMA. He'll even ask Congress to create a separate department of health with cabinet rank, and he'll appoint a physician as secretary. It'll be a new world."

"I love it," Letitia said.

"He promised me in Los Angeles. He'll do anything to destroy Jonathan Ridge."

"What is it between Chamberlain and Ridge that rubs off on me?"

"That's a grim story. Years ago, when they were both senators, David Chamberlain's son got caught up in a tragic blunder by the CIA. Chamberlain begged Ridge to intervene, but he refused, and in the end, young Bryce Chamberlain committed suicide. Chamberlain has been hell-bent for Ridge's scalp ever since. It's an obsession. You automatically became an enemy when Chamberlain thought you took the bribe from Ridge."

"Jonathan says I'm going to be indicted for murder and

multiple counts under RICO, and God knows what all. How do I deal with that?"

"I'll try to stop it. The original plan was, I would explain the President's alliance proposal to the executive committee tomorrow morning. At that point you would be arrested in front of the committee to make a big show of unity between the Chamberlain administration and the AMA. That's all changed now. I'll talk to the President's man this evening about the indictment. Tomorrow you and I explain everything together. We publicly close ranks with President Chamberlain and declare war on tobacco. That should make a big splash."

"You got a deal," Letitia said.

"You're dumping the tobacco cartel. They won't like it."

"Who cares. This is exciting. When will you know it's all set?"

"I'll call you later this evening," Joe said. "The President is a good man, and a fair man. He'll regret what's happened, and he'll make amends. He was only after you because he thought you were in cahoots with Jonathan Ridge. However, Luther will be indicted, and you may be required to testify."

"I know. I'm sick."

"Are you going home to Luther now?"

"Yes. I hate him, but I love and need him, and he loves and needs me. We've had a great run together. When all this unravels, I'll lose him. I don't know how I'll survive that."

"I'm sorry," Joe said.

"I'll have to alert Kate, of course. Whatever comes down tomorrow, it'll be a doozie. She'll have her hands full."

"She can handle it."

"Were they actually going to arrest me tomorrow?"

"That was the plan."

"Jeez. I'm damn glad I came to see you. Listen, Joe, I'm devastated. I feel betrayed and alone. And I'm scared. I know people are out to kill me."

"You're tough, Letitia. And you're smart as hell. You'll make it."

She rose to leave. He followed her into the foyer, and she turned and rested her hands on his shoulders. "We've had our differences," she said. "But I always liked and admired you. Now more than ever."

He smiled. "Thank you."

"You're an exciting man, Joe. I trust you. We could be great together." She pressed against him. "I might as well say it, I want to be your lover. I'll do anything you want. Satisfaction guaranteed. We can start now if you wish." She wrapped her arms around his neck and kissed him firmly on the mouth.

Gently, he loosened her grip. "Letitia, I'm seeing Kate."

The color drained from her face. "My God! I didn't know. . . . I'm so embarrassed."

"You had no way of knowing."

She pulled back and forced a smile. "Well, then, I'm going home now. Thank you for everything. Call me when you know about tomorrow."

❦

Jonathan Ridge entered the Oval Office and the door closed behind him. Across the room David Chamberlain sat behind the presidential desk studying a document. They were alone. Jonathan Ridge approached and stood before the desk. Neither man spoke. Then, not looking up, David Chamberlain said, "Senator Ridge, you have been indicted for murder in the first degree for the death of Mrs. Hawkins, along with multiple counts under RICO—racketeering, obstruction of justice, mail fraud, and wire fraud. Federal marshals will arrest you within the hour."

Jonathan Ridge, a frail old man—tight-lipped, pallid face expressionless, aging eyes unwavering behind the antiquated wire spectacles—stared contemptuously at David Chamberlain and said nothing.

David Chamberlain looked up. "Jonathan, this time it's no mistake. You're dead meat. Now get out before I throw you out."

[33]

KATE HAD SETTLED into her customary niche in the alcove bar at Mario's when Joe arrived. She was wearing the white cocktail dress he adored and the gold necklace, and in the ruddy lamplight the tanned skin of her bosom glowed fetchingly. The young man at the piano was playing a mellow "Stardust."

"You've never looked so beautiful," Joe said. He leaned down and kissed her.

"It's because I'm happy."

Within moments Duke Rodansky and Scott Ragan trailed in, by chance, together. "Good evening, gentlemen," Joe said and introduced them.

"I've heard a lot about you, Duke," Scott said.

"Likewise," Duke replied.

"Hello, everyone," Kate said cheerily.

"You're not smiling, Scott," Joe said. "What's the matter?"

"Jonathan Ridge committed suicide an hour ago."

"Good Lord!" Joe said.

"The President summoned Senator Ridge to the Oval Office late this afternoon. He informed the senator that he had been indicted for murder and racketeering and would be arrested within the hour. With that, Senator Ridge returned to his office and blew his brains out."

"He must have been guilty as hell," Duke said.

"He was guilty, all right," Scott said. "But I didn't expect suicide."

"This is crazy," Joe said. "Less than an hour ago, I had a surprise visit in my hotel from Letitia Jordan regarding Jonathan Ridge. He called her earlier this afternoon, evidently only moments before the President summoned him."

"Did she know about the suicide?" Scott asked.

"I think not," Joe replied. "She didn't mention it. But she did have a tall story to tell. Take a deep breath, my friends. Letitia convinced me that she had nothing to do with Grace's death, or Len Breslow's death, or the three million, or any of what we've been blaming her for. It was all Luther Agostelli's doing, and she knew nothing about any of it until Jonathan Ridge told her this afternoon. In other words, we've made a terrible mistake."

"You're losing me, partner," Duke said.

"Let's order," Joe said. "Then I'll explain." He turned to Scott. "I hope you remember your agreement to foot the bill, being from the White House and all."

Scott smilingly played reluctant. "Okay. Dinner on the White House."

"In that case I suggest champagne," Joe said. He notified the bartender who brought a bottle of Schramsberg, popped the cork, and after proper sampling and approval, filled four crystal flutes.

"A toast," Duke said. "May this be a memorable evening."

Then Reuben appeared bringing menus. "Good evening, Dr. Hawkins," he squeaked.

"Good evening, Reuben," Joe said. "How are the soft shells tonight?"

"Excellent. Bigger than usual."

Joe surveyed his companions. "Anyone object to Caesar salad and soft shells? No? Very good. That simplifies things. Forget the menus. The same all around, Reuben—extra anchovies on the Caesars—and fetch us when you're ready." Reuben departed looking satisfied.

"I'm glad everyone likes what Joe likes," Kate remarked. "He learned that maneuver from Pierre Globa."

They then huddled around the little table in the bar and sipped champagne while Joe related his conversation with Letitia. "We seriously misjudged her," he concluded. "Luther Agostelli is the villain. The only thing Letitia is guilty of is zeal."

"I'm glad," Kate said. "I've never fully accepted the accusations against Letitia."

"I've never liked Luther," Duke said. "He's such a laid-back little shrimp."

"Letitia is severely paranoid and manic depressive," Joe said.

"She practically dissolved in front of me. The woman put her trust in Luther. He betrayed her, and now she's terrified."

"It's tragic," Kate said.

Reuben then summoned them to the dining room for the Caesars.

"Is Duke up to date on everything else?" Scott asked.

"I briefed him this afternoon," Joe said.

"This obviously changes the plan for tomorrow," Scott said.

"She's committed no crimes," Joe said. "I told her I'd talk to you about her indictment. We'll have our meeting with the executive committee in the morning. She and I will lay out the whole thing, then we'll call the press."

"Sounds good," Scott said. "I think I can stop her indictment. However, the authorities may still want to investigate."

"Fair enough," Joe said."

"She's in for a rough time," Duke said.

When the Caesars were finished, the waiter brought big platters of butter-sizzling soft shells. Scott gingerly sampled the hot crab meat. "This is damn good."

"Joe's favorite," Kate said.

Then Joe said, "Scott, about tomorrow. It'll draw media attention. I hope the President's proposal isn't misunderstood."

"That's possible," Duke said.

"The President hopes this scenario will convince the AMA and the public of his personal commitment," Scott replied. "It's melodramatic, and the media will give it play. However, the President wants high visibility here. He believes Joe's personal credibility will prevail."

"I'll do whatever the President wants," Joe said.

"Count me in," Duke said.

Then Scott said, "Joe, in regard to Devlin, the police investigated and ruled him out."

"What about Devlin?" Duke asked.

"I thought Devlin might be Breslow's killer," Joe explained. "Breslow processed Devlin's expense accounts. If Devlin was cheating, Breslow could have blackmailed him, and Devlin could have hired someone to kill Breslow, just as Luther did."

"Do the police think Breslow's murder was related to his HIV?" Duke asked.

"Apparently not," Joe replied. Duke's question curiously puzzled him. "This was a well-planned, sophisticated execution, more in keeping with a hired killing than a crime of passion like a gay thing."

"Then, who killed him?" Duke asked.

"As of now," Scott replied, "the police have yet to make an arrest."

Then Reuben announced, "We have a superb chocolate mousse this evening."

"Wonderful," Joe said. "Cognac and coffee."

"This is sinful," Kate said.

"What the hell," Duke said. "We're sinners."

They devoured the rich dessert, and the cognac and coffee, then Kate said, "Dance with me, Joe, before we leave."

"Gentlemen," Joe said. "The lady wishes to dance."

"Of course," Scott said. He pulled out his cell phone. "Time to call the President. I'll get the check, and we'll meet in the foyer."

Joe and Kate moved into the alcove bar. "There's something I don't want the others to hear," he said. "Letitia came on to me this afternoon, big time."

"Oh, Joe. What did you do?"

"I simply said, 'I'm seeing Kate.'"

"Bless your heart."

"She didn't know about us. She was mortified."

"I can imagine," Kate said.

Then Joe asked the young man to play, and they danced. Softly, Joe sang:

> *Waking skies*
> *At sunrise*
> *Every sunset too*
> *Seems to be*
> *Bringing me*
> *Memories of you*

345

"I love it when you sing to me," Kate whispered.

"You're especially beautiful tonight," Joe said.

"I'm happy," Kate explained.

"Kate, please marry me."

Tears filled her eyes. "Oh, Joe."

"I love you very much."

She touched her nose to his. "I'm deeply honored. Of course I'll marry you."

"Stay with me tonight."

"My duffel is in the cloakroom," she whispered.

He smiled. "I like a woman who comes prepared."

"I love you, Joe. I'll love you the rest of my life."

"I'll call the taxies," Duke said.

"It's a pretty evening," Kate said. "Let's walk a bit?"

"That's a fine idea," Scott said.

"Spring is a lovely season in Chicago," she said as they started down the driveway.

"It's a perfect evening," Joe said.

"Perfect," echoed Kate. "And I'm the happiest girl in the whole world."

Then the muffled signal of a cell phone sounded. "It's mine." She extracted the little phone from her purse. "This is Kate." She listened and the color drained from her face. "My God! . . . When?" Horrified, she looked at her companions.

"What is it?" Joe said.

"Letitia Jordan and her husband are dead."

"What!"

"They were shot. An hour ago. At home. They were forced to lie on the floor, then shot in the back of the head. No robbery. No clues."

They huddled around Kate. "Who called?" Joe asked.

"Sarah Mason."

"Sounds like an execution," Scott said.

"Poor Letitia," Joe said.

"I can't believe it," was Duke's reply.

They stood in the driveway, shocked, groping for understanding. Joe put his arm around Kate and noticed a black Mercedes sedan at the curb with the shadowy figure of a man in the driver's seat.

"This was the work of the Toras," Scott said. "Letitia and Luther had become liabilities. It's that simple."

The driver's door of the Mercedes then swung open. A familiar looking Oriental man in a dark suit emerged. Joe strained to see in the dim light, then suddenly recognized the man. "My God! It's George! Look, Kate. It's George, from Tokyo." Joe waved. "George, what are you doing here?"

George Miyoshi moved swiftly, his face now clearly visible, devoid of expression. He whipped out an AR-15 and Kate screamed, "Look out!" George fired point blank and Scott crumpled. Kate lunged and the muzzle exploded like a thunderclap. Swiftly, instinctively, Joe kicked the weapon loose. It hit the driveway with a clatter. The young Japanese recoiled, stunned, eyes suddenly glossed with fear. Another kick and he screamed, doubled over, fell, clutched his groin, and rolled. Joe grabbed the weapon and emptied it into the contorted figure on the pavement. The crashing explosions of thirty-caliber cartridges reverberated down the street. George screamed once as the lethal fusillade ripped his body, then lay still, neck twisted, blood oozing from the gaping mouth, lifeless eyes staring at the sky, face blanching in the yellowish light of the streetlamps.

Kate lay on her back, her chest heaving with guttural, sucking noises. Blood soaked the white dress and bloody phlegm filled her mouth. The bullet had ripped a gaping wound through ribs and muscles. Pink lung bulged from the wound and blood spilled onto the pavement.

"Oh my God!" Duke cried out. A man ran out of Mario's. "Call the paramedics," Duke screamed. "Someone, call the paramedics."

Joe dropped to Kate's side. Her eyes found him and she fought to breathe. Her lips formed the words, "Help me." Her eyes rolled, and for a moment she lost consciousness, then she found him again. "Oh, Joe," she whispered.

347

"Hold on," Joe sobbed. "I love you. Oh God! Hold on." He tore away the remnants of her dress and with his bare hands tried to pull the ghastly, gaping wound together. God! She's got to breathe. She's sucking air. She's got to breathe. Pull. It won't come. The lung, the pink lung. The heart. Pounding. Bleeding inside. Can't get at it. She's dying. Got to breathe. "God! Hold on, baby. We'll fix it." Do something. Her breast. Her breast. He stuffed her torn breast into the bleeding wound. God! Her beautiful breast. Still sucking air. Tamponade. He tried to seal the wound with his bare hands and suddenly was struggling in that nameless, muddy stream in Quang Ngai with Sergeant Cobb, helpless, watching the lung bulge and blood spread on mucky water.

"Joe," Kate murmured. She coughed, and bloody phlegm bubbled oddly at the corner of her mouth.

"She needs a tube," Duke said. "The paramedics are on the way." He slid his jacket beneath her shoulders and cleaned the bloody phlegm away, and she seemed to breathe a little easier.

"She's bleeding to death!"

"I know."

"I can't get at it."

The people from Mario's gathered in silence and watched. Some cried.

"Hold on, baby," Joe whispered. "Please hold on. I love you. I love you." Her eyes moved. "I love you." So beautiful. Her poor breast. Her poor, beautiful breast. "Hold on, Kate. You can do it. Hold on. I love you. God! I love you. You can't die. You can't. God! I love you."

She moaned. Her eyes found him, and her lips moved, and again she drifted off.

"Please, Kate, please."

"Oh, Joe," she whispered, almost unintelligibly, her face the color of wax.

"Hold on," Joe pleaded. "Hold on. You can do it." He kissed her lips and she coughed hard, and with a deep sigh her eyes closed and the heaving stopped. "Oh, no!" Joe cried. He sucked bloody phlegm from her mouth, then squeezed her nose, sealed his lips against hers, and forced breath into her lungs. Her chest responded, and he thrust his hand between the ribs and grasped the slippery sac containing the heart. The contractions were feeble and wormlike, and the great muscle flaccid, drained of blood. He massaged the heart, then pumped harder, striving to make it beat, blew lungfuls of breath into her lungs, crouched over her still body, frantically pumping her heart, lips pressed to hers, infusing precious oxygen. "Hold on, baby. Don't die. Don't die. Hold on. Please, please, don't die."

"No pulse," Duke said.

In disbelief, Joe fought to instill breath and a heartbeat, and the people watching the grisly spectacle bonded in horrified silence. Then Duke touched the shoulder of his friend and whispered, "She's gone, Joe. Let her go. She's gone."

Then Joe relented. Blood smeared his face. Tenderly he draped his jacket over her shoulders, covered the bloody dress and the terrible wound, cradled her and smoothed her hair and kissed her, and sat on the pavement and rocked her, as she had cradled and rocked him on the warm sands of Red Beach, and cried. The people on the street embraced his agony.

"Joe! Look!" Duke suddenly cried out.

The door of the black Mercedes had opened, and an aging, bullet-headed, banty-legged Oriental in a rumpled suit emerged holding a folded silk scarf and a straw pallet. He unfurled the straw pallet and sat cross-legged on the sidewalk beside the Mercedes, the scarf on his lap, a surreal buddha under the sallow light of the streetlamps.

"It's Kajimoto!" Joe whispered, clutching Kate.

Kajimoto evinced no recognition. He rocked gently on his haunches, eyes closed, silent. Then he drew a compact Beretta from the scarf, and without hesitation put the muzzle to his temple and pulled the trigger. His body lurched, then toppled backward, and blood streamed onto the pallet.

Their faces spun out of reach, like tethered party balloons whipping in a whirlwind . . . Captain Hawkins . . . Sergeant Cobb . . . warm, beautiful Grace, blond tresses flailing her shoulders . . . Letitia and Luther . . . Kajimoto . . . George . . . Scott . . . Kate . . . sweet, loving Kate . . . all gone . . . now he was running, running, running . . . stinking quagmire . . . sinking . . . sinking . . . someone shooting . . . Kate crying . . . slipping . . . falling . . . crying . . . something wrong, wrong, wrong.

He awoke trembling, soaked in sweat, terrified. He searched the empty bed. No Kate. Turned on the light. It was midnight. Christ! He hated hotel rooms. He turned over and sat on the edge of the bed, gasping. Something was terribly out of place, terribly wrong. Duke. Where are you? That was it. Had to see Duke. Duke Rodansky's room was four doors away. Joe pulled on a robe, trying to shake off the nightmare, and hurried barefoot down the corridor. He hammered on the door, hammered again, and Duke's startled face appeared.

"Not now," Duke grunted.

"Now!" Joe said and shoved the door open.

Duke tried to stop him but was off balance, and Joe pushed his way into the room. Sitting on the bed was a stranger—a startled, muscular young man clad only in snug boxers.

"Jesus Christ!" Joe cried.

"What the hell?" Duke said angrily. "I know you're shook up, Joe, but what the hell?"

The young man snorted, "Get out."

"Please go, Joe," Duke said. "I'll talk to you in the morning."

"Duke!" Joe screamed. "You're a goddamn faggot."

Duke flushed and the young man whined, "I said, get out."

"Go to hell," Joe growled ominously.

"Be careful," Duke warned the young man.

The young man moved with a menacing flourish, but he was no match. Joe fired a rapier kick to the groin and the young man fell screaming to the floor. Joe then grabbed a wrist, wedged his foot into the axilla, and with a lightning twist, dislocated the shoulder. It was over in seconds, and the young man moaned and lay writhing on the floor, helpless, clutching his shoulder.

"Damn! I was afraid you'd do that," Duke said.

"Who told you Leonard Breslow had HIV?" Joe demanded.

"What do you mean?"

"You know what I mean. You let it drop last night at dinner. I didn't get it until now, in the middle of a nightmare."

Duke hesitated. "Len told me."

"I thought so. Were you boogering him?"

"For Christ's sake, Joe. Yes. One time. Three months before he died. He called to tell me he had tested positive and was going to turn in and disclose his contacts."

"You're a fucking switch-hitter," Joe said with abject disgust.

Duke tried to smile. "Let's say, I have eclectic tastes."

The young man groaned. "You're lucky I didn't kill you," Joe said. "You have a dislocated shoulder. Grit your teeth and I'll reduce it." The young man nodded and Joe grasped the arm, placed his foot firmly in the axilla, and skillfully snapped the head of the humerus into place. The young man flinched and gave a short yelp. "That's the dirty sock method. See a doctor tomorrow. Now get out of here."

The young man managed to slip into his clothes, then departed.

"Now," Joe demanded, "did Breslow try to blackmail you?"

"No," Duke replied. "I expected him to."

"He was going to disclose your name to the public health people?"

"That's what he said."

"When did he tell you?"

"Three weeks before he died."

"Did you contact him in the interval."

"No. What the hell is this, an inquisition?"

"Did you kill him?"

"C'mon, Joe."

"You're the only one besides Luther Agostelli with a motive, and the only one capable of killing him."

"Okay, I killed him."

"Any accomplices?"

"None."

"You did it solo. The choke hold."

Duke shrugged. "No problem. I'm an old wrestler, remember."

"Did you know he was trying to blackmail Letitia?"

"No."

"And Luther had hired a man to kill him?"

"I couldn't have known."

"Why the hell did you kill him?"

"Simple. I panicked about disclosure of the HIV thing. He was a pushover, and I thought I could get away with it. It was stupid."

"Then you persuaded me to hook up with the AMA."

"Yes. I shouldn't have pressured you. If I hadn't pressured, Grace would be alive, Kate would be alive. God knows, I'm sick about it."

"Been tested?"

"I'm positive."

"Shit!" Joe exclaimed. "What about Shirley?"

"She's negative, and I've broken off."

"Your wife?"

"Negative. Doesn't have a clue."

"And the queer you had in here tonight?"

"Don't know and care less," Duke said. "He's only a whore." Then he asked, "If you're satisfied, will you drink with me? I have Black Label in the minibar."

"Sure," Joe agreed without knowing why.

Duke poured the drinks and they sat down. Joe leaned back, staring at the ceiling.

"I'm sorry for what I've done," Duke said.

"Turn yourself in."

"I don't think so."

"Then I will."

"Listen, Joe. I'm a sinner. Something went wrong with my life. I've hurt people I love. Now I'm going to die of AIDS. I don't want to die of AIDS. And while I'm dying, I'll be facing murder charges. Not much of a future. Well, I'm not going to go through that. I have a two million dollar life insurance policy for Barbara and the kids, with no suicide exclusion. That's what I'm going to do, by God. Now."

Joe was too spent to respond.

"Funny . . . I feel better already." Duke withdrew a snub-nosed revolver from a satchel beside the chair. "Stay where you are, Joe. I don't want to kill you, but I will if you try to stop me. You're too fast. Christ! The way you unloaded on the Jap." He swigged the last of his Scotch. "I've given this some thought. I'm afraid to jump. Jumping would be spectacular. Out that very window, fifteen floors, Michigan Avenue, a long ride down. But I don't have the nerve, and I don't want to get smashed up. Poison is no good. Besides, I don't know anything about poison. A bullet in the head like Kajimoto is too messy. Unfair to the family. The best way is point blank into the heart. Sudden death. No mutilation. A little blood, that's all. Easy with the right pistol. This little Chief's Special will do the job. The snub-nose is easy to handle. I've practiced. That's what I'm going to do . . . now . . . so long, Joe."

He put the snub-nose to his heart and fired.

[34]

JOE FACED the bay window of his room in the Marriott staring at the vast, blue waters of Lake Michigan. A light squall had come at dawn, and now the sky was rain-washed clear and the sun reflected off the glassy lake with blinding intensity.

The chime in the foyer sounded, and Joe opened the door. In the corridor outside stood the President of the United States flanked by an entourage of Secret Service agents.

"Good morning, Joe," David Chamberlain said. His familiar, resonant voice tumbled into the foyer.

"Mr. President," Joe blurted. "Good Lord!"

They stood face to face, then they embraced, powerfully, silently, like gallant warriors in the wake of battle. "Is it really you, sir?" Joe finally asked.

"Of course it is," David Chamberlain strode into the room. "I couldn't let you go this alone." He inspected Joe's unshaved face. "You look terrible."

"I'm pretty beat, Mr. President," Joe said, then managed a smile. "Does the world know you're in Chicago, in this hotel, with me?"

"I hope not. I tried to keep it under wraps."

"I'm damn glad to see you, Mr. President."

"Joe, I'm absolutely sick about Kate, and Scott."

"It was horrible, sir."

"Scott called last night to fill me in on the Letitia Jordan matter. Two hours later I was notified that Scott and Kate had been shot dead, along with Kajimoto and his man, and Letitia Jordan and her husband. I was absolutely stunned." The two men settled into the sofa. "Joe, what happened?"

"Well, sir, last evening Kate and I, as you know, dined with Scott and Duke Rodansky. After dinner—we had just stepped outside the restaurant—Kate got a call on her cell phone that Letitia and her husband, Luther Agostelli, had been murdered. We were totally shocked. I remember Scott saying he thought it was an assassination. We were standing there on the sidewalk, more or less confused, when Kajimoto's man, the Jap, the one called George, ambushed us. He'd been waiting in a parked car. He pulled out an AR-15. Poor Scott got it first. He didn't have a chance. Kate lunged and took the next shot. Then I was able to stop the guy. Scott died instantly. Kate died a few minutes later, in my arms. Duke was unhurt. When it was over, Kajimoto emerged from the car, said nothing, sat down on the pavement in front of us, and calmly pumped a bullet into his brain."

"You loved Kate, didn't you?"

"I had just asked her to marry me."

"She took your bullet?"

"Yes, sir," Joe answered softly. "She died for me."

"I'll never forgive myself," David Chamberlain said. "I let you get in too deep."

"It wasn't your fault, Mr. President."

"Scott had a wonderful wife and two beautiful children. I called on them last evening."

Joe shook his head sadly. "I'm so sorry. I really liked Scott."

"I'll convey your condolences personally to Mrs. Ragan."

"Thank you, sir."

"How did you manage to kill the Jap?"

"I kicked his gun away, then shot him."

David Chamberlain whistled softly. "Masterfully understated, my friend. You're one good marine."

"Not good enough, sir. I lost Kate and Scott."

"We'll both take that to our graves," David Chamberlain said. "Rodansky was your friend?"

"A good friend."

"Where did he go wrong?"

"Duke was a college athlete, a successful neurosurgeon— married, two children, but he had problems. There was a black girlfriend in Chicago and a homosexual relationship with Leonard Breslow, and others. When Breslow found that he was HIV positive, he told Duke he was going to report his contacts. Duke killed Breslow to shut him up. It was purely coincidental with Luther Agostelli's attempt to kill Breslow."

"I understand he shot himself in your presence."

"That's correct, sir. He had recently discovered he was HIV positive, and he didn't want to die of AIDS. When I confronted him about Breslow, he decided the hell with it. He had a plan, had a thirty-eight in his duffel. I couldn't stop him. He would have shot me if I'd tried."

"Rodansky was not involved with the cartel?"

"He had nothing to do with the cartel."

"That coincides with my information. Scott briefed me yester-day before he came to Chicago. The police have evidence directly implicating Rodansky in the Breslow murder. They obtained a sweater belonging to Rodansky that matched a fiber found under Breslow's finger nail."

"Then, last night at dinner, Scott already knew Duke had killed Breslow?"

"That's right."

"He had no opportunity to tell me," Joe said. What a night-mare."

"You heard about Jonathan Ridge?"

"Scott told us."

"I hated the son of a bitch."

"I know, sir."

"Pierre Globa told you about Ridge and my son?"

"In Madrid. It was hard to believe."

"Yesterday was quite a day. We indicted three congressmen, not including Jonathan Ridge, and six tobacco executives. We clobbered the cartel. Then the Toras killed Letitia and Luther. I deeply regret that. I was dead wrong about Letitia. She was totally innocent. Her husband sold her out and got them both killed in the process."

"I'm sorry for her," Joe said. "She was a tragic figure—a remarkable, beautiful, talented woman betrayed by a twisted man she loved and trusted. But I have no pity for Luther."

"He signed their death warrants when he made that deal. The Toras never let go."

Then Joe said, "Letitia paid me a surprise visit yesterday afternoon. Jonathan Ridge had just tipped her off about the indictments. She came immediately to tell me that she had nothing to do with the death of my wife, or any of the rest of it. Two hours later she was dead."

"It's all very sad."

"Poor, poor Letitia," Joe said.

"Doc Kajimoto fooled us," David Chamberlain said. "He spent a lifetime establishing his reputation as a world-renowned physician. And it was all a charade. He was samurai to the bone. He hated Americans. The Tora Society is one of the most powerful crime syndicates in the world, and Kajimoto was a major player. We just learned that he controlled the Jeno Corporation, which, as you know, owns the patent on Y–1 tobacco. He had delusions of dominating the world tobacco market with Y–1. However, his story about your father was true. The so-called 'debt of honor' was real. He tried to pay the debt by brokering a deal between you and the Toras. Apparently the effort alone qualified as a good-faith attempt to save your life. Under samurai code, that satisfied the debt. But he still had to save face with the Toras, which meant he then had to kill you personally. Failing that, and having no way to escape after you stopped George, only one option remained—hara-kiri, seppuku. Death with honor, samurai style."

"He was extremely gracious in Tokyo," Joe said. "He liked Kate. Gave her a beautiful pearl."

"The long and short of it is, the man was slime."

"How did he get to Chicago?"

"He flew into O'Hare in his personal DC-10, four hours before the shooting. He had diplomatic credentials and was able to circumvent the red tape. Brought George with him. The plan was to finish you and beat it back to Tokyo before anyone realized what had happened. He didn't want the others. They were incidental."

"Did he really expect to get away with it?"

"I don't know. Perhaps he wanted it to end the way it did."

"Kajimoto was the last man I expected to see get out of that car," Joe said.

"Joe, you're taking Kate back to Montana?"

"Yes, sir."

"I'll have a plane fly you out. You can pick up your family on the way, if you wish, and return to Phoenix when you choose."

"Thank you, sir. I'd like to leave this afternoon. I don't want to spend another night here."

"Consider it done. By the way, my original commitments still stand. You decide what you want to do and when you want to do it. Take all the time you want."

"At this point, Mr. President, I don't know what to say."

"I called your mother this morning. We had a delightful chat." He smiled. "The lady squared me away. She let me know about meeting FDR when she received your father's medal of honor, and she made a point of telling me she regards FDR as the 'greatest president of them all.' She also said to remind you that we still have a lot to live for."

Joe smiled. "That's been her creed since she lost my father. And she certainly loved FDR. Thank you for calling her. I'm sure she was pleased."

David Chamberlain inspected the haggard countenance of his friend. "Are you okay?"

"Not really, Mr. President."

"Kate was an extraordinary young woman," David Chamberlain said. "Blue eyes, brains, grit."

"Now she's a beautiful memory," Joe said. "Funny. We danced to a song about memories before she died."

"She knew you loved her."

"The police took her away in a black, body bag, like in Vietnam. It was awful. She's in a cold drawer in the Cook County morgue." Joe struggled for composure. "I hate that. I witnessed autopsies there when I was a student. They'll lay her naked on a slab, gawk at her mutilated body, hose her off, cut her open, drop lewd remarks. I hate knowing those things."

"Concentrate on the good things," David Chamberlain said, speaking softly. "When Bryce died, I remembered his face as a little boy, then I had visions of him alone in a prison cell, hanging by a sheet. It devastated me. It helped for me to think about the good things." After a long moment, he added, "You'll deal with it, Joe. You're a survivor."

"I suppose I will, sir. I know I have a lot to live for—beautiful kids, a great mom, a great sister, wonderful friends. I want to go home, get back to work. I love what I do."

"It'll take time. You'll never forget, but you'll deal with it. I did. We all do."

"Yes, sir. I'll deal with it."

"Anything I can do before I leave?"

"I'll be okay. You've been wonderful, sir."

"I'll call in a couple of weeks. Perhaps you'd like to come to Washington. Bring your family. Let the kids run around the White House. We'll relax, have a quiet dinner, play some movies, sort things out. Be good for all of us."

"I'd like that."

David Chamberlain rose from the chair and handed Joe a card. "My private number. Call anytime, for any reason. Good-bye, my friend. Take care of yourself."

"Good-bye, Mr. President," Joe said. "Thank you for coming." They embraced warmly and, followed by his entourage, David Chamberlain swiftly departed. The room seemed empty without him.

❧

Oh, God, he was lonely. Joe turned from the foyer and noticed Kate's duffel on the chair where he had left it the night before. He looked inside and found the new alligator bag they had purchased in Singapore, still in its chamois wrapper, then a leather pouch containing the Mobe pearl, some fresh clothing—a skirt, new silk blouse, lingerie, all neatly folded—her kit of toiletries, and a lavender sachet with the tantalizing scent of ripe peaches. The silk blouse was soft and fresh, and he crushed it against his cheek, aching for more, but it was no good.

He moved to the bay window, still clutching the blouse, and bathed his face in the warm sunlight. Then it was over. He belonged at home. He looked to the horizon and gave a gentle smile. The big lake seemed as blue as the Mediterranean.